da Kid

Rich Kisielewski

WolfSinger Publications ⟨ Security, Colorado

Acknowledgements

This book would not have been possible without the assistance of a number of very important people. First on the list is Carol Hightshoe and WolfSinger Publications for her continued support of myself and Harry. Her editorial and creative genius turn every Harry book into a finished product we can all be proud of.

Thanks to Marge Simon for her imaginative art work that brings Harry to life.

Jeff Austin for allowing me to use Rich Valley Golf and Nolo's as an integral piece on the da kid story—I hope you and the entire RVG team enjoy the book as much as I enjoyed including you in this tale. And let's also hope Jon Fetterman enjoys playing the bad guy as much as I did creating his character—thanks for being a good sport.

My friend Ed Kurpiel—you can only hope to own your own golf course.

And Bill Burns who is far from little in many ways—here's one for you buddy…enjoy!

Finally, thanks to the "K" team for your continued encouragement and help with editing and story creation—you make my writing so much easier: Tara, Brian, Caitlin and most important my lovely wife Liz who puts up with both Harry and me.

Oh yeah—thanks Harry. See you again real soon…

Chapter 1

Eighteen years old. No, make that more like eighteen going on forty-three. He had seen, and done, and probably forgotten more "stuff" than any ten normal kids his age combined. Unfortunately, all of his streetwise wisdom and "*I can do dat better than you can, succa*" attitude don't add up to squat when the man lays the cuffs on you and drags your sorry butt down to the place with bars on the windows and three free squares a day.

Maybe I should jump back a few steps and let you in on what's going on here. My name is Harry because I'm told an aunt promised to lay some bread on me if my mom named me Harold. I don't believe it one little bit because I didn't see a single dime and, to my knowledge, neither did my moms.

Oh yeah, it's Harry, or should I say Harold Mickey Shorts, which wasn't my given name when I was ushered into this wonderful world of ours. My original name didn't cut it in my eyes and the Mick, Mr. Mantle, is my all-time favorite ballplayer courtesy of my dad. Plus, my original last name was way too long. Wearing tee shirts and shorts is how God intended us to dress, so that's how I came up with my new and improved name—" Shorts—which just happens to be a great conversation topic for the ladies.

By trade I guess you would call me a private investigator, but I'm not your ordinary run-of-the-mill, every-day private dick. Kizmet Incorporated is what my business card would say, if I had one. Mel had called and said he needed help. My help. For Mel, my ex-brother-in-law (EBIL for short) to ask Harry Mickey Shorts for help, any help, hell would have had to have frozen over and the "Devils" would have been practicing a long time for the upcoming hockey season. But, when I'm asked for help you best jump back because I'm coming through to do anything in my power to mend what needs mending.

Yup, here we go again…Harry Mickey Shorts style.

Chapter 2

"Who's the kid and what's he done?" is how I started the conversation when I walked into Mel's office the day after he had called me.

"Harry!" was the first thing I heard in return.

"Hey, Bunny. You're looking mighty delightful on this glorious day," I replied.

She came over and gave me a peck on the cheek.

Ms. Bunny Malone was Mel's erstwhile able bodied assistant. Her body was the primary able part with the rest of her assistant skills constantly in doubt. But what an able body she did possess, erstwhile or not.

"It's good to see you, Harry," Bunny said with a voice that made you want to do to her those things that float around in your head that you never get to do. And oh yeah, I've been there, done that, both ways. In my head, and…. I'm sure you get the picture and no need to elaborate.

"It's good to be seen, especially by you," I responded.

"Enough already," Mel interrupted.

Looking totally intruded upon, Bunny headed back to her desk. As traditionally occurs when I enter the premises, Bunny stopped at the file cabinet and bent over to get some supplies out of the bottom drawer. Her long shapely legs and cute tight ass were clearly defined for all to see; well, at least for Harry and Mel to observe. The short skirts Bunny favored didn't hurt the show one bit.

Post Bunny vision, I again said, "Who's the kid and what's he done?" to Mel.

Mel thought for a second, looked in Bunny's direction, and then said in my direction, "Let's go across the street and get a cool one. I'll tell you the story there."

"Cool," I replied.

"I'm heading out for a bit, Bunny," Mel told her. "Lock up when you head over to the open house if I'm not back by then."

"Sure," Bunny said. "And don't be such a stranger, Harry,"

she threw in my direction with a flutter of those big blue eyes of hers. That flutter started other things a fluttering every time she did it.

"Let's go," Mel said and he was gone with me close behind.

~ * ~

Once we had comfortably ensconced ourselves in the beeratorium across the street from Mel's office, cold beers in hand, Mel proceeded to give me the lowdown.

"The kid's in some kind of trouble," Mel started. "But that's not the part that has me worried the most."

"No," I said. "What does?"

"The kid's been in trouble for as long as I've known him. I coached him in the eighth grade and he was a real handful back then. All the talent in the world for a kid his age, but he couldn't give two shits. He showed up for practice when he felt like it and barely put in the effort when he did show up."

"He's not the only kid in the world that has "attitude" at that age," I said.

"You're right, Harry. But when he wanted to, he was light years ahead of the kids his age. He scored forty-two points one game without breaking a sweat. Didn't even play the last four minutes of the game," Mel said.

"You win?" I asked.

"That's just it. No, we lost by two," Mel explained.

"Why the hell didn't you play him at the end of the game?" I asked.

"That would have been a good idea, Harry. Problem was I called a time out with four minutes to play and he walked passed the bench and right out the door," Mel said.

"He just left the gym?" I asked in disbelief.

"Yeah, he just walked by the bench, past the end of the bleachers, and out the gym door. Adios kid, adios game."

"No shit?" I said.

"I shit you not," Mel replied.

Chapter 3

Our beers refreshed, Mel continued with his story.

"There were still two games left in the season and we were already assured of making the playoffs. Unfortunately, when the kid walked out of the gym that day that was the last I saw of him."

"What do you mean?" I asked.

Mel took a pull on his beer. "He didn't come back. Missed the next practice and he didn't show up for the next game. He didn't show up for the rest of the season. He was long gone."

"I assume you called his house. What about his parents? What did they say? You know his old man much?" I asked.

"Valid questions any putz would have followed through on, Harry. His parents filled out the necessary papers before the season started and never showed for a single game. They never picked him up after practice, either. Not one single time. I never met them and nobody answered the phone when I called on numerous occasions. Message only said 'Leave a message' and went beep."

"That's strange. What about the other kids? They know anything about him, like where he lived, who he hung with?"

"Equally as strange. The other kids said he showed up for school most days, at least enough not to get his butt in hot water. Didn't hang with any of them and kept to himself during school. End of the school day, he didn't even take the school bus. He just walked down the street and vanished," Mel said.

"Vanished, like in poof he's gone?" I asked.

"Like in now you see him, now you don't," Mel replied. "The kids I talked to said they knew nothing about him. A buddy of mine who knew somebody in the school's administration said the kid passed his tests and got mediocre grades—enough to pass. Parents never showed for any of the school nights or parent teacher meetings."

"Weird if you ask me," I said.

"Looking back on it, anyone who knew anything about it would have said weirder than weird," Mel agreed.

"And you never found out anything more about the kid?" I asked.

"Nope, eighth grade ended and he did a Houdini. He didn't enroll in either of the local high schools—St. Mary's or Manhasset High School. None of the kids saw him that summer and he was nowhere to be found in the fall," Mel continued.

After finishing my beer and getting another refill, I said, "So, we have an athletically talented eighth grader who bails on his team and does a Houdini at the end of the year. That right so far?"

"Right so far," Mel confirmed.

"He doesn't enroll in either of the two local high schools in the fall and nobody knows squat about where he went. Houdini act continues. So, how does he enter the picture after all this time and why are you concerned?" I asked.

"Fair questions, Harry," Mel replied. "You know me, if I coach a kid who puts in a fair effort I'll support the kid any way I can, for as long as I can. Some might consider it a character flaw in my otherwise perfect make-up: some think it's noble of me."

"Yeah, yeah," I said. "You going to get to the point before the keg goes dry?"

"The point, Harry. The point is—I lost this kid and for some reason he's resurfaced in my life. Maybe I should have said screw it, or him, and said it's none of my business. But I didn't and I'm in it now. And I need your help. You gonna help me or not?" Mel huffed.

I drank the rest of my beer and signaled for a new round.

"Calm down, Mel," I said. "You know I'll help you if I can. Gimme the details and let's see what we got."

Chapter 4

Before we continue, why don't I get the wheres and whys out of the way and give you a bit more info on Harry Mickey Shorts.

I hang my hat in Manhasset, NY, which is a little burg on the North Shore of Long Island. I've been there a few years—second time around—returned specifically to be close to my kids, and by necessity, my ex-wife. Things couldn't be better with the kids, Max and Briande, who are re-discovering their previously wandering father. Sherry, my ex, isn't constantly telling me to self-perform an act that normally requires two individuals to consummate, so I guess things are looking on the bright side there too. We even manage to "get together" on occasion if you get my meaning. Not to worry, I'm sure very soon she'll find some new reason to re-member what I did to her and the kids and revert to hating me again. It happens all the time.

As I said, my office is in Manhasset, L.I. in the back room I rent from my aforementioned ex-brother-in-law, a place called Pine Tree Realty. It really isn't a room but more like a desk we share. He owns the place and I use the phone and the address for mail deliveries. It happens to be real convenient and, as I just said, I used to live in the town in what seems like a lifetime ago.

I found myself seated at that very desk later that afternoon trying to make sense of what Mel had laid on me earlier in the day. The kid actually had a name and, after a little prodding, Mel finally produced said name—Billy Burns. I was afraid he would be "the kid" ever more, destined to remain nameless forever in the annals of time. A bit melodramatic maybe, but I'm prone to embellish-ment on occasion when I choose to amuse myself.

Anyway, it seems Billy Burns was currently residing in a jail cell in a small town in upstate New York. I knew the location since it was only a stone's throw from my parent's town of Cats-kill, New York. While Catskill had one traffic light, I was pretty sure this burg had none. It's just north of BFE (BumFuckEgypt) if you know where I mean. Guess that makes it NBFE!

By Mel's account, Billy found himself on the wrong end of a

con game he was perpetrating on some of the town's local yokels. Problem was; one of the local yokels was the son of the town constable and a member of the town's police department. Here's what Mel was told:

Billy and two other dudes roll into town in a beat up old minivan and park themselves next to the local playground. Some town guys are playing a friendly game of pick-up basketball when Billy and his dudes arrive on the scene. A couple of "Hey, how you guys doing?" and an innocent "Mind if we shoot a few baskets with you fellas?" leads to a little three-on-three game of hoops. Billy's team loses a few games and the locals are feeling real good whipping up on the new arrivals.

Yup, not a good thing for the local yokels.

Before Billy and his boys can get back in their van and head out of town, soundly demoralized, the locals suggest that maybe a small wager on one more game might be in order.

"No, we couldn't," Billy tells them. "You guys beat our brains in every game and we'd be throwing away the few dollars we have left that we need for gas to get back home."

Yeah you can...no we can't...sure you can...maybe we might...just one game for a few bucks...well, maybe one game for a few dollars followed.

A sound thrashing at the hands of the local yokels at five bucks a man lead to a second game, and before anyone knew what had happened, Billy and his boys were finishing an 11-0 whipping of the local boys for a thou a man.

"What the fuck just happened?" the local cop asked in astonishment as the game ended.

"Seems we just kicked your asses for a thou a man, buddy boy," Billy wise-assed. "Time to pony-up the dough," he finished.

Bullshit...not gonna happen...we been conned...pay up you small town welchers ensued. A push led to a shove, which led to Billy and his boys finding themselves in the local jail for assaulting a police officer. A routine search produced an open warrant issued in Cumberland County, PA, and Billy was in deep doo-doo.

"A lawyer buddy in town who coached with me back in the day caught wind of it and gave me a call," Mel had said. "Maybe I should look the other way on this one, Harry, but I'd kinda like to know what happened to this kid. Where was he between four minutes left in an eighth grade basketball game and getting arrested for conning a small town cop in a pick-up basketball game?"

Finding out "What happened" is something Harry Mickey Shorts was born to find out.

Chapter 5

"Who do you think you're bullshitting, Harry?" she asked.

"Bullshitting? You hurt me by saying those things, Sherry," Harry responded.

"Bullshit, Harry. That's more bullshit than the bullshit you just tried to shove in my back pocket," Sherry answered.

"Back pocket?" Harry said.

"Shut up, Harry. It was all that came into my head, especially when I'm trying to tell you to stop running that crap by me," Sherry said.

"Crap, what crap?" Harry tried.

"The crap about you not coming over here looking for something when we both know you are," Sherry answered.

"Are what?" Harry replied.

"Harry, if you are going to have any chance of getting what you want, here's what's going to happen right now. And I mean right now," Sherry started. "You are going to shut that big mouth of yours, take me in the back bedroom, bang my brains out, and then we'll see about what you actually want from me."

"Other than banging your brains out?" Harry dared to ask.

"Yes, Harry, other than banging my brains out. And you better be good."

"Deal," Harry agreed.

As a means of explanation for the above exchange, as previously established, Sherry is Harry's ex-wife. Harry had moved back to Manhasset, L.I. a bit ago to try and reestablish a life with his two kids—Max and Briande. Harry had skipped on them before they even knew they had a daddy and that they had been skipped on.

Sherry, well Sherry is part of the package deal.

Things had progressed nicely and the kids loved having Harry around. That is when he was around and not off gallivanting around the country trying to solve another one of his cases. He and Sherry had their moments, but they also managed to "get it together" on occasion to the enjoyment of both of them.

This was one of those moments.

~ * ~

Having had the chance to catch their collective breaths after their moment together, Sherry said, "Hmmm."

"Should I be looking around for your brains?" Harry asked.

Smiling, Sherry said, "Yes, Harry, I believe you should. I do believe you succeeded in banging my brains out as instructed."

"Enjoy it?" Harry asked.

"Hmm," Sherry hmmed.

"You weren't bad yourself," Harry complemented.

"Wasn't bad?" Sherry said.

"Okay, better than expected," Harry replied.

The whack to the side of Harry's head for that comment was well deserved.

"So, what is it you actually want, Harry?" Sherry asked.

"Information," Harry answered. "I need some information."

"About?" Sherry asked.

"A kid," Harry replied.

"Any kid?" Sherry asked.

"Well, no," Harry said. "I had one particular kid in mind."

"And how would I be able to help with this kid's information?" Sherry asked.

Harry hesitated and then said, "Well, the kid went through the Manhasset school system for a time. I was hoping to get a copy of his school records and any other info that might be available on him."

Sherry gave Harry that look. It was the look she gave him when she couldn't decide whether to break his neck, scratch his eyes out, or tear his "you know whats" off.

"What?" Harry said in self-defense.

"You just happen to know I'm kinda seeing the District Administrator and you think you can use me to get something you want from him. Is that right?" she asked Harry.

"Well, yeah," Harry replied. "Sounded like a good idea at the time I thought of it."

Smiling again, Sherry, said, "I was gonna dump the putz anyway. Might as well get something out of him for all the whiney washerwoman crap he tossed my way."

"That's my Sherry," Harry said.

"But it's gonna cost you, Harry. It's gonna cost you starting right now."

And their moment continued…

Chapter 6

When Harry latches on to a case, he latches on with both hands. He will use anything at his disposal to gather data, information, hearsay and nearsay that may pertain to the case. At the current moment he was making his initial foray into the Trundle Information gathering pool.

The Bayport Schooners are a minor league baseball team that plays in the Double A Eastern league. They play their games in surprise, surprise—Bayport, Long Island. Their owner is Mr. M. Randle Trundle, who is also the CEO of a major New York City conglomerate with businesses and holdings throughout the globe. He is the epitome of a BTBM—Big Time Business Mogul.

Not that long ago, Harry was a player coach for the Bayport Schooners. It involved a case he worked for Trundle, but that's a story for another day.

Harry was sitting in the owner's box watching the Schooners lay a pasting on the Erie, PA team. M. Randle Trundle was presently enjoying a hot dog and a beer in the seat next to Harry. He was also thoroughly enjoying watching the Schooners lay a pasting on the Erie team. As I just told you, it is his team.

"What are you doing out here today, Randle?" Harry asked Trundle. "You playing hooky again?"

"Playing hooky?" Trundle repeated with a "who me" look on his face.

"Yeah, that's what I said, playing hooky?" Harry repeated.

"For your information, Mr. Shorts, I'm here today as the owner of the Bayport Schooners looking in on one of my business investments. It is imperative you keep your eye on everything in your corporate empire at all times. It would do you good to learn from this visit and incorporate such behavior into your own day-to-day dealings," Trundle expounded.

Harry looked over at Trundle to make sure he had actually said that with a straight face. He had.

Turning back toward the field, Harry said, "I'm sure that is very sound advice, Mr. Trundle. Should I proceed to build my corporate empire beyond my present portfolio of business investments of, well, none, I will be sure to do so. I will also be sure to do so on a beautiful, bright and sunny day. I will also be sure to invest a portion of my extensive holdings in a hot dog and a beer to keep the vending community in the black."

Trundle looked over at Harry to make sure he had actually said that with a straight face. He had.

"Very wise indeed, Mr. Shorts. And so that we both may insure the vending community continues to remain in the black, how about I get us both another hot dog and a pair of beers?" Trundle said.

"Very fiscally prudent of you, Mr. Trundle," Harry answered.

"Bet they'll taste damn good, too," Trundle said.

"There is that as well," Harry replied.

Trundle looked over at Harry, Harry looked over at Trundle, and neither was sitting there with a straight face.

~ * ~

Hot dogs and beers secured, Trundle said, "So, what do you need, Harry?"

After licking a few drops of the golden nectar of the gods off the left side of his upper lip, Harry said, "Information, good old dig in the dirt kind of information. The kind of information your boys down in the basement can dig up like nobody else can."

"Just curious, Harry. Better than your Web Dude buds?" Trundle asked.

"Different, but I'd say for what they do best they are the best I've ever seen," Harry conceded.

"For that comment alone, done," Trundle told Harry.

"Thanks, Randle," Harry said.

"Let me deal with a quick issue down in the baseball office and then you can tell me what you're working on and how Trundle Industries can help," Trundle told Harry.

"Sure," Harry said. "I'll get us some replenishment reinforcements for your return."

"Dogs and beer?" Trundle asked.

"Dogs and beer, what else?" Harry confirmed.

Chapter 7

The Schooners were pounding away on the Erie SeaWolves much to the delight of the Schooner faithful who had come out to see them do just that. The Schooners delighted their fans more often than not.

"The boys are looking good today," Harry said to Trundle as he sat back down in the seat next to him.

"Well, I pay them to have fun and winning is fun," Trundle said.

"What's losing?" Harry asked.

"Why, it's bad for business, Harry. And as you know, baseball is a business when you come right down to it. It's fun for the fans and fun for the players when they win but, at the end of the day, it is a business we would like to see turn a profit. Plus, as you already know, Harry, I hate to lose. It isn't fun and the boys try their best to make me happy," Trundle said.

"Smart boys," Harry said.

"I agree with that assessment, Harry. Smart manager, too," Trundle added.

Harry nodded his head in agreement to that as well.

"So, at the expense of repeating myself, what do you need, Harry?" Trundle asked.

"Here's the Readers Digest version," Harry started. "My ex-brother-in-law came to me and said he needed my help. That of and by itself was a major leap on his part. Asking me for anything doesn't come easy for Mel."

"Having met Mel, I can see how that might be the case," Trundle added.

"Mel told me this kid he once knew was in some kind of trouble," Harry continued. "Mel continued by saying, *'The kid's been in trouble for as long as I've known him. I coached him in the eighth grade and he was a real handful back then. All the talent in the world for a kid his age, but he couldn't give two shits. He showed up for practice when he felt like it, and barely put in the effort when he did show up.'* But Mel told me he was light years ahead of the kids his age. He scored forty-two points in one game without breaking a sweat. Didn't even play the last four minutes of the game," Harry finished.

"Forty-two points in the eighth grade?" Trundle repeated.

"Yeah, and when Mel called a time out with four minutes to play, he walked right by the team bench and out the door," Harry said.

"He just left the gym?" Trundle asked with the same disbelief Harry had previously felt.

"Yup, he just walked by the bench and out the gym door."

"That would qualify as trouble in my book," Trundle said.

"You got that right. And when the kid walked out of the gym that day it was the last Mel ever saw of him. He missed the next practice and he didn't show for the next game. He didn't show for the rest of the season. He was long gone."

"What about school?" Trundle asked.

"Equally as strange," Harry said. "The other kids said he showed up for school most days, at least enough not to get his butt in hot water. From what I heard he didn't hang with any of them and kept to himself during school. End of the school day, he didn't even take the school bus. He just walked down the road and vanished, like in poof he's gone.

"A friend of Mel's who knew somebody on the school's administration said the kid passed his tests and got mediocre grades—enough to get by. Parents never showed for any of the school nights or parent teacher meetings."

"You know anything more about the kid?" Trundle asked.

"Nope. Mel told me eighth grade ended and the kid supposedly did a Houdini. He didn't enroll in either of the local high schools—St. Mary's or Manhasset High School. None of the kids saw him that summer and he was nowhere to be found in the fall," Harry continued the story.

"So, how does he enter the picture after all this time and why are Mel, and you, concerned?" Trundle asked.

"Mel, being Mel sometimes, feels he lost this kid and for some reason he's resurfaced in his life. I don't know why, but he thinks the kid needs his help. He turned to me and asked for my help as well," Harry said.

"Name it," Trundle said.

"I'll tell you what little else I know and I'm hoping your boys can fill in the substantial void in this kid's life between the eighth grade and now," Harry said.

"Done," Trundle agreed without batting an eye.

Chapter 8

Feet on the desk, a lukewarm half cup of coffee balanced on the arm rest of the chair, Harry was reading the USA Today when Mel entered the office.

"You get the worms or the birds beat you to them?" Mel asked.

Looking up from his paper, Harry said, "If you are implying I am up earlier than usual today, why shouldn't I be. It is another beautiful day in paradise, isn't it?"

"Paradise my ass," Mel replied.

"I hate to be the one to break the news to you, Mel, but your ass ain't nowhere in the vicinity of paradise," Harry told him.

"Blow it out yours," Mel responded.

After they had ceased laughing, Harry said, "So, where's the kid now?"

"Why?" Mel replied.

"I'm good, but I'm not that good, Mel. If I'm gonna look into what this kid's been up to, I need to see him and get something from him that points me in some direction to start. I got people working on it already, but you know how I operate. Rocks. I lift rocks and see what's under them. The kid is the first rock I need to lift," Harry said.

"He probably ain't gonna tell you jack," Mel answered.

"Depending on the beef, he may need a friend right about now. That is if he's even still there. Let me take a run at him and take my chances with what I get, jack or no jack," Harry told Mel.

"What makes you think he ain't still there?" Mel asked.

"If he's as good as you and I think he may be, he should be long gone by now, never to be seen in that particular upstate New York local venue again."

"He's not upstate anymore," Mel said. "My guy called and said he got moved south to the local jail where the warrant sat."

"You know where?" Harry asked.

"One of your old stomping grounds," Mel told Harry.

"Okay, where?" Harry asked.

"Cumberland County Prison in Cumberland County, PA," Mel replied.

"No shit?" Harry said in surprise.

"No shit is right," Mel said. "But my buddy said it's a small beef, so you better hightail it down there pronto if you're gonna catch him before he flies the coop."

"I'll be damned," Harry said.

"From your lips to God's ears," Mel said.

"Funny, you hump. I'll call my guy Tom down there and get a line on the kid right away," Harry told Mel.

"That's probably a good idea," Mel agreed. "If he's still around, getting a line on him now will make it a whole lot easier than chasing him in the wind later."

"If he's in the wind already, he's as good as gone," Harry told Mel.

"Happened once, it can happen again," Mel said without looking up from his beloved New York Times.

"If it does happen, or already did, he's history and you can write off that chapter in your autobiography," Harry said.

"When you're right, you're right, Harry," Mel told him. "You're still a dick-head, but in this case you're a *right* dick-head."

Chapter 9

Figuring there was no time like the present; Harry hit the speaker button on the phone and dialed his buddy-for-life in Mechanicsburg, PA. There were miles of history between Harry and Tom and Harry always enjoyed spending time with him. They had worked on a case not long ago and Harry figured there might be a small favor due on his side of the docket.

Even if there wasn't, Tom would drop whatever he was doing for Harry if it was humanly possible. Harry would do the same for Tom as well.

"Mechanicsburg Insurance Company—how may I help you?"

"Tom Naughton, please," Harry replied.

"May I say who's calling?"

"Of course you may," Harry replied.

Silence followed.

Harry waited.

"I'm sorry," the voice finally tried.

"Did you do something?" Harry asked.

"Excuse me!" was the reply.

"For what!" Harry answered.

Slightly flustered, the faceless voice said, "I, ah…Who may I say is calling?"

"Why, the party to whom you are speaking," Harry told her.

Muzak was all Harry heard next. He guessed he was on hold.

Mel looked over and gave Harry his "you're an asshole" look.

Harry nodded in agreement.

After waiting a few minutes, Harry heard the familiar, "Naughton" come over the speaker.

"Shorts," was all Harry said in reply.

"Harry, why do you have to fuck with people all the time? Especially a poor kid down here that got no chance to understand the shit you can put folk through," Tom asked.

"Well I don't know, Tom. Because I can, I guess," Harry told him.

"Just hang on there, Harry. She's new—I gotta tell the kid she

19

did good to put you through," Tom said.

"No problem, Tom," Harry answered.

Coming back on the line, Tom said, "How the hell are ya, Harry?"

"Better than a scarecrow in an overgrown cornfield without a single crow in sight," Harry responded.

"That good?" Tom asked.

"Yeah, that good," Harry assured him.

"You know some of us have to work for a living now, Harry," Tom said. "What can I do you for, or did you just call me cuz you're lonely and ya missed your good ole buddy?"

"Tom, I could use a favor," Harry told him.

"Harry, you know if it's humanly possible it's a done deal," Tom replied.

"I figured you'd say that, Tom. There's a kid got sent down to the Cumberland County Prison a bit back and I need to know if he's still there. If he is, I need ya to sit on him till I can get my sorry ass down there."

"That's it?" Tom said.

"That's all she wrote," Harry assured him.

"As I already said, consider it a done deal. If he's a kid like you said, I can have Cam help out with the "sittin' on him" till ya get here," Tom told Harry.

"That would work fine," Harry told Tom. "He's right around Cam's age I believe, and if I got this kid pegged right, they should hit it off fine. How is Cam?"

Cameron Naughton, Cam for short, was Tom's son and an integral piece in the case Harry worked for Tom not too long ago. While Cam seemed to have straightened his ass out and was on the right track now, his past had some pretty dark spots in it. He and Billy might hit it off at that.

"Cam's real good, Harry. Thanks for asking," Tom said.

Having given Tom the pertinent details, Harry said, "Call me when you know something, Tom. I hope to see ya soon, buddy."

Chapter 10

"How you be oh most favorite father of mine?"

That was what Harry heard when he answered the phone bright and early the next morning.

"Sleepy," Harry replied. "And unless I missed something, I'm not only your favorite father; I'm your only father."

"Nah, you didn't miss anything there, pops. But now that you mention it, the dude mom's been running with lately is getting pretty chummy," Max told him.

"Well, if she marries the dude it'd make my life a whole lot easier. No more brat kids to have to worry about for one thing," Harry said. He already had the lowdown on the current and soon to be departed dude.

"Mom getting married or not, me and Briande will haunt your life till your dying day. Maybe into your afterlife, too. That brighten up your day, poppyson?" Max asked.

"Music to my ears, Max. Like music to my ears—country music that is. And you just know how I just loves my country musicality so," Harry joked.

"Hey," Max said, "your American Idol chick's killing the country charts and winning every country award on every show. That's gotta count for something."

"I'll give you that one, Max. Now, what'd you wake my ass up for?" Harry asked.

"We have to postpone our doting father and devoted offspring Saturday soiree for this weekend," Max told him.

"What's up?" Harry asked.

"Mom's dude won some award and he has to go up to Boston to pick it up at a dinner his company is throwing. He invited mom, Bri and me to go with him and mom says it's a "you will go" no questions asked affirmative. Us youngins got no say in the matter it seems," Max told Harry.

Different dude Harry thought to himself?

"Does sound like it may be getting a little serious between your mom and this dude," Harry said.

"Happened before, it'll happen again," Max said.

"No walking down the aisle with this one?" Harry asked.

"Pops, you know mom better than any of us. She'll drag another guy along for a while, but she ain't giving up the ability to make your life more miserable than shit if she can help it. Yeah, she throws in a romp now and again, but her mission in life is to punish you for what she still sees as you leaving her and her youngins out in the cold," Max said.

"Out in the cold. What the hell do you...she...well, out in the cold? You guys got a house and she's got more money, twice the money I got. Romp—where the hell do you get off using the word romp with me and your mom in the same sentence?" Harry railed.

"Romp—as in me and Briande are out of the house and she's all smiley and happy when we get home. And, I might add, the new dude ain't been anywhere near the house. Yeah, romp it is and you be the romper, or rompee, or one of them."

"Stop growing up, Max. Pretty soon I'll be taking advice from you and that sister of yours instead of the other way around," Harry said.

"We'll be here for you, poppyson," Max assured Harry.

"Yeah, sure. Is my fellow romper around?" Harry asked.

"Yeah, but she's still sleeping. Out late last night with her dude man I think. And I gotta split for school. Later," Max said.

"Yeah, squirt. Later," Harry answered.

Romper.

Rompee.

I'm gonna kill that little bastard one of these days.

Chapter 11

"So, this dude the one?" Harry asked. "We talking like *Going to the Chapel* time or something with him?"

Silence filled the room.

"Max seems to think this one's more serious than the rest," Harry continued.

Silence continued to be her only answer.

Harry and Sherry were propped up against the headboard in Sherry's bedroom. They had just experience all the joys of another romp and were having a pleasant post-romp chat. At least Harry was chatting; Sherry hadn't said a word so far.

"What's his name? Dude, is it really Dude?" Harry asked.

"No, it's not Dude," Sherry finally answered. "It's Jeffrey. His name is Jeffrey Le Faire."

"Jeffrey Le Faire? His name is Jeffrey Le Faire?" Harry repeated.

"Yes," Sherry confirmed.

"I hope his nickname is Dude," Harry said with a smirk.

A quick jab to Harry's exposed ribs caused him much pain.

"That hurt," Harry said in obvious pain. "That hurt a lot."

"You got that right, dude," Sherry said with a satisfied smile on her face.

"That's bitchy!" Harry said.

"Fuck you, Harry," Sherry replied.

"Lest you forget, you just did, Sherry," Harry said with a satisfied smile on his face.

"I did at that. But I'm not sure I got it just right the first time," Sherry said.

Pointing to his injured ribs, Harry said with the most pained face he could muster, "I've been maimed."

"Well then let me kiss it and make it all better," Sherry said.

"That would be a start," Harry replied.

"I'll be happy to provide a start if you promise to provide a slam-bang finish," Sherry said.

"One slam-bang finish coming up," Harry replied. "And

speaking of coming up…"

~ * ~

Harry was in his car on the way down to visit his friend Tom and Tom's son, Cam. They lived in a small burg in Central PA called Mechanicsburg. It was only a hop and a skip from there to Carlisle which housed the Cumberland County Prison. The Cumberland County Prison presently housed one Billy Burns.

Tom had called Harry and confirmed Billy was still in the Cumberland County Prison. From his sources within the jail, Tom found out Billy was going to be released the day following Harry's original call. Unfortunately, there seems to have been a paperwork snafu and Billy's release would be delayed for several days.

"Good work, Tom. I'll be there in about an hour and I'm going directly to the jail," Harry told Tom over his cell phone.

Harry listened and then said, "Okay, tell your man Gordo I'm coming and to expect me this afternoon. Make sure they don't let Billy out before I get there."

Some more listening, and then Harry said, "Yeah, as soon as I get things squared away I'll give you a call. Thanks for all your help, Tom."

Chapter 12

"Any friend of Tom's is a friend in my book as well," Gordo said as he greeted Harry.

"Thanks, Gordo. I appreciate you meeting me and bringing me in. Prisons aren't exactly in my comfort zone," Harry told him.

"You ever been in one?" Gordo asked him.

"Visiting, yeah. And trust me, Gordo, that's the only way I ever want to be in one. I don't even like visiting them," Harry told him.

"Smart man, Harry. And you can take my word for it; you don't ever want to become a resident of this prison, or any other prison for that matter. Even the so-called country clubs are still prisons that don't let you out to go home for the night if you get the urge."

"Amen to that, Gordo, amen to that," Harry agreed.

"So, you here to see Billy Burns on a social call, or is it professional?" Gordo asked.

"Let's call it semi-professional for now," Harry answered. "Depending on how things work out and what Master William Burns wants to volunteer, maybe it turns more professional by the time we both leave."

"Good enough," Gordo said. "Your business is your business and you don't need me sticking my nose in it to muck shit up."

"Trust me, Gordo, sometimes mucking my shit up don't take much doing," Harry told him.

They both laughed.

"Here we go," Gordo told Harry. "Billy is actually a free bird already based on the call the warden got from the government agency. The paperwork is set up for signature and waiting for you to wave your hand for pen to hit the paper. Gimme the high sign and I'll put the word through to spring him."

"Thanks again, Gordo. I'll get through this as quick as I can and get out of everyone's hair," Harry told him.

"Harry, you take all the time you want. I started my shift two hours ago, so I'm here for another six hours at least. And the residents here, they ain't going anywhere either. Except Billy that is, and he leaves when you say so. Yell if you need anything," Gordo said.

"Okay, let's see what Billy Burns has to say for himself," Harry said.

Entering the meeting room, Harry was surprised by how claustrophobic it was. Maybe the "insideness" of it made it seem smaller and more confining than it really was. At least it did to Harry and he knew he was only there for a visit.

The room contained a six-by-four rectangular table with a chair on either side of the table. All three were bolted to the floor. Billy was seated in the chair across the table from Harry. He didn't get up when Harry entered the room.

"Who the hell are you?" was all Billy said.

"Maybe a friend," Harry replied.

"You here to let me out of this stinking shithole?" Billy asked.

"Well thanks, don't mind if I do have a seat," Harry replied.

"If you're here to let me out of this stinking shithole, you don't need to have no seat," Billy said.

"There's need, and then there's want. Maybe I don't need a seat, but I want a seat, so I'll take a seat," Harry said.

"Whatever," Billy mumbled.

"You don't know me," Harry started. "I walk in here, you have no idea why, yet you run that tough dude prison bullshit attitude at me like I'm supposed to shit my drawers right here and now."

Billy didn't even blink.

"So you know the ground rules, I talk, you listen. Then we talk to, not at, each other and then maybe I get you out of this stinking shithole. That agreeable to you, Billy Burns?" Harry asked.

"It's your dime," Billy answered.

Chapter 13

Billy looked at Harry like he had three heads, each with propeller beanies that were all spinning in unison. He had heard what Harry had said, every word of it, but he was having trouble processing any of it.

When Harry was done talking, he had sat back in his chair and waited for Billy Burns to say his piece. He was still waiting.

"So," Harry said trying to prompt a reply from Billy.

"So," Billy mimicked. "I'm supposed to believe a guy that coached me in the eighth grade thinks he fucked up because I walked out on him and the team and now he wants to make amends. Make amends for what? He didn't do the splitsareno on me…I split on him and the other kids on the team. And how the fuck did he find out about my current predicament in the first place?"

Harry just looked at Billy.

"And you. What's this got to do with you, and why? This guy Mel says jump and your ass is suspended in mid-air till he barks for your ass to hit the deck again. What's that about?" Billy continued.

Harry just looked at Billy some more.

"Key-R-Eyest on a crutch," Billy exclaimed in frustration.

Harry figured it was time to fill in a few of the missing blanks.

"Mel's my brother-in-law, well, my ex-brother-in-law to be precise. He periodically gets a bug up his ass that he has to solve some problem of the world; in this case it's your world. Since I'm a licensed Private Investigator, I get enlisted to assist in his world class problem solving excursions. Usually ends up costing me, but my ex would kick my ass if she heard I refused to help Mel. So, I help," Harry explained.

"This is weirder-n-mongoose shit," Billy said.

Perplexed, Harry said, "And you've seen mongoose shit?"

"That was a very long story that turned out very profitable for yours truly," Billy answered with a smile.

"I guess I'll have to take your word for it," Harry said.

"You got a punch line to this little tale of yours?" Billy asked.

"The punch line is Mel thinks he lost you somehow and he didn't, doesn't like it. Think of it as unfinished business from your not so distant past," Harry said.

"This is turning into an honest to goodness cluster fuck," Billy replied. "I mean it. First we beat some small town nobodies out of a few bucks and I end up in this god forsaken rat hole over a trumped-up two-year-old beef I had nothing to do with in the first place. Don't get me wrong, I done some shit in my day. But these here two are unadulterated bullcrap with a capital B," Billy said.

"If I may ask, how'd you get bailed out of here so fast?" Harry asked.

Obviously caught off guard by Harry's question, Billy hesitated momentarily and then chose to ignore it all together.

"Alright, here's a request you either take or leave. Give me a few days to run some stuff down, and if I don't come back with something solid for you to consider, you walk and I don't follow," Harry offered.

"Something solid for me to consider? What the hell is something solid for me to consider? I don't owe you, or Mel, or anyone else from that part of my past life diddly squat. There's nothing for me to consider because you ain't got nothing, and never will have anything I'd be interested in. I don't even know you from a hole-in-the-wall. And Mel, never mind Mel. All I want is out of here and I'm in the wind again," Billy said.

At that moment, Harry's cell phone rang. He listened, smiled, and said thanks. He then turned to Billy and said, "Billy, it's for you."

Chapter 14

Handing the phone back to Harry, Billy said, "How in the unholy name of fuck me did you pull that little stunt off?"

"Stunt," Harry replied. "What stunt would you be referring to?"

"Try this on for size, Harry Shorts. I'm here what, three days, and you show up from out of nowhere. You run this 'Mel feels bad' soap opera shit by me and then you pull off a stunt I didn't think anyone could ever pull on me," Billy said.

"I still don't know what "stunt" you're talking about," Harry told him with a shrug of his shoulders.

"How'd you get Edie to call me? And on your cell on top of it all," Billy said.

"Oh, that stunt," Harry said.

"Yeah, that stunt," Billy confirmed.

"Let's just say I know some people in the right places who know some people in some more right places," Harry replied.

"I don't know who you are Harry Mickey Shorts, but if you can get Edie to call me on your cell here in the Cumberland County Prison after, well, after some time, and it's suggested I listen to what you have to say, then I'm all ears," Billy told Harry.

"Solid," Harry said. "I have a bud who lives close by. We'll crash at his place for a few days and play it as it falls after that. Sound good to you?"

With that, Harry waved his hand in the air.

"What's that for?" Billy asked.

Before Harry could answer, the door opened and Gordo entered. He walked over to Billy and handed him his official walking papers.

"You are now free to go, Mr. Burns. It is our understanding you will be leaving with Mr. Shorts and do not require a means of transportation. Is that accurate?" Gordo asked Billy.

Looking as surprised as he should be, Billy answered, "Yeah, I guess that's accurate. Is it, Mr. Shorts?"

"On the button," Harry answered.

Billy turned back to Gordo and said, "On the button."

Gordo looked at Billy with his best no-nonsense look and said, "Then let's get you processed out of here so you can get the fuck out of my jail and don't you ever come back. Harry will be waiting for you just outside the door."

Billy stood and said, "Getting the fuck out, boss. Never coming back, boss. Be getting out right 'bout now, boss."

Gordo nodded at Harry and started for the door. Billy followed close behind wanting to make sure he got the fuck out before Guard Gordo changed his mind.

Harry was right behind them.

~ * ~

The Gold Datsun B210 Honeybee (circa 1976) with the HoneyBee painted on the side was sitting in clear sight of the prison entrance/exit. It was impossible to miss it. Harry was headed toward it when Billy turned to Harry and said, "So what now, chief?"

"As I said, I got a buddy down here who's gonna put us up for a day or two while we put our heads together and get a plan in place. His son Cam is about your age and you two can hang a bit while we're here," Harry told him.

"A plan to do what?" Billy answered. "Who says I need a plan? Who says I need you to help me put a plan in place as if I needed a plan in the first place? I don't even know you. Your Mel story could be pure bullshit and my ass could be going down a road it don't want to travel."

Billy looked away and gave out a huge sigh.

Looking back at Harry, Billy said, "Why do you think you need to try and help me, Harry Mickey Shorts? Never mind need to, what the fuck are you doing it for? You don't know me from Adam and all of a sudden I become your pet project like saving the rain forests or some endangered specie."

Not knowing exactly how to respond to Billy's queries, Harry thanked his lucky stars when his cell chimed.

"Shorts," he said.

After listening for a good minute and a half without saying a word, Harry said, "Give me an hour and I'll call you back on a secure land line."

Chapter 15

"Harry, you good for nothing hound dog, get your ass in here," was how Tom greeted Harry when he opened his front door.

"Good to see you too, Tom. This here is Billy Burns who I told you about," Harry replied.

"Welcome, Billy Burns," Tom said extended his hand toward Billy.

Billy shook Tom's hand but didn't know what to say.

"Talkative sumbitch, ain't he," Tom said to Harry.

Harry looked at Billy and then back at Tom.

"Put both of your hands in your pockets," Harry told Tom. "Grab your wallet with one and your balls with the other. If you don't, young Billy Burns is libel to be leaving with the whole shooting match and you won't even know it till he's gone."

"Balls and all?" Tom asked.

"Balls and all," Harry confirmed.

Tom looked at Billy with the "that true" look guys give each other when they're looking for confirmation of a particular notion.

Billy just hunched his shoulders.

"Reckon it be true then," Tom said.

Tom put both of his hands in his pockets and smiled.

Just then Tom's son Cam walked into the room. He walked over to Harry and gave him a high five.

"Been awhile, Harry. All's cool in Shortsland?" Cam asked.

"All's cool," Harry replied. "You good?"

"Gooder than good," Cam said. "Me and the old man here got it going on and the life flick be humming solid."

"Cam, this here is Billy, Billy Burns. Why don't you take Billy downstairs and blow out his ear drums like you do yours with that rock shit you call music," Tom told Cam. "I gotta talk with Harry for a spell, then we can get something to eat."

"Cool. Come on, Billy. Let me show you my set-up and you can pick some tunes to listen to," Cam told Billy.

Cam gave Billy some kind of multiple hand shake, palm slapping, finger gripping greeting and they proceeded down to the basement.

"Beer?" Tom asked Harry.

"Was the pope once Polish?" Harry answered.

"His Popeski he was for sure," Tom replied.

"Then a beer it is," Harry confirmed.

"Done deal," Tom said.

"You get the brews while I make a call. The phone cleared?" Harry asked.

"Cleared it just this morning, Harry. Help yourself while I get us some suds," Tom told Harry.

"Thanks, Tom."

Harry went into Tom's den and dialed a number. He hung up after two rings, waited a minute, and then dialed the same number again.

When the call was answered, Harry listened for a solid four minutes and then hung up without saying a word. He had what he needed.

Tom was sitting in his recliner in the living room when Harry reentered the room. Tom offered Harry a beer and Harry sat down on the couch across from Tom.

"You get what you needed?" Tom asked.

"I got a second confirmation of what I already knew. So yeah, I got what I needed," Harry told Tom.

After Harry was done giving Tom the short version of what he knew, Tom agreed with Harry's plan and direction.

"You need my help?" Tom asked.

"Not yet, Tom," Harry told him. "Maybe later, sometime down the road, but not yet."

"Cool. Let me get Billy and Cam and let's get this party going," Tom told Harry.

Chapter 16

Tom, Harry, Billy and Cam were seated in Tom's living room all with beers in hand. Harry figured beers would make the next fifteen minutes go down a lot easier for Billy; and for himself as well.

Tom just liked his beer.

Harry wasn't sure how to get started, so he sucked it up and just began. He had a story to tell and a captive audience to tell it to.

"Billy, I'm gonna lay some shit on you that I've had confirmed by two separate parties. It's nothing you don't know, at least most all of it I presume. I don't know any other way to get into it than get into it, so here goes.

"Your mother and father, whose names were Edie and Paul Burns, were a "best-of-the-best" con artist team who ran ahead of the law and everyone else for a very long time. Eventually, like most, they were caught in the act. When given the choice of either going to jail or helping their country, they chose country. They were recruited by the government and, from what I'm being told, you hardly saw them after you were twelve years old."

Harry stopped to assess how Billy was handling what he was saying. He also stopped to have a slug of his beer.

"They traveled extensively from when you were small. An aunt was supposed to watch you for them but it seems she didn't do a very good job of it. You learned from listening to and observing your parents when they were around and you were considered a naturally gifted "grifter" at an early age. A con artist, a shamster, a whatever you needed, or wanted to be. You were a chameleon of sorts. This next part is somewhat of a "grey area" in the information I have, but it is believed you often participated in "jobs" with your parents when they were around and had the need for your gifts of athleticism and "cutesy" childlike gab."

Harry sipped his beer and visually scanned the room. Tom and Cam looked transfixed. They seemed to be hanging on every word Harry was saying.

Billy sat, drank his beer, and listened with what Harry would have considered a casual interest akin to someone hearing a story about somebody they didn't know for the first time.

Now talking not just to Billy but to Tom and Cam as well, Harry continued to spin his tale of, um, Harry wasn't sure exactly what it was a tale of.

To a large degree, Billy was self-taught. Wherever he found himself he read everything he could get his hands on—legally or otherwise. He passed his GED at age sixteen. Why—his answer when asked that very question was, "because he felt like it." No other reason, he just felt like it. He applied to a small college in Indiana and got in. He didn't enroll, and when asked why not, he said, "I've learned all I need to know on the street. What could some college professor teach me that would be useful on the street?"

"Why'd you apply then?" he was asked.

"Do you remember what you replied when you were asked?" Harry asked Billy.

"Just to get in," Billy answered. "I think I said 'Just to get in' if I remember the conversation correctly."

"That's what I was told you said," Harry confirmed.

"So what?" Billy said.

"So what?" Tom repeated. "So what! Some kids, especially around some of these parts here, they'd give their right nut to get into a college. They'd give their other nut to be able to pay for it, too."

"Whatever," Billy said matter-of-factly.

"Whatever! What-fuckin-ever! I need another beer," Tom railed as he got up and left the room.

Cam followed his dad.

Billy yawned.

Harry just shook his head.

Chapter 17

Five minutes later Cam came back from the kitchen with a round of beers for everybody.

"Billy couldn't help taking what was out there to be taken. It is what it is, he was what he was. He was a street kid making it on the street any way he could," was how Harry restarted the conversation after Tom returned.

When Tom looked at Billy to see if he could get a reaction to what Harry had just said, Billy looked back and shrugged his shoulders.

Harry decided to jump back in before Tom could be Tom.

"This next part is pretty sketchy," Harry said. "From what my sources have been able to splice together, a grifter by the name of Frankie, or Jon Francis Fetterman to be exact, saw Billy doing a little scamming and decided to watch the kid. Much to his surprise, the kid had talent, real talent, talent that reminded him of himself at that age. Enough raw talent that he decided he had found the "him" he had been looking for. The "him" being someone he could mold, and teach, to be the best of the best. Better than him, better than anyone he had seen, and he had seen some pretty good ones in his day."

Billy smiled as Harry recited what he had been told about Frankie Fetterman.

"Yeah, the kid could be the one," is what my source has been told Fetterman said about Billy.

Billy continued to smile.

"Any truth to what my source was told, Billy?" Harry asked.

Billy thought for a minute and then said, "There are sources and there are sources. If I believed everything I was ever told by a so called source I worked with I'd have been locked up a long time ago. Probably for good. You trust the sources you trust until they tell you something you don't trust. I've been on the other side and you provide information as a source until you have to provide information your connection shouldn't believe. You just know what's right and what's not."

Harry listened to what Billy said, thought for a minute, and then said, "Very sound logic, Billy. Unfortunately, in the midst of your very sound logic you neglected to answer my question."

"That's right, he didn't," Tom agreed.

Cam looked confused.

"Billy?" Harry said.

"Let's just say some sources are able to hit the nail right on the head," Billy said.

"And mine?" Harry followed up.

"Yours," Billy said, "I'd hang on to yours if I were you."

"Good enough," Harry conceded.

"I don't know about you guys, but I need to take a piss and stretch my legs," Tom broke in. "Let's do that and maybe lighten things up a bit afterward."

"Good idea, Tom," Harry agreed. "At least about the piss part."

Chapter 18

With squirts completed and legs stretched, the boys were back in Tom's living room looking for Harry to take the lead.

Harry complied.

"Why don't you regale us with some of your exploits so as to 'lighten the mood' as Tom suggested," Harry said in Billy's direction.

"I can do that," Billy said after thinking for a minute or two.

"An easy one is the Stain Trick," Billy started. "You're in a crowd and a person eating a hotdog will brush against you leaving a glob of mustard or ketchup on your clothes. He will apologize profusely, and frantically try to remove the stain. Meanwhile, his partner (me) has pilfered the luggage you put down, or picked your pockets."

"It's that easy?" Harry asked.

"Yeah, it's that easy," Billy said. "A word to the wise, if someone starts cleaning a stain on you, aggressively hold onto your belongings, retreat, and clean yourself off in a less-crowded spot."

"Another one," Harry said.

"Sure," Billy said with a smile that said all believe in me, boys. "How's about the Bump Dump. Again, the fraudsters use physical contact. One thief will bump into you hard enough to knock you into his partner, who falls to the ground. While you and the fallen partner are scrambling to get him back up, the first thief pretends to help while rifling your pockets or handbag. You have to always suspect no-good hanky-panky when strangers bump into you. Hold onto your valuables and move away as quickly as possible."

Billy looked at the group and smiled.

"Another is the Metal Detector Hustle," he continued without being prompted. "Thieves working in pairs watch for targets approaching airport metal detectors and are especially fond of those carrying laptop computers. One thief waits until the victim places his bag on the conveyor belt that goes through the X-ray machine, then cuts in line in front of the victim and intentionally sets off the metal detector, causing a delay and distraction. Meanwhile, the thief's partner who was waiting on the other side of the metal detector, he snatches the victim's bag with his laptop when it passes through and immediately disappears among the crowd."

"That really sucks," Cam said.

"What the hell are you supposed to do against something like that?" Tom asked in obvious disbelief shit like this could be so easy.

"To defend against this trick, again, whenever possible, you should always travel in pairs," Billy responded. "One friend should pass through the detector two places ahead so he can collect all of the carry-on bags."

"And if you have to travel alone?" Harry asked.

"If they want you, you're probably SOL," Billy responded.

"Shit Outa Luck," Harry said.

"You got that right, sucker," Billy confirmed.

"And you've participated in these, these…this thievery?" Tom asked.

Billy's smile faded as he thought about what Tom had just asked him. A minute later, he responded.

"Tom, you have to remember what Harry just told you a few minutes ago. My parents were a "best-of-the-best" con artist team who ran ahead of the law and everyone else for a very long time. From an early age they used me in their scams, their tricks, their act. I was a stage prop to distract people's attention at first while they did their stuff. Little by little they taught me how to be a part of the game until I could do most of their scams myself," Billy replied.

"How old were you then?" Cam asked.

"When I could pull off the scams on my own, or with my crowd?" Billy asked.

"Yeah, on your own. How old?" Cam repeated.

"Eight, maybe nine," Billy replied.

"Get the fuck outa here," Tom said. "No way no eight-year-old snot-nosed kid could pull off scams like you just told us."

"Get me another beer and I'll enlighten you some more," Billy said.

Chapter 19

With the boys properly beered up all around, the group settled in for more of the educational "Billy Burns How to Scam the World" exploits.

Billy started again.

"Let's do the Pickpocket with Newspaper job," Billy said. "I couldn't do this one until maybe two or three years ago."

"Why not? What's so hard about the Pickpocket with Newspaper job?" Tom asked.

"I'll explain it and you'll immediately see the problem," Billy said. "A man pretending to read a newspaper bumps into you. As he makes a big deal of apologizing, he uses the newspaper to shield your view from his picking your pockets or handbag. Always be suspicious of any stranger who enters your personal space. Hold onto your wallet or bag, and move quickly away."

"Ah," Tom said when Billy was done.

"Cam?" Billy asked.

Obviously without an answer, Cam said, "I don't have an answer."

"How about you, Harry?" Billy asked.

"My guess would be you finally got tall enough to hold the newspaper high enough to pick the mark's pocket or handbag," Harry said.

"Give the man a cigar," Billy replied.

"Smartass," Tom said to Harry.

"Why thank you, Tom," Harry replied with a smile.

"Got any more?" Cam asked enthusiastically.

"Don't you be going on getting no ideas in that thick skull of yours, young man," Tom said.

Cam stuttered a few words, looked down and shut up.

Tom looked at Harry, then back at Cam.

Harry and Tom started cracking up at the same time.

When everyone had settled down again, Billy began his spiel once more.

"Let me tell you about the first scam I ever learned. My mom and dad had this one down to a science and I was the perfect foil for them to utilize. It's called Mobbed and Robbed," Billy said.

"Did you say Mobbed and Robbed?" Harry repeated.

"Yeah, Mobbed and Robbed," Billy confirmed. "This one is especially popular in crowded tourist locations, big cities and the like. A horde of children would run up to a tourist, asking for change or a picture. As the kids tug on their intended victim—me included in the group—begging and pleading, several people stand behind the victim. That would be my loving parents in this case, rummaging through packs and pockets. The well-trained kids are taught to choose targets that cannot easily flee such as infirmed elders and pregnant women."

"That's just wrong," Tom said.

"There's no way the victim could get away from something like that," Harry added.

"To some degree, you're right, Harry," Billy said. "If it ever happens to you, start yelling and keep yelling your lungs out for help as you move away from the little thieves."

"Unbelievable!" Tom said.

"Okay, here's another one," Billy said. "It's called 'The Sandwich' by those that can pull it off. As the mark tries to disembark from a crowded subway or train, someone getting on will bump into him, or her. He pushes you into his partner behind you who will pick your pocket while you are flustered. To counteract this one, be on guard: keep your hands over your valuables and don't let bumps and jostling deter you. If you feel a hand in your pocket, grab it if you can and yell "Thief!" The English word is understood almost everywhere."

Shaking his head, Tom stood and informed the group it was, "Time for another piss break."

Chapter 20

Relieved, but not relieved, Tom returned to the room.

"You got any more?" he asked Billy.

"Couple more and we'll call it a day," Billy replied.

"Why am I not surprised," Tom responded.

"My parents used this one when they, or should I say we, were on the road. It is somewhat risky, but produces big time results if you get lucky," Billy started.

"Risky? How risky?" Cam asked.

"You'll see right away once I describe it to you. I bet you've heard of it before and maybe even heard somebody say they were the victim of the scam," Billy said.

"I hope nobody I know said that to me," Tom said with hope in his voice.

"It's the 'Fake Road Accident' deal. My parents enhanced it by using me as the bait when I was only, oh, I guess I was maybe seven or eight. Here's how it goes traditionally: A group of thieves create a fake roadside accident, usually on a rural highway and often involving at least one "victim" sprawled out in the road, blocking your path. When the Good Samaritan stops and gets out of his car to see if he can help, he is robbed of his possessions, his car and perhaps his life."

"His life?" Harry asked incredulously.

"Your parents actually killed people to pull off this scam?" Tom added.

"With you as the bait?" Cam blurted out.

"Whoa, guys," Billy said. "My parents didn't kill anyone, ever, at least not that I know of. Or, at least not that I knew of when I was with them. But, you have to understand this is a very dangerous scam. You have to trust your instincts. If this happens to you, try driving around the victim, slowly and determinedly, but leaving no doubt that you will not stop, even if people put themselves in your way.

"One last one," Billy told them. "It's known in the trade simply as Rental Car Break-Ins. Thieves in tourist areas know rental cars are often full of cameras and luggage. They watch airport rental car offices looking for the tourist that's renting a car that's loaded down with "*stuff*". They watch hotel and motel parking lots, restaurants and diners, and anywhere else they can easily case looking for rental cars."

"Shit, now it ain't even safe to rent a car no more," Tom said with obvious disgust.

"You're right, Tom," Billy agreed. "Your defense is to minimize the chances of your car being a target. If there is a rental company sticker or license plate frame on the car, remove them. Do not leave signs of your tourist status, such as maps or luggage, visible in the car when you park it. And when you arrive at your hotel ask them where the safest place to park your car is."

"Well, shit. I ain't renting cars no more," Tom said. "Or if I have to, I ain't bringing more than a change of clothes with me if I have to."

"That's a bit drastic don't you think, Tom," Harry said.

"Drastic my ass," Tom replied. "I'm supposed to know what the hell I'm doing and this kid could probably strip me naked, swipe my tidie-whities, dress me back up and sell me my own drawers for twice what they're worth."

"Well, Tom, after hearing young Billy here tell it, you might be right after all," Harry said.

The three of them looked at Billy who just smiled.

"Tom," Billy said, "to prove you're right about what you just said, here's your watch and wallet back."

Chapter 21

Tom and Harry were sitting in Tom's living room. Cam and Billy had escaped back to the basement to listen to more music and do whatever. Tom was still shaking his head.

"Did you hear the shit that came out of that kid's mouth?" Tom asked Harry.

"Yeah, I heard," Harry replied.

"People actually pull that stuff on other people. No, they're not people, their scum," Tom started. "They're the scum of the earth to treat other folk like they're dirt and do shit like that to 'em.'"

"People get by any way they know how, Tom. You know that. You've been around. Some of them would steal their mother's last nickel and convince their dad it was worth ten cents if they could get it past him. Your scruples, what you were taught and how you go about your life, it don't mean anything to them. They have a different way about 'em and whatever it takes to survive they just do it, no questions asked, or answered," Harry said.

"That don't make it right," Tom said.

"No, it don't, Tom. I agree with you one hundred percent," Harry replied.

"And to think his parents taught him some of that stuff. Let him do it to other folk. Hell, they used him in their stealing to get over on folk. Not right, Harry, it's just not right," Tom lamented.

Harry realized his beer was empty and got up to get refills for both Tom and himself. When he got back he could see Tom wasn't feeling any better about what he had heard.

After passing Tom his refill, Harry said, "Let me tell you some other stuff I learned about Billy Burns. Well, not really about Billy, but it might lend itself to understanding who, or what, Billy Burns has become during his eighteen years on this earth."

"I'd surely appreciate that, Harry, cuz I ain't got a very good feeling about that boy right about now" Tom said.

Harry took a long pull on his beer and then started in.

"I already told you Billy's parents were a "best-of-the-best"

43

con artist team who ran ahead of the law and everyone else for a very long time. There's more to that story, truth be told. As I said before, their names are Edie and Paul Burns. Edie's father had wanted a boy after having twin girls and he named her Edie. Not short for Edith, but short for Edward. It's kinda similar to the Jonny Cash "A Boy Named Sue" scenario."

"No shit?" Tom asked.

"I shit you not," Harry confirmed.

"Edie's two sisters, who were twins, were named Mary and Jane. Their mother left for good when they were small and their father was a drunk. He often offered them to his friends by saying 'Any you guys want a Mary Jane?'"

"Now you're pulling my leg," Tom asked.

"Nope," Harry told Tom. "The two sisters left the day they turned sixteen leaving Edie alone with her father. She was just shy of fifteen at the time and was gone long before her sixteenth birthday.

"The official police report says Edie's father got drunk and "*fell*" down a flight of basement stairs. He wasn't found for a week and it was believed he lived a good part of that week with a broken back in what was also believed to be severe pain. The second step going down to the basement seemed to be in need of repair and could have caused his fall. The investigation termed the death "*possibly suspicious*" but nobody was ever charged in the incident."

"You thinking, maybe…" Tom thought out loud.

"Tom, right now I ain't thinking nothing, at least I'm trying not to," Harry replied.

"But it seems kinda…" Tom continued.

"Yeah, it sure smells like it," Harry agreed.

"What about this Paul Burns fella?" Tom asked.

"Funny thing about him," Harry said. "Paul Burns doesn't exist before he married Edie Molloy. You know my sources are as good as they come, better even. They came up empty when they went looking for Paul Burns. Who he was before that day is anybody's guess, yours is as good as the rest of us," Harry told Tom.

"I'll be damned," Tom said.

"Probably," Harry replied.

They laughed mighty hard over Harry's comment.

Chapter 22

Resigned to what they had to deal with, Tom and Harry decided to do what they would normally do under these circumstances.

"Let's get the boys and get us some grub," Tom said. "If it comes to it, we may have to drink heavily to wash this shit off our hands and out of our minds."

"Sounds like a plan if I ever heard one," Harry agreed.

Tom walked over to the basement door and yelled down for the boys to hightail it on up and get their sorry bones into the truck.

They did just that.

Once they were settled in his truck and under way, Tom asked, "Nolo's good with everybody?"

"Good by me," Cam answered.

Looking confused, Harry asked, "What's Nolo's?"

"My bad, Harry," Tom replied. "Nolo's is the name they gave to the restaurant and bar over at Rich Valley Golf Course. You and me played there a while back before they had the upstairs properly laid out and named. We had a beer but no grub. They spruced the place up and named it Nolo's Bar & Grille."

"Any good?" Harry asked.

"No, Harry, the food tastes like shit and the booze rots your gut. I just go there cuz I got shit for brains and don't know no better," Tom smirked.

"Don't be a horse's ass, you turd. You know what I meant," Harry said.

"For your information, Harry, the food's as good as you are gonna get around these parts and most other parts as well. The owner's son-in-law, whose name just happens to be Nolo, puts out a spread you are just gonna love. Every darn bit of it. They also got some real good beers on tap and the price is right, too," Tom bragged.

"Okay with you, Billy?" Harry asked.

"It involves food and drinks and I'm not buying. What's not

45

to like about that," Billy replied.

"We'll see about the drinks, but it sounds like we have ourselves a winner. Nolo's it is," Harry said.

"Then Nolo's it will be," Tom confirmed.

They pulled up to Rich Valley and parked down the hill around in front of the pro shop. Tom wanted to stop into the pro shop before they went up to eat and, what Tom wants, Tom usually does.

As they entered the shop Tom stopped short and shook hands with a guy who was about to leave the shop.

"Jeff, this here's my buddy, Harry. You know Cam and that there is Billy," Tom told the guy.

Turning toward Harry, Tom said, "Harry, this here is Jeff Austin. Jeff owns this cow pasture he passes off as a golf course and the place upstairs we're gonna chow down at in a few."

"Please to meet you, Jeff," Harry said as he shook Jeff's hand.

"You too, Harry," Jeff said in reply. "Cam, Billy," he continued.

"If you're headed upstairs we'll be up in a few. Fire up some grub and prepare to pour us a few cold ones," Tom said to Jeff.

"I'll be there waiting," Jeff replied.

"Hey Larry, you got any room tomorrow for four hackers who wanna tear up this poor excuse for a golf course?" Tom asked the guy behind the desk.

"I'll assume the other three guys with you are part of the "four hackers" you want a tee time for," Larry said to Tom. "You, you can't even qualify as a hacker the way you butcher the ball around a fine golf course such as we have here at Rich Valley."

"Any time you wanna part with a few of those green backs you keep squirreled away in your wallet you just let me know,' Tom replied.

"I may have to get Kevin and he and I will kick your butt and poor Cam's butt along with yours to the tune of multiple cool ones upstairs," Larry replied.

"Any time, Larry, any old time you and your boy feel the urge," Tom said with a smile.

"Ten a.m. do for you?" Larry asked.

"Ten o'clock will do just fine. You got enough clubs my guys can borrow tomorrow?" Tom asked.

"We'll rustle some up for Harry and Billy if they need," Larry said.

"They need," Tom replied. "And thanks for the fine service and pleasant conversation."

Larry just shook his head and walked away.

Tom and the boys left the pro shop and headed upstairs to Nolo's.

Chapter 23

Tom poked his head into the bar area and saw Jeff seated at the end of the bar talking with a few guys.

"We're gonna sit outside if it's alright with you, Jeff. Okay with you Hope?" Tom said to the lady behind the bar.

"Head on out, Tom," Hope replied. "We'll get somebody out there right away."

Tom led the boys through the bar and out to the outside seating area overlooking the course.

"This is cool," Harry said as they grabbed a table and sat down.

From the rear of the patio they were on, Tom pointed and said, "That there is the three-hole course Jeff put in as a practice area for those not quite ready for the main course. We use it sometime to work on our iron play and you'll find kids out there all the time."

"I didn't know you played, Cam," Harry directed at Cam.

"The old man got me started on that par three course out there and I took a real liking to the game. I still suck, but I'm learning," Cam replied.

"He keeps up the way he's going and he'll be kicking my butt all over the course soon enough," Tom said.

Cam smiled.

"That's the driving range and the front nine over there. The front's kinda flat and fairly wide open if you remember, Harry, but the trees Jeff planted, plus letting the rough grow out, is making it a bunch tougher than the last time we played it," Tom said to Harry.

"Back get any easier?" Harry asked.

"Kicks my ass severely every time I go out there," Tom lamented.

"You have a game, Billy?" Tom asked.

"I play some," Billy answered.

"That usually means my wallet gets plenty lighter I go up against somebody says 'I play some' with a straight face," Tom said.

"How some is "some" if you don't mind me asking?" Harry asked.

"Some," Billy replied.

"That good, huh," Harry said.

"Some," Billy replied again.

"Well, we'll see come tomorrow," Tom said.

"They have any lefty clubs?" Billy asked.

"Actually, one of my neighbors plays with lefty clubs. I'll fix it with him tonight," Tom replied.

At that point the door opened and Nolo walked over to their table.

"Hey, Tom," Nolo started. "Jeff says you guys want some food and maybe something to drink."

"Foods a yeah, drinks are a definite," Tom said. "Two Magic Hats for my buddy Harry here and me, the usual Pepsi for Cam."

Billy looked at Harry, Harry looked at Billy, and Billy said, "Make it two Pepsis."

"If you would like I can put together some of what we have in the back and you can each get a sampling of what we have here at Nolo's. That way Harry and Cam's buddy can get a flavor for what Nolo's has to offer," Nolo offered.

With no objections from the table, Tom said, "That works for us, Nolo. Be sure and bring some of the Steak Quesadillas you know I just can't do without every time I come here."

"Coming right up," Nolo said as he turned and left.

Chapter 24

After the beers and sodas were delivered, Harry toasted Tom on his choice of beer and welcomed Billy to the best Mechanicsburg, PA had to offer.

"I'm just making conversation mind you," Tom started which Harry knew from experience could be trouble, "but where have you been to since you left that fancy Long Island town Harry lives in. And how'd you get by?"

"Here and there, this and that," Billy responded.

"That it?" Tom followed up.

"That's about the size of it," Billy said.

"You were round about fourteen the last time them folk set eyes on you. From fourteen to eighteen and all you got to say for yourself is, "Here and there, this and that" and nothin' more?" Tom continued.

Billy sipped his soda and sat quietly.

"Nothin'," Tom repeated.

Billy still sipped his soda and continued to sit quietly.

Tom looked at Billy and then said, "Harry," as he turned and looked at Harry.

"What the fuck do you want from me?" Harry asked.

"Make him say something," Tom urged.

Harry looked at Billy and said, "Say something."

Billy said, "Something."

Tom was about to jump out of his seat when Nolo and one of his helpers came out onto the deck with a round of appetizers to start the group on their way.

"Here's a taste of our appetizers and a healthy helping of Steak Quesadillas for you, Tom," Nolo said. "Please enjoy and we'll be back later with some entrees to keep things going."

Cam finally joined in and said, "Thanks, Nolo, it looks great. Thanks, Chad."

"No problem, Cam," Nolo replied. "I'll have some additional refreshments brought out right away."

The food diverted Tom's attention and they all started on the appetizers like they were a pack of starved wolves. Billy reached for the plate of Steak Quesadillas before Tom had a chance to grab his share and got a 'Don't even think about it' look from Tom.

Billy backed off the Steak Quesadillas and hit the spring rolls instead.

With their plates full and liquid refills in place, Harry took the lead.

"I'm curious myself, Billy. Mel tells me he last saw you in the eighth grade and nobody saw head nor tail of you after the school year ended. Since you didn't enroll in high school in the area, one can only assume your family moved or you hit the road on your own after that. Care to enlighten us for amusement sake if nothing else," Harry started.

Chad came back outside and over to the table before Billy could reply to Harry questions.

"Can I get you guys anything else right now?' Chad asked them.

Billy reached into his back pocket and took out his wallet, produced an ID, and handed it to Chad.

"I'll have one of what they're having," Billy said pointing to Harry's beer. "Magic Hat I believe is what they are having."

Chad looked at the ID, looked at Billy, and then handed him back his ID.

"One Magic Hat for Billy Burns coming right up. Anyone else need anything?" Chad asked.

The rest of the table was too busy looking at Billy to respond.

"I'll take that as a no," Chad said and departed.

"Sometimes a boy needs to be a man and this here was one of those times," Billy said to the group.

The group continued looking at Billy too surprised to respond.

Chapter 25

Billy had his Magic Hat and the appetizer plates had been cleared from the table. Entrees were promised in a bit.

Harry looked at Billy and said, "May I see your identification?"

Without hesitation Billy responded, "No."

"Ah, no?" Harry replied.

"Yeah," Billy responded immediately. "An N and an O combined means no. You don't understand no?" Billy asked.

For the second time Tom looked like he was about to jump out of his seat but Harry put up his hand to signal I got this.

"I'm fully conversant with the word 'no' in the context you have used it," Harry started. "I'm also fully conversant with the laws regulating underage drinking and the use of false identification particularly when used in the act of committing a violation of the state liquor codes."

"Makes you pretty conversant, doesn't it," Billy responded.

"It does. May I see your identification?" Harry asked again.

"Ah, no," Billy replied. "But, to make you happy, I will give you the Readers Digest version of 'Where in the World was Billy Burns?' for the last four years. Deal?" Billy asked.

Harry looked at Tom, who looked at Harry, who then looked back at Billy and said, "Deal."

"Four years is a long time to account for," Billy started. "Actually, it wasn't really four years; it was more like six months, then a one-year increment, another year increment and then a year and a half spell. Before you go asking a bunch of dumb questions, let me explain."

Billy sipped his beer and then continued.

"When eighth grade ended we, that being a me and my parents "we," we hung out for the summer and through the fall doing stuff that stayed under the radar. They were still going strong as a team and had been home maybe half the time for the last two years. They decided to spend some "quality time" with their son and we traveled some, did jobs some, and practiced a lot."

"Practiced?" Tom interjected.

"Yeah, practiced," Bill responded. "I was good at most of the cons we pulled up to that point but the tougher they got, the more we needed to work on them to be perfectly assured I could handle my end of the action. We were traveling to different places so I could get a feel for what was required at different venues and registering for school never happened. I probably wouldn't have stayed if I had registered; so no big loss."

"Why not?" Cam jumped in.

"Why wouldn't I have stayed if I had registered? You have to be around to go to school and we were moving fast, and often, back then. Dad wanted to hit it big and maybe get out if they could. A few good scores and they probably would have put the act in mothballs and laid low for a few years," Billy said.

"Coupla questions if I may?" Harry said. "They made enough to finance a semi-retirement? Why quit if they could make that much dough—they had to be pretty young? And what happens to you if they do go quiet?"

"Those are some good questions, Harry. They made a steady take over several years and then they got into something that paid real good money. One mighty big score if I had it right. Second, the shit they got into had the potential to blow up if done wrong and they would have been on a much longer vacation if it did. Free and clear on the state's dime with three squares, etc. And me, I guess I would have gone underground as well. Didn't happen, so no real answer to that one," Billy responded.

Nolo appeared with several trays of food. Tom led the way and everyone filled their plates with a sampling of the different entrees Nolo had placed on the table. More beers and Cam's soda came with the entrees.

Billy continued as they ate.

"With the first six months now gone, the next one-year increment in my life started. Mom and dad went off to make one of the scores dad thought they needed and that was the last I saw of them. I hung by the house waiting for them to return, but they didn't. When word came down through what dad called his disaster recovery channel, it was time for me to bail and hit the road. I closed up the house and got word to the agent dad had put on notice beforehand to sell the house and put the proceeds in an account in the Caymans. Me, I vanished."

"What do you mean vanished?" Tom asked.

"Vanished as in hit the road not to be seen in those parts ever again," Billy responded.

"How old were you?" Tom asked.

"As they say, I was fifteen going on thirty and I was in the wind," Billy told them.

Chapter 26

The talk subsided and food became the priority. Everyone hit it hard and there was nothing left when they were done.

"Man, that was great," Harry said.

"The fish stew, both the veal and the chicken chesapeake, they were all something else," Billy chimed in. "And those potatoes, what'd they call them? Volcano potatoes? They looked like little mountains about to erupt. Pretty damn good if you ask me."

"Nolo can put out a spread, can't he? The food is that good all the time and he changes the menu with the seasons to keep things fresh," Tom told the group.

Sips of beer and soda were consumed all around.

Harry got them back to the subject at hand.

"Billy, you said you were fifteen and in the wind. How the hell does a fifteen-year-old vanish on his own? Where'd you go, what'd you do?"

Tom was nodding his head in agreement with what Harry was saying while Cam was eyeing the cutie that had just come out onto the deck.

"First, I wasn't out there on my own," Billy started. "And, I wasn't out there at all in the beginning. After mom and dad split and they didn't come back I used the cash stash we had in the house and hid out at home. I bought what I needed at night and used different get-ups to go out during the day."

"You mean disguises?" Tom asked. "And for how long?"

"Yeah, being able to use multiple disguises was part of how you stayed unnoticed when you cased out jobs or wanted to be someplace without being there. Shit, we had a whole room in the house set up to do our disguise work. It took me a week to dismantle it, pack it up, and ship it to our storage facility in Jersey," Billy explained.

"That is unbelievable," Tom said.

"It was soon after that I decided to split the scene myself. They were gone way too long and I knew they weren't coming back. The day after Christmas I grabbed whatever cash was left, set the alarms, locked the doors and hit the bricks," Billy told them.

"Nobody came looking for you all that time?" Harry asked.

"Oh yeah, they looked," Billy replied. "All sorts of people came to the house. The cops stopped by for about a month every other day, then once a week, and then they just stopped coming all together. Guys in a black sedan drove by for a while. They came to the door a few times. G-Men was what I assumed from their black suits, short hair and stupid looking sun glasses. Then, nobody came and I was able to go about my business as I pleased."

"Where'd you go?" asked Tom.

"Here and there," Billy said. "I tapped the people I knew from my time with mom and dad until I finally heard they got pinched. Nobody heard or saw them after that and the word on the street was they got caught by the big guys. That happens and you're going away. But it was weird, they just vanished into thin air and my street connections had no clue where or why."

"Here and there?" Harry redirected Billy.

"Yeah, here as on Long Island and in the Village downtown New York with people in the business who did me a solid and took me in. There as in Atlanta, Chicago, LA. Anywhere where somebody was going and I could grab a hitch and hang while they were there. I knew enough to get by and build a small stash of my own until I could get hooked up with the right spot to hit something bigger."

"Did you?" Harry asked.

"What?" Billy asked.

"Did you hit it big?"

"Harry, I got caught hustling the wrong country fucking bumpkins in Podunk Nowheresville USA. Do you think I hit it big?" Billy responded.

"Point taken," Harry replied.

"I had it though," Billy added. "Fetts had it going on and I was right in the middle of it. Right in the damn middle and a part of the play. I had it and then it was gone. Fetts taught me and let me in and then cut me out dry as a bone in nothing flat."

With that Billy got up and left the table.

Chapter 27

Nolo had visited them and replenished their liquid refreshments before Billy returned from his visit to somewhere. Cam had started to chat up the young chickie and was beginning to make his move. Her big as a brick-shithouse boyfriend entering the picture shut that down pronto.

Billy sat down at the table and picked up his beer. Any discussion on where he had gone was obviously not in the cards.

Harry was pretty sure he knew the who part, but to make sure everyone was on the same page, he started with, "So, who's Fetts, what was the play, what'd you do and how'd you get cut out?"

"Don't bullshit me, Harry. You may not know the play but you know who Fetts is. Jon Francis Fetterman, sometimes known as Frankie Fetterman, other times know as Fetts, never known as someone to be trusted. In this case, the last part proved to be very, very true," Billy said with emphasis on the last part of his statement.

"What went down?" Harry asked.

"Bullshit went down is what went down. I ran into Fetts, or should I say Fetts ran into me, when I was bummin' around LA waiting for my connection to finish his thing so we could head up to San Fran. He was either being sloppy or wanted me to know he was trying to lift my wallet in a straight bump and grab. I caught his wrist and he started laughing his ass off. Strange reaction to throw at someone who just caught you with your hand in the proverbial cookie jar I thought."

Billy stopped to enjoy a bit of his Magic Hat and try and gauge what Harry and Tom thought of his story so far. Plus, he was afraid he was going to have to jump into the fray if Cam pushed his luck any further with Miss Sweet Cheeks of the hulking boyfriend.

Blank stares from Harry and Tom combined with Cam turning his attention back to their table gave Billy the heads up to push on.

"Once he finally stopped laughing, Fetts told me he had been watching me do my "thang" and I was better than he thought I'd be. He said he had been turned on to a kid who might be what he was looking for and decided to find out if they were right. I was the kid and I had passed his little test," Billy continued.

"That seems to jive with the information I got and we discussed earlier at Tom's house," Harry said.

"That would seem to be the case, Harry," Billy agreed. "From there we started shooting the shit and I ended up crashing at Fetts place for most of the next year. He had a crib in LA and a place he ran his "business enterprise" from just this side of Las Vegas."

"His what?" Tom asked.

Before Billy could answer Tom's question, all hell seemed to break loose. Cam had yelled, "Screw you, asshole," at Mr. Body Beautiful boyfriend who obviously took offense at Cam's attention toward his girlfriend and had jumped up to advance on Cam. Before he got two feet Chad came out of nowhere, knocked him to the ground, and told him not to move if he knew what was good for him. Harry was holding Cam back and Billy had gallantly grabbed hold of sweetie pie to protect her from any possible harm to her body. As order was restored, Billy continued to protect the apple of Cam's eye and she seemed to be nestling in against his chest quite comfortably.

Harry gave Billy a look and he let her go. Based on his smile, a kiss on his cheek was more than enough reward for Billy.

Chad escorted sweetie's boyfriend from the premises with Nolo's assistance. She followed and then Harry and his crowd left as well.

"Let's head back to my place before Cam here gets all out asses kicked," Tom said to the group.

They all agreed and off they went.

Chapter 28

"Maybe it would be best to take a little break from this crap," Harry said to Tom once they had gotten back to Tom's house.

"That's not a half bad idea," Tom agreed. "I'll send Cam and Billy down into the basement to blow out their eardrums and you and I can figure out what our next steps are gonna be."

"That'll work. I'll get us some refreshments and you get rid of the boys," Harry told Tom.

When Harry returned to the living room Tom was emerging from the back of the house without the boys.

"Here's a cool one. Let's cop a squat and jaw on where we go from here," Harry said.

"That boy's a handful," Tom started.

"Ah, which one?" Harry asked.

Tom thought on that for a second and then said, "Both of them I guess."

"Yeah, I think you may have hit that one right square on the head. Well, maybe, could be," Harry semi-agreed.

"Cam was just being Cam," Tom said. "He thinks with his Jonson some times and it can get him in a pickle more often than not. He's getting better, but he's still Cam."

"He'll get there, Tom. Remember where he came from and his days traveling with that posse of his. Those days, if he had continued in that direction, would have led him to no damn good for sure. And long term at that," Harry continued.

"I just don't know about Billy," Tom said. "I got myself a bad feeling about that one. I hope I'm wrong, but I don't think I am."

"He's different, I'll grant you that. But, if you take into account how he grew up and what his life has been like, I bet there's a half-way decent kid hiding somewhere in there. He doesn't come across as mean or vindictive, or the kind that would stab you in the back before he stole your wallet. He'd steal your wallet in a heartbeat, but you wouldn't know it happened," Harry said.

"Maybe," Tom kinda agreed. "You may be right about that kid. But, I ain't turning my back on him, and I'm keeping a hand on my wallet when he's around."

"Fair enough," Harry agreed. "You watch the boys for a spell while I tend to something?" Harry asked.

"Sure, Harry. I'll leave the back door open for you in case we hit the sack before you make it on back. I'll get you up in the morning so we can get over to Rich Valley early enough to hit some balls before we play," Tom replied.

"Thanks, Tom," Harry told him.

~ * ~

The time Harry spent in Central Pennsylvania helping Tom with a bitch of a case Tom had signed on for was not all work and no play. Harry had made the acquaintance of several members of the opposite sex during his work on the case in a manner that belongs to Harry, and Harry alone. As long as he was back in the vicinity, no reason not to say hello to at least one of his, well, prior acquaintances.

Once he left Tom's house and was on the road, Harry dialed a number he hadn't forgotten.

"Guess who?" he said when the person answered.

It took a moment until the person on the other end of the phone realized who it was. Then Harry heard, "No Sugar Tonight?"

"I sure hope there's sugar and a whole lot more," Harry replied.

"The garage door is open if you remember where it is," the voice replied.

"I'll find it," Harry replied. "How could I possibly forget?"

Chapter 29

Harry navigated the Honey Bee toward his destination and entered the garage ten minutes later. The garage door had indeed been left open. He was hoping it wouldn't be the only thing he would enter that night.

The door into the house was also left open, so Harry went in. There wasn't much light in the back of the house, but Harry could see well enough to find his way into the kitchen. Standing on the other side of the island in the middle of the room was Harry's acquaintance.

"Madame President and General Counsel I presume," Harry greeted her.

"It's been a while, Harry," she replied.

"It has. One doesn't easily forget though," Harry answered.

"No, one doesn't, at least not some things," she said.

Neither of them had moved as of yet.

"You look good," Harry commented. "And that, ah, whatever you're wearing becomes you."

"Thank you, Harry. It was easy to throw on after you called," she replied.

"And from what I can tell it might be just as easy to remove as well," Harry said.

"It might at that if one intended," she replied.

"Might one intend, Ms. Metzger?" Harry asked.

"One might," she replied as she turned and headed for the back of the house.

From a previous visit Harry knew there in lies the lady's boudoir and he surely did intend.

~ * ~

"It was just as I remembered it," she said as they lay back among the pillows which were propped against the headboard.

"Which time?" Harry asked.

"Our last night at Visaggio's," she replied.

"No, I meant which time tonight," Harry replied.

"All of them," she replied without thinking. "Maybe the last one, the third time I think it was, was the best."

"They're all the best when it's with you, Maddy," Harry answered.

"That's sweet, Harry," she said.

"And I'm very glad there was sugar tonight," he replied.

She smiled.

"What brings you to Mechanicsburg?" she asked.

"I'm here on a bit of business I guess you could say," Harry replied.

"That's somewhat vague," Maddy replied.

"My ex-brother-in-law got a bug up his butt and I'm afraid it's gonna cause me a pain in my butt. It's a favor to him and he doesn't ask me for much, so I'm doing it," Harry replied.

"You staying long?" she asked.

"Not more than a few days this trip, but I may be back," Harry replied.

Maddy looked up at Harry and said, "It would be nice to see you again before you leave if you can swing it."

"It would and I'll do more than swing it," Harry answered.

Maddy smiled again.

"I know they say the third time's a charm and all that, but I'm thinking I may want to try my luck at a fourth if you're game?" Harry said with his own smile in place.

"A fourth time would be lovely, Harry. I'm thinking me ending up on top would make it just divine," Maddy replied.

"What the lady wants the lady shall have," Harry said.

"Then, as the lady says, let's get it started," she replied.

They did, and she did, and it was.

Chapter 30

"Wake up you worthless piece of shit," was the first thing he heard and what woke Harry the following morning.

"And a good morning to you too, Tom," Harry replied.

"What time'd you roll in last night?" Tom asked.

"Late, or early, depends on your point of view, I guess," Harry answered.

"Well, we're up and ready to get some breakfast before we hit the links at Rich Valley. You do remember we are playing at ten this morning," Tom said.

"Yes, I remember, Tom. I'm tired, not brain dead. Give me twenty minutes and I'll be ready to roll," Harry replied.

"We'll load up the truck and be waiting on your sorry butt outside," Tom said as he headed back up the stairs from the basement where Harry had crashed.

~ * ~

As promised, twenty minutes later Harry was showered, dressed and out of the house. He hopped in the truck and they headed out to grab a hearty breakfast at the local diner.

Once they were all seated in a booth they grabbed menus and prepared to order. Tom never looked up over his menu when he addressed Harry.

"So, what'd you do last night, Harry? You seem to be walking a bit stiff like this morning," Tom said.

Harry lowered his menu and gave Tom a look.

Ignoring Harry's don't ask look, Tom said, "You head somewhere for a little workout maybe?"

Harry continued to give Tom the same look.

"You are kinda stiff this morning, aren't you, Harry?" Tom continued.

"I'll be fine," Harry replied.

Harry didn't appreciate Tom's line of questioning or the shit-eating grin that filled his face.

"You gonna stop now, Tom?" Harry asked.

"Well, stop what?" Tom said in defense. "I, well, we're all

concerned for your health and well being. If you went out last night and got yourself hurt in some way we'd be mighty upset and worried. Maybe overexerted yourself in some way, maybe?" Tom concluded.

Tom's smile was getting bigger every second. Even Billy seemed to be enjoying the exchange.

Somewhat exasperated by Tom's badgering, Harry said, "If you must know, Tom, as long as I was down here I went over to see an acquaintance I met a bit ago and got caught up some. That's all, nothing more."

"Caught up some? You were gone a mighty long time to just be catching up some." Tom pushed.

"Tom," Harry said in his cut the shit voice.

"Just saying is all," Tom concluded as he raised his menu again.

With that the waitress appeared and they ordered enough breakfast for an army. Billy was unsure what or how much to order at first, but once the orders started flying he jumped in with gusto.

Orders placed, Tom said, "Even though I think Billy here is a sandbagger three times over, me and Cam will take on you two if you think that's fair, Harry."

"What are you playing to these days, Tom?" Harry asked.

"I'm a seventeen from right there at Rich Valley," Tom replied. "You can see it right there on the handicap board in the shitter along with Cam being a twenty-two."

"That makes you and me even then, Tom," Harry said. "What's your handicap if you have one, Billy?"

Billy hesitated a minute, then said, "I don't get out much but, if I had to pick it, I'd say maybe a ten or so on a good day."

Tom looked at Billy and he had that 'I know you're bullshitting me, son' look on his face.

"Ten it is then. You give us five a side and we'll adjust at the turn. Sound okay?" Tom directed at Harry.

"Good enough to start, Tom," Harry agreed just as their food arrived.

Billy just sat there and smiled.

Chapter 31

When they got to Rich Valley, Tom checked everyone in and set Harry up with rental sticks from the club and Billy with his neighbor's lefty clubs. Tom scraped up shoes for both Harry and Billy from the members, bought some balls, gloves, and tokens for the practice range for everyone.

Once they were properly outfitted, they hit the range to warm up before playing. Harry hit his small bucket of balls and watched Billy do the same. Billy showed the athletic form of a true athlete no matter what the sport, but there was something about his swing that struck Harry as odd. Harry noticed Tom was watching Billy as well.

Harry took a break and walked over to where Tom was standing.

"What do you think?" Harry asked Tom.

"About the kid?" Tom asked.

"Yeah," Harry replied.

"The kid can hit a golf ball," Tom said. "There's a natural smoothness to the flow of his swing that hackers or even medium handicappers don't have."

"I agree," Harry said.

"But," Tom added.

"But, there's something about his swing that's there, but it's not there, and I can't put my finger on it yet. It's just a feeling I have," Harry said.

Tom thought for a full minute or so and then he said, "To me it's like watching somebody do something that he's not used to doing. He can do it all right, but it's not natural. The kid can smack it for sure, and it's pure, but it looks like it should be even better. That make any sense, Harry?"

"Something like that, Tom. I can't put my finger on it either, but I know it's there, just like you're feeling," Harry agreed.

"Better stop yappin and finish hitting your balls. We tee off in fifteen minutes and I wanna putt a bit. These greens are faster than shit through a goose," Tom told Harry.

"Okay, Tom," Harry said as he walked back over to finished his bucket of practice range balls.

After they putted for a few minutes they headed on over to the first tee. Cam was unusually quiet but Tom had told Harry earlier Cam was really trying hard to learn the game and got keyed up before they played. "A hole or two in and he's fine. Kid stuff," Tom had told him.

Billy on the other hand was walking around like he didn't have a care in the world. He wasn't in jail and somebody was fronting the bill, so I guess he had no cares at all at that very minute.

Tom threw a tee in the air to see who would tee off first. It pointed at Billy when it landed, so he was up first. Harry would follow and then Tom and Cam.

As Billy was addressing his ball, that "*cush*" sound a beer can makes when you pop the pull top filled the air.

Everyone turned toward Tom who said, "It's noon somewhere in the world! Might as well join the crowd."

The rest of them decided to join Tom and "*cushes*" filled the air.

Larry was standing on the golf cart apron outside of the pro shop just shaking his head at Tom and his buddies.

Chapter 32

Cans safely stored in the carts, Billy returned to addressing his golf ball. The first hole at Rich Valley was a slight dogleg right with an elevated green. Not real long but there was a marshy area on the right that would swallow your ball if you tried to cut the dogleg and came up short. It would also grab it if you just plain hit a bad shot.

Billy hit a three wood off the tee and smacked his drive with a slight draw to the elbow of the fairway. It looked smooth and the result was perfect. Harry hit next and pulled his drive left into the rough between the first and third fairways. Not bad, but not Billy good. Cam hit his drive short but in the fairway and Tom gave him a high five. Cam smiled.

"Good drive, Cam," Harry told him.

"Thanks, man. I usually donate one to the marsh shit over there every time we play," Cam replied.

Tom hit last and drilled one right down the center and long.

"Where the fuck did that come from?" Harry asked him.

"Been working on my game some," Tom replied.

"I'll say," Harry answered. "You get a job over at MechInsCo. and you're out here hitting golf balls all day instead of working like the rest of the folk around here."

"Don't be ragging my ass just cuz you hit that dribbler into the rough over there," Tom replied with a laugh.

"Lotta golf to go my man. We'll see whose buying when we're done," Harry said as they took off in their cart.

They came to the fourth hole with Harry and Billy one hole up on Tom and Cam. Harry took one look down the fairway and let out a soft moan. He remembered the hole from the last time he and Tom had played it.

"That moan left over from last night?" Tom asked.

"What the hell do you know about moans you old dog. You ain't got none in a hound's age," Harry said in reply.

"This dog ain't that old, Harry. And you'd be surprised what went on around these here parts once your ass cleared out of town," Tom answered.

Cam was shaking his head over in the cart.

"What the hell you shaking your head at, boy?" Tom said toward Cam.

"Walls in our place ain't that thick, pops. And that lady you're seeing got herself a mighty good pair of lungs on her she does. Hell, the neighbors know when you're getting a piece," Cam replied.

"Ain't that something," Tom said. "Is 'Getting a piece' any way to talk to your dad? Kid deserves a good whipping for that and, if he wouldn't kick my ass instead, I'd give him one."

Even Billy laughed at that one.

"This here is a mother of a hole, Billy," Harry said. "Two hundred twenty-five yards to the waste bunker with out of bounds on the left and the right. There's a sand trap long and left of the green that you don't want to be in. You go first so I can drag it out as long as I can."

Billy nodded and teed up his ball. He hit some kind of utility club he found in the bag and launched it high down the left side dropping it ten yards short of the crap.

"Nice shot," Tom said. "Two pars and one lip-out for another to start and now that drive—you're hitting it pretty good for a ten handicap."

"Must be the enjoyment of the fine company that's doing it," Billy responded.

"Fine company my katookis. Hit the damn ball, Harry," Tom said somewhat frustrated.

Harry lined up and hit a high lazy slice into the neighboring property that was guarded by signs that said in slightly different words—KEEP YOUR ASS OFF MY PROPERTY!

Cam followed with a weak liner down the right side but in play. Lucky it was since Tom proceeded to hook his shot left back onto the third green and way out of bounds.

"This game can really suck," Tom said as they took off down the cart path toward their balls.

Chapter 33

The rest of the front produced some fairly uninspired play. One hole was won by Cam and Tom when Cam drained a thirty-foot putt on the par 5 eighth for a birdie. Billy had short putts on six and nine to win each hole but he missed them both. That left them all square after the front nine.

"Let's stop in to the pro shop and get us some more cool ones for the back nine, Harry," Tom said.

"Sounds like a plan," Harry agreed.

While Tom paid for the beers, the boys went in to take a squirt. Harry hung with Tom and offered to pay but Tom wasn't hearing any of that.

With their cool ones in tow, Harry and Tom headed back out to the carts.

"Funny how Billy missed them two easy putts on the front that woulda won holes for you two. He made the other ones like that to halve the holes but missed the ones to win them other holes," Tom said to Harry.

"And?" Harry replied.

"Just saying is all," Tom replied with a shrug of his shoulders.

"You're never just saying, Tom. I catch your drift and I'm gonna give the kid the benefit of the doubt for now. Let's see what happens on the back," Harry said.

"He's all yours, Harry. You deal with what you gotta deal with or let it be if you say so. Don't make any difference to me cuz we're gonna whip your asses on the back nine anyway," Tom told Harry.

"We'll see, Tom, we'll see," Harry replied.

The boys came out right then laughing and slapping at each other. They jumped in the carts and off they went to play the back nine.

~ * ~

Based on Cam's birdie on the eighth hole, he and Tom still had the tee. The tenth hole was another bitch of a hole and was playing dead into the wind to boot. It was playing just over 150

69

yards that went downhill from the tee, over a small pond at the base of the hill, and then sharply back uphill. If you didn't carry the ball onto the green it would normally roll all the way back down the hill leaving you a very tricky pitch to a sloping green.

Cam chose a five iron, let it fly, and wished he hadn't. His ball sliced severely to the right and into the water in front of the eighteenth hole.

Tom shook his head and teed up his ball.

"You hit a five?" Tom asked.

"Ah, yeah," Cam replied.

"Knowing that help you out, Tom?" Harry asked with a straight face.

Tom just looked at Harry and didn't say anything. He stood over his ball looking at the trees behind the green trying to gauge the wind. A slow and deliberate backswing followed by a mighty lash produced a high arcing shot just right of the green. It settled in the rough but it could be seen from the tee.

"Nice shot, Tom," Harry said. "What'd you hit there?"

"A club," Tom replied.

"Really?" Harry said.

"Yup," Tom replied with a straight face.

"You heard the man, Billy. Hit 'a club' and you'll be right there," Harry told Billy.

"A club it is then," Billy replied as he headed for the tee box.

Billy rolled a ball onto the tee and didn't bother teeing it up. He took one quick look at the green and took what looked like a long lazy swing. The ball flew like it had eyes and settled about five feet past the hole.

"That there's a mighty nice shot, Billy boy," Tom said.

"Thanks, Tom. I couldn't have done it if I didn't know to hit 'a club,'" he said.

Harry couldn't help himself and burst out laughing. Even Cam was smiling behind the cart where his dad couldn't see him.

"Glad to help out," Tom said.

Harry was still laughing when he hit his ball into the pond at the bottom of the hill.

Chapter 34

The back nine at Rich Valley can be much testier than the front. It gets especially interesting when you reach the fourteenth tee and continues on right through number eighteen.

At the fourteenth tee box, Tom said, "Let the fun begin."

Harry and Billy had the honors after Billy drained his birdie putt on ten and they halved holes eleven through thirteen.

"What's this do?" Billy asked.

"It kicks my ass every damn time," Cam replied. "Going on in from here all these holes do it to me right through me hitting my damn ball in the water on eighteen near every damn time."

Tom nodded his head agreeing with Cam's lament.

Billy looked at Harry for a bit more help than that.

"Correct me if I'm wrong, Tom, but if I remember this hole it goes out 150 yards and then goes directly left 150 yards. You can cut off tons of yardage if you fly it over the trees on the left. But if you cut too much you're in the trees along the left side. Don't cut it at all and you're either in the trap long or in the shit. Miss it altogether and you're in that overgrown crap right in front of you short of the fairway."

"That pretty much says it all," Tom agreed.

Billy took it all in and then pulled a five wood from the bag.

"Just right of the trees on the left with a gentle fade will work?" Billy asked.

"If you can do that you'll be sitting pretty," Harry told him.

"Okay then," Billy replied.

Billy lined up on the left side of the tee and hit his ball on a high arc that cleared the trees on the left side by five yards with a gentle fade. They saw it bounce in the fairway which would leave Billy in perfect position for his second shot to the green.

"Eat shit and die, kid," Tom said after seeing Billy hit his shot.

"Thank you, Tom," Billy replied with a smile.

Harry hit a five iron to the middle of the fairway playing it very safe. He would have had to draw the ball around the trees to duplicate Billy's shot. He had tried to draw the ball twice earlier with very little success. Safe was the correct play.

Cam took a three wood but didn't hit it anywhere close to the way Billy had hit his shot. While Billy hit a controlled shot that moved from right to left, a fade for a lefty, Cam hit a slice, not a fade like Billy. It moved left to right sharply just inside the trees on the right and not controlled at all. Finding that ball would require much luck.

"Seen that shot before," Tom said.

"Yeah, too many times," Cam agreed.

Following Harry's lead, Tom fit a five iron to the middle of the fairway to make sure they had a ball in play. It landed about ten yards to the right of Harry's ball, but it was in play.

There is luck and then there is luck. They found Cam's ball which was the good luck, but where they found it was the other kind of luck. The ball had come to rest in a section of thick tall grass that would have required the strength and skill of a Tiger Woods to hit any kind of useful shot. Tiger Woods Cam wasn't. He wasn't even in the same universe.

Two mighty (at least for him) lashes of the club later and Cam was done with that hole. At least he followed the main mantra of all high handicap golfers—don't get hurt!

Tom, Harry and Billy all hit their approach shots on the green and two putts later the hole was halved. Cam did an excellent job of tending the flag while the other three finished the hole. And, he didn't get hurt doing it.

Billy won the fifteenth hole with a fifteen-foot birdie putt to put them two up in the match. Tom came right back and won the bitch-of-a sixteenth hole with a chip-in from off the back of the green for a birdie of his own. Seventeen was halved and they arrived at the eighteenth tee with Billy and Harry up one over Tom and Cam.

"Good finishing hole," Tom told Billy. "You need to hit a good drive to make sure you can clear the water at the bottom of the hill just beyond where the fairway ends. It's the water you saw from the tenth tee if you remember. Three tiered green and a bitch-of-a trap to the right of the green."

"That all?" Billy asked.

"Actually, no," Tom said. "The green slopes pretty severely

from back to front and the pin is on the bottom tier if I remember right. If you're long you might struggle to two putt. Or if you're Cam, you might struggle to three putt!"

"Thanks, pops," Cam said.

"They've seen you putt, Cam," Tom said.

"How about you dig out the last of the beers and we get this round over with?" Harry said. "I can't wait to get back to the clubhouse and enjoy a few cool ones courtesy of my good friend Tom."

"Ain't over till it's over," Tom reminded Harry.

"You're right there, Tom," Harry said. "Billy, let's end this sucker so we can enjoy the spoils of victory."

"Sure thing, Harry. Can I borrow your driver?" Billy asked Harry.

Chapter 35

Harry heard what Billy said but it didn't seem to register. He looked at Tom to see if Tom had heard Billy and was having the same reaction. Tom was looking at Harry the same way.

"Um, Billy, did you just ask me if you could borrow my driver?" Harry asked him.

"Ah, yeah," Billy replied. "It's a loaner anyway, so what's the problem?"

"Well, other than you're a lefty, and I'm a righty, and you've been hitting lefty clubs and mine is a righty club, other than that I don't see any problem. You see any problem. Tom?" Harry said.

"Other than what you just said, no, I don't see a problem," Tom replied.

"Yeah, well, you asked me to end this sucker and I figured I would. Can I hit your driver or not?" Billy asked.

"Sure, have at it," Harry answered.

"Can I share your glove?" Billy asked.

"You want my balls, too?" Harry asked.

"Somebody else probably wore out your balls pretty good last night, Harry, so I don't think Billy would have any use for them," Tom said.

"Fuck you, Tom," Harry directed at Tom.

"Harry, somebody else probably wore out your dick pretty good last night as well, so I doubt you'd be any good. I'll pass," Tom said.

Harry couldn't help but laugh.

Turning back to Billy, Harry said, "Take the driver and knock yourself out. When we're done you can explain what the hell is going on here."

"Sure, Harry, no problem," Billy replied.

While swinging lefty over the first seventeen holes Billy had hit his drive about 225 yards on average. He hit it mostly in the fairway and moved it left to right, or right to left, when he needed to. He switched to the other side and set up as a righty using Harry's driver for the eighteenth hole. He took one practice swing, stepped up to the ball, and launched a rocket down the right side that flew past the 200-yard marker like it had wings. In all, it looked like it went about 250 to 260 yards. Essentially, a picture perfect drive.

"Holy mother jumping jeepers," Tom exclaimed. "What in the name of hell frozen over was that?"

"Um, a drive," Billy answered.

"A drive?" Harry repeated. "You switch from lefty to righty and launch a flaming screaming-meemie like that and all you can say is 'A Drive!'"

"Yeah, I used your driver and hit the ball from the tee box down the fairway. I believe that's what you refer to as a drive in golfing terminology," Billy answered.

"Screw this," Tom said as he pushed past Billy and Harry and teed up his ball. Obviously pissed, he wailed at his ball and sent one flying to the right a good forty yards off line. "Shit, shit, dick-wad shit," he said as he stormed over to his cart.

Cam tried to hit his drive but he was laughing too hard to make contact. His ball squirted thirty yards to the left.

Harry hit one about 200 yards down the left side and quietly walked back to his cart so as not to piss off Tom any further.

They rode out to their balls.

Cam hit his ball back into the fairway but was still a good 190 yards out. When they got to his ball, Tom jumped out of the cart, grabbed a club, and without a practice swing stepped up and took a huge swing at his ball. It must have been dirty when he hit it but it wouldn't be any longer. It flew directly into the water in front of the green.

"Shit, shit, humpin' dickwad shit," he said as he stormed back over to his cart and took off down the fairway. Cam, who was standing ten yards from the cart, watched as he drove away. Not knowing what else to do, he started walking to his ball in the fair-way.

By the time everyone was done hacking and slashing their way to the eighteenth green, Tom lay five twenty feet above the hole. Cam had hit a pretty good third shot over the water and lay four right in front of Tom's ball. Two tough putts down the hill to the front pin placement awaited them. They got a stroke on the hole and it looked like they would need it and more.

Harry had chipped to within ten feet right of the pin leaving him with a big right to left break in his putt. And Billy Burns, he had hit his second shot right handed to within three feet of the cup directly below the hole leaving him an easy putt back up the hill. Tom missed his putt and missed the come backer for a three-putt which was duplicated by Cam. Harry two-putted for a bogey before Billy calmly drained his putt for a birdie to close out the match just as Harry had instructed. And, he did it lefty.

They all shook hands. As they walked off the green, Tom said to Billy, "Son, you got some splaining to do."

Chapter 36

"This Magic Hat is going to taste especially good. Thanks, Tom," Harry said once they were seated up in Nolo's and refreshments had been served.

"Screw you, Shorts," Tom replied. "And you, too, you son of a bitch sand-bagging no-good lefty-righty swinging prick."

Billy raised his glass in a toast of thanks to Tom.

Tom didn't smile or return the gesture.

"Okay, spill it," Tom said.

Billy took a long sip of his Magic Hat and let out a contented sigh.

Cam was drinking an O'Douls so he could pretend he was one of the boys tossing down a few cool ones.

"Well?" Tom said.

Billy put down his glass and prepared to tell his tale.

"I could always use both hands for just about everything I did. Always could since I was a little kid. I could shoot a basketball equally as good with either hand. I could throw a baseball or football the same with either hand. Switch hit in baseball—no problem. So naturally golf was more of the same. That's what made me some money and that's when Fetts screwed me out of my big payday."

Billy consumed half of his beer to wet his whistle.

He continued.

"Here's how the deal went down. It was the best con I had ever seen and it turns out my mom and dad were the masterminds behind it. I didn't get involved until after they were out of it and I never knew they were originally in it until much later.

The con involves golf hustlers who target a specific golf course and run a sophisticated scam on a number of the course regulars. They don't go after the country club courses. No, they target small local clubs that cater to the average Joe looking to hit the little white ball and chase it down the fairway, into the woods, or wherever it goes. They insert players to win some and lose some with the average players letting themselves get beat more often than they won. Quietly they let it be know they wouldn't mind playing for some serious dough.

Word spreads and eventually they get around to the best players at the course. You lose some money to guys that think they can actually play the game and they will want more. A lot more. So much more they can't see themselves getting sucked in before it's too late. The stakes go up, their new suckers miraculously start to play the game like Nicklaus, Palmer and Woods all rolled into one, and their wallets end up filled with nothing but air. After taking them for all their money, the cons go after the club's ownership who are now in deep as part of the initial fleecing."

"And you were part of this "con" as you call it?" Tom asked.

"You asked for the story and now I'm telling you the story. You want it or not?" Billy said.

"Sorry, kid. Go on," Tom said.

"Anyway, Fetts worked me into his crew doing some easy stuff first and then it got a little more sophisticated. I was making some dough; enough I could get myself a small place to go and hide when I needed to get away from it all. Needless to say, I didn't know Frankie was on to me and had the place watched and wired tight as a drum."

"He bugged your place?" Harry asked.

"Yeah, he did," Billy answered. "You have to understand he didn't trust anyone including the boys who had been with him from day one. It was a way of life and not an uncommon trait. I was a newbie and had background in the game from when I was a young kid. Frankie knew it. You don't trust anyone and especially when the stakes get to the point the "golf con" reached."

"How high did they get? What are we talking about on average?" Tom asked.

"They'd get the club owners who weren't conglomerate people but local businessmen who built or bought a golf course. They maybe had a pro shop business, a driving range, and sometimes a snack shop or small bar and grill as part of the set up. The real value was in the real estate. After getting control of the club outright they sold out to a group that developed the land for housing, or malls," Billy told them.

"They'd actually take over the club? Like own it lock, stock and barrel?" Tom said.

"Yeah, you got it. Fetts had guys that could beat your brains in at cards, darts, horseshoes or any other betting angle that existed. And rest assured they would do it all day and all night long. They'd practically move in and pound you into the financial ground. Pound you into submission. The end game was when they got you on the course for the mega bucks after losing to you for pretty big sums of money. Then there's a turning of the tide and you find yourself getting yourself in deep to them after a few freak shots win a round. You're so confident up to that point you don't see anything coming. All of a sudden you're all in for your life and surprise, surprise—your club's gone."

"And you helped him do this?" Harry asked.

"Yeah, I did two of them almost back to back. Then Fetts screwed me out of my share and I ran. I hit the road and never looked back," Billy said.

Chapter 37

Harry and Tom were looking at Billy like he was an alien from outer space with two heads and ten arms and legs. Even Cam was eyeing Billy in a different light.

Harry finally spoke up.

"So if we got this scam right, Billy, a guy or group of guys who own a small golf course one day, don't own it the next day. They just lose the club, all of it, to a bunch of crooks who basically steal it from them."

"Ah, yeah," Billy agreed.

"What about the police, or lawyers, or I don't know, somebody that could stop them from scamming the club right out from under them? Nobody could help them?" Harry asked.

"Help them what?" Billy said. "He, or they, lost enough money to Fetts and his boys that the only thing they could put up was the club. The second one I worked was just that—the club against all their prior losses in one round of golf. I was the key that finished the deal."

"What do you mean you were the key?" Tom asked.

Cam was keenly interested by now and was practically leaning out of his chair to get closer to what Billy was saying.

"I'm saying I was the final piece to the puzzle. I was the one that made the difference when the final round of golf was played. The last one I worked went down like this: I hung around the club playing some small matches with the bigger players as a lefty with a ten handicap. I'd win a few but mostly I kept those guys happy and the owner of the club very happy. I stroked his ego and made him believe he owned my ass on the golf course. He was a five handicap and I couldn't beat him for nothing."

"You played as a lefty?" Tom asked.

"Yeah, only as a lefty. I'd wear cut off jean shorts and beat up old golf shirts two sizes too big. My golf shoes were two different colors. But I could play enough that the guys let me hang around, tee it up, and took my money with no questions asked," Billy continued.

"Nobody ever asked where you lived, where you came from, or where you got the money to play em?" Tom asked.

"Nah, they just let me tag along and took me for some chump change when they couldn't get a bigger game. They'd let me do some odd job shit to scoop a few bucks now and again. You have to understand, for this scam to work you have to target small clubs that get a reputation for hustlers, or guys that don't mind playing for some serious scratch. Guys that think their shit don't stink and they're invincible," Billy continued.

"And the owners? What about them?" Tom asked.

"Billy thought for a second and then said, "You have to re-member I was only personally involved in two club takeovers. But the two clubs had owners that played to low handicaps and not exactly Einstein IQ's. One was a single owner who was part of the group I played with and where I hung on the periphery. He was just too fucking arrogant to know his ass was blowing in the wind and his club was as good as gone. The second club had two brothers as owners and only one played golf, but not well enough to play for the stakes he did. The other played poker and played very badly for higher stakes than he should have as well. The combination of the two brothers' faults was lethal."

Nolo appeared at that moment with a plate of appetizers for Tom and his group. Refills of their liquid refreshments followed.

"Anything else I can do for you guys?" Nolo asked.

"No, I think we're good, Nolo. Thanks for the eats, they look great," Tom replied.

"No problem, Tom. Just yell if you need anything," Nolo said and left.

"Why don't we eat some of this good looking food and relax for a bit," Harry suggested. "Maybe pick it up later on back at Tom's house."

"Good idea, Harry. Pass me the spring rolls before Cam eats every last one of them," Tom said.

Chapter 38

When they got back to his house, Tom filled his old beat up cooler with Rolling Rock beer and took it out to his back yard. After properly emptying their individual piss tanks, the rest of the troops followed.

Rock in hand, Harry said, "So, Billy, why don't you go on where you left off at Nolo's. I think you were explaining the two times you helped steal a golf club from the owners."

"Steal's the wrong word to use, Harry. There was no theft involved. Nobody out and out "stole" anything. The owners were big boys that got in way over their heads and weren't smart enough to quit before they lost everything. Nobody put a gun to their heads and nobody threatened them. They chose to continue down a path that led to their ultimate demise and loss of their "assets" in the end," Billy explained.

"Did you say they lost their asses?" Tom asked. "It sounds like they sure as hell lost their asses and everything else, too."

"Assets, Tom. Billy said they lost their assets," Harry corrected.

Cam had had enough of this talk and said, "I'm heading over to the pool hall on the Pike. You wanna come and hang, Billy?"

"No, but thanks, man. I'm going to stay here a little bit longer. Maybe I'll catch you over there a little later and we can hang," Billy told Cam.

"Sure, dude. You know where it is?" Cam said.

"It's a pool hall on the Pike which I assume is the same Carlisle Pike we were on today. I'll find it," Billy answered.

"Down," Cam said and he split.

Harry passed out another round of Rocks and said, "Lay it out for us, Billy. How did it go down? Take me through one of the scam deals from point A to point Z and end of ballgame for the owner."

"Okay, here goes," Billy said. "Once he had the con locked in one hundred percent solid, Fetts sends his boys out scouting small clubs he heard had action if you wanted it."

"Action?" Tom interrupted.

"Action in that world means there's money in play. There's gambling of some sort, or multiple sorts like poker or horses or in this case higher stakes golf. Gambling of the kind Fetts could manipulate the outcome with little back end chance of loss for him. Enough play that if you had the goods you could make a killing and get out unscathed. Smart money emptying out the pockets of dumb money. They were looking for those characteristics tied to a smallish golf club where the owner(s) were part of the equation. Once they had a sniff, they descended like a pack of wolves and took them to the cleaners."

Billy had some of his Rock and looked for some kind of reaction from Tom or Harry on what he had just told them. Confused looks on their faces told him to go on and clarify it for them.

"The last one I worked was a golf course in Ohio with a small restaurant and a fair sized driving range. The course was in pretty good shape and got a mediocre amount of play, the driving range was underused, and the restaurant had okay food at okay prices the locals liked to frequent. But, and this is the key, the restaurant was the site for the Saturday night poker game with some pretty good stakes; there were ten or twelve guys who liked to play golf for money and had what looked like plenty of expendable cash to play with. The owner was a big player in both. Since there was no country club close enough to go to they made this course their own country club with the owner catering to his boys.

"Fetts locked in on it and put his move in play. He sent two guys in to see how good the golfers were and had them lose enough money to get them invited back to play whenever they wanted. That led to an invite to the poker game and they did the same—lost enough money to get themselves invited back when they were around. Since they said they were salesman handling the territory, they made trips back every two weeks. It took them three months to have the lay of the land totally scoped out and be confident enough of their chances for complete success—con style."

"Three months?" Harry said.

"A con of this magnitude takes time to put in place, Harry. Every detail had to be perfectly planned and the right person has to be assigned to each piece of the puzzle to make sure nobody screws up and sinks the whole deal. In the end it took almost six months from the first round of golf (point A) to the club belonging to Fett's shell company (point Z)," Billy told them.

Tom said, "This is just blowing my mind. I can't believe this shit happens out there and could happen here, too."

"Trust me, it happens," Billy told him. "You don't hear of it because the guys that lose don't want it out there what they did and the transaction is hush, hush with nobody the wiser. The club is sold to another entity for a bargain just to unload it or it becomes a housing track or a mall, built by a company who gets the land for what they consider a steal."

Harry's cell phone rang then and everyone else got up to take a breather.

Chapter 39

"Hey, daddy-o," is what Harry heard when he answered his phone.

"Max, my favorite son," Harry answered.

"That's right, pops. Where you be?" Max asked.

"Central Pennsylvania—same place I did that job not long ago," Harry told Max.

"Well, you can hang out in that beautiful part of the country for a bit but your butt had better be back here Saturday for your next Saturday excursion with me and Briande," Max said.

"It's on the calendar and ingrained in my brain. Wouldn't miss a Saturday with my favorite two kids for the world," Harry told Max.

"Uh, you already missed some," Max reminded him.

"That's past and ancient history my little punk son. It will never happen again," Harry assured Max.

"Yeah, sure," Max said. "Just make sure your presence is accounted for at nine o'clock on Saturday and it's at our front door."

"Take it to the bank, Max" Harry replied.

~ * ~

Harry went back inside and found Tom and Billy in the living room enjoying a good laugh. Things sure can change quickly is what popped into Harry's mind.

"What the hell are you two fools laughing at?" Harry asked them.

"You of course," Tom told Harry.

"Me?" Harry asked.

"Yeah, you," Tom confirmed.

"I'll play—why me?" Harry continued.

Tom looked at Billy who gave him a 'why not' shrug in return.

"Why not?" Tom said. "I was telling Billy here about the job you helped me with at MechInsCo. and your two-way shenanigans on the lady front."

"You were?" Harry asked.

"Yeah, I sure was," Tom confirmed. "And I was telling Billy that unless I was plum loco, you had yourself one of them Deja Vu things with the moms the other night."

"Oh, you were," Harry said. "And what makes you think you know what I did with my time you old coot?" Harry asked.

"Harry, how long have I known you? Answer—too long is the answer. And how many times have I seen you after you got your rocks off and wandered on back to the roost afterward. Answer—too many times for my own good, and yours too probably. So, don't you think I know where you were and what you did when you wandered off?" Tom said.

"Coulda been something or someone else," Harry answered.

"Her daughter Chrissy ain't here right about now and the moms is the only other sure thing you got around these parts. Ergo, as the highfalutin folk don't never say, moms be the one," Tom concluded.

"If that was the case, and I'm not saying it was, what the hell's so funny about that?" Harry asked.

"Told ya so," Tom said to Billy.

"Alright, I owe you ten bucks," Billy answered.

"What?" Harry asked.

"That's what we was laughing about," Tom told Harry. "I told Billy you'd get all huffy if I pegged it right who you was boffin' the other night and he said no way. I said you wouldn't want anyone else to know about your twosome down here and he started laughin' his ass off. I couldn't help myself but join in."

"Yeah, well, fuck the two of you," Harry replied.

"That's another tenner you owe me," Tom told Billy.

Billy shook his head in disbelief and said, "The man knows you better than you know yourself, Harry. I'm outa here."

Billy left to go meet Cam just as Harry was about to take a playful swing at Tom.

Chapter 40

Harry and Tom were having coffee and reading the newspaper at the kitchen table the following morning when Billy walked into the kitchen.

"Coffee?" Tom asked him.

"Yeah, that'd be cool," Billy answered.

"It's on the stove and the mugs are in the cupboard; help yourself," Tom told him.

"No need for you to get up or put yourself out on my account," Billy told Tom.

"No worry, I'm not," Tom answered.

Harry looked up from his paper, nodded for Billy to help himself, and went back to his coffee and paper.

After getting himself a cup of coffee, Billy said, "Where's Cam?"

Without looking up Tom answered, "He went over to the office early to catch up on a few things. I'm heading over there in a few minutes and you and this pain in the ass reading my paper and drinking my coffee are out of here."

"We are?" Billy said more to Harry than to Tom.

"Yes, you are," Tom said as Harry again looked up from his paper.

"Yes, we are," Harry concurred. "I have some business to attend to in New York and you have a long lost friend to get reacquainted with. Pack your stuff and we're out of here shortly."

"Did you forget, Harry, I don't have any stuff. Whatever I had was in the van and my boys took off with all of it. What you see is what I have pretty much."

"Yeah, I forgot," Harry said. "We can stop on the way out of town and get you some "stuff" to replace the stuff you don't have any more. But, before Tom splits for the office, why don't you finish your explanation on the golf course con."

"Man, I almost forgot we didn't get to finish last night. Not much left to tell I guess. Fetts' two boys get themselves locked in tight with the "in" group at the club and gradually introduce two more players into the mix. Slowly the two new guys from Fetts' team target the top two or three club guys who have the most money and the biggest egos combined. They add the owner, or owners, to the mix and then dig them a hole they can't get out of. In that one the girls they bring with them start doing their thing and secretly put together a picture show of the clubbies that would make a porn star blush.

"It all comes down in one fell swoop and the club flunkies fall away with their collective clocks cleaned to leave the owner(s) with their dicks swinging in the breeze. That only leaves the secret weapon to be unveiled to secure the club outright."

"What's the secret weapon?" Tom asked.

"Not what, but who," Billy told them. "Fetts' boys set up the final golf match with the owner and, if he's on his own, they let him pick whoever he wants to play with as his partner. If there's more than one owner they play together and they got them even easier. A match to give back everything they have lost up to that point is arranged against the ownership of the club if they lose. Having no choice with what they are in the hole for by then, the owner(s) agree. Only on the day of the match, one of Fetts' boys doesn't show up. In the job that I worked, I was known around the club as a know-nothing kid with about a ten handicap—as a lefty—who liked to gamble but always lost when he played better golfers with money on the line."

"And you just happen to be conveniently "around" on the day in question?" Harry added.

"Yup, that's right, Harry. I was in plain sight on the putting green when Fetts' guy showed up alone. The owner was a five handicap and the player he chose to be his partner was a two, maybe a three, handicapper. He was in deep to Fetts' boys as well and was looking to get even, too," Billy recapped for them.

"What happened?" Harry asked. "Was it set up in advance that you would replace the missing guy?"

"Yes and no," Billy replied. "Fetts' guy tried to cancel the match but the owner wouldn't hear of it. He and the other guy started yelling at Fetts' guy and I walked over to see what was happening. That was set up in advance so I would be there and available. The owner yelled at Fetts' guy and said he'd "get him" if he didn't give him a chance to get even. I thought he was going to blow a valve right there. Fetts' guy was supposed to "look threatened" and scared and blurt out, *"Okay, okay, calm down. I'll take Billy here and we'll play."*

"Just like that Fetts' guy is gonna give in, pick somebody out of the hangers-on, and let them have their way?" Tom asked.

"That's what it was supposed to look like. In actuality, it was always set up for me to be the other player in the final match," Billy told them.

"And they agreed?" Harry asked.

"I had played the better player several times and he beat my brains in every time. I had never beaten the owner for money with or without strokes. They let me be the replacement in a heartbeat," Billy said.

The phone rang and Tom went off to answer it. Billy and Harry refilled their mugs while they waited for Tom to finish his call.

Chapter 41

Tom returned from his call and also refilled his mug. He, Billy and Harry sat back down at the kitchen table and Billy continued his story.

"So once everyone had calmed down and it was decided I was to be the replacement, the three other players headed for the first tee. I knew what was coming but it shocked the shit out of the owner and the other club guy. Another one of Fetts' guys rides up to the tee with a set of clubs on the cart. He gets out of the cart and goes over to say hello to Fetts' guy. As he does, his windbreaker flops open displaying this fucking howitzer of a gun he had in a holster under the jacket. The owner and his partner see it and practically shit themselves right there."

"Where were you?" Tom asked.

"I was off to the side waiting for this little show of strength to play itself out. The owner's partner liked to pretend he was a tough guy but seeing the gun and understanding the intent of showing them the gun, Mr. Tough Guy went pansy-time pronto fast," Billy replied.

"What happened next?" Harry asked.

"When the muscle left I walked over and got into the cart. The owner must have noticed the clubs on the cart and said, "Hey, Billy, wrong cart. Those are right handed clubs on there." I told him no problem; I'd play with them this time."

"The owner looked at his partner, the partner looked back, and together they knew they had been had. They were as good as done right there and then," Billy said.

"Did they try and back out, or protest you playing right handed, when they knew you as a lefty?" Harry asked.

"The owner started to say something but quickly shut up when Fetts' guy turned and looked in the parking lot at the guy with the howitzer for a toy. He just shook his head and told his partner to get in the cart and play," Billy told them.

"How bad was it?" Tom asked.

Billy laughed.

"We played from the blue tees and I hit first. My drive came to rest two yards short of the green just beside the trap. I chipped up to two feet and sank the putt for a birdie on my way to a round of four under par sixty-seven. My partner shot one over par. We won thirteen of the eighteen holes and halved the other five," Billy said.

"They didn't win a hole?" Tom asked.

"It would have been hard for them to win any holes with the owner shooting eighty-four and his partner shooting a ninety-four. The poor dude threw up his guts after the fourth hole when they went down four and he knew he was soon to be out a ton of cash. I just hope he had it to lose.

"When the round was over Fetts' guy met howitzer man in front of the pro shop and they hustled the owner into the building. I heard they had Fetts lawyer sitting there with the paperwork to turn over the club and the owner's lawyer as well. The lawyer had been invited to the meeting and escorted there by another of Fetts' boys who was partial to Glocks, I was led to understand."

"The deal was finalized right there and then?" Harry asked.

"The paperwork was waiting and the owner signed away his club on the spot. I was told he got in his car immediately and left for parts unknown, as instructed, never to return to the club again. Anything Fetts didn't want would be boxed and sent to the owner's lawyer on his behalf," Billy concluded.

"What about you?" Harry asked.

"I was long gone by the time the ink dried on the contracts. My share was supposed to be sent to me in a week or so at a P.O. Box I rented for such payments. When it didn't show up, I called Fetts to ask him what was up. Howitzer answered the phone and kindly informed me my services were no longer required. He was instructed to tell me Fetts thanked me for my excellent work on behalf of him and his organization. When I asked where my share of the last deal was, Howitzer man laughed and hung up the phone."

"That meant no payment for Billy Burns?" Harry asked.

"No payment for Billy Burns and, if I wanted to question the outcome, I could speak to Mr. Howitzer personally if I so chose," Billy replied.

"You did not so choose?" Harry said.

"Correct, Harry. I did not so choose," Billy answered.

"That kinda bites, doesn't it?" Tom said.

"Yup, it sure bites the big one," Billy agreed.

Chapter 42

Harry and Tom said their goodbyes and Tom was off to the office to tend to MechInsCo.'s security needs. Billy thanked Tom for his hospitality and asked him to say "yo" to Cam. Cam would understand Billy told Tom.

"Anyone else you want me to send greetings to at the office," Tom asked Harry.

"No, I'm good," Harry told him.

"Suit yourself," Tom replied and he was off.

"Let's hit the road, Billy Burns," Harry said. "We're gonna stop and get you some 'stuff' and then I will drive us to New York. Once there you will spend some time with whomever you're gonna spend time with, including Mel, and I'm gonna take care of what I need to take care of. You can hang at my place while we figure out what to do with you."

"What makes you think you need to "do" something with me?" Billy said with emphasis on the word "do."

"All in good time, Billy Burns, all in good time."

~ * ~

With the needed stuff secured for Billy, Harry pointed the HoneyBee north and they were on their way. Exactly what Harry was going to "do" with, or for, Billy was still a mystery to Harry. The only thing he knew was that he had to reunite Billy with Mel and he had promised Billy's mom he would make sure he stayed put long enough for a family reunion to occur. A family reunion Harry couldn't wait to see.

Big Mel came first.

Harry's Saturday with the kids came second.

A family reunion was somewhere in line behind those two, but when remained an unknown for now. And if Harry played his cards right, maybe, just maybe, Harry would have a reunion of a different kind with one of the Manhasset ladies of his life.

Harry's thoughts were interrupted when Billy asked, "What's with this Saturday thing you do with your kids?"

Harry thought about how he should respond to Billy's question and then said, "It's a thing I started a little while after I re-turned to Manhasset and reappeared in my kids' lives. Once a month, if I'm in town, the kids get to put together a day with their dad doing whatever their little minds can concoct. There are no holds barred as long as they remember I'm paying and both of them plus me get equal enjoyment out of the day, and night, if it goes that long. It often does. Part of my enjoyment is the me pay-ing part. So far all of them have been a blast."

"That's pretty cool," Billy said.

"Yeah, it is," Harry agreed.

"What's in store for this Saturday?" Billy asked.

"That's part of the beauty of them. They don't tell me what we are going to do and the day unfolds as we go along. They love it and I kinda get a kick out of seeing what their little devious minds can come up with," Harry told Billy.

Billy turned and looked out his window. Harry had the feeling Billy was thinking about his childhood as it was and realizing he had missed out on what other kids can and do experience.

"Earth to Billy Burns," Harry said to bring Billy back to the here and now.

There was no response from Billy.

"Hey, Billy!" Harry half-yelled.

Billy came out of his insta-coma and turned back to Harry.

"Sorry, Harry, I guess you caught me day-dreaming," Billy said.

"No problem, Billy. You going off in your thoughts is noth-ing unusual for me. Is there anything you want to do in New York that I could help set up for you?" Harry asked.

"Well," Billy said, "I suppose I have to see Mel and get that over with as soon as possible. That way if he kicks my ass for bail-ing on him I can recuperate and get on with whatever I'm going to do. I could try and find some of the kids I played ball with before I split. Nah, they wouldn't know me from Adam and wouldn't care either. I don't know, Harry. Can I think on that for a while?" Billy concluded.

"We're in the car for another couple of hours, Billy. You give it some thought and I can make a few calls either from the car or when we hit Manhasset if you come up with anything," Harry told him.

"Okay, Harry," Billy replied and went back to looking out his window.

Chapter 43

They were still at least an hour from Manhasset if they didn't hit much traffic. Since it was still early enough to get in before rush hour, Harry decided to stop and stretch his legs for a bit. Billy had slept the last part of the way and Harry had to wake him when they hit the rest stop.

"We there already?" Billy asked when he came awake with a start.

"Nope," Harry replied. "I need to stretch my legs and I'm gonna drain the well and grab a soda while we're here. Come on in with me and grab something to drink."

"Sure. I'm kinda thirsty and I could use a squirt break myself," he said.

They went in, hit the rest stop head, and then grabbed some sodas and a few bags of munchies to keep them happy until dinner time. Harry had promised Billy a good down home Manhasset meal when they hit town. What exactly constituted a down home Manhasset meal remained to be seen.

They cruised into Manhasset off the Long Island Expressway since the other roads into town had traffic tie-ups. On occasion the radio news stations were good for something. As they turned on to Shelter Rock Road Billy couldn't believe his eyes. He remembered the construction and building that went on before he left for parts unknown but, seeing what was there now, he was floored. There wasn't a single inch of the entire stretch of road that wasn't covered by some form of housing or active construction site.

"This sure ain't the Manhasset I remember," Billy said.

"It wasn't the Manhasset I remembered when I got back into town and it hasn't stopped changing since then," Harry told him.

"Hard to believe," Billy said.

"Get used to it, kiddo. You come up with anything you want to do while we're here in Manhasset while you were catching z's?" Harry asked.

"After I'm done catching shit from Mel I think I would like

to just walk around town and see what's happened to the place. It's been a long time and I want to get a feel for the area as it is now. That cool, Harry?" Billy asked.

"All's cool, Billy. You have the address and your ass had better be standing on the porch at six-thirty sharp or your time with Mel will be a birthday party compared to what my ex will do to you," Harry told him.

"Understood," Billy replied. "I'll be there by then or I'll be in the wind."

"Better be a strong wind behind your back," Harry said.

Billy smiled at Harry's remark.

~ * ~

They cruised into Manhasset down Plandome Road and stopped across the street from Mel's office. Billy looked over at the place he had known a long time ago and blinked a few times.

"Didn't change much, did it?" Billy said.

"Mel hasn't changed much, his place hasn't changed much, and the whole street's pretty much the same as five or so years ago. The rest of the town has changed quite a bit as you saw coming in, but Plandome Road has remained pretty static," Harry said.

"Well, I guess it's that time," Billy said.

"Relax, kid, Mel's tough as shit on the outside, but when he sets his eyes on you after all this time, the toughness is going to melt right away," Harry told him.

"You think so?" Billy asked.

"Sure," Harry replied. "Or, he'll jump across his desk and kick your ass like it's never been kicked before."

Billy stared at Harry with a "you shitting me or what" look on his face.

Harry looked back and said, "Come on, it'll be fine."

Billy wasn't so sure.

Chapter 44

Harry entered Mel's office first with Billy following close behind him. He was figuring if Mel threw something he could hide behind Harry until he could make it back to the door and run for his life.

Harry started the conversation with, "What's cooking, Mel?"

Mel looked up from his desk. "Harry, what the f...?" before he stopped in mid-word. The look of confusion on his face as he looked past Harry to the person hiding behind him said more than words could express.

"Is it?" Mel asked.

"Is it what?" Harry answered to be his usual pain in the butt self.

"Sir," Billy whispered from behind Harry.

"I'll be damned," Mel exclaimed.

"So your wife says," Harry told him.

"Billy Burns?" Mel asked.

"Ah, yes, sir," Billy answered.

"Ask and you shall receive, master," Harry said. "You have but to command, my sire, and your every wish will be fulfilled. I live to grovel in your dust, to..."

"Harry, shut the hell up, will you?" Mel threw at him.

"Shutting up as commanded, master," Harry dead-panned.

Mel gave Harry his "look."

Harry saw it and shut up.

"Come out from behind that babbling idiot, Billy," Mel said.

Billy stepped out from behind Harry, walked over to Mel and put out his hand.

Mel stood and shook Billy's hand.

"You need me to go back in, coach?" Billy asked Mel.

Mel looked at Billy and then said, "You can play for my team any day, Billy. But first, I'm gonna kick your ass for screwing up my one shot at a championship," as he grabbed Billy in a playful head-lock.

Concerned at first, Harry quickly realized Mel was playing and jumped on the two of them causing all three of them to tumble onto the floor.

~ * ~

Order restored, Mel was behind his desk talking to Harry and Billy. Billy wasn't sure all was right within Mel's world but he was willing to give it a ride for a while.

"So, I've been wondering the same thing all these years. Why did you just walk out of the gym during that game and where the hell did you go?" Mel asked Billy.

"Why?" Billy repeated. "Why did I just walk out of the gym during that game at that time? Well, damned if I know. There was a timeout and I just walked off the court and didn't feel like playing any more. I didn't have to, so, I didn't. I split."

"Just like that? Nothing more—you didn't feel like it so you split?" Mel asked.

"Yeah, that is if I can remember what happened that far back. I didn't wanna play anymore, so I just didn't," Billy answered.

"I'll be damned," Mel exclaimed.

A repeat of the "look" stopped Harry from repeating his prior comment.

"What made you think you could just walk away from the game, your teammates, and me without a word?" Mel asked Billy.

Billy thought about what Mel had asked. When he was sure he knew what he wanted to say, he said, "Right now my answer would be different; back then the answer was I did what I wanted, when I wanted, how I wanted. I was mostly on my own and ran my life my way, not anybody else's way. A know-it-all fourteen-year-old kid's way. May not have been cool, but it was what it was."

Shaking his head in disbelief at what he just heard, Mel said, "Where'd you go?"

"When I left the gym I went home. When school ended we laid low for a time. When I had to, I took what I could carry and I hit the bricks. Where did I go? Nowhere, I guess, and everywhere," Billy said.

"At fourteen you hit the road?" Mel asked.

"Fourteen's just a number," Billy responded.

"And what about your parents? What did they say?" Mel

asked.

Upon hearing Mel's question, Billy sat for a minute. When he was sure he knew what he wanted to say, he said, "My parents hadn't been around much, if at all, for the past year or so. Didn't see them before, so no need to hang around and wait for them to be seen later. I didn't need them, or anybody else, so I split for parts unknown."

"I'll be damned," Mel exclaimed.

Harry knew to be quiet.

~ * ~

They talked for another fifteen minutes about nothing in particular. Harry had things to do and left Billy with Mel in his office with Billy's promise to be at Sherry's place at 6:30 sharp. Mel confirmed he would be wise to be there and be on time, or else.

As Harry walked up the street toward his apartment he couldn't help but wonder what the immediate future had in store for him, and for young Mr. Billy Burns.

Chapter 45

With plenty of time to spare, Harry left his apartment and started on his way to Sherry's house for their 6:30 dinner. Just as he had told Billy, there was no way his ass wasn't going to be there on time, if not early.

Harry knew Sherry very well and exactly what she was capable of if you crossed her in any way. He didn't care to go down that road today or any time soon for that matter. He wouldn't mind traveling down a different path with her, one that would please them both, but the "I'm late" road he would avoid like the plague.

As he was about to cross the street directly across from Sherry's house, Harry felt a car creeping up behind him. It parked and before Harry could turn around Billy emerged from the driver's side of the car.

Harry looked at Billy as he joined him and said, "Ah, nice wheels, Billy. If you wouldn't mind me asking, where'd you get them?"

"Borrowed them," Billy replied.

"Borrowed them?" Harry questioned.

"Yeah, I borrowed them," Billy replied. "I was with some guys and I didn't want to be late for dinner; so yeah, I borrowed them."

"Who do they belong to?" Harry asked.

"Some guy," Billy replied.

"Some guy?" Harry asked. "Like, what guy? Like a guy you were with earlier? Like a guy you knew before and he had no problem lending you his wheels after how long? Like, what guy?"

"Ah, just some guy," Billy replied.

"I don't want to know, do I?" Harry asked.

"Probably not, Harry. But not to worry, he'll have them back; nobody's the wiser and nobody gets hurt none," Billy told Harry.

"Yeah, I don't want to know," Harry told him.

"It's almost six-thirty, Harry. I would think we best hustle our asses inside," Billy said.

Harry didn't answer. He just shook his head and started across the street.

~ * ~

Max answered the door as soon as Harry knocked.

"Hey, poppyson. Cruise on in here," Max said.

Harry stepped into the house followed by Billy.

Giving Billy some room, Harry said, "Max, this is Billy. Billy, Max."

"Hey, Billy. I've heard a little about you. Nice to meet you," Max said.

"You too, Max," Billy returned.

Sherry came in from the kitchen followed by Briande. The Airedales were in the back yard howling up a storm trying to get at the new meat.

Ever the great host even though it wasn't his house any more, Harry said, "Sherry, I'd like you to meet Billy. Billy, this is my lovely ex-wife, Sherry, and my favorite daughter, Briande."

Billy shook their hands and said, "It's a pleasure to meet both of you. Harry couldn't say enough good things about you, all of you."

Sherry looked at Harry, then back at Billy, and said, "Billy, in case you haven't figured it out yet, my darling ex could charm the pants off Mother Superior if he put his mind to it. I'm sure everything he said about me was all peaches and cream."

"With sugar and a cherry on top," Billy said with a smile wide enough to charm Mother Superior.

"Cute," Sherry said. "You two must get along real fine," Sherry said as she turned her gaze on Harry.

Trying to change things up and lighten the mood, Harry said, "Can a guy get something to drink around here? And, before you ask, the kid's got ID making him legal that's better than the real thing."

Taking a closer look at Billy after Harry's comment, Sherry said, "Max, go on out to the kitchen and bring in the pitcher and glasses on the counter. Get you and Briande some soda, too."

Max bowed and shuffled backwards saying, "Yes um, mam, I'se be getting dose refreshments right quickly, mam."

Sherry went to swat Max but he was too quick for her.

"You see what you've done, Harry," Sherry said to him.

"Me, what?" Harry replied sheepishly.

"You know he gets that from you, daddy," Briande said. "He thinks he's so funny."

Max could be heard laughing in the kitchen.

Billy was taking it all in and smiling—on the outside. Thoughts of what he might have had, but didn't, were running though his inside.

"What the hell are you smiling at?" Sherry threw at Billy.

"Well, you guys, what else?" Billy answered.

Sherry thought, understood, and smiled.

Chapter 46

Acting as butler and bartender for a day, or night, Max distributed his and Briande's sodas and poured Absolute Gimlets for Harry, Billy and his mom. He didn't spill a drop. After that he hustled back into the kitchen and brought out the goodies—pigs in a blanket, mini-Reubens and a crab dip specifically requested by Briande.

"Thank you, Max," Sherry said to her son with obvious pride.

"Yeah, good job, bub," Harry chimed in.

Max beamed.

The little bastard is growing up way too fast, Harry thought to himself and he couldn't help but realize he liked it to some degree.

"Welcome back to Manhasset, Billy," Sherry said as she lifted her glass in toast.

"Thank you, Sherry, I guess," Billy replied.

"You guess?" Sherry repeated. "You don't sound so sure about that."

"Let him be, Sherry. The kid just got back..." Harry started before Billy cut him off.

"It's okay, Harry. She's right. I didn't sound very positive because I'm not, I guess. I mean I think...I, ah, I guess I don't really know what I think," Billy said.

"Been a long time," Harry said.

"Yeah, it has," Billy agreed. "And it surely wasn't on the best of circumstances that I left Manhasset, my home. I never really expected to see this town again. I thought it was part of my past and I was on to other adventures, other places, other things. But, you never know, you know?"

"One never knows, Billy. One just never knows," Harry said.

"Mini Reuben anyone?" Max piped in.

Everyone looked at Max and the room erupted in laughter.

"Hey, what'd I do?" Max asked.

"Nothing, Max, nothing at all," Harry said. "Welcome back to Manhasset, Billy," Harry continued as he lifted his glass in Billy direction.

"Thanks, Harry. And I'll take one of those Reubens, Max," Billy said.

~ * ~

They were seated around the table enjoying a fine dinner prepared mostly by Max and Briande. There were indications Sherry had supervised, but the actual individual courses starting with the hors d'oeuvres already consumed were decided on, bought, cooked and served by the two kids.

So far, they were a big hit.

Max had handled the salad course and decided on hearts of lettuce, crumpled bacon with a hint of chives and a honey Dijon French dressing. Mini pop-ups slathered in garlic butter accompanied the salads.

Max was cleaning up the salad plates while Briande worked on the main course. She and Max had put their heads together to decide on the entrée while Briande made the decision on the accompanying pieces. She was struggling to get it all to come together at the same time.

"That was a great salad, guys," Sherry said. "Is there anything I can do to help?" she asked in Briande's direction.

"No thank you, Max and I have everything under control," Briande replied as she gave Max a look that could kill.

"We're on it, mom," Max said when he saw Briande's look. "None d'you worry."

Max scurried over to the stove to see how he could help before Briande brained him with a pan.

"Let me get us a coupla beers and some wine for Sherry," Harry said as he got up from the table. As he approached Briande to see if he could slyly help out, her stare told him to run to the fridge and sit down quickly if he valued his life.

Harry ran like his life depended on it.

Chapter 47

"What did you just say? And where the hell did you hear that shit if I heard you right?" Fetts asked.

The guy standing before Fetts wished he had kept his stupid-assed mouth shut for once. He glanced to the right hoping to get some support from his brother but, at the moment, his brother was intently investigating the shoelaces on his sneakers. It was obvious no help from him was forthcoming.

"Did you hear me, asshole?" Frankie yelled. "I said, 'What did you just say? And where the hell did you hear that shit?'"

"I heard you the first time, Frankie," Mutt replied. "I ain't deaf you know."

Calmly, Fetts repeated, "What did you just say? And where the hell did you hear that shit?"

Before answering, Mutt again looked back at his brother Jeff, but his brother never picked up his head. He never looked up at Mutt at all.

"I said we heard he was let out and we missed it. Billy got out of the jail in Carlisle when we heard he was gonna be there for a while longer for sure. That's right, ain't it, Jeff?" Mutt said.

Fetts looked at Mutt like he couldn't believe he was hearing what he was saying. He heard the words, but he didn't believe him.

"That right, Jeff? Is what your dumb-ass of a brother just told me true? Are you both telling me you lost Billy?" Frankie asked.

When Jeff didn't respond, Frankie continued, "The two of you are trying to tell me that you don't know when Billy got out, how he got out, who got him out and where he is now? Are you two dip-shits of a pair of worthless brothers of my two-timing no-fucking-good ex-fucking wife really trying to tell me that?"

Looking like he wanted to crawl up his own asshole and hide, Jeff said, "We're sorry, Fetts. We had our guy all over him like you told us to, but he just wasn't there when our guy went to check on him last week. I swear to god we had it covered!"

Fetts looked from Jeff to Mutt, and back to Jeff, all the time shaking his head in utter disbelief.

"Your guy. Your fucking guy. Your no-good same-as-you worthless piece of shit of a guy. You two had better get your guy and between the three of you find Billy again and find out how he got out, who got him out and where he is now. Do it and do it fast. And I don't want to see your worthless asses anywhere near me until you do. Do you understand that? DO YOU TWO FUCKING MORONS UNDERSTAND THAT?" Fetts screamed.

The two of them ran for the door as Jeff said over his shoulder, "We heard you, Fetts. We're on it and we'll find him, and fast."

~ * ~

Believing the conversation was over, and for his hearings sake he was thankful it was, Yeomans took off his headphones and shut off the tape recorder. He jacked out the cassette and labeled it "LAS VEGAS—Fetterman/Billy Burns #12." He opened the cassette tape holder case and inserted the cassette in the slot next to the tape labeled "LAS VEGAS—Fetterman/Billy Burns #11."

Taking out his cell phone, Yeomans dialed the number he had dialed numerous times every day for the last three months. Hearing the connection click on from the other end he said, "Mutt and Jeff are on the road to meet up with their guy. They have been instructed to find Billy."

Yeomans listed for a full minute and then said, "You got it. I'll continue until I know they have located him and reported same to Fetterman."

Yeomans disconnected and put his phone back on the desk. He picked up his copy of the newest "da" novel from the popular private detective series and began to read.

Chapter 48

Beers and wine adequately served, Harry re-started the conversation in Billy's direction. The minor commotion at the stove was ignored by all at the table.

"What did you see and do today, Billy?" Harry asked him.

"See and do?" Billy repeated.

Harry looked at Sherry. She looked back at him.

"He always do that?" Sherry asked.

"You get used to it," Harry told her.

Looking back at Billy, Harry said, "Yeah, Billy, see and do. It's a question people ask other people to find out who they may have been with during the day. As in Who'd you see today? What did you do today? Like that," Harry concluded.

Sherry nodded in agreement.

"Who'd I see?" Billy repeated. "Just some guys, that's all. And we didn't do much of anything."

"You see now, that's very helpful, Billy. That clears it up perfectly for us," Harry said with just a hint of sarcasm in his voice.

"Perfectly," Sherry agreed.

Before Billy could respond to their digs, Briande announced, "Dinner will now be served," as she and Max began bringing plates over to the table.

Briande placed the platter with the main courses in the middle of the table and stepped back to admire her masterpiece. Max had the potato and vegetable dishes and placed them on either side of the main course. He stepped back with Briande so she could describe the coming feast to the big people at the table, including Billy.

Briande spoke.

"For our main course this evening we have a choice of either a meat entree or poisson which she pronounced perfectly en Francais. The Salmon is a Wild Sockeye Salmon poached in butter and white wine with just a hint of parsley. It will be complemented perfectly by the garlic mashed potatoes and green beans almandine you see before you." As she looked at Harry, Briande said,

"For the meat lovers in the crowd, we have a filet mignon pre-sliced for your dining ease with a red wine sauce you will adore."

With that, Briande stepped back to allow Max his eight seconds in the sun.

"As we have no confirmed wine consumption planned for our meal this evening, we offer for your pleasure a selection of three choice beers that will enrich your dining experience immensely. The first is a Blue Moon we believe is the lady's preference and either a Magic Hat #9 or Becks for the gentlemen who have joined us this evening. The Becks is of course the imported variety from Germany and not the swill bottled here in the United States," Max concluded.

Max then stepped back to join Briande.

Harry looked at Sherry, who looked back at Harry, who also looked at Billy before he stood and gave Briande and Max a standing ovation. Sherry and Billy joined him much to the kids delight.

Max high-fived Briande and said, "Let's eat!"

Chapter 49

To put it in its most simple terms, dinner was CONSUMED! It was devoured by all as if they hadn't eaten in a week and wouldn't be eating again for another week. They ate, they drank, they laughed, and then they ate and drank some more. They ate until every last morsel of Briande and Max's creation had disappeared from the table.

"You gonna lick your plate, Harry?" Sherry asked.

"I would, Sherry, but I want to save a tiny bit of room for dessert," Harry replied.

Looking up from her plate, Briande said in a panic, "Dessert?"

Briande looked at Max, who looked back at Briande, who had nobody to look back at. It's not good to be the last one in the look-at line.

"You do have an utterly scrumptious dessert planned for us, don't you, Briande?" Harry asked.

When there was no response from Briande, Harry turned his attention to Max and said, "Max?"

Max never looked up from whatever had attracted his attention down in his lap.

"Sherry?" Harry said.

"Don't look at me, Harry. I'm just sittin' here a-eatin', and a-drinkin', just like you two fellas," Sherry replied.

"Billy?" Harry threw at Billy.

"What, me?" Billy said. "I'm the deadbeat runaway kid, remember."

Shaking his head, Harry said, "Why is it I always have to be the one stuck holding the bag?"

"Because you do it so well," Sherry answered.

"Yeah, sure," Harry replied.

"I didn't know this was going to be so much fun," Billy threw in.

"Shut the hell up, Billy," Harry told him.

Briande continued to look absolutely mortified while Max

continued to play invisible man while he inspected his fly.

"Oh, hell, if I have to save the day like I have always done…" Harry said before Sherry interrupted him by saying, "Need I remind you my savior, there have been times too numerous to mention in your sordid past that your ass wasn't anywhere near here to save a damn thing!"

"What, no smile while you berate my ass in front of our guest?" Harry answered.

"Harry, may I remind you that our guest just described himself as 'the deadbeat runaway kid.' And I only smile at you when there's a reason to smile at you," Sherry said with half-a-smile.

"And I do so enjoy giving you a reason to smile," Harry replied.

Sherry smiled.

"Now, if I may," Harry said as he took out his cell and dialed a number.

"Now," was all he said when he connected.

Two minutes later the door bell rang.

"Will you get that Briande? Help your sister, will you, Max," Harry said to the two of them.

Reluctantly, Briande got up and went to the front door. Max scurried after her to get away from the big people who had no dessert.

"What the?" was all Briande said when she opened the door.

Harry and Sherry were standing in the kitchen doorway grinning like two kids who had just raided the cookie jar. The real cookie jar.

"Well, aren't you going to let them in?" Harry said.

Briande, looking speechless, stammered out, "But who, ah what, ah…"

"Max, help the man bring in his stuff, will you?" Sherry asked Max.

"But who, ah what, ah…" Briande repeated.

"The who, the what, and the why will all become crystal clear in a minute," Harry told them.

Max grabbed the big box on the porch and followed the man dressed like a chef into the kitchen.

Briande finally rejoined the here and now, closed her mouth and followed the crowd.

Chapter 50

Once everyone was back in the kitchen, Harry started, "Max, Briande, this is Humbert. Humbert, I introduce to you my favorite two children, Briande and Max."

"And I am to assume from what you have told me they are your only two children, Harry?" Humbert asked.

"As far as I know," Harry smirked.

Sherry gave him a good shot in the arm for that comment.

"I will ignore that," Humbert replied.

To Max and Briande, Humbert said, "My two lovelies, your parents have arranged for me to be with you here today in your mother's lovely home to help you complete the feast you have prepared for them and their guest. Come, let us begin while the 'big people' do what big people do to amuse themselves. Come, tout suite," Humbert said.

Briande and Max went with Humbert over to the kitchen counter while Harry, Sherry and Billy adjourned to the living room to continue their imbibing of the finer liquid enjoyments of life.

"I have to tell the both of you I think this is one of the cooler things I have ever seen," Billy told Harry and Sherry. "Mind you, my experience with families and cooler things is somewhat limited, but this would be up there no matter where I'd been and what I'd seen before."

"Thanks, Billy, that's very sweet of you," Sherry told him.

"What about me?" Harry said.

"You'll get your sweet later, Harry," Sherry told him.

Harry smiled at the thought.

Billy and Sherry sat in the living room while Harry went off and got them all a new round of beers.

"Has the town changed much since you've been gone?" Sherry asked Billy.

Thinking for a second, Billy responded, "You know it has and it hasn't. That may sound strange, but I feel like I've never left and I feel like a stranger, too. It's weird, as if I can't explain it like I'd like to. You know what I'm saying?"

"I haven't traveled that much and never for very long, but I think I can relate to what you're trying to say," Sherry told him. "The town hasn't changed much, but it has. The big changes are obvious and you can't miss them. But there are little things that you don't notice and then some time later you say, "When did that happen?" Yeah, I totally get you."

Harry returned with their liquid refreshments to see Sherry and Billy nodding their heads in agreement.

"Did I miss anything?" Harry asked.

"More then you will ever know, Harry. More then you could possibly ever know," Sherry replied.

Sherry and Billy clinked their bottles together and enjoyed a sip of their beers.

~ * ~

The sound of a crash coming from the kitchen followed by a "Sacre Bleu" caught their attention.

"Everything all right in there?" Sherry yelled into the kitchen as she was beginning to rise.

Sticking his head around the kitchen doorframe into the living room, Max said, "All's cool in here. The plate was an old one and Humbert was teaching Bri and me how to say "sacrifice the blue plate" in French in case we ever needed it again. All's good."

Max disappeared back in to the kitchen.

Less than five minutes later Briande appeared in the doorway and announced, "Mother, father, Billy, dessert will now be served."

Once everyone was again seated at the table, Briande and Max came from the back of the kitchen pantry dressed in white chef's outfits and wearing chef's hats. Briande had hers cocked slightly to the left giving her an air of confident nonchalance.

"I'll get the lights," Max said.

Hearing that, Harry blurted out, "Oh shit!"

"Relax, poppyson, this is gonna be too cool for words," Max replied.

Chapter 51

"Gentlemen, mother," Briande started, "to complete the evening's dining we have for your enjoyment…"

Max beat out a drum roll on the kitchen counter accompanied by Humbert's French version of "Toot-ta-doot-to-doo" in advance of Briande proclaiming, "…Bananas Foster."

Hearing that, Sherry blurted out, "Oh shit! The House."

"Madame Sherry, Messieurs Harry and Billy, observe and be truly amazed," Humbert announced.

As if they had been doing it for years, Briande and Max produced a flaming Bananas Foster unsurpassed by few before them. Chef Briande combined the ingredients expertly with the assistance of Chef Max who deftly lit the dish and swirled the flaming pan to the delight of all. When the show was over, Harry, Sherry and Billy were served their Bananas Foster in beautiful bone china dishes delivered with care by the Chefs de Shorts.

Humbert applauded their showmanship and deliverance causing beaming smiles to adorn their faces. In unison, they hugged Humbert who beamed in return.

The oo's and ah's that went along with the big people consuming their dessert convinced the kids they were a success. The high-five each received from Humbert completed the evening perfectly.

~ * ~

The kitchen looked like a hurricane had blown through, but that could wait. Humbert had packed up his goodies and went off on his merry and very well compensated way. They all sat in the living room listening to Melissa Manchester on the sound system—vinyl on a turn table of course. Beers were being consumed along with Shirley Temples for the dual budding chefs.

"Thank you, that was very nice, daddy," Briande said to Harry. "And you too, mother," she continued.

"Yeah, moms and pops, it was out there like we've never been before," Max contributed to the graciousness.

"It was nice having you here as well, Billy," Briande told Billy.

"Well, it was my pleasure and I thank both of you for one of the best evenings I have had in a long time. And not just the meal, either," Billy told them.

It was Sherry's turn to beam and she did so, proudly.

Billy continued.

"Your dad has told me about the special Saturdays you guys have together and I think they sound great. I know I may be way out of line, but I would like to take the four of you on a "Saturday out" to thank all of you for making me feel at home here in Manhasset."

Silence filled the room.

"I believe I may have caught everyone by surprise here, haven't I?" Billy finally asked.

Harry was the first to regain his ability to speak and said, "Well, you did catch us by surprise. At least you caught me by surprise and, by the looks on the other faces in the room; I'd say you were right all around."

Nodding of heads in unison confirmed Harry's assumption.

"Sorry about that. I just want to do something to thank all of you and, most of all, you, Harry. I want to do the right thing with no strings attached, no payday today or down the road. I just want to say THANK YOU! Thank you. Thank you for treating me like the eighteen-year-old kid I should be and not who I have become," Billy told them.

Before they could say anything, Billy finished with, "We can make it a Sunday out so it's different than your day out."

Sherry spoke up and said, "I'm sure I speak for all of us when I say we would be thrilled to have a Sunday out with you. I'm a bit apprehensive trying to imagine what you may have planned but, at the same time, excited to see what you may have planned. Right kids?"

"Let's do it," Max said.

"It would be our pleasure," the Miss Briande responded.

Sherry looked at Harry with that look which prompted Harry to say, "What the hell; what can possibly go wrong!"

"Sunday it is then," Billy said.

"And may God help us, every one," Harry added.

Chapter 52

"Are you sure? If you're bullshitting me, or just yanking my chain, I'll kick your ass until I can't raise my foot one more time," Mel said to the guy sitting across from him.

"What you can get for the office we're sitting in, the building it sits in, the business you have built over the years plus the state of your investment portfolio makes it possible," he said.

"What are we talking here?" Mel asked.

"It's not an exact figure and won't be until we unload the business and the building but, conservatively speaking, I'd put your net worth without the house at around three to three and a half mil," his advisor told Mel.

"Three to three and a half million dollars!" Mel said in amazement.

"Now who's bullshitting who," Roger said. "You've been tracking your portfolio every day for more years than either of us wants to count. The only unknown was what the business would bring and when the right time to sell it was."

"Maybe," Mel replied sheepishly, or as sheepishly as Mel was capable of.

"Maybe my ass," Roger replied. "You could probably tell me to the penny what the portfolio was worth as of close of the markets yesterday. The last offer for the business didn't get you to where you needed to be, but this one does. Once the Kings sold out and closed up shop your office became the number one target in town. I got the offer yesterday and it's as good as you are going to get. Now's the time to sell," Roger told Mel.

"You're sure?" Mel asked.

"Mel, I've been tracking the regional and national sales of real estate businesses and building sales within one hundred miles of here for five years. The economy sucks but there are still people out there with big bucks willing and able to buy when the time is right and the commodity is right. Your commodity is hot and these people are willing and able. Say the word and you and the wife will be sitting on the deck of your new beach house, drinking

Mai Tais, and looking at the ocean before you know it. I have a buyer for your house and negotiated a good deal on the beach house you love, too," Roger told Mel.

"You've been busy, Roger. You're really serious about this, aren't you?" Mel asked.

"Serious as you are when you're reading that fucking New York Times you so love to devour," Roger answered.

"That serious?" Mel asked.

"That serious," Roger answered.

"Who's buying the business? They legit?" Mel asked.

"They're as legit as they come, Mel," Roger answered. "Madison Holdings is part of a New York conglomerate and from what I see, among other things, they manufacture money. In big bunches, all day, all year."

"When?" Mel said.

"When what?" Roger answered.

"When do I have to decide? How long can I have to think it over?" Mel asked him.

Roger bent down, reached into his briefcase, and pulled out a stack of papers. He placed them on the desk in front of Mel and said, "The offer sheet for the business and building, the offer sheet for your house, the bid paperwork for the beach house are presented for your review and signature. You can review them as long as you want, Mel; but, if it was me, my hand would be scribbling my John Hancock on the paperwork in front of you right quickly. As a package you're making a killing all around."

"You make it sound like I can't do anything but sign them, Roger," Mel said.

Roger sighed, looked Mel right in the eye, and then said, "Mel, I'm your financial advisor and have been for twenty years. I've been your friend for longer than that and I'm proud to be able to say that. You've busted your ass for a long time. You've put your kids through college, you built a very successful business, and you have friends that like you for some reason. They respect what you have done and I, and they, would love to see you and your beautiful wife go off and enjoy life. Go eat, drink, shit and be merry."

Mel looked at Roger, thought for a long minute, then picked up the phone and dialed a number.

"Hon, you wanna go to the beach?" Mel said into the phone.

He listened for a bit, said, "Okay," and then hung up the phone.

Looking Roger directly in the eyes, Mel said, "Do you need a special pen to sign these papers?"

Roger replied, "Yeah, it requires a special retirement pen and I just happen to have one right here in my pocket."

Chapter 53

Harry heard the car pulling into the driveway that led up to his garage apartment on George Street. It was just before 8:45 am on Sunday morning and right on time. When he looked out his front window over the deck facing the street, he didn't know what to make of what he saw. He walked out onto the deck to get a better look.

It wasn't a car. It wasn't a station wagon. It wasn't a van. It was a...Harry didn't know what the hell it was. It stopped in front of the garage doors right below Harry and Billy emerged from the driver's side door.

Seeing Harry standing on the deck looking down at him, Billy said, "Hey, Harry."

Harry continued to look at the "whatever" it was that was currently sitting in the driveway.

Billy saw where Harry was looking and yelled up to him, "What's the matter, Harry? You confused about something?"

"Confused? Nope, not confused," Harry said. "Well, maybe a little," he continued.

"Come on down and I'll explain the ride to you. Plus, we're gonna be late if you don't hustle your ass," Billy told him.

"I'm hustling, I'm hustling," Harry responded.

Emerging from the side door, Harry came over to where Billy was standing and took another look at the "whatever."

"Good to see you bright and early on this beautiful Sunday morning," Billy started. "Harry, let me explain what we have here. This is a vehicle with a truck chassis base for maximum ground stability and a van'ish upper body for maximum passenger space. The engine is pristine muscle with four hundred and fifty horses under the hood to get you where you want to go and the whole thing could withstand a machine gun/mortar attack if necessary. Hopefully, that won't be necessary," Bill concluded.

"Yeah, all what you just said," Harry said. "And, in case you haven't noticed, it looks like shit."

"And much effort was expended to make it look that way,"

Billy told Harry. "Would you steal something looking like that?"

"Steal it?" Harry answered. "I don't even want to be seen near it, never mind in it. Steal it? For what reason?" would be my answer looking at it."

"Precisely," Billy responded.

Harry just looked at him.

"Come on, get in and let's hit the road. You don't want to be late, do you?" Billy asked him.

"No, I don't. But getting in this thing ain't high on my list of preferred things to do right about now either," Harry replied.

"Where's you sense of adventure, my man?" Billy asked.

"My sense of adventure will be flying right out the window as soon as Sherry gets a look at this *thing*," Harry told Billy.

"You worry too much, dude. All's gonna be cool," Billy told Harry.

"You truly don't know Sherry at all, dude," Harry replied with emphasis on the *dude* part of his statement.

The inside of the "whatever" surprised the hell out of Harry. It was just like the inside of a large minivan and immaculate. It had bucket seats up front and a triangular set of buckets in the rear with a built in cooler between the two sets of seats.

Seeing Harry looking at the cooler, Billy said, "It's for long rides when you would prefer not getting out of the vehicle except for gas."

"Convenient," Harry replied.

"Very. May we go now?" Billy inquired.

After opening the cooler and seeing it was stocked to the brim with enough of somethings for everyone, Harry said, "Let's go, my man."

Chapter 54

Here's how it went down when we pulled up in front of Sherry's house at the appointed and agreed upon time of 9:00 am "sharp" on Sunday morning.

The kids came running out of the house—well Max ran, Briande approached in her newly found teenager of note walk—and both stopped dead in their tracks when they saw the "whatever" sitting at the curb. Sherry was the last one out of the house and, upon turning toward the street after locking the front door, also stopped dead in her tracks, pointed at the "whatever" and said, "What in the holy mother-in-law of fuck is that thing, Harry?"

In response, Harry shrugged and said, "Whatever!"

Sherry wasn't amused.

"Harry, I'm not getting in that *thing*. The kids aren't getting in that *thing*. We aren't going anywhere in that *thing*. Not gonna happen, Harry. Not now, not ever. Not in that whatever you call it," Sherry continued.

"Whatever," Harry replied.

Sherry wasn't amused.

Billy made an attempt to save the day.

"Hey, guys. It's great to see you this morning," he started with a smile that could light up hell on a bad day.

Sherry wasn't amused.

Billy trudged on.

"Come on over here and let me show you what this actually is. The "whatever" as Harry calls it. Come on, come on," Billy urged.

Max walked over to Billy's side; Briande approached cautiously and Sherry came half way.

"Come on over here, Sherry. It won't bite…much," Billy told her.

"Biting isn't what I'm afraid of," Sherry told Billy.

Harry walked over to Sherry, grabbed her hand in his, and walked her over to the "whatever" sitting by the curb.

Having everyone's attention, Billy pointed to the vehicle and said, "I'd like you all to meet Grubby. Grubby, say hello to the nice people,"

A low grumbling sound from somewhere deep in the bowels of Grubby startled Sherry. She took one full step back.

Max laughed.

Briande didn't.

"Well, that's no way to great new friends, Grubby," Billy said to the "whatever" as if it could hear him. "Say hello nicely, Grubby."

From the same place as before in a somewhat friendlier voice came, "Hello nicely, Grubby."

Sherry took another full step back. Harry continued to hold her hand.

Max laughed again.

Briande didn't, but she did crack a very small smile.

"Harry tried to lighten the mood by saying, "Nice tricks, Billy—does it fetch?"

"Fetch, no; most everything else, yes," Billy replied.

"Like what?" Max asked.

"Well, let's see," Billy replied. "To make your mom feel a little better about Grubby, let me show you what would happen if we thought someone was trying to harm us in some way."

Billy took his hand out of his pocket and pressed a button on the small remote he was holding in his hand. A metal shield dropped down covering all of the windows except the front windshield. That was then covered by a plexiglas shield that looked like it was three feet thick.

"Grubby may look like a heap of junk, but nothing, and I mean nothing, can penetrate Grubby if he feels threatened and doesn't want to be breached," Billy told them.

"Sweet," Max exclaimed.

Billy pressed another button and two small openings appeared on the sides of Grubby pointing forward. Two more opened doing the same thing toward the rear.

"Sherry, they are there to allow the machine guns mounted within Grubby to defend him if necessary," Billy told her.

Max's eyes widened as his mouth dropped open.

Billy concluded his little demonstration by saying, "That's a small example of what Grubby can do. If you need sound deterrent, Grubby deters."

A press of another button and Grubby let out a one beat shriek that nearly scared the poopies out of everyone but Billy, including Harry.

Regaining his wits, Harry said, "What the hell would you need that for?"

"One never know, Harry, one never know," Billy replied.

Chapter 55

Confidence somewhat restored, the group climbed aboard. Even Sherry was mildly impressed when she saw the inside of Grubby.

Harry rode shotgun.

"Are you going to tell us what you have in store for us today?" Sherry asked Billy.

"Fun, plenty of good old fun and enjoyment," Billy responded.

"That's it?" Sherry asked.

"What could be better than fun and enjoyment?" Billy asked.

"Yeah, Sherry," Harry piped up.

"Yeah, mom," Max chimed in.

Sherry looked at Briande who just shrugged her shoulders.

"Okay then," Billy said. "Contrary to the normal beginning to your Saturday affairs, we have mobile eats for our breakfast feast. Briande, if you would reach behind you and grab the hot boxes in the back there we can get this party rolling. Harry, why don't you dole out the drinks from the cooler."

"Cooler?" Max said.

"Relax, pipsqueak," Harry told Max. "We have some milk, some Orange Juice, water and other juices. Breakfast drinks."

"Oh," was all Max said in reply.

"Oohs," could be heard coming from the rear of Grubby.

"Good eats?" Harry asked.

"Very nice eats," Briande replied moving far away from her normal expected response.

"Well then, pass some of those eats up here and let's put the feed bag on," Harry said.

From there they ate and drank to their hearts content while Billy drove.

"You going to have anything, Billy?" Harry asked.

"Nah, I'm good," Billy replied.

"Suit yourself," Harry said. "More for me and Max, right Max."

"You got that right, pops," Max agreed.

"What's in this box?" Briande asked from the back.

"I assume you are referring to the cold box," Billy said. "That would have the breakfast dessert."

"Ah, dessert?" Max said.

"Yes, breakfast dessert," Billy told Max. "What better way to conclude breakfast than with dessert, especially chocolate filled éclairs."

"Holy mackadoly!" Max exclaimed. "I'm liking you and riding in Grubby better every minute."

"Yum," Sherry was heard to say from the rear.

"You had better pass some of those up here before I figure out how to turn those machine guns in your direction," Harry said.

"Oh daddy, these are to die for," Briande gushed.

"Screw this," Harry said as he turned and jumped into the back of Grubby.

Billy drove on and smiled.

~ * ~

Order was restored and everyone was back in their appointed seats once all the food was gone. Billy had continued motoring Grubby down the Long Island Expressway toward their destination.

"Not gonna tell us where we are going?" Harry asked.

Billy didn't answer.

"How about we play twenty questions?" Max said.

Billy thought for a sec, and then said, "Alright, that'll work. You guys think of your questions and I'll think of how I can answer them."

"But if you don't know the questions, how are you going to come up with your answers?" Briande asked Billy.

"Imagination, Briande, imagination," Billy replied. "Imagination is what I am. It's what I'm made from and made of."

Chapter 56

Grubby exited the LIE and was motoring down the Brooklyn Queens Expressway through Queens toward Brooklyn, hence, the Brooklyn Queens Expressway.

"What state?" Max asked.

"Is that question number one?" Billy asked.

"Yup," Max answered.

"New York," Billy replied.

"Are we going into New York City?" Briande asked.

"That's number two and, if you mean Manhattan, the answer is no."

"Somewhere in Queens?" Sherry asked.

"That's number three and no," Billy replied. "Are we having lots of fun yet?"

"Are we having lots of fun yet?" Sherry repeated.

"That's number four and no, not lots yet," Billy replied.

"Hey, that's cheating," Briande said.

"I assume you're asking if that's cheating—no, it isn't, and that's number five," Billy said with a smile.

"Are you kidding me?" Sherry said.

"No," Billy replied, "and that's number six."

"Don't say another word," Harry said to the group.

Billy started to hum what sounded to Harry like an old Beatles tune.

"Okay, question number seven—is it one of the five boroughs but not Manhattan or Queens?" Harry asked.

"Yes," Billy replied.

"Well, that leaves Brooklyn, the Bronx and Staten island. How about I try Brooklyn," Harry said.

"Bingo. Give the man a cigar," Billy replied.

"Might I assume attempting to get any more information on precisely where we're going and what we'll be doing might prove to be somewhat impossible?" Harry asked.

"That would be question number eight and my response would be in the affirmative. You can try, but I'd save the rent if I were you," Billy told him.

Harry turned to Sherry and the kids and said, "I guess we're just going to have to wait and see what young Mr. Billy Burns has in store for the Shorts clan."

"Mr." Billy said with an upturned eyebrow.

"I use the term loosely," Harry replied.

"Very loosely," Billy agreed.

"Are we close to where we are going?" Briande asked him.

Billy looked in the rearview mirror at Briande and said, "Yes we are, Briande. We should be there very soon."

"And did we need this vehicle, I mean Grubby; did we need Grubby to get there, wherever it is we're going?" Sherry inquired.

"Yes and no," Billy replied.

"Yes and no?" Sherry repeated in the form of a question.

"No, in that we could have taken any means of transportation to physically get to our final destination. Yes, in that I feel much more comfortable riding in Grubby to get there, plus the people we will be seeing are used to seeing Grubby enter the space," Billy replied.

"Well, that clears it up nicely," Harry interjected.

"I'm glad we're all on the same page," Billy quipped.

"Did all that mean something?" Max asked.

"Yeah," Harry said. "Don't ask any more questions. Keep your eyes open, your head down, and remember, we're going to have plenty of good old fun and enjoyment, kiddo."

"Okay, pops, I'm all over it."

Chapter 57

They rode in semi-silence for the next half hour with the only sound coming from the stereo system nobody could see. In order, they heard Van Morrison, Madonna, Jethro Tull, Maeve Brennan and David Bowie. How Billy knew they were all Shorts family-faves and to play them was anyone's guess.

Billy informed them he had met Bowie in his travels and dug his sound so he was added to the list, too.

Also, the sound of Sherry's ever increasing pounding heart filled the vehicle as well. The worse the neighborhoods they drove through got, the louder the sound.

The area they traveled through could best be described as old warehouses with abandoned cars and trucks littering the streets and very few people in sight. Not totally deserted, but it was no thriving thoroughfare either.

"Those gang colors?" Max asked at one point toward the end of their travels.

"Yes they are, Max. And very observant of you I might add. They are the young gentlemen we contract with to provide protection including day and night safety for our people," Billy said.

"Protection and safety from what?" Sherry asked rather shakily.

"This and that," Billy answered.

Before Sherry could say anything else, or faint, Billy maneuvered Grubby in the direction of a double-doored warehouse. It could have been two warehouses joined together based on its size. As they approached, the doors opened and Billy drove Grubby into the warehouse.

"Where are we?" Sherry said.

"We're entering your darkest nightmare, mom. Do-doo, Do-doo," Max said in his best devilish voice. Rod Serling would have been proud.

"That's not even close to funny young man," Sherry responded by whacking Max in the side of the head.

"Was that worth it?" Harry asked him.

"Yeah," Max replied. "Did you catch the look on her face?"

"Shut it, kiddo," Harry warned him for his own good.

"Okay, we're here," Billy announced.

"Yeah, but where's here?" Harry asked him.

"For a while, it was my home away from home. For a time, when I was here in the area, it was home, period," Billy replied.

As they got out of Grubby, Billy was met by a tall, blonde bombshell who gave him a hug like she hadn't seen him in a million years or she missed him a whole bunch. Maybe both.

"Billy, you look good, man. How've you been?" she asked him when they finally disengaged. "You've been gone way too long."

"I'm good, Tips. At least I am now," Billy told her.

"Now?" she asked.

"Long story," Billy said. "Nothing major, just a hassle more than anything."

Gesturing toward his guests, Tips said, "They cool?"

"Yeah, they're cool," Billy told her. "This is Harry Shorts, his kids Max and Briande, and that there is Sherry."

"She with you?" Tips asked him with a hint of trepidation in her voice.

Billy laughed.

"Nah, I should be so lucky. That's Harry's ex-wife and she's a cool lady. They've been real good to me and, in fact, Harry's the one that helped me with my small problem shall we say," Billy told Tips.

"People that are good for, and to, Billy are welcome here any time," Tips told them. "Has he told you where you are and what we are?"

"Ah, no, he hasn't told us anything up to now and lord knows we've tried," Sherry answered Tips.

"Typical Billy," Tips replied as she gave Billy a look.

Billy just shrugged his shoulders with an "it's me" shrug.

"Well, welcome to 'The Place' and let me show you around," Tips told them.

Chapter 58

Tips led the way with Billy and the rest of the crew close behind. They went through a side door and entered a room that smelled heavenly.

"Oh, my," Sherry said. "What is that aroma?"

"Welcome to what we call our 'Chocolate World/Mini-Chef Kingdom' among ourselves. Billy probably fed you already on the way over, but there's always room for chocolate," Tips said.

Looking around, Max said, "Chocolate, and chocolate, and more chocolate."

"Right you are, Max," Tips replied. "We make other goodies besides all things chocolate, but I decided chocolate would be the choice for today. It is Billy's favorite," Tips said with a smile meant more for Billy than the rest of them.

Fearing they would have to shield the kids eyes in a minute, Harry asked, "By the way, Tips?"

Tips thought for a second and turned toward Billy.

"Do I have to?" she asked him.

"Yup, you do," Billy replied.

"Alright, if I have to," Tips said reluctantly. "There are several versions of how I came to be known as Tips. The first, and possibly the closest to the truth, is the fact that for a time I hustled for tips in a, shall we say, place of gentlemanly delight. I choose not to count that one as accurate. Second, and the most unsettling to me, is a certain portion of my anatomy that "stands out" and draws undue attention from the male population."

Billy smiled and Tips gave him a look that could kill.

He un-smiled quite quickly.

Without drawing undue attention to himself, Harry discreetly peeked. He agreed with the assessment whole-heartedly.

Turning her attention away from Billy and back to Harry and the rest of the clan, Tips said, "The third and actual reason I'm called Tips is due to a particular activity I can perform that most people can't. I will now demonstrate."

Tips dropped to the floor and did ten push-ups supporting

her entire weight on the tips of her fingers. She jumped back up and said, "And that is why I am called Tips."

"Among other things," Billy said to himself just a tiny bit too loud.

Tips gave him a swift whack to the side of his head.

~ * ~

"Sherry, where's Max?" Harry asked realizing he was nowhere to be found.

"Well, I don't know," Sherry replied.

"Max," Harry called out.

The sound gave him away. It was the sound of lips smacking when they encounter something that pleases their palate and every other part of them as well.

"Max, what the hell are you doing over there?" Harry yelled.

Peeking out from behind the counter, Max showed a face so covered with chocolate you could barely tell it was him.

"Max!" Sherry exclaimed in shock.

"It's okay," Tips said. "That's what I made them for. Chocolate is made to enjoy and this is one instance where neatness does not count."

Max took another bite of the chocolate Éclair with dark chocolate filling that was squirting filling from all sides.

"Shall we?" Tips asked.

"Oh, we shall," Harry replied. "You can bet your bottom dollar we surely shall."

And they all did for all they were worth.

Chapter 59

After wiping her lips with a paper napkin, Tips looked good as new. Sherry and Briande did the same with equal results. Harry and Max on the other hand needed the sink and a serious amount of water to get themselves un-chocolated.

"What is this Place?" Harry finally asked.

"As I said, this is what we call our 'Chocolate World/Mini-Chef Kingdom' among ourselves," Tips started. "You just experienced the 'Chocolate World' portion in all its glory."

"How'd you get to know how to do that?" Sherry asked.

"We had several desert chefs come in and spend the time to teach me and two other people how to throw a few things together in a pinch," Tips replied.

"Tips tends to be somewhat modest when she describes her culinary prowess," Billy threw in. "She can throw a few things together with the best of them I can assure you."

"You can say that again," Max said.

"Thank you, Max," Tips said.

"What do you use it for?" Briande asked.

"We use it to entertain guests such as yourselves," Tips started. "We also have need on occasion to put together an affair or some such event as part of what we do. Making our own food protects us from outside sources we would rather not have to deal with."

"What else can you make?" Max asked.

"We say 'Mini-Chef Kingdom' as part of how we describe this section of our set-up, but we can whip up anything you could possibly dream up. You will get to see a small inkling when we have lunch later," Tips told them.

"Cool," Max said.

"Shall we show them a bit more of our little hidey-hole?" Billy threw in Tips direction.

"Sure," Tips replied. "You get started and I'll clean up a bit in here. We have a job soon and I need everything in good working order."

Turning toward Harry and the rest of the Shorts clan, Billy said, "Okay, I guess you're stuck with me for a while. Let's head on out the way we came in and I will show you some of the other things we can do here."

"You gonna define 'The Place' a little better for us at some point?" Harry asked.

"Maybe, maybe not. We'll see," Billy replied.

"Fair enough," Harry replied. "Lead on then and we shall blindly follow."

"I have the feeling you don't do anything blindly, Harry," Billy said.

Harry just smiled knowingly in return.

"Just shut up and follow him, will you, Harry," Sherry scolded.

"Yes, dear," Harry replied.

"You know I hate that 'Yes, dear,' shit, Harry," Sherry scolded him further.

"Yes, dear," Harry replied as he ran past Billy to avoid the wrath of Sherry.

"Whoa," Harry said as he entered the next room. "What the hell is this place and what's it for?"

As the rest of them entered, they all had a similar reaction.

"Come on in everyone," Billy answered. "This is what we affectionately call our "Primp Palace/Muscle Up" room. As you can see, all walls and the ceiling are covered by mirrors. Mirrors as far as you can see, and see, and see…"

"And see…" Harry continued.

"And see some more," Tips threw in.

"Did I hear you right when I heard "Primp Palace/Muscle Up" room coming from your mouth, Billy?" Harry asked.

"You heard right, Harry," Billy confirmed.

"Splain, please," Harry said.

"Sure, we can do that, Harry," Billy replied. "Care to start us off, Tips?" Billy asked her.

With the slightest nod of her pretty head, Tips started, "Be glad to, Billy."

Turning her full attention to the group of curious newcomers, Tips said, "This is our 'Primp Palace/Muscle Up' room."

They waited.

"It's where we Primp and Muscle Up," Tips continued.

They waited some more.

"When we need to Primp and Muscle Up," Tips finished.

They would have waited a long time if Billy hadn't cracked up and Tips followed in his laughter.

"Tips gets off doing that," Billy said. "She asks me if she can do it and we let her do it if she's been real good lately."

"I'm always 'real good' and you know it, Billy," Tips responded.

"I'll let that one slide, Tips," Billy said.

"Look around for a bit and then we can explain what goes on in here," Billy told them.

Chapter 60

Sherry and Briande had given the Primp Palace a thorough "Look See" while Harry and Max explored the "Muscle Up" portion of the room. Each twosome had given a cursory viewing of the other functional portion of the room to be polite and nosey.

They returned to where Billy and Tips were sitting, sipping sodas, all of them wide eyed and question full.

"Wha'd you think, Max?" Billy asked Max.

"That's some set up you got there. I've never seen anything like it. Not even on TV or in the movies. Pieces of it here, other pieces of it at another time, but never together," Max replied.

"Harry?" Billy asked.

"Same here," Harry replied. "It's a hell-of-a set up."

"Okay, cut the small talk bullshit," Sherry blurted out. "I'm dying here. What the hell is this place?"

Tips laughed and Billy followed suit.

Briande looked at Sherry in surprise while Max gave her points for cutting the shit and getting to the point.

Harry smiled at his ex-wife and remembered how he so loved the fiery, no crap side of Sherry.

Tips stood and said, "It's just what we said it is. The guys and gals, we all use the Muscle Up side of this particular part of our home base to keep strong and fit. When it calls for it, the guys hit it hard to add that extra needed edge that may save the job or their lives. You can't find the array of equipment we have here or the depth of equipment anywhere else. And we all know how to use it."

"Lot of hard cash went into building this room for our group to stay in the kind of shape they need to be in. Without it we'd all have to be on the outside getting what we need and people see what they see. No need for it and we don't. The family does its thing here," Billy said.

"Family?" Harry inquired.

"Later,' Billy answered.

"It's dynamite," Max gushed.

"Thanks, Max," Billy replied.

"And the other half?" Briande asked.

"That's my side of the room," Tips said. The ladies can follow me while the men stay and muscle up some."

The ladies followed Tips while Max and Harry followed Billy.

~ * ~

It was probably thirty to forty minutes later when the three ladies walked back into the area where the guys had been muscling up big time. Sweat flowed and muscles ached, but the guys were all smiles.

Looking up as they approached, Harry whistled and said, "Hubba hubba!"

"Mom!" Max exclaimed in a somewhat shocking tone.

"Briande!" Max said. "That you?"

"Gentlemen, may I present Madame Sherry and Mademoiselle Briande. Ladies, the sweaty guys," Tips said.

"Holy shit!" Harry blurted out.

"This is the product of what we affectionately call our "Primp Palace" for obvious reasons," Tips explained. "When you want, or need, to doll it up, the people we have here can doll you up with the best of them. And fast."

"You ain't just whistling Dixie, sweetheart," Harry said.

"You like?" Sherry asked Harry.

"If there weren't people here I'd give you "I like" like you never seen before, kiddo," Harry replied.

Even through the make-up and get up, Sherry blushed.

To change the direction, Tips said, "We can do almost anything here—even make a silk purse out of a sow's ear if necessary. I did a little beauty work along the way and lead the effort in this particular area of our kingdom."

"She's being modest," Billy threw in. "Nobody is better than Tips when it comes to making you look like a million bucks."

Tips blushed just a shade at that remark.

"We're gonna get cleaned up some while you take the ladies back and get them back to normal," Billy said to Tips. "We'll meet you next door if you think that fits?"

"Next door it is. Fifteen minutes enough time?" Tips asked.

"Fifteen it is," Billy answered.

Chapter 61

It turned out to be more like twenty-five minutes before the ladies met the guys at the entrance to the "next door" Billy had just mentioned. They are female you know.

"Oh, it's you again," Harry threw in Sherry's direction which earned him a nasty pinch of his ear lobe.

"Come on," Billy laughed. "Let's see what 'next door' has in store for you."

They followed Billy through the double doors with Tips bringing up the rear. It was Max who saw the neon sign hanging from the ceiling first. The sign blazed "He/She Turbo Golf" in bright orange for all to see.

"He/She Turbo Golf?" Sherry stated as a question.

With that Billy waved his arm and the other side of the room illuminated.

"Ohhhhh," Briande said.

"Yeah, Ohhhhhhhhhhhhhh," Max agreed.

Even Sherry was impressed as evidenced by the look on her face.

Billy took the lead.

"What we have here are ten golf video set-ups complete with five courses utilizing the best equipment with the highest resolution on the market. The mats give you the feel of grass and the tunnel effect that surrounds each set-up really focuses you in on what is in front of you. Any club you want, we have. Any direction you need, we can provide. The ten instructors we have access to at any time are the best in the business minus a few big names. Thoughts?" Billy concluded.

The four of them looked dumb struck.

"It looks amazing," Harry said finally.

"Every golf hustler on the East Coast has been through here," Billy told them. "And trust me, they pay big bucks and are happy to do so."

"Turbo?" Sherry asked.

"Glad you asked, Sherry," Billy said. "Each round is set to

end thirty minutes after you hit the ball off the first tee. The screen tells you how far to the green from where your ball stops and what condition it is in. You grab a club and hit without thinking—over and over again. You have to finish eighteen holes in thirty minutes or your round is over without finishing all eighteen holes. Golf—Turbo style."

"That can be done?" Briande asked.

"My best is twenty-two minutes at Pebble Beach," Billy responded.

"Wow!" Max said.

"What about putting?" Harry asked.

"Let's hit some balls and then we'll go over to our putting area," Billy replied. To make it easy I will set up a three-hole mini to show you how it goes."

~ * ~

The four of them selected the clubs they wanted and set themselves up on one of the mats. After a few practice swings to get the feel of the clubs and the mats, Billy said, "Are we ready?"

"Nods all around meant they were ready to give it a whirl. Of the four, Sherry looked much less ready than the rest.

"Okay then, let's see what you got," Billy said.

The screens came to life and they found themselves standing on the first tee at Pebble Beach. In the lower left corner, the screen showed the wind as calm, sunny sky and temperature of 83 degrees.

"Ready, GO!" Billy said.

They each swung the club and the mini-round was on. Harry and Max hustled to grab a club and hit balls as soon as their shots came to rest. Sherry and Briande were still in awe at how life-like the game portrayed the course and its speed. Seven minutes after they had hit their first shots a bell sounded and the screen went dark.

"What the...?" Max exclaimed.

"That's the equivalent of a thirty-minute round for three holes," Billy told them. "Well, not really, but I cut you some slack since it's your maiden voyage into the land of Turbo Golf, Billy World style."

"How'd we do?" Sherry asked.

"Well, let's get a drink, check your score cards, and see what we all did on our first pass at He/She Turbo Golf," Billy answered.

Chapter 62

Properly hydrated, they were back in front of their screen anxious to see how they had performed. Well, at least Harry and Max were. Sherry and Briande each doubted they were going to like what they saw.

As the screens came back to life, Billy stepped in front of the four of them to decipher the results. Sherry was first.

"Seems you didn't quite grasp the Turbo aspect of the game to its fullest, Sherry," Billy started. "You finished the first hole after eleven shots and you were seventy-five yards from the green on the second after taking seven shots. Progress was made I guess you could say."

Max started to say something but stopped abruptly when Harry gave him a look that said, "Not if you ever want to eat again."

"First time, Sher. Not an easy task either," Harry comforted her.

Sherry didn't look overly comforted. She looked like she wanted to have another go at it right away, as in right now.

Turning to Briande, Billy said, "You took one less shot on the first hole after taking three to get out of the bunker. You did finish the second hole and did very well taking only eight shots to reach the green."

"Good job, kiddo," Harry told her.

Briande nodded her head in Harry's direction in appreciation.

Billy moved on to Max next.

"Good job, Max," Billy started. "You had an approach to the third hole remaining and took eighteen shots to that point. The six on the par five second hole is pretty good for your first go-round at Turbo."

Harry high-fived Max and Briande said, "Not bad, Max."

Sherry took a practice swing with the club she had in her hands.

Billy next turned to Harry.

"Have you played simulated golf before, Harry?" Billy asked

him.

"A few times," Harry replied. "Not in a few years, though," Harry added.

"You showed some familiarity with the concept and a fair golf game as well. I'm sure the Turbo speed threw you a little, but overall you did quite well," Billy told him.

Sherry scowled and swung the club a little harder.

"You hit the first green in regulation and would have done the same on the par five second hole, but your approach flew the green. Your chip there would have left you a very tricky putt. On three you hit it in the bunker, but you blasted out to ten feet. Overall, ten strokes or anywhere under ten stokes is great the first time you play under these conditions," Billy told Harry.

Max high-fived Harry. Briande did the same as Sherry continued to scowl in the background.

"Not too shabby for first timers I'd say," Billy told the group. "Let's go take a peek at our putting area and then you can reward yourselves with a treat."

"Cool," Max said expressing the sentiment for the whole group.

Sherry reluctantly put down the club.

"She doesn't like to lose," Harry whispered to Billy as he led them through a really cool looking sliding glass door set-up.

~ * ~

Once inside, Billy said, "This is our putting area."

"Holy crap!" Max said.

"Is that real grass?" Briande asked.

"Yes, it is," Billy replied. "We have special lighting that tricks the grass into thinking its outside in the sun. Our watering system simulates the natural elements of a perfect outside environment that promotes daily growth. We mow it twice a day to keep it in the best shape we can. Our greens keeper came from one of the top clubs in the south."

"Real grass?" Sherry said in somewhat disbelief.

"Go ahead, walk on it," Billy told them. "Feel it, too, if you want."

"It's real grass," Sherry repeated herself once she had felt it.

"Yep, thirty feet by forty-five feet of real grass," Billy repeated.

"Kinda flat," Max said.

"It is now, Max," Billy agreed. "Everyone come over here and I will demonstrate the best part of our little indoor wonder."

Chapter 63

They followed Billy and stood behind him as he picked up a remote control that had been on the podium off to the left. Billy pressed a series of buttons and the green seemed to come to life. The entire green rose in some spots and dipped in others.

Billy held out his hand, palm up, and said, "I present to you the first green at Pebble Beach."

"No shit," Harry said.

"No shit," Billy replied.

"How'd you do that?" Briande asked.

"Magic," Billy told them. "That and hiring the best engineer we could find to make it happen."

"Can we try it?" Max asked.

"What good is having a green if you don't putt on it," Billy replied.

"Oh, man" Max said.

"Grab a putter from the rack over there and give it a whirl," Billy told them. "I think we have the putter you each use."

And they did; and they did, putt that is. And they enjoyed the shit out of putting on real grass, indoors, just like they were on the first green at Pebble Beach.

"They're fast as can be," Briande said.

"Fast doesn't describe this green," Sherry said as she rolled a ball off the green into the depths of neverland.

"Don't worry, Sherry, we have more golf balls. Plus, you're not the first person to roll a ball off the green. We'll find it," Billy told her.

"This is something else," Harry said.

"Yeah, Harry, it really is," Billy agreed.

~ * ~

The snack they rewarded themselves with was as much a surprise as everything else that had occurred since they had arrived. Tips and her helpers arrived just as they left the putting area to escort them to a place where they could freshen up. When they came back the snack was waiting for them.

Billy disappeared for the time being leaving them in Tips' capable hands.

Once they were seated, Tips asked, "You guys hungry after your hard day of golf on the links?"

"You bet," Max piped up.

"Well then, let's get you fed," Tips replied.

Helper #1 came in carrying a tray filled to the brim with every fruit known to mankind. Well, maybe not every fruit, but those known to mankind and not on the tray were the ones they all agreed they didn't like, or want, to begin with. In the middle of the tray was a dip that tasted like nothing any of them had ever tasted before and enhanced the flavor of the fruit even more with each piece they tasted.

Helper #2 brought each of them a milk shake the size of what looked like a gallon jug. To no one's surprise, all four were the favorite flavor of each of them.

After they were done pigging out to their hearts content, Helper #3 brought out a tray of warm towels to clean off their hands and faces. From their look of contentment, you could tell their tummies were full and their bodies refreshed. Their smiles were broad enough to light up the putting green.

"Anything else we can get for you guys?" Tips asked.

"Permanent residence?" Max asked with a smile.

Tips smiled and replied, "Sorry, Max, visits are permitted and it gives us great joy to make you guys happy for a day. Permanent residence I'm afraid isn't in the cards. Plus, I'm sure you'd miss everyone, wouldn't you?"

"Oh, they can stay, too," Max the know-it-all replied.

Everyone laughed.

With that, a man they hadn't met before appeared and asked if they were ready to move on.

"Lead on, kind sir," Briande replied.

Chapter 64

Harry, Sherry, Briande and Max were led down a long hallway and told to continue around a sharp bend that lay ahead of them. As they did, they were joined by another person they hadn't met before. He looked somewhat familiar to Harry, but he was pretty sure he hadn't had the pleasure.

In a faint British accent, the gent said, "It is a pleasure to meet all of you. Have you enjoyed your stay with us so far?"

Hesitantly, Harry replied, "It's been great, but who may I ask are you?"

"Quite right, quite right indeed," he replied. "I'm William and I will be your guide for the next leg of your journey here today. Please follow me."

With that, William turned and proceeded farther down the hallway. They were then led through a door about ten feet ahead of them on the right. Stepping aside, William said, "After you if you please."

Harry pleased so he held the door as Sherry, Briande and Max entered.

"Trusting aren't we then, sir," William said to Harry.

Harry gave him a look before he followed the others inside. The door closed behind him with no William in sight. In fact, there was nothing in sight since the lights went out the second the door closed.

"Don't move," Harry immediately shouted. "Sherry, Briande, Max—don't move. Stay right where you are."

"Harry, we aren't moving an inch until you fix this and get the fucking lights back on again," Sherry shouted. As her voice rose, she continued with, "And I want them on this very instant, Harry. You hear me, Harry Mickey Shorts? Lights back on right NOW!"

With that, a spot light shone on a single figure across the room. It was quick, but Harry thought it was William. A second later, a second spot highlighted Tips across the room from William. One second, two seconds, and then the lights slowly came up illuminating the entire room again. Not full illumination, but bright enough to see Tips standing next to a mirror that showed the reflection of William sitting in a chair in front of it. Behind him, someone was doing something to his face.

"What the hell is going on?" Harry asked.

Tips waived at them and said, "Come on over, guys. Let me re-introduce you to someone you already know."

Harry and the gang slowly made their way toward Tips. Harry's motto of 'You trust your mother but you cut the cards' was in play.

When they finally made their way across the room they could see the person working on William's hair. To be more precise, she was removing William's hair, or hairpiece to be more precise. It was the best hairpiece Harry had ever seen and had been expertly applied as well.

"Tips?" Harry queried.

"In due time, Harry," Tips answered.

Once the hair piece was gone the girl applied some additional cream to William's face that obscured his face almost entirely except for his eyes and mouth.

Harry started to laugh and Tips said, "Don't, Harry."

Catching himself, Harry said, "Okay, Tips. I'm cool."

"What the hell, Harry?" Sherry said.

"You'll see, Sher. Give it a minute," Harry answered.

Three minutes later, Sherry saw.

William was transformed into Billy Burns.

"Well I'll be a..." Sherry started.

"You already are, Sher," Harry finished for her.

~ * ~

Hair, face, padded jacket and pants removed, Billy Burns stood and took a bow. Tips was smiling the smile of a job well done. A job very well done indeed.

Also smiling, Billy said, "This area of our little hideaway we call "Now u see him..." and you can finish the rest."

"That was something out of the movies," Briande told the group.

"The people we have working in this area came from the movies, TV and the theater. A number of them were on Broadway themselves but prefer the behind-the-stage theatrics more," Tips informed them.

"It was the eyes, wasn't it, Harry?" Billy asked.

"What eyes?" Max asked.

"Billy's eyes," Harry answered. "With his face covered in that cream all I could see were his eyes and his mouth. His eyes gave him away."

"Well I'll be a..." Sherry started.

"As I just said, you already are, Sher," Harry told her.

Chapter 65

They were all back in what Max referred to as the "food room" enjoying some coffee for the big guys and sodas for Max and Briande. The inevitable question that was bound to be asked was posed by Briande.

"So, who owns this, ah, whatever this whole thing is?" is how she finally phrased the question.

"That's a good question, Briande," Billy started. "We like to think it belongs to everyone that does what we do. We're all welcome to come here and improve ourselves and help be as prepared as we can to do what we do."

"Nice convenient answer," Harry said, "But who 'owns' it is what Briande and all of us are asking?"

"Well, when you put it that way," Billy started, "Then the answer is, technically, Tips and I own it."

"It's Billy's," Tips chirped in. "It was his idea, he got the space and designed the layout. He supplied the seed money and secured the remainder of the financing needed to get it done. He says it's "ours" because he gave me a share after what we've been through together in the past. You help each other and then you "*help each other*" if you know what I mean."

"It's really owned by a shell company of a shell company that a lawyer I know watches for us," Billy informed them.

"Not to be too direct and nosy, but you cover your nut at the end of the day?" Harry asked.

Billy looked at Tips, who looked back at Billy, who looked back at Harry and said, "We've had it in operation for two full years plus this year. After a slow start, last year we almost broke even and we're running ahead this year as word continues to travel among the people we want to hear of its existence. We better make money this year because all I got's tied up in it now. Plus, Tips hasn't made dime one yet and she's the one that watches the shop most of the time."

"It's an amazing place," Sherry said.

"Thanks," Tips responded.

"The only piece you didn't see is what we refer to as "Game Galaxy" where we have one of just about every Pin Ball Machine, Space Ride, you-name-it-game. It's for our eye-hand coordination and helps a lot," Billy told them.

Max looked disappointed when he heard they wouldn't see it today.

"Another time, okay, Max? I promise," Billy told him.

"That's okay, Billy," Max replied not too convincingly.

"Well, I better get you guys back home," Billy told them. "You may find it hard to believe, but it's almost seven o'clock."

"Are you kidding?" Max asked. "It seems like we just got here."

"Thank you, it was really a great day," Briande said.

"Yeah, mondo cool," Max said.

"I can't believe I'm saying it, but it was mondo cool," Sherry told Tips as she gave her a big hug in thanks. "You too, Billy," who also got a Sher hug.

"You guys are welcome back any time," Tips told them.

"Grubby awaits," Billy said to get the group moving.

"I got Shotgun!" Max yelled.

Harry gave him a look and Max said, "Maybe not."

"Next time when you and me hit the road without the old folks," Billy told Max.

"Over my dead body," Sherry said.

Everyone laughed and they headed for the exit.

"See you all soon," Tips told them as she handed Sherry a goodie bag for the ride home. "Just a little something to tide you over during the ride."

"I get first pick," Max said.

"Over my dead body," Sherry repeated.

Everyone laughed again.

Chapter 66

Harry was sitting at the desk in the back of Mel's office when the phone rang. Mel wasn't in yet and when Mel wasn't around, Harry usually let it go to the answering machine. For no other reason than he just felt like it, Harry picked it up.

"Harry Mickey Shorts, can I help you?"

"Hold please," was what Harry heard in return.

He couldn't do otherwise, so Harry held…and he held…and he held some more. Just before he got tired enough of holding and hung up, he heard, "Connecting."

"Harry?"

"Yes," Harry answered.

"It's Randle."

"Randle," Harry said, "If I don't know your voice by now…"

"Sorry, I was distracted by something else when I picked up the phone. Or should I say someone else," Randle Trundle replied.

"Haven't replaced her yet, have you?" Harry asked.

"Replaced who?" Trundle replied.

"Replaced who? Like we don't both know who you haven't been able to replace yet. You can't replace Ms. Timmons so don't try to, Randle. Just accept the fact she's doing your bidding elsewhere and find the best you can and get done what you need done," Harry told him.

"Right as usual, Harry. But that isn't why I called," Randle went on.

"And you called why?" Harry asked.

"Since I've been out of the country for the last week I didn't get a chance to see if you got the information you requested."

"Yes, it was received and much appreciated. It was right on the money and more," Harry said.

"Good," Trundle replied. "Anything else you need you just have to ask. And by the way, there's a possible day of hooky in the wind for next week if you are interested."

"I'm interested," Harry replied. "And, just so you know, I

miss Ms. Timmons, too."

"Thanks, Harry, I know. See you soon," Trundle said as he hung up.

~ * ~

He wasn't sure it was the right thing to do, but he always did it when he was working on a case. This wasn't an official case and he wasn't getting paid to work on this case, but it had a "case" feel to Harry. So he turned on the PC and started a case file on the non-case he was semi-working on.

"Billy the Kid" didn't sound like the right name for the case.

"Mel's Case" didn't work for Harry.

"Mel's Kid" sounded even less right.

For want of any better idea, he named the case file "Little Billy Burns" and moved on. It didn't take long, maybe fifteen minutes, and he had updated the case file with everything he knew to date. He attached the information he had received from Trundle's boys and the one from his own Web Dudes to the file. With nothing more to add for now, Harry dated the entries and closed the file. Just as he did, Mel came into the office.

"Anything new?" Mel asked Harry.

"In the Middle East? The price of soap suds in Poland? On the potential whereabouts of Elvis? The Yankees are still the best team on God's green earth," Harry tried.

"Is it necessary to break my stones every chance you get, Shorts?" Mel replied in frustration.

"No, but it does brighten up my day," Harry replied with obvious joy.

"And I need this why?" Mel said.

"Because you love me so. And should you have forgotten, you asked for my help and I'm complying," Harry replied.

"Just tell me, will you, Harry?" Mel tried.

"Because you asked so nicely, I will," Harry said. "What do you want to know—everything or just the highlights?"

"The highlights will do," Mel replied.

"Okay," Harry said, "Buy me breakfast over at the diner and I will give you the highlights of the case we are officially calling "Little Billy Burns" now and forever more. That is unless I think of a better name and then it won't be called…"

151

"Shut the fuck up, Harry. Shut up, get your ass across the street to the Manhasset Diner, and order breakfast. Then give me the details and then shut the fuck up again," Mel said.

"Shutting up here now, Boss. I'se shuttin' 'er up and shufflin' on over to the diner right quick now, Boss Man. You'se be seeing me…" Harry said as he ran out the door.

Chapter 67

Harry waived to the waitress as he walked to the back of the diner. Before long the eggs over easy, bacon, white toast with coffee and OJ would be placed down in front of him. Mel would get his usual placed before him as well—no need to ask, same as Harry.

"Spill it and don't piss me off while you do," Mel told Harry as soon as he was seated across from him.

Harry was about to reply "Spillin' it Boss" but thought better of it. After all, Mel was between him and the door.

In concise and abbreviated fashion, Harry updated Mel on everything he had learned about the life of Billy Burns and all who were connected to him. He left out a few details, but nothing that mattered much. He debated about it, but in the end he ran down their day at the warehouse for Mel as well. He completed his rundown just as breakfast arrived.

They did their salt and pepper, sugar and milk work and got down to some serious eating. Half way through Mel looked at Harry and said, "That all?"

Harry wiped his mouth with a napkin and said, "Everything that needs to be said for now. There's more little shit that doesn't really matter and some stuff I'm still running down. But, you got the major lowdown that I know so far."

Mel lowered his head and proceeded to finish his breakfast. Harry thought that was a pretty good idea so he did the same.

When Mel was done, he looked at Harry and said, "So, what does it mean?"

"Mean?" Harry repeated.

"Yeah, what does it all add up to? The kid has this, this, I don't know what to call his life and then he up and splits on his own at fourteen. He's in the wind and hustles his way through four years and nobody says boo. What the hell does all that mean?" Mel said.

"Mean?" Harry repeated again. "It don't "mean" nothing. What is says is you have a kid that was in "the life" probably since he could walk and he's still there, just on his own now. No, not on his own, he's in his life now. He's with his people and making it happen any way he can. He's got a business venture if you want to call it that and trying to make that happen for him and Tips. He's trying is what it means. He's trying to survive the same as you try and survive, and I try and survive, and every other shitbum or King-Of-His-Own-World tries to survive. Any way they can is how."

Mel shook his head and said, "So, what do I do?"

"You," Harry said, "you do what you been doing. You do your thing day after day and hope the New York Times rings your number one day and you ride off into the sunset with the wife in tow. As far as Billy Burns goes, you did your thing with him when he was fourteen and now he's somebody else's problem. You're out—he's not your "problem" any more."

"He yours?" Mel asked.

"If you mean problem, no he's not my "problem" either. Somehow I'm in it if I can figure out what "it" is and how I got there, but he's not a problem for me. Don't know what's coming down the road, but I sure as shit hope it doesn't develop into a problem for me," Harry told Mel.

Mel just sat there and looked at Harry for a long minute. Finally, he shook his head just a titch and then said, "If you say so, Harry. The kid, no he ain't a kid anymore and probably never was a kid in the way we think of kids that age; well, he's on his own and there's nothing I can do about it. Nor should I. I just wanted to, to ah, shit, I don't even know what it was that I wanted or expected to do."

Harry looked Mel in the eye and said, "You did the best thing you could do; you cared. That's a ton more than anyone else did for that kid."

Nodding, Mel said, "You're probably right, Harry. I gotta get back to work. If you didn't owe me a lifetime's worth, I'd say I owe you one. But, thanks for your help anyway, Harry."

"Don't mention it big guy," Harry replied.

~ * ~

Mel got up and left the diner in a hurry. That was cool except for the fact he didn't leave any money on the table. Since he had to front the bill, Harry figured he might as well add it to the expenses on the case. Nobody was gonna pay the expenses, but at least it kept everything neat and tidy. That would be Harry Mickey Shorts—neat and tidy at your service!

Chapter 68

The two paying cases Harry had been working on, before the Billy Burns so called case popped up, kept him busy for the next three days.

Harry didn't particularly like following some dude around waiting to catch him banging some broad so he could report back to the guy's wife he was cheating on her. He didn't like it, but it paid bills and it was easy work. At least this one involved a drop-dead gorgeous broad who didn't mind the back seat of said cheating husband's car. With the pictures mailed to the soon-to-be-rich-and-divorced wife-client, Harry moved on to case #2.

Case #2 was a bit trickier than the first and, if he had to work at all, more to Harry's liking. Most of the work was done by the Web Dudes Harry employed when he needed information most other people can't get. The Dudes could get anything, on anything or anyone if it, or they, existed. How, Harry didn't know and it cost him an arm and a leg every time he used them, but they delivered without fail. Plus, the cost was just an expense passed along to the client who didn't say peep one as long as they got what they wanted. And in this case they got what they wanted and Harry was happy to bill them accordingly.

Cases solved and nothing but time on his hands, Harry decided he would indulge himself in his one true passion in life— baseball. Well, now that you come to think about it, there were a few other things Harry could get passionate about, and the one in particular he really liked involved another person. Baseball involved no one and everyone who was there at the time.

Harry yanked on some strings that hung before him and set up a day at the ballpark for both him and his current non-problem. When he told Billy what he had in mind Billy jumped at it with gusto.

"That's really cool, Harry. You can do that?" Billy asked.

"I can and I did," Harry had replied. "Be at my place at eight sharp and we will get some grub from Micky D's for the ride before we head out."

"I'll spring for the grub," Billy told Harry.

"You bet your ass you will, kiddo," Harry told him.

~ * ~

The ballpark was the home of the Bayport Schooners in, well of course, Bayport, Long Island. It was the #1 franchise in the Double A Eastern League and the baby of Mr. M. Randle Trundle.

As they entered the park, Billy asked Harry, "Did you really coach and play for the Schooners?"

"Is that such a far out possibility you doubt it could have happened?" Harry replied.

"No, I just, ah, I was only saying, ah..." Billy stammered.

"Forget it, Billy," Harry said, "Let's go inside and see what's in store for us."

Billy was impressed when they entered the player's entrance and the guy at the door nodded hello to Harry. Once inside Harry knew the way and led Billy down the hall to the player's locker room.

As they entered, Billy stopped dead in his tracks and said, "Holy shit, this is like a major league locker room."

"Mr. Trundle does things first class all the way in everything he does, Billy. When you meet him you'll see for yourself," Harry told Billy. "And by the way, how do you know what a major league locker room looks like?"

Ignoring Harry's last question, Billy said, "Meet him?"

"Yeah, meet him. As in he's there, and you're there, and you're there together. Then you say hello and you met him. Like that," Harry replied.

"Fuck you, Harry," Billy said.

"No thank you, Billy," Harry replied.

They both laughed.

"Harry Mickey Shorts," Harry heard from behind him.

Smiling, Harry turned to greet the General Manager and field general of the Bayport Schooners. They shook hands like old friends.

Turning to Billy, Harry said, "Billy, I'd like you to meet Mr. Curran, the best coach and baseball man you are ever going to meet. Coach, this is Billy Burns."

"Pleased to meet you, Billy," Coach Curran said. "Anyone Harry brings to our ballpark is welcome here any time."

"It's my pleasure, Mr. Curran," Billy responded.

Curran waived to a guy in the back of the room and said, "Hey, Tommy, come on over here and take care of Billy while Harry and I catch up."

Billy didn't know what was up, but he went off with Tommy while Harry and Coach Curran went off in the other direction.

Chapter 69

Harry was sitting in the owner's box behind first base watching the players prepare for today's game. They were just getting ready to start infield practice when Billy came out onto the field. He was dressed in the Schooners home whites with the number 73 on his back just below the name that said Billy Burns.

Coach Curran met Billy as he ascended from the dugout and introduced him to several of the players. Ray Jask, the starting shortstop for the Schooners, handed Billy a glove and they trotted out onto the field. Billy positioned himself behind Ray as infield practice got started. One of the assistant coaches ran the starters through a set of drills and then called for the second teamers to take their positions. Playing shortstop with them was Billy Burns.

They ran through a full set of drills starting with fielding several ground balls and a straight throw to first. They followed that with two sets of double plays that Billy handled flawlessly. Outfield cut-off drills came next and Billy nailed a throw to the plate like he had been doing it all day every day. When they finished up with a slow roller and throw to home plate Billy came off the field with a smile wider than the Grand Canyon.

"Quit your grand-standing and grab a bat, kid," one of the coaches told Billy.

Billy did as he was told, dropped his glove and grabbed a bat, but the smile stayed.

Batting practice started with Billy in the cage first. Harry knew what was coming when the batting practice pitcher wound up and knocked Billy right on his ass with the first pitch. High and tight, right where he wanted it. Billy got up, dusted himself off, and lined the next pitch into left field for what would have been a clean base hit. The smile never left his face.

While Harry enjoyed watching Billy enjoy the thrill of being on a professional baseball field, M. Randle Trundle sat down in the seat next to him.

"That the kid I've been watching?" Trundle asked.

"You been here long?" Harry asked him.

"Long enough to watch the kid handle himself quite nicely," Trundle replied.

"He does have that natural feel about him, doesn't he?" Harry answered.

"He does," Trundle agreed. "There's a small difference when you watch him and compare him to the guys we throw out on the field for the Schooners, but not much. It wouldn't take long for him to compete with the Single A guys we have and probably excel at that level. How far he could go would probably be up to him."

"You have to remember he's only eighteen and hasn't played organized ball in several years," Harry threw in.

"Makes it even more interesting, doesn't it," Trundle observed.

"It sure does. Shame he's pointed in a different direction that I'm afraid will eventually get his ass in a sling he may not be able to get out of. His luck has held up to now, but sooner or later they all meet up with the wrong guy, in the wrong place, and they end up either behind bars, or worse. It seems to be in his blood from what I can tell," Harry told Trundle.

"You may be right," Trundle replied. "But people have been known to change if the situation presents itself. What are you going to do about it?"

Harry looked at Trundle and was at a loss for words which didn't happen to Harry very often. Not often at all in fact.

"Do about it?" Harry asked.

"Yes, Harry, do about it. Do you not understand what that means?" Trundle asked him.

"Well, sure, I understand what that means. But it normally implies one has the ability to "do something about" whatever it is that is in question. I don't know that I have the power to "do something about" Billy's future. I really don't," Harry answered Trundle.

"As usual, you underestimate what you can and can't do in certain situations, Harry. Look inside yourself and say, 'Do I want to do something about it' and follow your heart. It will lead you to the right conclusion most of the time. You've done it before, probably without even knowing it. It served you well then, and will do so again in the future. Trust me, and trust yourself," Trundle told him.

Harry again found himself stuck for what to say.

Seeing Harry's dilemma, Trundle said, "Dog and a beer?"

Harry replied, "The sun's shining, we're at the ballpark, a dog and a beer it is."

Chapter 70

Billy joined them in Trundle's box and they enjoyed watching the Schooners pound on their opponents. Back in civies after his time on the field, beer and dog in hand, Billy couldn't have looked happier.

"Enjoy you time out on the field?" Trundle asked Billy.

"It was an outright blast, Mr. Trundle. I haven't had that much fun in a long, long time," Billy told him.

"We're glad we were able to provide you with a blast," Trundle replied.

"Thank you," Billy said, "thank you very much."

"Harry and I were just talking about you before you got here," Trundle continued. "I was asking Harry what was on the horizon for you now, in a roundabout way."

Harry drank his beer and ignored Billy and Trundle. If they're not there he can't be brought into the conversation. In theory that is.

After looking at Harry who continued to ignore everyone and everything but his beer, Billy said, "That's an interesting question, Mr. Trundle. Out of curiosity, what did Harry decide was "on the horizon" for me?"

"Harry was somewhat noncommittal on the subject you could say," Trundle informed Billy. "He gets that way on occasion and it takes him a little while to provide some meaningful reaction to my inquiries. It isn't often mind you, but it happens."

So as not to be excluded from the conversation entirely, Harry piped in with, "Great game, huh guys?"

Trundle considered Harry's comment and then said, "As you have often reminded me, Harry, and rightfully so, baseball is the greatest game on this God's green earth."

Billy considered Trundle's comment, looked over at Harry, and then said to both of them, "Harry, I think you may have something there."

~ * ~

Harry dropped Billy at the corner of Plandome Road and

Andrew Street as requested. As Billy was about to exit the car, he turned to Harry and said, "I don't know what's "on the horizon" for me, Harry, but I do know what's right behind me has taught me a great deal about people, life, and what can be out there if you want it and you got the guts to go after it. I'm not saying I'm gonna go all "normal" on the world, but there's plenty for me to think about."

Perplexed, Harry again found himself short on words.

"Nothing to say, Harry. Just wanted to let you know I was thinking, that's all," Billy said as he opened the door and split.

Harry thought to himself, *I hope I'm doing that kid some good, because he's sure as shit got me confused at times.*

Before he could get moving his cell rang and Harry answered it.

"Shorts."

"Care to drop them?"

"Drop what?" Harry answered.

"Your shorts," the caller asked.

"Right here in my car?" Harry responded.

"I hope not."

"Then where?"

"The kids are out and won't be back for several hours. I'm standing in my bedroom with the fan blowing on my naked body. You know what that does to my body, don't you?"

"Ah, yeah, I sure do," Harry replied as he envisioned the result.

"Then get your ass over here, drop your shorts, and do what you do," the caller panted.

"Doing as instructed post hastily," Harry replied. "And don't shut off the fan!"

Harry aimed the car in the appointed direction and hit the gas. He was sure as hell hoping that was Sherry on the phone.

Chapter 71

"You dumb shits find him yet?" Fetts asked Mutt while his brother Jeff looked on in deep fear.

Mutt hesitated too long before he answered and Fetts repeated in stronger fashion, "I said, did you dumb shits find him yet?"

"Yes, sir, we found him," Mutt replied.

When Mutt didn't say anything else Fetts figured he was going to have to pry it out of him one word at a time.

"And where is it that you found Billy, Mutt?" Fetts asked him.

"Jeff found him," Mutt replied.

On the verge of an explosion, Fetts said, "And where was it Jeff found him?"

Mutt thought for a few seconds, then he said, "Was actually both of us what found Billy."

With the quickness and viciousness Fetts was known for, he backhanded Mutt with a shot that landed him on his ass. He looked at Jeff who didn't move a muscle, frozen in his boots.

"Get up," Fetts told Mutt.

When Mutt didn't move fast enough, Fetts grabbed him by his shirt and yanked him off the ground.

"Now, think before you speak, Mutt. Where did you and Jeff find Billy? And where is he now?"

Jeff was about to open his mouth when Fetts raised his hand and said, "Don't say a word, Jeff. If you know what's good for you, keep your trap shut."

"He's in Pennsylvania," Mutt blurted out. "We's found him in some Podunk little town down in PA like."

"PA like, or in Pennsylvania?" Fetts asked Mutt.

"Ah, in PA," Mutt responded. "Mechanicsburg, PA's where we found him."

"How did you find him and what was he doing in this Mechanicsburg, PA?" Fetts asked.

"Ah, we didn't really find him like. This fella we knows been looking for golf places for us like you told us to keep looking for,

Fetts. Golf places that would be like the other golf places we been to before. He says he saw'd Billy playing at this Rich Valley place one day he was scoutin' for us, I mean for you. He ain't there now, though," Mutt told Fetts.

"That's good, Mutt. Now where is Billy if he isn't in Mechanicsburg, PA?" Fetts asked them.

"I think he's back up in New York, I think," Mutt responded.

Frustration was starting to creep back into Fetts' bones again.

"And why would you think he's back in New York, Mutt?" Fetts asked him.

"Grubby," Mutt replied.

"Grubby?" Fetts asked.

"Yeah, Grubby," Mutt said.

Fetts was now approaching his boiling point again.

"Mutt, tell me everything else you know about Billy—Billy in New York, Grubby and anything else you can remember," Fetts told Mutt. "And Jeff, if you have anything to add you do it when Mutt is done. You hear me?"

Jeff nodded too scared to say a word.

Looking back at Mutt, Fetts said, "Go ahead, Mutt."

"This other guy, not the guy we knows who found that there Rich Valley golf place in PA, but another guy says he saw'd Billy's ride Grubby some place in New York. He didn't say exactly where in New York, but it was in New York he saw Grubby. So's, Billy musta been there too, with Grubby. If Grubby's someplace, Billy's there, too. Grubby don't go noplace without Billy doing the ridin'," Mutt said.

Fetts took in what Mutt had just told him and looked over at Jeff.

"You have anything to add?" Fetts asked Jeff.

"What Mutt said," is all Jeff could get out.

"Okay, that's good. Now get ahold of your guy in New York and tell him to find Billy. Then get your other guy who found that golf place in PA to send me everything he has on this Rich Valley. Does he know what I'm looking for?" Fetts asked Mutt.

"He know," Mutt replied.

"Good. Now do it and get the fuck out of my sight until you do what I just told you two nimwits to do. And even god won't be able to help you if you fuck this up, Mutt. You too, Jeff. Now get," Fetts told them.

Quick as they could, they get while the gettin' was still good.

Chapter 72

Harry was enjoying his morning coffee on the deck off the living room of his garage apartment on George Street. He had just opened the morning paper and had taken a second sip of his coffee when he heard a familiar voice from down below.

"Harry? You up there, Harry," he heard again.

Harry got up and went over to the railing that looked down on the driveway. He was fairly sure it was his neighbor from one of the apartments in the main house and, yup, there she was.

"There you are, Harry," he heard.

"Good Morning, Sandy. What has you out this early in the morning?" Harry asked her.

"Just being neighborly, Harry," Sandy replied with a big, bright smile. "I was up early and decided to bake a batch of sweet buns and I thought you might like to try them."

"Your buns are sweet, Sandy," Harry replied with a smile. "And you know I would try them any chance I get."

If possible Sandy's smile got even bigger and brighter.

"Come on up and let me check out those buns of yours, Sandy," Harry said.

"All of them, Harry?"

"You bet your sweet buns, Sandy, every one of them," Harry replied.

~ * ~

Later that afternoon Harry was back out on his deck with the intention of finishing the paper he had started that morning. Sweet buns, all of them, had consumed the entire morning right through lunch. The fact lunch had been served in bed followed by more sweet buns of both varieties didn't bother Harry one little bit.

Just as he finished the sports pages, Harry's cell chirped.

"Shorts," Harry answered.

"Hold please," was what Harry heard in shades of Déjà Vu from not that long ago.

Seconds later, Trundle came on the line.

"Sorry to bother you, Harry," Trundle started. "I have a small problem I would like you to rectify for me if you can."

"You name it and it's done," Harry replied.

"My son seems to have gone missing from his confinement and I need him returned discreetly. You understand the complications involved here, don't you, Harry?" Trundle asked.

"Oh, yes, I understand completely, Randle. Do you have any idea of the how's and where's involved?" Harry asked.

"Neither, Harry. I just got word he's missing and I need him found, and yesterday was too late. The plane's waiting for you at Teterboro and Charles should be at your door in a matter of minutes. Can you leave immediately, Harry?" Trundle asked Harry.

"I'm packing a bag as we speak and I'll be waiting downstairs when Charles gets here. Don't worry, Randle, I will find him and I will put him back where he belongs," Harry assured Trundle.

"Thank you, Harry. Charles has cash and a credit card for you. Whatever it takes is a pittance so long as he is returned. I will deal with him after that," Trundle told Harry.

"It's as good as done, Randle. I will call you when I'm on my way back," Harry told Trundle as he hung up the phone.

The phone rang again almost immediately. Fairly sure it wasn't Trundle calling back, Harry said "Shorts."

"Hey, Harry, it's Billy. What's shaking?"

"Hey, Billy," Harry replied. "I have an emergency I need to deal with and I'm heading out of town for a few days. Where are you now?"

"I'm in Jersey taking care of a few things. Why?" Bill asked.

"If you're up for a little diversion, meet me at Teterboro as soon as you can get there. Do you know where it is?" Harry said.

"I can find it," Billy replied. "And yeah, I'm not doing much right now and a little diversion sounds cool right about this time."

"Okay, I will see you there in about an hour, give or take," Harry told Billy.

"Be waiting on you, brother," Billy said as he disconnected.

~ * ~

With visions of sweet buns dancing in his head, Harry zipped his bag and headed downstairs to meet Charles. What lie ahead was a mystery of sorts, but mysteries were what got Harry's giddy-up giddy-upping.

Chapter 73

Charles was the primary driver for Mr. M. Randle Trundle. Charles drove for no one else but Randle, unless Trundle dispatched Charles to take Harry where Harry needed to go. Today was one of those days.

The Violet, not Purple, Rolls Royce rolled up the driveway and stopped next to Harry. Charles got out and said, "Harry, it is good to see you again."

They shook hands as only old friends do.

"Good to see you too, Charles. I appreciate you coming out here to turn around and drive me back to New Jersey," Harry told him.

"Ain't no place on earth too far to go for you, Harry. You know that, don't you?" Charles said.

"Like it was the only thing I know, Charles. Still good of you to do it anyway," Harry replied.

"Thank you, Harry. I appreciate that," Charles told Harry.

"Then let's hit it," Harry said.

~ * ~

Billy was sitting in the waiting area when Harry arrived at Teterboro. Charles would normally drive Harry right out to the plane, but Billy changed that.

"Been waiting long?" Harry asked Billy when he came up alongside him.

"Couple—not long. I've been admiring the clientele that frequent Teterboro Airport and find them quite interesting," Billy told Harry.

"Don't get any ideas, Billy. You screw around here with these people, and they catch you, your ass is grass. Dead crab-grass grass," Harry told him. "There's more security here than even you can imagine. Trust me, they'd get you before you turned to hightail it out of Dodge."

"I said I was admiring, that's all," Billy answered Harry.

"Yeah, well, stop admiring and grab your bag. We got a plane to catch and I have a job to do," Harry told Billy.

"Right behind you boss man," Billy said.

"That's what I'm worried about—you behind me and I can't see what you're doing," Harry replied.

"You worry too much, Harry," Billy told him.

"Three things," Harry said. "One—it's my nature; two—it's what I get paid to do; and three—it's you we're talking about."

"Points well taken," Billy replied. "Let's go and fix your shit and get back to New York. By the way, where are we headed?"

"Arizona," Harry told him.

"That's gonna be a bit of a trip. Maybe I'll catch a few while we bird it across the country," Billy told Harry.

"Suit yourself," Harry said. "I'll wake you when we get within spitting distance of the airport."

As they entered the plane, Billy looked around and said, "Holy shit, Harry, you spring for this?"

"It's one of Mr. Trundle's. The job is a favor for him so he's getting us where we need to go. Beats flying commercial any day," Harry told Billy.

"I'll say," Billy agreed. "Maybe those winks will have to wait. We get anything to eat on the way out to Arizona?"

"Eat and drink, Billy. First class all the way when you fly as a guest of Mr. Trundle," Harry replied.

"This Mr. Trundle is a pretty good guy to know, you know, Harry," Billy said.

"That he is, Billy, that he is. I'm a lucky guy to have made his acquaintance and even luckier to be his friend," Harry told Billy.

Chapter 74

When the plane landed they were met by a limo waiting for them beside the plane as they disembarked. A rather imposing guy was standing beside the car holding the rear door open for them.

"Welcome to Arizona, Mr. Shorts. My name is Arnold. I trust your flight was satisfactory?"

"The flight was perfect. This is Billy," Harry told the guy.

"Hello, Billy," Arnold greeted him.

"Arnold," Billy greeted him in return.

"Step inside the car and I will see to the bags," Arnold told them. "There are refreshments in the cooler on the floor."

"That you Arnold," Harry said as they stepped inside the car.

"Pretty nice," Billy commented once he had himself situated.

"As I said on the plane," Harry replied, "first class all the way when you travel as a guest of Mr. Trundle."

"You said fly, Harry," Billy corrected.

"Huh?" Harry queried.

"You said "First class all the way when you fly as a guest of Mr. Trundle" while we were on the plane. Fly, not travel, that's what you said," Billy told Harry.

"Keep that shit up and for you it will be walk, not fly, back to New York when we're done out here," Harry warned.

"I've walked, flown, rode, driven, hitched, hid and done just about every other "get there" mode you can name. So, when we're done out here you can fly back to New York in your fancy jet without me. I'll manage, Harry. Trust me, I can manage," Billy told him.

"I believe you, Mr. Touchy," Harry answered.

Their back and forth was disturbed when Arnold got in the front seat and fired up the limo.

"Comfortable, gentlemen?" Arnold asked.

"Yeah, we're good, Arnold. Thanks," Harry told him.

"Good, then we will be on our way. Relax, have something to drink, and I'll have you at the hotel in no time."

Billy lifted the top of the cooler and perused its contents. He told Harry, "We have your soft drinks, your orange juice for the healthy minded traveler, and your after twelve favorite—beer. But not your average beer guzzlin' piss water beer, Harry. This is top of the line stuff."

"Magic Hat #9," Harry said matter-of-factly.

Billy looked at Harry in that how-the-hell-did-you-know-that way, then said, "How-the-hell-did-you-know-that, Harry?"

"It's my current beer of choice and I introduced Mr. Trundle to Magic Hat #9 not that long ago. As I said before— 'first class all the way when you fly/travel as a guest of Mr. Trundle.' The man doesn't miss a beat," Harry informed him.

"You can say that again, Harry. So, Magic Hat #9 for you?" Billy asked.

"It is twelve somewhere in the world if not here, Billy. No sense in letting a good beer go to waste sitting in a cooler in the back of a big-assed limo, now is there?"

"When you're right, you're right, Harry," Billy agreed.

With that, Billy popped the top on two Magic Hat #9's and handed one to Harry. Harry took it and said, "To Mr. Trundle and to new friendships," as he held out his bottle towards Billy.

"To Mr. Trundle and to welcome new friendships," Billy said as he touched the top of his bottle to Harry's.

They drank, two friends sitting in the back of a big-assed limo like they'd been doing it their whole lives.

Chapter 75

Arnold told them, "We're ten minutes out."

"Thanks, Arnold," Harry replied.

Billy turned to Harry and said, "What exactly is it we have to do out here in Arizona as a favor to Mr. Trundle?"

"First of all, the "we" is reduced to the "me" when we refer to the "to do" out here in Arizona. The "you" in the "we" will be confined to making some phone calls trying to get a line on a guy's whereabouts while I try and get a line on how he got to be wherever he currently is in the first place," Harry informed Billy.

"I don't get to do no detecting like the "big shot" Private Detective Harry Mickey Shorts?" Billy asked.

"Detect this, Billy, and detect it good. You sit by the pool ogling the T&A while you talk on the phone looking all important and like that. You wait until I give you a possible name he's under and then you try and find my guy if you can. You don't move from the pool and you don't "detect" at all on your own other than what I just told you to do. You got that "little shot" non-Private Detective Billy Burns?" Harry instructed.

"Phew! Touchy fucking touchy, aren't we now," Billy scoffed.

Harry looked Billy right in the eyes and said in the sternest voice he could muster, "Billy, I don't give a rat's ass what you have done in your life before this very minute, I really don't. But this is very serious and real world shit that could blow up in the blink of an eye and piss all over the very nice parade I got going for myself. Don't, I repeat, don't give me any cause to doubt my decision to bring you along with me. Not one iota of a reason. Clear?"

Without hesitating, Billy replied, "Clear, Harry. Clear as a cloudless sky over the far away mountain tops of..."

"Shut the hell up, Billy," Harry told Billy.

"Shutting up, Mr. Private Detective Man," Billy responded.

"Why do I do these things to myself?" Harry asked nobody.

"Cuz I'm absolutely irresistible," Billy replied to the same nobody.

Harry just shook his head as Billy smiled.

~ * ~

Unpacked, Harry called Arnold who was on call for the duration of their stay in Arizona. Arnold told Harry he would be waiting downstairs in two minutes.

"Get the phone book from the night stand and find yourself a spot by the pool where you can watch the lovelies and not be heard. I will call you as soon as I have something," Harry told Billy.

"Lunch?" Billy asked.

"Yeah, you can order lunch," Harry told him. "Put it on the room but just for yourself and not for any of the lovelies you may see by the pool. You're undercover, Billy."

"Undercover?" Billy asked with that sneaky smile he could project.

"Not those covers, Billy. P.I. undercover," Harry told him.

"I was just playing with ya, Harry," Billy replied.

To save himself the murder rap, Harry left.

~ * ~

As a means of background, Harry had helped Trundle with a prior case that culminated with Trundle's son being whisked off to Arizona in lieu of a stay in one of the federal governments more restrictive housing units. Being privy to all of the intimate details, Harry was the perfect person to ensure he was returned to his prior accommodations.

Harry was sitting across the desk from the Assistant Vice President of Operations and Administration at PharmCo. Inc. Harry was told the Vice President of Operations and Administration at PharmCo. Inc. was unavailable at the moment.

Harry wasn't pleased.

"He's unavailable at the moment?" Harry asked.

"Yes, Mr. Shorts. Mr. Blother is unavailable at the moment."

"Mr. Thompson is it?" Harry stated and not asked. "This Mr. Blother, he's unavailable at the moment as in he's taking a piss and will be available shortly. Or, he's unavailable at the moment and there's no shot in hell I'm gonna see him any time soon?"

It was indeed Mr. Thompson and he blinked several times

without responding to Harry's question.

"I see it's the latter," Harry surmised.

Several more blinks from the Assistant Vice President of Operations and Administration at PharmCo. Inc., but still no verbal response.

"I'll take that as a yes. Now, here's what I need: who helped Teddy Trundle leave this building yesterday and where is he, or she?" Harry said stated as a demand not as much as a question.

After the responding first blink from Mr. Thompson, Harry stood and said, "If I find out you had anything to do with this, I will bury your Assistant Vice President of Operations and Administration at PharmCo. Inc. fucking ass. If I find out you're covering for someone, like the Vice President of Operations and Administration at PharmCo. Inc. perhaps, I will bury your previously mentioned fucking ass. And if I have to come back here and discuss this with you again, I will kick your Assistant Vice President of Operations and Administration at PharmCo. Inc. fucking ass. Clear?"

Thompson didn't blink and Harry had what he wanted.

"Thank you for your time, Mr. Thompson," Harry said as he showed himself out of Thompson's office.

~ * ~

Back in the car, Harry called Billy.

"P.I.'s are US."

"Very funny, Billy," Harry said.

"Lunch was great and the lovelies as you so aptly named them are even better. How goes the clue hunt, partner?" Billy asked.

Harry sighed.

"Here's what I need, Billy. Call every hotel within fifteen miles starting with the top of the line and work your way down. I doubt you'll get very far before you find our guy," Harry told Billy.

"Top of the line?" Billy asked. "Not some sleaze bag flee-bitten roach motel the bad guys usually go to hide out until the coast is clear?"

"Not our guy, Billy. He'll be in swank city hiding out until the coast is clear," Harry answered.

"I'm on it, partner," Billy said. "Name?"

"Billy, we're not partners. And name—your name is Billy and my name is Harry. And the guy you're looking for will be registered under the name of Blothers. Probably Theodore Blothers."

Chapter 76

Arnold found Harry a Mickey D's and pulled up to the drive-through window. He ordered Harry a Big Mac, small fries with extra ketchup packets and a large Root Beer. Just as Harry was finishing the last of the fries, his cell rang.

"Harry."

"Billy."

"You undercover but not incognito?"

"Something like that, Billy," Harry replied.

"Got him," Billy said.

"Let me guess—Four Seasons?" Harry guessed.

"You suck, Harry," Billy replied sounding rather put off. "I find the guy and you already know where he is."

"It was just a guess, Billy. I started from the top and that's as good a top as I could think of," Harry told him.

"You still suck, Harry."

"Address?" Harry asked.

Billy gave him the address and told Harry he was registered under T. Blothers, not Theodore Blothers as Harry had thought.

"You did good work, Billy. I'll be back before you know it, but I don't want to catch you "undercovers" when I get back. You got that, Billy?" Harry said.

"Shit, Harry, you do suck big time," Billy whined.

~ * ~

Arnold pulled the limo in front of the Four Seasons and Harry told him to wait in the car someplace close by. "I won't be long," he told Arnold.

Harry walked up to the front desk and asked the very attractive young lady behind the desk if he could speak to the manager on duty, please.

"And this would be in reference to?" the very attractive young lady behind the desk inquired of Harry.

Harry leaned over the front of the desk as far as he could and whispered, "It's a secret between him and me," and winked at her.

Blushing like a schoolgirl caught with her hand between her

legs, she picked up the phone and whispered something Harry couldn't hear. She promptly left the desk.

Two minutes later a rather attractive young man in a manly kind of way came around the corner and approached Harry.

"I'm Mr. Smith, the manager. You are?"

"Well, Mr. Jones, of course," Harry responded.

Doubting he was Mr. Jones, Smith said, "What is this in reference to, Mr., ah, Mr. Jones? And may I see some identification, please?"

"Surely, Mr., ah, Mr. Smith," Harry replied.

Harry reached in his pocket and produced a small card case which he opened and then extracted a single card. He handed it to the manager.

Mr. Smith read the card and said to Harry, "Government Services?"

"Yes, Mr. Smith—Government Services. And the government would appreciate your assistance in a most delicate matter," Mr. Jones told him.

"Government Services? What Government Services?" Smith asked.

Harry smiled at Smith and said, "You know the old joke 'I would tell you but then I'd have to kill you.' Not that bad, but close."

Mr. Smith took just the slightest step back from Mr. Jones.

"Now, what the government would like is the room number of a guest registered here in your hotel—a T. Blothers—and a pass key to open the door to his room. Can you assist me and Government Services with this most delicate matter, Mr. Smith?"

"Ah," Smith uttered.

"I can assure you there will be no disturbance and myself and Mr. T. Blothers will be gone from your hotel before you know it," Harry told him.

Without saying a word, Smith turned and scurried behind the desk accessing the computer as fast as his fingers would allow. Shortly thereafter, Smith handed Harry a piece of paper with Blother's room number and a pass card to access the room.

On behalf of the government, Harry thanked Mr. Smith and headed for the elevator bank. Soon he was standing in front of Room 432 where he put his ear to the door to listen. The TV was on and Harry was ready. He inserted the card in the slot and pushed open the door.

"What the hell...?" Teddy blurted out just as recognition reached his brain.

"Hello, Teddy," Harry said.

"Harry Shorts. Well I'll be damned," Teddy replied.

"Not that bad, Teddy. But, your sorry ass is going back where it came from, and where it belongs, thanks to the I-don't-get-why generosity of your father, Mr. M. Randle Trundle," Harry told him.

"We can't make a deal?" Teddy asked Harry.

"The only deal that's going to be made is the one that dumb ass Blothers had better make if he knows what's good for him. If your dad gets his hands on him after he helped you get away he'd be in for some very rough going I'm afraid," Harry told Teddy.

Teddy took a quick look around the room.

Harry followed his eyes and said to him, "It would give me great pleasure to find you stupid enough to try and get out of this, Teddy. Please try something so I would be required to subdue you in the most earnest matter I could conjure up. And trust me, Teddy, I can conjure up some very ernest ones."

Resignation was all over Teddy's face.

"Now put on some clothes and cover up those god-awful ugly boxers you're wearing. We will then leave the hotel in a civilized manner and return you to whence you have come and belong. We good with that, T. Blothers?" Harry asked.

T. Blothers began to dress so Harry and Teddy could be on their way. Harry was certain T. Blothers would live on no more.

Chapter 77

Harry got back to the hotel and found Billy not undercover, but overcover, lying on the bed watching TV while munching on mini-bar goodies a plenty.

"That shit's expensive, Billy," Harry said in greeting.

"You're very welcome for my help, Harry. It was no problem and I was happy to be of service to Mr. P.I. himself," Billy replied.

"I'm so sorry to have put you to such a burdensome task, Billy. I fly you across the country in a private jet, put you up in a fancy hotel where you got to sit by the pool, suck on some suds, and imagine what you would do to every babe that walked or swam by. Then you force yourself back to your swanky room where you consume a fortune in mini-bar shit watching"—Harry looked at the TV and shook his head— "watching porn in the middle of the afternoon."

"It was and continues to be a mighty struggle, Harry," Billy replied.

"Asshole. Get your shit and let's go. We're gonna get something to eat and then get the hell out of Arizona. The plane's gonna be ready in an hour so make it snappy," Harry told Billy.

"What, we don't even get to spend the night on our first "Big Dick" road trip? That sucks," Billy complained.

"I've had enough of Arizona already," Harry replied. "I'd just as soon ditch this place and sleep on the plane if I have to. Unless you'd care to find your own way back, you will, too."

"As much as I was looking forward to doing some "undercover" work with one of the subjects I surveilled this afternoon, a ride back on the "this be the way to travel" flying machine will have to overrule any further surveillance," Billy replied.

"For a first time P.I. helper-boy you're catching on pretty quick, Billy," Harry told him.

Smiling broadly, Billy replied, "Well, fuck you very much Mr. Big Time P.I."

With a smile just as big and broad, Harry said, "You are quite fucking welcome, Billy."

~ * ~

Tummies filled, Harry and Billy hit the road back to the "this be the way to travel" plane for their trip back home. Harry settled in with a brew and the day's newspaper while Billy did the same without the newspaper. Peppering Harry with questions between sips of beer was his idea of how to pass the time.

Frustrated by Billy's interruptions, Harry finally put down the paper and turned to face Billy.

"Billy, ask me your questions and I'll give you whatever answers I can. Then, shut the hell up and leave me alone to enjoy this fine mode of transportation in peace. Deal?" Harry asked him.

"Deal," Billy responded.

"So ask," Harry told him.

"What's with you and Sherry?" Billy started.

"We're divorced," Harry answered.

"And?" Billy continued.

"And what?" Harry replied.

"And you guys may be divorced but you seem to get along fine. What's up with that?" Billy asked.

Harry thought a few seconds, then said, "We were married, I fucked up, she finally threw me out. End of story," Harry said.

Again Harry thought for a few seconds, then said, "The kids I love to death and I'd do anything for them. They're the reason I came back and they're the reason I stay. There will never be anything more important to me than those two kids; not now, not ever."

Billy looked at Harry while he considered what Harry had just said. Coming to some revelation in his head, Billy said, "Sounds like you got your head on straight where Max and Briande come in, Harry. Those kids are cool and I'm thinking that having kids, if they turned out like them, that'd be pretty cool. Yeah, maybe someday…" Billy trailed off.

"That's an interesting statement coming from you, Billy," Harry said.

"You're right, it probably does sound like something from out of left field coming from me. Up to now kids have been nothing more than a distraction to be used in some con or game. It's what I knew growing up and what I've known ever since. You and your kids gave me a view I haven't had the opportunity to see before now and it gives one pause to think and consider what could be if one wants it."

"Life's strange like that," Harry told him. "You never know what it's going to throw at you and you also don't know what to catch. Just thinking about kids in a different light is a move in the right direction, Billy. There might be hope for you yet."

"Yeah, maybe, Harry. Maybe," Billy responded.

Chapter 78

As they deplaned in New Jersey, Harry was surprised Charles wasn't there to greet them. A car was there as they hit the tarmac, but the driver standing next to the limo was foreign to Harry.

"Mr. Shorts?" the driver asked.

"That would be me," Harry responded.

"It is a pleasure to meet you, sir. Charles has spoken of you often and it is a pleasure to have the opportunity to be of service to you. My name is Jonathon," the driver said.

"Pleased to meet you as well, Jonathon. This is Billy," Harry replied.

"Pleased to meet you as well, Billy," Jonathon replied. "Where will I be taking you today, Billy?" He asked.

Billy looked at Harry before answering.

"He's with me for today, Jonathon," Harry replied.

"Splendid," Jonathon answered. "Let me get your luggage and we can be on our way. There are refreshments in the back for the ride. Please help yourself and we will be off shortly."

~ * ~

Harry and Billy were getting comfortable in the back of the car, cool ones in hand, when Jonathon got back in. In a jiff they were on their way.

"Can I stop anywhere to get you something to eat?" Jonathon asked.

Harry replied, "Thanks, but we ate on the plane. The cool ones should tide us over until we get back to Manhasset."

"Good enough," Jonathon replied. "If there is anything I can do during the ride please let me know."

"Will do," Harry told him.

"So, what's next?" Billy asked Harry.

"Right now I don't have a next," Harry answered.

"Well, in that case, I have a thought," Billy replied.

"Just one thought?" Harry said.

Billy smiled and said, "Never just one thought as you would expect, Harry. But I have one specific thought that would pertain to the circumstances that envelop us at this time."

"Envelop us?" Harry repeated.

"Yeah, envelop," Billy started. "It means..."

"I know what envelop means, Billy. I was more eluding to the "us" part of the "enveloping us" in your statement," Harry answered.

"Perhaps I have overestimated where we are, Harry. Perhaps I have assumed more than I should," Billy said.

Harry sat back and took a long pull on his beer. He considered what Billy had just said and considered how he might respond. One more shorter pull on his beer and he was ready.

"Billy, we haven't known each other very long," Harry started. "If it weren't for Mel we probably never would have crossed paths at all. Where we "are" in the whole scheme of things is a question I don't have an answer for right now. I like you, Sherry likes you, and the kids like you. Shit, I think even Mel may tolerate you which is saying a lot."

Billy didn't know what to say so he did the best thing possible. He kept his mouth shut and waited for Harry to continue.

"That being said, I can listen to your *thought* and see where it takes us, if anywhere," Harry finished.

When Harry didn't say anything else, Billy determined it was his turn to talk again. After a short pull on his beer, Billy said, "Thanks for that, Harry. This may be a loony idea, but it's one I think I need to take a shot at. You can either agree that it is loony-toons and run for the hills, or you can think about it and get back to me later on. Either way, I'm gonna find a way to make it happen with or without your help and let the chips fall where they may."

Harry looked out the window to see where they were. Seeing they had a long way to go before they reached Manhasset, Harry said, "Okay, spill it, Billy. I'm gonna get another beer just in case I need one. Let me hear your brainstorm and we can figure out what goes after that."

"Fair enough," Billy said as he proceeded to lay out his idea for Harry.

Chapter 79

Mel was sitting at the kitchen table having breakfast with his wife when he laid the shock on her. He pushed his plate away and finished his coffee.

"Carol Ann, that is exactly what he said when we talked. He gave me all the figures and what it would take to get the house we always wanted. It's all there; all we have to do is say yes. The business, this house, most of what's in this house goes except for whatever you feel you have to have. The new place is furnished with stuff that's practically brand new. And it's nice, too. Just the kind of stuff you would pick out for a beach house if you were to furnish it yourself. Plus, anything you don't like we get rid of and replace it with whatever you want," Mel told her.

Carol Ann sat there stunned, clearly unable to speak.

"It's what we've been talking about for years," Mel told her.

"And we'd have enough money to go on living like we do now? None of that scraping by shit so we can say we're retired. We could travel, see the kids whenever we wanted to?" she asked.

"The only thing that would change is the sound of the ocean instead of the Long Island Railroad when you open the windows or door," Mel told her. "Walk half a block and sand replaces sidewalk, just like we dreamed of long ago and have talked about ad infinitum ever since, well, since we got close enough to talk about it. Only now it's not just talk, Carol Ann. Now it's say yes and we are there before you know it."

"We really could do it?" Carol Ann asked.

"As God is my witness, may he strike me down if I'm lying," Mel responded.

"Don't push your luck, hun," Carol Ann said.

"Good point," Mel agreed.

"Do the kids know?" she asked.

Shaking his head, Mel said, "Nobody knows but you, and me, and the man that counts the beans for us."

Carol Ann looked at her husband in a way she hadn't done in a long time. After a spell she said, "Mel, this is big what you just unloaded on me. Real Big! It's not a "Where should we go on vacation?" or some other minor conversational subject we occasionally banter over. This is a "What are we going to do with the rest of our lives and where are we going to do it?" subject. It's major."

Mel picked up his empty coffee cup, put it back down, and said, "I know that, Carol Ann. That's why I wanted to make sure the numbers made sense and trust me, I checked not twice but ten times. It is real and we can do it if we want it to happen. All we, you and I together, all we have to do is say yes. We say yes and the process gets put in motion as we sit back and plan the rest of our lives. No business bullshit, no daily hassles other than what time do we want to go down to the beach and what time are cocktails before dinner."

"That's it?" Carol Ann asked.

"That's it," Mel answered. "Free as birds to shit on life instead of having life shit on us for a change."

"What about the kids? What about your sister, and Harry, and their kids? What about...?" Carol Ann said.

"They aren't going anywhere, Carol Ann. They will all go on living just as they did before. Plus, now they will all have a place to visit if they want to go to the beach and mooch off the old farts who retired when they wanted to and not when they had to," Mel told her.

"I don't know what to say," Carol Ann told Mel.

Mel took his wife's hand and said, "You say yes, I make a call, then we begin the rest of our lives."

Carol Ann smiled and said, "Yes!"

Chapter 80

Fetts was sitting in his shithole of a so-called office he used when he needed to get away by himself and think. He had his "official" office where he would meet with the rest of his crew and the clients of his façade businesses. But now, Fetts needed to think, and he needed to think alone.

Fetts needed to put things in perspective.

Fetts needed to get his ducks in a row

Fetts needed to plan.

Fetts needed to make some decisions.

Fetts needed...he needed...well shit, he needed to kick some ass and make a big score. He needed to let the world, his world, know he was still a player. He needed to make sure people knew you couldn't fuck with Jon Francis Fetterman and not feel the consequences. Fetts needed to be "the man" in as big a way as he could.

Fetts knew what he needed to do and he was going to get it done.

~ * ~

Ms. Bunny Malone had a very strange habit of giggling that then led to all out laughter at what some people might consider a very strange time. This was one of those times.

The first time it had happened Harry didn't quite know what to do. Since that time, it had happened again several times and he wasn't always sure what he should do.

"I can't help myself," Bunny had told Harry. "You get me going and once I get to a certain point I guess my body, my mind and my whole soul get over-happy and I finally get giggly and then I get to laughing. I just flat out lose it all together and I can't help myself. There's no other way to describe it but you just plain fuck me silly, Harry Mickey Shorts. Yeah, that's it, you just plain fuck me silly."

Not knowing what else to say, Harry warily said, "And I assume this is a good thing?"

Bunny smiled up at Harry and said, "Oh, yes, Harry, this is a very good thing. It was a good thing today, and it's a good thing every time it happens. At least it is for me." Sitting up with a look of concern on her pretty face, she said, "It's good for you, too, isn't it, Harry?"

Harry smiled at Bunny and said, "Oh, yeah, Bunny, it's plenty good for me as well. I may not be laughing like you on the outside, but trust me, I'm having a damn good time inside, and outside, and every which side you can think of."

With that, Bunny shimmied on down under the covers and Harry was fairly sure a good time was about to be had by all—inside, outside, and every side you can think of.

~ * ~

Bunny was gone. Harry would have liked to bask in the glory of the memory, but he needed to put a few things in motion if he was going to help Billy with his looney-toons plan. The more he thought about it, the more he thought it could work.

He almost liked it.

Yeah, it could work. It would take some maneuvering, but he was pretty sure they could pull it off. They had the know-how and Billy had more than enough incentive for all of them; but there was still one piece they didn't have. That would be Harry's job. It would be Harry's job to secure the last piece to the puzzle, ensure the back end would be covered, and nobody would get hurt after the fact.

"Sumbitch could actually work, I reckon," Harry said to nobody.

Chapter 8.1

Jon Francis Fetterman wasn't a gambler by nature. It's true he had an operation set up in Las Vegas which could lead one to insinuate Fetts liked to try his luck now and again, but one would be wrong. As he could be found presently doing, he did sit at the blackjack table now and again to pass the time. He did wager on the outcome of the cards. He did win and he did lose. But he didn't gamble.

Fetts sat at the table and he thought.

Fetts sat at the table and he planned.

Fetts sat at the table so nobody would bother him in his thoughts and his planning.

Fetts sat at the table and he...

"Hey, Fetts."

Fetts didn't move. He didn't turn around to see who could be stupid enough to bother him while he sat at the blackjack table. Everyone knew you didn't bother Frankie Fetterman when he didn't want to be bothered. Everybody knew.

"I said, hey, Fetts."

Fetts wondered who could be so fucking ignorant as to bother him at the tables. He had to find out, so he turned his head ever so slightly to get a look at the asshole bothering him at the table.

When he turned, the guy again said, "Hey, Fetts."

Now it made sense.

"Germ," Fetts muttered under his breath.

"You busy, Fetts?" Germ had the balls to ask Fetts.

"No, Germ, never too busy for you," Fetts replied.

Never too busy for the guy who controlled Vegas. Not all of Vegas, obviously. Only the portion of Vegas that lived under the radar when you needed something. The portion of Vegas that allowed you to go about your business without anyone knowing what you had to work with and where it came from. The portion of Vegas Fetts needed to run his business if he wanted to be successful and eventually rich enough to leave Vegas behind.

Germ was that guy.

Like a germ that invades your body and renders you helpless to its ravaging effects, Germ could render your efforts in Vegas helpless. Germ controlled the "stuff" you couldn't get but had to have.

Germ was a ravaging germ in the underbelly of the City of Sin.

"No, Germ, never too busy for you," Fetts repeated when Germ gave him that look.

"Good, Germ told Fetts. "Care to buy me a soda?"

"Sure," Fetts replied.

"The bar in ten," Germ said and walked away.

~ * ~

Harry was halfway through his second Magic Hat #9 when Billy joined him at the bar. He had expected him about thirty minutes earlier, but Harry knew by now Billy wasn't a slave to the clock.

"Your poison?" Harry asked Billy.

"Yours," Billy replied.

Harry nodded to his bud and the bartender brought Billy a Magic Hat.

After an initial sip, Billy asked Harry, "You talk to your guy?"

"Yeah," Harry replied.

"And?" Billy asked.

Harry smiled before he said, "My guy would be most delighted to play."

"And you?" Billy asked.

Harry smiled again before he said, "I too would be most delighted to play."

"Then play we shall," Billy replied.

~ * ~

Germ never touched his drink. Neither did Frankie. Germ commanded and Fetts had no choice but to agree. He would pay the outrageous sum Germ demanded in return for what he wanted. He either paid or he had to kill Germ once and for all. It would happen eventually, but not yet. For now, Fetts paid the piper and would have to bide his time…until it was time.

Chapter 82

It was close to midnight when he sat down across from her. She never heard him come in or cross the room to where she sat. How he could appear and disappear like that baffled her to no end, but that was Billy. Since the very first day she had met him and every day since, that had been Billy.

"You rang?" Billy asked Tips.

"In a matter of speaking," Tips replied.

"It has to be something pretty important for you to put the word out in the manner you did," Billy told her.

"I didn't know how to get to you without letting them know," she replied.

"Cell phones off the approved list these days?" Billy asked her.

"Oh yeah," Tips started. "I call you on your cell and you don't answer. I wait for you to return my call and you don't. You know you won't. I know you won't. So, I call you back and the cycle repeats itself."

Billy didn't respond.

Tips thought about giving up but trudged on.

"Finally, after the third try with the same result, I put the word out through the guy I'm not supposed to go through and you eventually show up like you did just now," Tips told Billy.

Not surprisingly, Billy didn't respond.

Tips sighed.

Satisfied her little pout session was finished, Billy said, "I'm here now. What's the emergency?"

"It's the same thing it always is, Billy," Tips tells him. "Only this time you have to listen. This time we're close to the end and I don't know what to do to fix it if you won't listen. You have to help, Billy. It isn't a big deal to anyone that comes here and all you have to do is say okay and we're back on level ground."

"They're our friends, Tips. They're who we are, who we were and who we're going to be. It's why I, we, started this place and it's why we keep it open. It's for them and all the other "wes" out

192

there who need it," Billy replied.

Tips shook her head as she said, "And it's going to be gone unless you get that thick skull of yours out of your ass and pay attention to what I'm telling you. We are about to go under and I can't stop it unless you let me. Let me do what I have to do, what I can do, and we will be fine. Trust me for once, Billy. Everyone is willing to pay what they should instead of the pennies you charge them to use this place and the services we provide. They know we're going under and they're begging me to keep it open. They need it, Billy. We need it, Billy. I need it, Billy."

Billy looked away and stared off into space. He'd heard the plea before and turned a deaf ear every time. He created this place for the rest of the Billy's out there because he could and he wanted it to be for them.

"Please, Billy," Tips cried. "Please let me do this for us and for the rest of our people who need it. If not, we all lose. You, me, we all lose, Billy Burns."

Billy turned back toward Tips and said, "Get whoever you need together and let me know when. I'll talk to them and let them tell me what they want to do. I want to hear it from our kind and they will tell me how to go forward. You and them, Tips. Okay?"

"Okay, Billy. I'll get them together as quick as I can and tell the financial people we're working on the solution. I'll fix it with them until we get straightened out. Thanks, Billy," Tips told Billy.

"You could have gotten me without the tears you know," Billy said.

"Yeah, I know," Tips told him. "But it was good practice."

Billy smiled as he got up, kissed Tips on the forehead, and left as quietly as he had come in.

Chapter 83

Ted entered the pro shop a little before ten on Tuesday morning just as he had been doing for six years now. You could set your watch by it. Five minutes to ten on Tuesday morning, every Tuesday morning, from early March through some time in November.

The weather got manageable and Ted started his golfing season. The weather started to get too cold and Ted's season was over at Rich Valley until next March. You could bet on it.

"Hey, Larry," Ted said as he ambled up to the desk.

"How's it going, Ted?" Larry replied as he always did.

"About half," was Ted's normal reply.

"You gonna ride eighteen?" Larry asked.

"Did the Pope used to be Polish?" Ted replied.

They both smiled. They had been saying exactly the same thing to each other every Tuesday morning for as long as Larry could remember. Ted did the same on Thursday mornings and played with the boys on Saturday mornings, too.

"You have a game today?" Larry asked.

"Nah, Lenny's got some bullshit thing at the Y his wife's got him doing this morning. I'm going solo today," Ted replied.

With that a guy came into the pro shop and walked up to the desk where Larry and Ted were having their weekly chat.

"Can I get on?" the guy butted in.

Ted turned and looked to see who this guy was who had the balls to interrupt he and Larry's weekly give and take.

"What?" the guy said to Ted. "Can't a guy ask if he can get a game around here?"

"This your first time at Rich Valley?" Larry asked him.

"Yeah, first time," the guy confirmed. "A guy told me it's alright and you can get a game if you're looking for one."

"You looking for one?" Ted asked him.

"I could be," he replied. "My buddy Twins bugged out on me and I'm going it solo today."

"What are you playing to?" Ted asked the stranger.

"USGA eight point one," he told Ted. "You?"

"I'm a three point one," Ted replied. "You got your USGA card?"

"If I need it," the guy said. "You?"

"Same," Ted replied.

"Wanna play?" the guy asked.

"Why not," Ted told him.

~ * ~

At the first tee Ted learned the new guy's name was Buddy, or so he said.

"You care to make it interesting?" Ted asked Buddy.

Buddy looked at Ted and said, "I don't usually gamble much, but we can make it a small wager to be friendly. What did you have in mind?"

"Oh, I don't know. How about a two dollar Nassau?" Ted asked.

"That's friendly enough," Buddy told Ted. "I suppose I can donate a few bucks to a guy on his home course the first time I play it. After all you're giving me a game after my pal bugged out on me."

They agreed Ted would give the new guy five strokes and they could readjust at the turn if they needed to. As they would come to find out, any readjustment would have been futile. Ted shot a mediocre 78 for his game while Buddy found Rich Valley a bit tougher than he expected and shot a not very good 86. Could have been a 96 if Buddy didn't hit a half dozen great chips and sink a few longish putts.

Ted and Buddy enjoyed a beer up at Nolo's after their round. Buddy grudgingly paid off his Nassau bet and bought the first round.

"Come by again if you're looking for a game," Ted told Buddy half-way through their first beer.

"That's mighty neighborly of you, Ted," Buddy replied. "Couldn't have anything to do with the fact you kicked my ass out there today, now could it?"

"Of course not," Ted said with a smile.

"I will and maybe bring my friend along, too. He's a bit more prone to wagering a buck or two on a game. Hell, he'll wager a buck or two on most anything, but he does love his poker game most of all."

Ted looked at Buddy and said, "We may be able to accommodate your friend in more ways than one."

~ * ~

After several more cool ones, Buddy left Nolo's with a ten o'clock tee time on Thursday. He and Twins would be enjoying a friendly round with Ted and one of Ted's fellow Rich Valley golfing buddies. As he reached his car, Buddy hit a speed dial number on his cell. After two rings it was answered.

"Fetts, its Buddy. Rich Valley is in play."

Chapter 84

The sound of a baseball meeting a baseball bat is a very distinctive sound, indistinguishable to most, but loved by some. It was such a sound that had Harry's undivided attention on this particular beautiful day. The orchestration of a pre-game workout had always fascinated Harry. Each player was in a pre-determined spot doing a particular drill, or exercise, or warm-up routine that was particular to the position they play. Harry had never embraced the beauty of it when he was a player and he regretted it now.

"Hey, Harry," was what brought Harry out of his reverie.

Harry turned to face the voice of a friend he had a need to see at times. "Hey, Harry, you got nothing better to do than sit in the stands of a two-bit baseball club with a two-bit Assistant General Manager?"

"As it turns out, nope," Harry replied.

"Still have the best General Manager and Field Manager that ever played or coached the game?" Harry asked.

"Harry, Coach Curran is what you said and ten times more. And yeah, we still got him, we love him, and we hope to have him for a long time to come," Richie replied.

"Tell him I'll stop in and see him before I leave today," Harry told Richie.

"You staying for the game?" Richie asked.

"The sun's shining, balls are flying, and as far as I know bears still shit in the woods," Harry replied.

Richie smiled at Harry and left to do what the Assistant General Manager and Marketing head of a top notch Double A minor league baseball team does to fill his day. Harry didn't exactly know what that was, or care much either, but he did consider Richie a bud and he hoped he always would be.

~ * ~

"Shorts," was what brought Harry back to earth the next time.

Harry knew that voice and took ten seconds to process the voice, connect it to a face and a person, then say, "Mueller."

"Nothing better to do?"

"Nope," Harry replied.

"Nice day for a game."

"Yep," Harry replied.

They sat in silence for a good ten minutes enjoying the display of artistry that transpired on the field. Neither moved; they just watched the ball fly, the players run, and what was to be.

Finally, Harry turned to Mueller and said, "You come here often, fella?"

That brought a smile to Mueller's face which didn't happen very often.

"Nope," Mueller replied without looking at Harry.

That sat for several enjoyable moments of baseball splendor, then Harry said, "Been awhile since you helped out with that case I had."

"Yep, it has," Mueller replied.

"Need something?" Harry asked.

Mueller finally turned to face Harry and said, "Me, no. You, what I hear."

"You in a position to do that?" Harry asked Mueller.

"What I do," Mueller replied.

"Probably could use some," Harry told Mueller.

"The Man says it happens, "It" happens. You know it, I know it, and they are going to know it," Mueller told Harry.

"Yeah, I know," Harry said. "Later then?"

"Yeah, later," Mueller replied as he got up and left.

Harry watched Mueller leave and smiled.

A baseball game, several hot dogs with the always present partnering ballpark beers, and all was right with the world. Harry enjoyed them all plus the come to be expected victory by the Bayport Schooners in resounding fashion.

Chapter 85

Tips was never so nervous in all her life. She had played in some tricky gimmicks and pulled off a few solo savers she desperately needed to survive but, in all her done-dats over the years, this one topped the cake. This one was not just for her, it was for Billy, too.

If Billy only knew.

They came because Tips asked. They came because they needed the warehouse and what it gave them. What it allowed them to do, and learn, and perfect without the fear of what could or would, go wrong. And what would happen then. They came for the person that gave all that to them. Mostly, they came for Billy.

Tips chatted with the ones who came the most and also the ones that came infrequently. She welcomed those who had never been there even once but had heard about it and came because they felt they had to. Tips was the welcoming wagon, hostess, manager and chief bottle washer. They all knew it and they loved her for it. But, and there was no bigger but, there was nothing for them here and never would have been without Billy.

They came for Billy and would help Tips prove that to him.

~ * ~

An hour is a long time to wait when you don't know how long you're going to be waiting. Unless you're in a job, show up at midnight usually means sometime after dark and before daylight. They weren't jobbin but word was out for them and they all showed just before or right after the little hand on the clock reached the top.

But where was Billy?

The chatter started that Billy wasn't coming.

The chatter grew impatient.

The chatter said Billy didn't care and they could do whatever they wanted, but they couldn't tell Billy what to do.

The chatter stopped chattering at Tips and wondered if she really had a handle on Billy, or if he cared.

The chatter pissed Billy off to no end.

Somebody whistled and the chatter stopped.

Everybody looked around to see where it had come from. They all wanted to know who thought they were bigger than them, so important they could whistle and everyone should jump and stay in the air until told to come down.

Plus, where the fuck was Billy.

They got their answers when the newcomer nobody knew stripped off the padded flannel shirt and dirty-haired wig and said, "So I'm here, what'd you want to tell me?"

They had come for Billy and he was there in the usual Billy unconventional fashion.

They gawked at what they could never understand and never duplicate. That's what and why they had come; they came for *this* Billy.

~ * ~

It was dawning a new day when they wrapped up what they had come to do. More than one hundred strong they shouted their message in whispers Billy heard loud and clear. They said it, they cried it, and they implored it until it couldn't be said any more.

WE NEED THIS!

WE NEED YOU!

WE NEED US!

Tips was in tears when they were done and couldn't believe the way they had poured their hearts out to her and to Billy. They needed the love this place gave to them and would beg, borrow and steal any amount it took to keep it afloat. Money is only money and anybody can get it if they need to. But the love that banded this group together trumped all else.

It didn't matter what they were charged, we will get it they had said.

It doesn't matter how much it costs; it isn't nearly enough they had said.

It isn't the what, or the how much, they had said; it's the who, and that's us, and most importantly it was the who that had made this for them, and gave it to them, and was one of them.

They had come for Billy and they gave of themselves freely to Billy.

Billy heard and arm-in-arm with Tips, he cried.

They would charge what they needed, and only what they needed, and together the brotherhood and sisterhood would grow stronger for it.

Through the tears Tips kissed Billy in triumph.

He should only know.

Chapter 86

Thursday morning proved to be another beautiful day in paradise. Well, as a means of clarification, it was the little burg called Mechanicsburg in Central Pennsylvania, so maybe paradise was stretching it a bit. But, the sun was shining, the birds were singing, and it was a day.

Buddy and Twins pulled off Rich Valley Road and went down the hill to the Rich Valley Golf Course parking lot. They parked the beat up ride they had arrived in and moseyed on over to the pro shop for their 10 o'clock tee time. As they went, Buddy could see Ted over on the driving range hitting what looked like flop shots with some kind of wedge.

Pointing to Ted, Buddy told Twins that was their current #1 pigeon. He guessed the big guy hitting balls next to him was Ted's partner for their round. The big guy was pounding his driver long but not necessarily always straight.

Twins looked back at Buddy and smiled.

"Don't smile and don't fuck this up, Twins," Buddy told him. "Our time will come and in spades."

Buddy checked them in with a guy named Jeff who Buddy learned was the owner. Buddy told Jeff he liked the course and he was glad to be back to give it another try.

"You want range tokens?" Jeff asked Buddy.

"Nah, me and Twins just walk up to the first tee and whack away," Buddy told Jeff. "No sense in practicing lousy shots on the range when you can hit them on the course I always say."

Buddy looked at Twins who was nodding his head in agreement.

After having chatted with Ted late on Tuesday, Jeff smiled at Buddy and let them go off on their merry way.

~ * ~

Ten minutes later Buddy and Twins were on the first tee as Ted drove up in his cart. Buddy had been right as the big guy on the range next to Ted was in the other seat with him.

"Hey, Buddy, good to see ya again," Ted said as he got out of the cart. "This here is Big Joe but you can just call him Joe."

Buddy reached out and shook Ted's hand and then turned to Joe.

"Big Joe?" Buddy said to him.

"My cousin plays here too and he's named Joe as well. To make life easy people refer to me as Big Joe when they're talking about me and just Joe when they talk about my cousin," Joe told Buddy.

"Fair enough," Buddy replied as he shook Big Joe's hand.

"This here is Twins," Buddy said as he pointed to Twins.

"Pleased to meet both of you," Twins said ever so politely as he shook both of their hands.

"Twins?" Ted threw at him in the form of a question.

Twins smiled and said, "It's a bit of a long story maybe I can relate later over a cool one should you boys care to."

"Sure enough," Ted said. "We can play ourselves some golf, then retire up to Nolo's and maybe have a few cool ones and listen to your story."

"Works for us," Buddy said.

"Buddy tells me you're not opposed to a small wager now and again," Ted tossed in Twins direction.

Twins looked at Buddy and then turned back toward Ted before saying, "I've been known to place a few bucks on the line, Ted. You have something in mind?"

"Well, as I told Buddy here on Tuesday, I'm about a three and Joe here plays to a tad better than that. Buddy had a bit of a tough day his first time out here but he told me he was an eight handicap—what are you playing to?"

"I don't play near as much as Buddy, but he and I hit the little while ball about the same I'd say," Twins told Ted.

Ted thought a minute and then said, "Well, then, how about better ball and we'll give you boys four strokes on the front to see what that does for us. We'll figure out the back at the turn. Sound good to you boys?"

Buddy looked at Twins who shrugged back at Buddy.

"Sounds fair enough. How much?" Buddy asked.

"Ah, how's five dollars a side and the losers buy when we get back to Nolo's?" Ted asked.

"As long as Joe here doesn't drink a keg on us, that'll do fine," Buddy replied.

With that, Ted tossed a tee in the air to see who would hit first.

Chapter 87

Nolo's had a better than average selection of beers on tap. Ted stuck to the same Lager he had had on Tuesday while Joe went with a Gin and Tonic. Buddy, who was buying, had a Magic hat #9 and ordered a Jack and Coke for Twins who had stopped in the head.

"Looks like my buying's getting to be a habit," Buddy told Ted as he handed him more of his hard earned cash.

"Must be bad luck," Ted told him as he readily accepted his winnings.

"Or a bad golf game, or partner, or a good heaping of both," Buddy lamented.

"A good heapin' of what?" Twins asked as he came back into the bar.

"Ted here thinks it's my bad luck having to buy twice in a row. I told him I thought it was more likely a bad golf game, or partner, or a good heaping of both," Buddy answered Twins.

"Well, the partner part of it was surely true today out there on the course," Twins said with an audible sigh.

"I still can't believe you shot a ninety-two," Buddy told Twins.

Ted looked at Joe while the two losers had their chat. Joe smiled back at Ted as he rubbed two fingers together in the accepted gesture for cash money.

"Who you bullshitting," Twins threw at Buddy. "Your ass didn't play a heck of a lot better than me, now did you?"

Twins picked up his Jack and Coke and drained it in one gulp.

"Gimme another of these there, ah…" Twins said to the bartender.

"It's Hope," she responded. "Another Jack and Coke coming right up."

Joe "ahumed" in Twins direction who quickly took the hint and forked over what he owed him.

"Thanks there, Twins. Maybe you'll fare a little better next time we play, that is, if you care to give it another go some time," Joe told Twins.

"Yeah, well, we're gonna need more strokes if you two fuckers are gonna shoot two and three over par and take our money. Me and Buddy will kick your asses with a couple of more strokes. Right, Buddy?" Twins half-slurred.

It looked like the four or five beers on the course and 1½ drinks he just threw down was starting to take its toll.

Seeing the possibility of a problem, the owner Jeff came over from the other end of the bar to mediate.

"Hey, I'm Jeff. I own this place. Can I buy you and your buddy a drink?"

Twins looked at him at the same time Buddy got up and pushed Twins away from the bar and out into the hall. A loud shouting match could be heard coming from the hall.

A minute later Buddy and Twins came back into the bar.

My apologies, folks," Buddy said to all in attendance. "Twins here just hates to lose and gets himself worked up at times; right Twins?"

"Yeah, I'm sorry," Twins said. "I played so bad today and it gets the better of me. You don't have to worry none about me— I'm harmless and just plain stupid at times.

"Okay, Twins," Buddy told his pal. "Let's me and you hightail it on out of here. We done enough damage for one day plus we have that poker game to get to tonight and you could use a little sleep before we head over."

The word poker had Jeff and Ted looking at each other.

"You boys play a little poker do you?" Ted asked.

"Love to play," Buddy answered. "Any time we can find a game we jump in with both feet, now don't we Twins?"

"I love to play," Twins told Ted. "Wish I could play a speck better, but I can give up my money with the best of them. I get lucky now and again though and so does Buddy here."

"Well, we play a small game on occasion here," Jeff told them. "Maybe you boys would care to join us some time?"

"Well that's mighty neighborly of you, Jeff. Twins and I would love to play some cards with you and your boys. You just let us know when and, if we're in town, me and Twins would be glad to donate to the cause," Buddy replied.

"We'll do that," Jeff replied.

"Another game next week?" Ted asked them.

"Tuesday should work for us again, Ted," Buddy said. "But Twins here is right when he said we're gonna need a stroke or two more to make it more competitive. We can't be giving you our money every time we play, now can we?"

Ted looked at Joe who gave Ted an affirmative nod.

"I'm sure we can work out something that would make everybody happy, Buddy. See you boys on Tuesday," Ted said.

"Then Tuesday it is," Buddy told them as he and Twins departed.

~ * ~

Buddy could hear laughter coming from the bar as they left the building. He would have been surprised if he didn't.

"You hustle over and get the car and I'm gonna call Fetts and give him the lowdown on how today went," Buddy told Twins.

"Cool," Twins answered Buddy. "And be sure and tell Fetts I can't be fucking up my golf game like this for too long. I'm gonna have to kick some ass right soon and you had better believe Big Joe is gonna have one sore ass and some empty pockets when I'm done with him."

Chapter 88

Shooting hoops alone was something Billy had done a thousand times and never tired of it. He was up at the Manhasset High School b-ball courts and had been there for half an hour when a group of guys got out a car and joined him. They went to the other end of the court and started shooting around.

Billy shot and moved while he watched the other guys do the same. The "nothing but net" that had been the end result of his shots previously had turned into the occasional good shot coupled with plenty of clanks and enough air balls to make him look like he was just another guy shooting bad hoops.

This was not lost on the guys shooting hoops at the other end of the court.

A bad pass from the other half of the court brought the ball down to where Billy was standing under his basket. He picked up the ball and tossed it to the guy coming his way.

"Thanks, man," the guy said to Billy.

"No sweat," Billy replied.

"We just messing around. You wanna game?" the guy asked Billy.

Looking hesitant at first, Billy reluctantly said, "I'm not that good and I don't want to screw up your game."

"Like I said, we just messing around," the guy told Billy. "We need another guy to run. Come on over and we can give you a game. Don't worry none; it's just a few guys playin' some hoops."

Billy agreed and said, "Thanks, man. I'm Billy."

"Andre," the guy told Billy. "The big guy's Willy and the little guy's name is Shorty. He my cousin and don't pay him no mind. He thinks he can play and runs his mouth like it's on fire some time."

"Cool," Billy told Andre as they joined Willy and Shorty at the other end of the court.

When introductions were over they proceeded to shoot for another ten minutes. Then Andre said, "Billy, you and Willy against me and my cousin for a little two on two. Okay?"

Billy looked at Willy who shrugged his shoulders as if to say, "S'awright with me if you're cool with it."

"Sure," Billy replied. "Let's run."

They played games to ten points with single points for each basket. It was clear from the get go Andre was the player but his cousin Shorty wasn't bad either. Willy was tall but couldn't shoot, and couldn't jump—a bad combination. Billy and Willy lost three games in a row and it wasn't even in the ballpark of close.

"You boys warmed up yet?" Andre asked Billy.

"Ah, yeah, I guess so. Why you asking?" Billy replied.

Andre sheepishly said, "I was just thinking maybe we give you and Willy two points a game and we play for sumpin."

"You been kicking our asses every game. How we goin' to beat you now that money on the line wit only two points a game?" Willy replied.

"You never know?" Andre answered Willy.

Billy smiled inside and said, "Three points. How much?"

"I donno. Ten bucks?" Andre answered Billy.

"Okay, kiddo. Three points, ten bucks, my ball," Billy agreed.

Andre smiled and handed Billy the ball.

Willy was on the court to touch the ball and give it back to Billy. When Andre agreed Willy didn't have to even touch the ball, Billy ignored him and told him to stay out of his way. Billy hit two jumpers and then drove around Andre for a layup. He next hit three straight shots from beyond the top of the key as Andre and Shorty tried to push him further from the basket. The game ended when Billy drove around Andre, passed Shorty, and dunked with two hands.

Andre stood there looking at Billy like he was seeing an apparition.

As Billy started to walk off the court he turned to Andre and said, "Dude, when you gonna hustle somebody, you best be damn sure you know who you trying to hustle. Otherwise, your ass gonna get fried time or two. Keep the ten and buy yourself a lesson."

As Billy walked away, Shorty pointed at his cousin Andre while laughing his ass off hysterically.

Chapter 89

Fetts hung up the phone and smiled. Like the cool dude he used to watch on TV, Fetts also liked it when a plan came together. The baited hook was in the water and the fish were nibbling like he hoped they would.

No, like he knew they would.

The fish always did. They couldn't help themselves. Even when it was too good to be true and all they had to do was gobble it all up, the fish nibbled and then hit the hook for all they were worth. Unfortunately, their "worth" was soon to be his and he would love it like he loved it every single time.

Fetts dialed another number and waited. After four rings he hung up, waited a minute, and then he dialed the same number again. This time it was answered on the first ring.

"It's Fetts."

"Yeah."

"It's on."

"When?"

"Give me a few weeks to lock it down and then I'll call you to finalize."

"Same terms?"

"Same terms."

"Done," the caller finished and the call terminated.

Fetts was going to say something else but he didn't get the chance. He so needed to be in control of things and his frustration boiled over when dealing with him. If he had a choice he wouldn't, but Fetts wasn't big enough to go it alone. At least not yet he wasn't.

He needed him.

He used him for what he needed while biding his time.

He wouldn't always need him and he rejoiced with the very thought of it.

Fetts would someday be the "him" and he wouldn't need anyone else to get it finished. They would come to him, Fetts, and he would dictate how it went down. Fetts would be the man and he would be the one that took the biggest slice.

He would be the one that would say "Done" and hang up the phone.

~ * ~

Mutt again told Jeff he was stupider than dirt. It was the third time he had told him so today. Fetts needed them to do a job and why Jeff continually fucked it up was something Mutt couldn't figure out. The fact Mutt was fucking up the job along with Jeff didn't occur to him.

"Why you have to say that to me?" Jeff said to Mutt. "I'm doing what you tole me to do before."

"Then why haven't you done it?" Mutt asked him.

"You tole me we had to look for Billy and we been doing that. You and me been looking for him for three days now and just 'cause I haven't seen him don't mean it's my fault. You been looking with me and you ain't seen him. Have you, Mutt?" Jeff said.

"We're looking but that's not what Fetts told us to do. Fetts told us to *find* Billy and then have Billy yell at Fetts. We have to get Billy to call Fetts and we can't do that less we find him, now can we you dumbass dummy? Can we?" Mutt yelled.

Jeff shrunk down to half his size just like he did every time Mutt yelled at him that way. Never mind he was doing what Mutt told him to do, he still got yelled at. Never mind Mutt was doing it with him like he always did, he still got yelled at. One of these days he wasn't going to take it and he'd yell back. Maybe he'd do more than yell back. Maybe he'd...

"Come on," Mutt yelled again. "Gimme the phone and I'll make some calls to see if we can find out where that butthead Billy is hiding out. If we have to we'll put out the word and we'll get him then."

"But that's gonna cost us," Jeff answered Mutt.

"No, that's gonna cost you from your share of the job cuz you can't do what you're told," Mutt told Jeff.

"I don't like it when you do that," Jeff told Mutt.

"I don't give a rat's ass what you like or don't like you dipshit. Now give me the phone and drive the car," Mutt said to Jeff speaking to him as if he was two years old.

Jeff did what he was told while he silently steamed inside.

Chapter 90

Ted and Jeff were sitting at the bar in Nolo's after the place had closed down for the night. Big Joe was still there but had disappeared from the bar area ten minutes earlier. When Joe had to spend alone time he needed it for as long as he needed it.

"You want me to find somebody to check these guys out?" Ted asked Jeff.

"No need," Jeff told him. "I have it covered and you can go ahead and see if they want to join the game Saturday night."

"You sure?" Ted asked him.

"You fleece these guys for chump change on the course and I'll handle the Saturday night game. We'll see where we go from there. You can handle that I presume?" Jeff asked Ted.

"No need to wrack my cage, Jeff. I can do it and Big Joe will do as he's told," Ted replied.

"Alright then," Jeff told him. "I may join you for a round with these two jamokes if the stakes get any higher. Maybe they have more cash to lose than we think and I want a piece of the action if they do."

Big Joe came back in and bellied up to the bar. He looked like he had his head together which was a good thing with him. When Big Joe went off kilter you had best be somewhere else if you valued your hide.

"Nice playing out there today, Joe," Ted told him. That brought a smile to Big Joe's face.

"Thanks, man. I like playing good and winning money from stiffs like we played today. I coulda played like shit and we still woulda took their money. Tuesday we'll take more," Joe told Ted.

"Don't get too cocky. We can play like shit and then they'll be the ones raking in the dough," Ted replied.

"Yeah," Jeff threw in. "You get shit like that in your head and before you know it these new guys will be leaving with Rich Valley money and we aren't having any of that. Play tough, and play smart, and the bucks are going in your pocket, big guy."

Big Joe smiled again.

Ted walked around the bar and refilled their glasses.

"To marks like those two guys," Ted toasted.

"Yeah," Big Joe yelled.

Jeff didn't say anything.

Thirty minutes later Jeff closed up and headed back toward his place. Ted and Big Joe were on the right track and would serve the purpose for now. These two guys named Buddy and Twins, or whoever they actually were, were playing it just as he had expected them to. If it played out as planned they would be there on Saturday night and dump some cash to his regular poker group.

Dialing the number he had been given he waited for the guy he had been dealing with to pick up.

"Yeah," he heard when it was answered.

"It's Jeff at Rich Valley. It went as you said it would today and the next step is in play. I'll know for sure on Tuesday. Anything more I can do?"

After listening for a minute, Jeff hung up the phone and nodded in agreement. There was nothing else to do but let it play itself out however it was going to fall. If the people he was talking to knew their shit, it would all fall into place and all he had to do was what he was told.

Chapter 91

Fetts had his "A" crew together and they were going over the current operation that was in play. He probably didn't need these guys to be involved but, if this was to be the last operation before they took down the big prize, he wanted his best involved for a live test run.

"This one is small potatoes compared to a few of the ones we already blew through. The plan is the same though—we set up the marks, we lay down dead for them, and then we make our moves slow and easy. When the time comes we explode on their asses like the Fourth of July. Buddy and Twins are already greasing the skids for us," Fetts told the group.

"We going in like gangbusters and raping and pillaging like usual?" one of Fetts boys asked.

Fetts evaluated the question before he formulated and articulated his answer to the group. He understood where his guy was coming from and it was a good, aggressive question. He wanted the group hungry, but he didn't want them to be overly aggressive until they needed to be.

"We go at it like we usually do and play it as it comes. If the marks get aggressive, we get aggressive. If they slow play it and we need to push the stakes to make it happen, then we can go in that direction. We've done it before and we'll do it again," Fetts finally told them.

It was his poker ace Keough that spoke up next. Having played with and taken down some of the best back room players around, Keough knew from where he spoke. And he wasn't afraid to speak up when he needed.

"We go in and take their money at the table before we get the course action set up nice and tight and we could blow it."

"What the fuck do you know about course action, Keough?" Nobs challenged.

Keough glared at Nobs.

"Don't give me that poker face shit, asshole," Nobs challenged.

Fetts sat back and watched the exchange between two of his main guys. It wasn't always his way to let the boys duke it out in front of the rest of the boys but, every now and then, some lively interaction was probably good for them. How long and how far he would let them go at it was the tricky part.

"I'll give you more than a poker face, you two-bit hacker prick," Keough challenged Nobs.

The "hacker prick" remark seemed to really set Nobs off. He jumped up as if he was going to go after Keough which prompted two of his guys to follow suit. Keough wasn't backing down and rose to accept the challenge.

Fetts had seen enough.

"All right, boys. When the job's over you two can go off into the desert and beat the living piss out of each other. I don't give two shits what you do. But when we have a job on the line, you had both better button it up and pay attention to business. I catch either of you wandering from the target and I will personally see to it you don't play here or anywhere else ever again," Fetts told them.

When they continued to glare at each other, Fetts said, "Did I make myself clear enough for you two lamebrains?"

Keough and Nobs sat down in unison and nodded to Fetts.

"Good," Fetts said to the entire group. "Now let's go over the details once more and get this job in motion. I want their money and I want Rich Valley Golf Club in my pocket before the month is out. We all on the same page here?"

Heads nodded plus "We're on it" from several guys told Fetts they were focused again. Buddy would move it along and Fetts would be there soon enough to take the prize down. He needed to finish this deal if he was going to land the big fish he was after.

"Okay, boys, get to it. I will see you at wherever this Rich Valley place is soon enough," Fetts said as he rose to leave. "And mind my words boys. There ain't no room for fucking up here and there ain't no room for internal fighting. We are one solid group with one purpose in mind. We are not, I repeat *"not,"* going to cowboy this shit because somebody gets a bug up their ass. Do your jobs and we take it for our own. One of us fucks up and we all can go down and I'm not going down!" Fetts told them.

Chapter 92

Harry had to meet Billy in an hour. They had finalized their plans with everyone who had a piece of the action and they were ready to head back to Tom's place to set it in motion. Harry had one immediate problem to deal with before he could get on his way to meet Billy—Sherry's head.

"Sherry, babe, I told you I have to get moving," Harry told her.

There was no response from Sherry in reply.

"Sher…oh, man…SherryohmanSherry," Harry groaned.

Lifting her head slightly, Sherry asked, "Did you want something, Harry?"

Without hesitation, Harry answered, "No, Sherry, I don't want to interrupt. Please continue with what you were doing."

"Okay, Harry, but only if you insist. I could stop and…"

"Oh, I insist," Harry told her. "I truly do insist."

"Very well than, Harry. You will tell me again if you need to leave and you want me to stop," Sherry said.

As Sherry resumed her activity Harry felt no need to reply.

~ * ~

With their backs propped up against the headboard, Harry and Sherry rested. Harry still had to meet Billy, but it was now just thirty minutes to their agreed meeting time. After what had just transpired over the last hour or so, Harry was going to be late.

Picking up his cell phone, Harry dialed Billy's number.

"Yeah, Billy, it's me, Harry," Harry told him when Billy picked up.

"Hey, Harry, everything cool? Plans the same—we still heading down to Pennsylvania?" Billy asked him.

"Ah, yeah, but I need about another hour. Something came up and it had to be handled," Harry told Billy.

Harry looked over at Sherry who was handling it again hoping it would come up again. Harry tried to discourage her with a wave, but gave up when it was obvious Sherry wasn't going to stop.

"You still there, Harry?" Harry heard Billy saying when he returned his attention to his cell.

"Yeah, I'm here, Billy. I'll get this thing done and meet you at the same place we said. Give me an hour and a half and I'll be there," Harry told Billy.

"Sure thing, Harry," Billy replied. "Do what you need to do and I'll be ready when you get there. And Harry, say hi to Sherry for me."

The phone went dead.

Harry laughed which prompted Sherry to ask him what he was laughing at.

"Nothing, Sher," Harry told her. "And by the way, what the hell do you think you're doing?"

"Well, you told Billy you needed an hour and a half which is more than enough time to get it done and still meet him. I'm looking to be done, and if you're going to be the doer, something's going to have to "come up" and I'm just helping it along," Sherry told Harry with that smile of hers.

"For the third time?" Harry asked her.

"When things come up, Harry, they come up. Now time's a wasting and if you're gonna get her done, I suggest you cut your yapping and get her done. Her is ready and it looks like you're rising to the challenge," Sherry said.

Harry shrugged in defeat and said, "Since you seem to have things well in hand, and I do have a bit of time, let's get down to it and I will do my very best to get her done."

"Like before?" Sherry asked.

"Like twice before," Harry answered.

"You're the best, Harry," Sherry told him.

"Everybody's gotta be good at something," Harry told her.

"Lucky me," Sherry purred in response.

Chapter 93

Harry picked up Billy just a bit after the time they had agreed upon. It was a rush getting there when he did, but he managed it.

"Everything good, Harry?" Billy asked once he had stowed his gear and was inside the HoneyBee.

"All's good," Harry replied.

"Busy day?" Billy inquired.

"A bit," Harry answered warily.

"Feeling good though?" Billy continued.

Harry thought Billy was smiling but he didn't want to look over at him.

"Yeah, I'm feeling pretty good. If you want to say something, Billy, go ahead and say it," Harry told him.

"What's to say?" Billy replied. "You had things that needed to be handled and I assume *it* got handled to everyone's satisfaction. Everyone was satisfied when all was said and done, weren't they, Harry?"

Harry looked over at Billy who was grinning from ear to ear.

"You got some balls for an eighteen-year-old snot nosed kid there Billy boy," Harry said with a small grin of his own.

"Speaking of balls, Harry, how are yours feeling right about now?" Billy asked.

"Not that my balls and how they are feeling is any of your business but since you asked, they're none of your fucking business. But if they were, they're feeling tired but GGRREEAATT!" Harry responded.

Billy roared with laughter and Harry joined him.

"Yours?" Harry asked.

"Not bad, but obviously nowhere as good as yours," Billy replied.

~ * ~

They rode in silence for a bit, each to his own thoughts. They had agreed on the direction they would take and a loose game plan to start. How and when they would get to the meat of the plan, if they even did, was a bit sketchy. How Harry and then Billy would insert themselves into the game was going to be tricky, but they thought they could maneuver their way in. Only time, luck, and their own skills would tell the story.

Harry brought them out of their personal reflections.

"What's with you and Tips?" he asked Billy from out of the blue.

"Huh?" Billy replied.

"You and Tips," Harry repeated. "What's the deal?"

"The deal? Well, Tips runs the warehouse..." Billy started before Harry put up his hand and cut him off.

"No, Billy not the warehouse. I know you set it up and Tips runs the warehouse. What's the deal with *You* and *Tips*?" Harry said emphasizing the *You and Tips*.

"I don't know what you're asking, Harry," Billy told him.

Harry shook his head in disbelief and then said, "Billy boy, you are either dumber than dirt, totally blind, or in deep denial. Maybe it's all three now that I think about it. Tips obviously has the hots for your skinny ass to the point where I think she may actually believe she's in love with you."

Billy looked at Harry like he hadn't understood a single word Harry had just said.

"You're trying to tell me that you, Billy Burns, able to scam tall buildings in a single bound; you haven't seen the way she looks at you? The way her total being changes, lights up, when you are in the room? If you haven't, man, maybe you ain't as good as I think you are," Harry told Billy.

Billy sat there speechless. Not a single word.

"Billy, when this shit is over, you had better high-tail you ass back to Brooklyn and figure out what you got with that lady. If you don't, sooner or later she's gonna decide you don't care and move on to greener pastures. And, my man, from what I saw in that one afternoon, it's going be your loss and a big one," Harry told him.

Billy just continued to stare ahead and not say a word.

Chapter 94

Having stopped for something to eat on the way down, it was getting dark when Harry pulled the HoneyBee into Mechanicsburg, Pa. He and Billy would be staying with Tom for the night until Harry got something set up for him and Billy.

"Harry, Billy, get your asses in here," Tom said when he saw them after opening the door.

"Good to see you too, Tom," Harry told him as he and Billy entered Tom's house.

"Even though I knew you guys were coming down you still caught me by surprise," Tom told them.

"It's good to have a place to crash for the night before we get something setup for the long haul. Thanks, Tom," Billy told him.

"Bullshit on your thanks, Billy. You and Harry are welcome in my house any day of the year for as long as I'm suckin' in air. After that even," Tom said.

Billy smiled knowing Tom meant every word of it.

"What's a dude gotta due to get a beer around this dump?" Harry asked.

"He can walk his ass into the kitchen, reach in the fridge, take out a beer and open it," Tom answered Harry. "And while you're there, get us one, too."

Harry smiled, walked over to Tom and gave him a hug like he hadn't seen him in years. "Same old Tom," Harry told Tom.

"And getting older and thirstier every minute you stand there yappin' and not getting me that beer," Tom answered.

"I'll get the beers while you two play huggy bear and shit," Billy said as he walked toward the kitchen.

~ * ~

Beers in hand they sat in Tom's living room planning the how's and when's of the next few weeks. Tom spoke up and told them, "I got you two set up in a pair of shitholes about ten minutes from Rich Valley. Same complex but different cubby holes."

"Shitholes?" Billy asked.

"Well they're shitholes compared to the palatial digs Cam and I call home," Tom said with a laugh. "It will do for the short haul and look inconspicuous enough so as not to call any attention to either one of you."

"Inconspicuous?" Harry said with a raised eyebrow.

"Yeah, inconspicuous," Tom repeated. "It means nobody gonna see or care about your sorry ass as it probably should be."

"That's an ego lifter if I ever heard one," Harry told Tom.

"Your ego's bigger than the ocean and don't need no liftin'," Tom told Harry. "And him," pointing to Billy, "he don't need it less than your ass does from what I seen of him."

"Thanks," Billy said before he drained half his beer in an appreciative gesture.

"Enough ego shit," Harry said. "Let's get down to business and make sure we got a half-way decent plan in place before we all get our asses toasted by being too dumb to watch said asses properly."

"Amen to that," Tom toasted with his beer.

Half an hour later they all agreed they had the makings of a pretty good plan in place. They would need to play it out one piece at a time and shuck & jive as the playing field changed, but the basis of the plan was sound. Or, as sound as it could be before Billy made the first call and set the ball in motion. Then they would be able to move from got-a-plan to plan-in-place. And if it all fell into place the "got" would be a big time "gotcha" that would solve multiple problems for multiple parties.

"One more cool one and then let's get some shut eye," Harry told Tom and Billy. We're going to have to hustle to finish the set up if we are going to move ahead this weekend."

"I'll get 'em," Billy told them.

"About time you did something useful, kiddo. Or should I just say kid?" Harry teased him.

Billy gave Harry the evil eye before he turned, gave him the one fingered salute, and laughed his way into the kitchen.

Chapter 95

Harry and Billy had breakfast with Tom and Cam the following morning before Harry drove them to their new digs. Tom was telling them the truth—palatial they weren't, but they would suffice for the short time they needed to be there.

"Let me dump my stuff and I'll come back to your place so we, you, can make the call to Fetts," Harry told Billy.

"That's cool," Billy told him.

"After that I'll make the other calls and then we can see where we stand. If we need to start the improvising we can start the improvising," Harry told Billy.

"I'm with ya, Harry. See ya in a few," Billy told him.

In less than five minutes Harry knocked on Billy's door.

"That was quick," Billy told Harry.

"When you don't travel with much it doesn't take long sort it out," Harry told him.

"Same case here," Billy told Harry. "You ready?"

"Question is, are you ready, kiddo?" Harry asked.

Without a thought Billy responded, "Harry, the call part's a piece of cake. What's behind it is different. Real different. Fetts been fucking with people all his life and he doesn't think twice about any of it. He just takes what he wants, from who he wants, and moves on to his next conquest. It's about time somebody else took from him and gave him a dose of his own medicine."

"Well said, doctor," Harry agreed with Billy. "Where's the phone from?"

"Found it," Billy replied.

"Found it?" Harry asked.

"Yeah, found it," Billy replied. "It was there, then I found it in my pocket as I walked away. So, I found it."

"There?" Harry queried.

"Yeah, there, then my pocket, now here," Billy explained.

"Any reason to go on with this?" Harry asked.

"Nope, none," Billy answered.

"Call," Harry told him.

223

Billy set his newly found phone to speaker and dialed the number. It rang five times before it was answered.

"Who?"

"An old friend," Billy answered.

"Who?"

"An old friend," Billy answered again.

The call disconnected.

"What the hell was that?" Harry asked Billy.

"If Fetts doesn't expect the call or recognize the number that's calling, he doesn't answer. It's SOP for him," Billy told Harry.

"So you were just screwing with him?" Harry continued.

"I suppose you could call it that," Billy replied.

"Why?" Harry asked.

"Well, why not?" Billy replied matter-of-factly.

Harry shook his head and said, "Kids."

Billy smiled at Harry and hit redial. As it did before, it rang five times before it was answered.

"Who?"

"An old friend," Billy answered.

Silence.

"You know which one," Billy told Fetts.

"Why?"

"You know why," Billy answered.

Fetts didn't reply, he just laughed.

The phone went dead.

"Now what?" Harry asked.

"Now, we wait," Billy replied.

"Wait. Wait for what?" Harry asked.

"We wait for Fetts to be Fetts," Billy replied.

Chapter 96

They waited. And they waited. And they waited some more. Then, a phone rang somewhere in the room. It wasn't the "found" phone, it wasn't Billy's other phone that sat on the bed, and it wasn't Harry's cell phone. It was a cell phone ringing somewhere in the room and Harry had no clue where.

Billy obviously knew what phone and where.

"Billy?" Harry posed in the form of a question.

"Harry," Billy responded.

"Oh, don't you try and play Fetts' games with me you little prick," Harry threw back at Billy.

Billy smiled and casually walked over to the bed, lifted the mattress and extracted a cell phone.

"The phone," Billy said as he showed it to Harry.

Harry was clearly trying to maintain his composure. If he didn't, he might strangle Billy right there and then.

"The phone," he repeated.

"Yeah, the "phone"," Billy said. "The crew phone. Fetts' crew phone to be precise. The only phone we were to use when we were on "the job" and only Fetts called on "the phone" as we called them.

"Fetts is calling you?" Harry asked.

"Follow along, Harry," Billy said. "This is the job phone. It's "the phone" that only Fetts called on. The phone rang, ergo, Fetts is calling. Or, it could be a wrong number."

It was also "the phone" that had stopped ringing.

"If it was "the phone" and you knew it was Fetts calling, then why didn't you answer it?" Harry asked Billy.

"Playing hard to get," Billy told Harry.

"Tips may not have anything to look forward to after I kill your ass, Billy," Harry told him.

The phone rang again. Billy waited three rings and then answered it.

"Who?' Billy said.

Harry sighed.

"You know damn fucking well who the hell this is," was the reply they heard through the speaker, plenty loud and clear.

"Is that you, Fetts?" Billy replied.

"Yes, it's Fetts, Billy Burns," Fetts said with struggled constraint.

"It's good to hear from you, Fetts," Billy replied. "How have you been? And by the way, I hope you have been taking good care of my money?"

Harry and Billy heard nothing for the next thirty seconds save the snorts and muffled cursing of a very pissed off human being.

"Your money?" was what they heard next.

Billy let that sit for a good thirty seconds.

"Yeah, my money," Billy finally replied.

Sounding surprisingly calm and composed, Fetts replied, "My money is my money, Billy. If you have some belief that some of it belongs to you, why don't you come out here and take it from me."

"Oh, Fetts, we both know that wouldn't do. I made you a ton in your little swindles and all I wanted was the small share that was mine. You decided to keep my share and I'd like it back," Billy said equally as calm and collected.

Harry raised both of his hands in the well known "what the fuck?" gesture. Billy shrugged it off.

When Fetts didn't say anything immediately, Billy continued.

"How's this grab you, Fetts?" Billy said. "I help you with the Rich Valley job, then I help you with the "BIG SCORE" you've been planning for years that gets you out. You give me the money you owe me and double my usual take for the next two and we call it Even-Steven."

When Fetts didn't say anything immediately, Billy continued.

"Don't be so surprised, Fetts. This ain't the little Billy Burns you thought you could fuck over so easily. My ear's to the ground and my network works the angle circuit good as yours—better maybe. I know your hooks are into Rich Valley and I'll help set them up and help you reel them in. Then together we do the "BIG SCORE" and you ride off into the sunset or maybe become big man in town if that's where you got your sights set. Either way, I get paid my fair share with back pay if you catch my drift."

This time it was Billy who hung up on Fetts before he could

reply.

Before Fetts could hit redial his other cell rang. Unfortunately, it wasn't Billy calling him back—it was the Germ.

Chapter 97

"Jon Francis Fetterman I presume?" is what Fetts heard when he answered his cell.

"Yeah," Fetts replied.

"The Jon Francis Fetterman who asked for my help?" Germ continued.

"Yes, it's me, Germ," Fetts told him.

"Since I dialed your cell I assumed it was you, Frankie," Germ replied.

Fetts hated Germ more and more every time he had to talk to him, or had to listen to him, or both.

"And it is, Germ," Fetts told him.

"The information you asked for was very difficult to obtain, Fetts. Your little ventures have become much larger ventures over time and your targets more elusive. Nothing the Germ can't handle of course, but obviously they become much more expensive the more elusive they become," Germ told Fetts.

Fetts had no desire to appease Germ's need for adoration and groveling from those he viewed as inferior to himself. The silence that lengthened indicated he would have to do so, whether he wanted to or not.

"I understand that Germ and I appreciate what you do for me," Fetts told Germ.

"Do you, Fetts? Do you really appreciate what I do for you? Really appreciate it?" Germ went on.

If he could get his hands around Germ's throat at that very moment, there would be no more Germ Frankie thought to himself. Calmly he said, "Yes, of course I do, Germ."

"Good, Frankie, because I would hate to think I wasn't appropriately appreciated for the fine service I provide to my clients," Germ said with just enough sarcasm in his voice to piss Fetts off royally.

"The information, Germ," Fetts said.

"The information you requested is in the usual spot safe and sound from other prying eyes," Germ told Frankie.

"Thank you, Germ," Frankie forced himself to say.

"Payment?" Germ asked.

"Normal method in one hour," Frankie assured Germ.

"It better be," Frankie heard followed by complete silence and then dead air.

Chapter 98

Saturday night, all dressed up with nowhere to...wait, Billy did have somewhere to go. Not only did he have somewhere to go, he was there. Billy was sitting in Nolo's over at Rich Valley at one of the two tables they had set up in the back room. Two tables of No-Limit Texas Hold 'em poker: seventeen players who each paid the $25 entry. Seven hundred fifty in chips and no rebuys. You bust out and you go home.

Billy had learned to play along life's highway on the road to where he was today and he could play with most amateurs. Pros were a different story, but he had paid his dues and he could challenge enough of the backroom pros. This group that met at Nolo's every Saturday night after the place closed down was considered the lower end of the players Jeff and his partner invited to play in their games. A few drinks, some poker, a night out with the boys. Be lucky enough to win and you took home a decent chunk of change for a $25 investment.

The big boys played on Wednesday nights once Nolo's closed down. Same deal only the buy in was a lot steeper at $500 and rebuys were $1000 for the same seven hundred fifty in chips that you got for your $500. Don't like the rules—don't play. Next chump is ready to take your place. They paid and they played.

Billy was content to lose his $25 for the last three weeks while he learned the house rules and how the regular group played. Tonight was going to be different. He had played with this crowd long enough and knew he could take them. Tonight he started his advance to the big game where Fetts' boys were doing their thing.

"You're pretty lucky tonight, Billy," Dominick told Billy after he won another fairly large sized pot.

"That's what it is, Dominick, all luck," Billy told him.

"All luck?" Dominick responded.

"Well, mostly," Billy replied.

They played for another half hour with nothing extraordinary happening. Smallish pots shared by several players and nobody making any significant move. Then there was the game changer.

At Billy's table, Billy was under the gun and he had called one of the small stacks who was in the small blind with about 250 in chips and had gone "All In."

The big blind thought for a minute and announced he was also going "All In" with the rest of his chip stack of 450 chips. Billy now had his chance to make his move. He had limped in with pocket Queens and he too followed suit when he moved "All In." He wanted to smile but controlled the urge.

The rest of the board folded and Billy showed his Queens. The small blind had KQ of hearts and the big blind had a pair of 10's. Billy had them dominated and needed to avoid a King, 10, or a bunch of hearts.

The flop was no help to anyone. The Turn card was a Jack of spades that hit nobody. When the dealer turned over the two of clubs on the River, Billy had won the pot.

The two tables then merged with the final nine players.

Over the next hour Billy hit two more big pots as the table got down to five players. He had the biggest stack now and began to play aggressively, but he really hadn't been bullying anyone up to that point. He decided it was time to seize control of the game.

Billy raised at every chance he had and stole several blinds. The small stack went all in after one of Billy's raises and Billy had him dead. When he turned over his Aces he had the small stack's Jacks covered big time. An Ace on the turn sealed the deal and Billy added to his lead. Ten minutes later the same scenario unfolded only this time with Billy's pair of Kings outdistancing a pair of tens. It was now down to three players.

Jeff wandered in from the bar to see what was happening. As Nolo was one of the three left, Jeff had a small interest in the outcome of the game. On most nights he couldn't care who won.

Billy raised again from the Big Blind and the other two players went "All In" if only to shorten their misery. Billy called and obliged by hitting a nine on the River for a straight. End of game with Billy taking in the winnings.

After giving Nolo the proper amount of good try and you'll get them next time, Jeff told Billy, "Nice game."

"Thanks, Jeff," Billy answered back. "Everyone gets lucky once in a while."

"That it, just luck?" Jeff asked him.

Billy wasn't sure where the question came from and where it was going, if anywhere. But he couldn't ignore it, so he said, "Yeah, I guess so. Why you asking?"

"From what I heard the other players saying and from the small bit I saw, you played a different game tonight from the last few times you were in here. Tom vouched for you and said you were alright. I hope he didn't send in a card shark to clean up on my friends. This is a friendly game and I'd like it to stay that way," Jeff told Billy.

Jeff had said it just loud enough so the rest of the guys still hanging around could hear him.

Stuttering just a bit, looking and sounding like a scolded child, Billy said, "I didn't mean nothing by it, Jeff. I just got some cards for a change and got a little aggressive with my betting, I guess. I'm sorry if I done something wrong."

"Nothing to it, Billy. No problem. You got lucky tonight and the other boys probably played their usual brand of shit-ass poker. Maybe they were feeling sorry for the kid and let you win one time. They'll probably kick your ass next Saturday," Jeff told Billy again just loud enough for all to hear.

Billy looked down at his shoes.

"Come on, I'll buy you a soda pop," Jeff told him. "In fact, soda pops for all you boys," Jeff told the group as they headed for the bar."

As the group moved into the bar, Billy stayed a few steps back and whispered to Jeff, "One more week, one more ass-whipping, and then I move to the Wednesday game."

"That's the plan, Billy, that would be the plan," Jeff replied as they caught up with the rest of the boys to enjoy their soda pops.

Chapter 99

Billy had been playing at Rich Valley for the last three weeks about three or four times a week. When asked why he wasn't in school or out working someplace, Billy replied, "School didn't suit him much and neither did working. Neither ever did."

Once two weeks ago and again last week Billy had finally hooked up with Jeff's partner for a friendly game. Jeff had paired them up when his partner's usual golf flunkies had bailed on him at the last minute. They either had something else to do or didn't feel like losing money to one of the club's owners on that given day. Plus, the "money" games he played were set for particular days of the week

Jeff did play, but he didn't like to play for money on his home course, at least not that often. That didn't seem to bother his partner none, or at least it wasn't visible if it did. Billy heard there was fairly big money changing hands regularly.

The first time Billy played with him Jeff brought Billy over to the first tee from the putting green where Billy was wasting time practicing his putting. Jeff had started to make the introductions when his partner interrupted him in mid-sentence.

"Name's Edie Kurpiel," he had told Billy. "Some of my friends call me Fast Edie but you can call me Kurps like most people do."

"Glad to meet you Mr. Kurpiel. I'm Billy Burns," Billy said extending his hand toward the owner.

"Mr. Kurpiel is a nice touch there Mr. Billy Burns, but I'm Kurps and you are Billy if we are going to chase the little white ball around this here converted cow pasture Jeff swears is a golf course. That cool with you?" Kurps said to Billy as he took his hand.

"Right by me, Kurps. You're up," Billy told him.

"We gonna make this interesting?" Kurps asked Billy.

"We could," Billy replied.

"What do you play to, Billy Burns?" Kurps asked him as he reached into his cart and popped open a Coors.

"About a ten," Billy told him.

"Good, that makes us about even," Kurps lied. "Beer?"

"Why not," Billy replied taking the can of Coors from the owner.

"Five bucks a hole too steep for you, Billy?"

"Only if I lose most of them," Billy replied with his widest smile.

Kurps smiled at Billy and said, "I like you kid. Let's play."

"Your honor," Billy told him.

"It usually is," Kurps replied as he teed up his ball to get the party rolling.

And roll the party did. They picked up six more beers at the turn and Fast Edie called the pro shop later to have them bring another six pack out to them at the fifteenth tee. Billy did his thing and had Kurps up by two holes through fourteen. Kurps ten handicap was much closer to a five and Billy had to make a few long putts to be down only two holes.

Billy was playing him lefty and Fast Edie was true to his name downing Coors faster than Billy.

When they got to the eighteenth tee Billy found himself down only one hole. If they halved the last hole he would owe the co-owner a small five dollars.

Knowing it was coming as sure as he was going to grab the last Coors from the bag of ice, Kurps said, "Care to make this last hole a bit more interesting?"

"How interesting?" Billy asked him.

"The guys I've been playing with the last few weeks would say '*As interesting as you like, Kurps*,'" he replied.

"And?" Billy asked.

"It's been pretty interesting," Kurps replied.

"For who?" Billy continued.

"Well, I guess I'd have to say it ended up more interesting for them than for me more times than not," Kurps replied. "Just not in a good way."

Billy thought on that for a second and then said, "I don't think I'm in that league, Kurps. In fact, if I got this pegged right, I'm way out of that league. How's ten bucks sound?"

Kurps laughed and said, "Sure, kid, ten bucks it is."

Billy missed a five foot put to halve the hole and they rode back to the clubhouse laughing like two old friends. Billy would have to find out how interesting was interesting to gauge where Fetts was in his game plan.

Chapter 100

Harry and Tom were sitting at the bar in Nolo's, just two local guys having a beer or two at a local watering hole. Ted was sitting two seats down from Tom engaged in what looked like a heated discussion with a fairly big dude he was calling Joe.

Harry overheard Ted say to Joe, "No, that's not going to happen, Joe. I'm not playing golf with Buddy and that asshole Twins tomorrow or any other day for that matter. Not their so-called "friends" either—no way, not gonna happen. And if you know what's good for you, you'll stay clear of all of them, too."

"Come on, Ted," Joe started back in before Ted cut him off.

"Joe, I'm in deep to all them fucks and I got more money than you'll ever see. Two other of the boys are in the same boat and I hear Fast Edie is flushing more green down those boys' toilet than you ever saw before. You ain't got the scratch to play in that league and I'm getting out before I'm in the toilet myself. And my resources don't come close to Kurps, either," Ted told Joe.

"But…" Joe started before Ted cut him off again and said, "No more, Joe."

"But I already set it up," Joe told Ted.

Clearly upset at what Joe had just said, Ted told him, "Then you had better unset it up because I'm not playing. Not tomorrow, not the next day, not any other day. Those boys sucked us in and they're bleeding us dry and if I lose any more and I'll be bone dry. You hear me…bone fucking dry!"

His head hung low, Joe told Ted, "We lost money we don't have to those two last time we played and they want it."

"We who? What the hell are you talking about, Joe? Who's WE! How much money?" Ted practically screamed at Joe.

The whole bar was listening now.

Joe just sat there with his head hung low.

"Who and how much?" Ted repeated almost in a whisper.

Joe finally raised his head and said, "Me and my cousin Donny. We lost more money than we have between us and they want it. Our business don't throw off that kind of bucks and now it's gonna be lost, too."

"How much?" Ted pushed him to answer.

"Ten thousand," Joe told Ted.

"Ten thousand dollars! You lost ten thousand fucking dollars to those thieves. How the hell could you two assholes lose ten thousand bucks in one golf game?" Ted asked him.

Joe hesitated and then said, "We were in deep to them already and we thought we could get even. They gave us extra strokes and we played for two hundred a hole plus junk—you know, sandies, birdies, shit like that. They played out of their asses and we tried doubling up a few times. We got to the last hole down five grand and went double or nothing."

"What the hell were you thinking?" Ted asked Joe.

"I was probably half drunk and my cousin was worse. Those two guys were drinking worse than us but it didn't seem to bother them none. Like they weren't even drinking, you know. We lost the eighteenth hole and ten grand. Ten grand we don't have and they want that and the rest of the money we own them or a chunk if not all of our company. They said they don't give two shits which it is, but they want it now," Joe said looking like he might start crying any minute.

"Buddy?" Ted asked.

"Yeah, Buddy and some other guy we played once before," Joe confirmed. "He said he'd have some guys on us and we'd give them our company or that wouldn't be the only thing we'd have to worry about."

"They threatened you and your cousin?" Ted asked Joe.

"Sounded like a threat to me, Ted," Joe told him. "What the fuck I'm gonna do now, Ted? Huh? My wife and kids, man. My cousin's wife will cut his balls off if her father doesn't get to him first. We're both toast and I need to get that money back, Ted. I'm out thirty large total, maybe more, and I gotta have that money or my business is gone. Gone, Ted, Gone!"

Ted looked at Joe, looked down at his drink, and truly didn't know what to say. When he continued to say nothing, Joe got up and left the bar.

As Joe passed by them, Harry looked at Tom, who looked back at Harry. Neither of them knew what to say the same as Ted.

Chapter 101

Billy had been the fourth person to sit down at the table for his first go at the "big game" at Nolo's. The table filled and since Billy had played golf with Fast Edie, he was prepared when he boomed into the room trailed by a plume of smoke from the monster of a cigar he was chomping on.

What Billy wasn't quite prepared for was Buddy coming in right behind Kurps trailed by a guy he was all too familiar with. Billy was surprised to see Keough here at Nolo's. Billy knew Keough was Fetts "poker guy" who came in to finish off the kill after guys like Buddy and Twins had set them up for the taking.

Why Keough now?

How bad was the previous action and why was Fetts using his ace for a play in the fucking sticks of Pennsylvania?

Were the rumors of Fetts' "BIG SCORE" really true and could this be the dress rehearsal for that one?

What the hell was Billy doing at the table if this was going down?

All those questions raced through Billy's mind in a flash as soon as he saw Keough. Questions Billy had no answers for and questions that truly scared Billy. Billy didn't scare easily, or often, but this was one of those times. The biggest question in his mind was what the hell did he do now? If Fetts knew Billy would be at the game, was he expecting him to help fleece the other players at the table? If he didn't know, well, that would be bad. Bad because Fetts didn't have tabs on Billy like he would expect Fetts to have. Or maybe Fetts didn't care, yet.

Questions and no answers. Billy sure needed a Harry Mickey Shorts QAS right about now.

Billy thought about just leaving under some false pretense and getting out of the game before he blew his plan and fucked over whatever game Fetts was playing. But that wouldn't work. You don't get yourself invited to the big game and then bail before it even gets started. No, Plan B was needed, but Billy didn't have a Plan B at the moment.

Before Billy had a chance to act the last guy sat down at the table and Billy was stuck. He'd have to wing it and see which way the Fetts wind was blowing. If he was lucky, this was just a "set-up" game and the big score wasn't until next week or the week after. When Keough showed he was there to play for real and Billy could only hope he didn't have a role in this play they had set up.

Still thinking, Billy heard, "We gonna play us some cards or we gonna sit here all night playing with ourselves," Kurps boomed.

"Cards it is," Nolo replied. "Let's shuffle up and deal."

A round of cards were dealt and Billy ended up with the first ace giving him the button as dealer. That would give him a few hands to try and size up how Fetts wanted his boys to play it and maybe get a handle on how he would play it as well. Or so he hoped.

It didn't take long. The second hand saw Kurps raise, Buddy re-raise and Keough call. Kurps called and everyone else folded. To Billy, it looked like it was on.

Billy had no idea how much money was sitting at the table, but he was sure it was a ton more than the five hundred dollar buy-in each player put up to get in. For this game, re-buying chips was open ended.

The Flop came out Ten of Hearts, Nine of Diamonds and Two of Diamonds. Kurps was first to play and he bet fifty. Buddy looked at his hole cards again and raised the bet to one hundred dollars. Keough never took his eyes off Kurps and just called. Kurps had his eyes glued on Keough as well and called when it was his turn.

The Turn card was the Jack of Spades.

Kurps checked, Buddy checked behind him and Keough did the same.

The River card was the Four of Diamonds.

Kurps checked his hole cards, looked at Keough and said, "I'm All In."

Buddy didn't hesitate and folded.

Keough's eyes were still locked in on Kurps. He smiled at him and said, "You smooth checked your straight on the Turn and now you want me to throw in the rest of my chips thinking the Four of Diamonds made your hand."

Kurps didn't even blink.

"I make you for KQ giving you a pretty nice hand, Kurps," Keough told him. "I should probably fold don't you think?"

Kurps didn't respond.

"Well, there's more chips where these came from," Keough said. "Maybe I'll call. You want that, Kurps?"

Again, Kurps didn't respond.

"Okay, I call," Keough told Kurps.

Kurps reached down and turned over his unsuited KQ giving him a straight to the King just as Keough had said. He smiled.

Keough looked down at Kurps cards, looked up, returned his smile and then turned over his cards. He laid the Ace and Six of Diamonds on the table giving him an Ace high flush. Keough had won the hand.

Kurps turned to his partner Jeff and said, "Give me another thousand in chips."

Chapter 102

In Fetts' camp Keough may be the man, but Billy was no slouch at the felt table either. The stakes were proceeding to well above any game he had played in to date and could have caused him mucho harm if he wasn't absolutely careful beyond careful.

Billy was careful—well beyond careful, but not chicken-shit either. He won one pot that netted him close to six hundred dollars and another that had a total of close to five bills. Buddy was down a few hundred, but Keough made up for Buddy's losses and much more on top.

Kurps luck was flowing downhill like a runaway freight train along with his chips. It had been that way most of the night. It was now past two am and he had been hitting the Grey Goose hard the last hour.

The game was now down to four players. Ted had just left the game after absorbing a punishment at the hands of Buddy and Keough, mostly Keough. Billy had a big enough stack he could handle the one hundred/two hundred blinds, but not for much longer. He was about to bow out as well.

That would leave Kurps, Buddy and Keough.

Jeff and Nolo had been playing bartender for the night while trying to keep Kurps on an even keel. He was down a bundle along with the load he was putting on with no stop in sight. When Jeff tried to get him to slow down, Kurps told him, "Do what you're told and get me another fuggin' drink."

The normal house rules had been lifted and chip availability was now open ended. You didn't have any chips in front of you, you just asked for more. That was not good news for Kurps in his current state.

"Deal the fuggin' cards fur Christs's sake, will ya," Kurps tried to say.

Billy could see Buddy give Keough a look he knew all too well. They would find a way to go in for the kill and finish off Kurps for good. It was decision time for Billy: was he part of the plan, Fetts' plan, or would he find a way to save Kurps from himself.

A Win for Billy was a Loss, and a Loss by Kurps was a Win for the bad guys. Kurps was probably going to be out bucks either way.

It was Keough's turn to deal and Billy knew for a fact he could be an absolute magician with the cards. Kurp's current state didn't demand Keough's skills, but there was no reason for him to take any chances. This was the hand that would stick the knife in Kurp's back and Buddy would be the one twisting it, with Keough's help of course.

Keough dealt and Billy could see Kurps was having trouble focusing on his hole cards. He had no problem betting though— Kurps raised to two thousand.

Billy was stuck big time now. He knew Keough would give him enough cards to stay in but not enough to beat Buddy. If he folded, Buddy and Keough would know something was up. If Kurps was as drunk as he seemed, and Billy couldn't understand how he got that bad that fast, he'd hammer the pot thinking he was golden. All roads led to Shitsville and they were motoring there at top speed.

Billy was stuck and reluctantly said, "It's a crying fucking shame but you guys are just blowing me away with these dollars. It's bullshit, but I gotta fold."

Keough looked up at Billy for a split second, took a quick glance toward Buddy, and then back down at his cards.

Buddy was next and he thought for a good long minute before he shook his head and said "I call."

Keough called over to Jeff and asked him for another ten thousand in chips. Jeff looked over at Kurps but there was nothing he could do. He had to give Keough the additional chips When your partner makes the rules you go along for the ride whether you like it or not.

Chips delivered, Keough called.

The Flop was Ace of Diamonds, Jack of Clubs and four of Clubs.

Without any hesitation Kurps bet three thousand.

Equally as fast, Buddy called.

Keough called Kurps three thousand and raised three thousand.

Kurps smiled and called. Buddy did likewise.

The Turn card was a blank—the eight of hearts.

Kurps thought for a long time and then checked. Buddy and Keough took little time and followed suit.

The River card was seemingly another blank—the deuce of diamonds.

Kurps looked at his hole cards and called "I'm All In!"

"How much?" Buddy asked.

Billy counted the chips and said, "Sixty-four hundred."

Buddy nodded his head, checked his cards, and called making the pot just over thirty-seven thousand dollars.

Keough looked at his hole cards, thought for what seemed like eternity, then tossed his cards in the muck and just said, "Nope."

"Read 'em and weep you fuckers," Kurps bellowed as he turned over his cards—an Ace and a Jack giving him two pair, Ace high.

Nice hand, but Billy knew he was dead meat.

Buddy said, "Nice hand there, Kurps. I don't have any high cards like those, but my two little ones will do," he said as he turned over a pair of deuces giving him three deuces and the winning hand.

Kurps stared at Buddy's pair of deuces in disbelief. Then he rose from his chair and stumbled out of the room without saying a word.

Game over.

Chapter 103

It was now late Sunday morning just a bit before Nolo's was scheduled to open for the day. Jeff was sitting at the bar nursing a beer while talking to Ted and Nolo.

"We have to figure out how bad this is, Ted," Jeff said.

"It's bad, Jeff, real bad," Ted told him.

"Spell it out for me," Jeff answered.

"You take me, Joe, his cousin and all the other boys together and we're in to them for close to seventy-five grand; maybe as much as a hundred. Really, I don't know how much it is because each of them could be bullshitting me big time. I got a ten thou marker outstanding and who knows what Joe has out there. He got loaded one day and doesn't know how much that marker is worth. His cousin's an unknown too. I could scrape mine up if I had to, but Joe, he doesn't have it. His business is as good as theirs," Ted told Jeff.

"Shit," Jeff said to Ted and Nolo both. "How the hell did this happen. I barely played with them and I'm more than ten grand in the hole. All my money's tied up in this place and I can't get another damn nickel out of Kurps."

"What about Kurps? How bad is he off?" Ted asked Jeff.

"How the fuck would I know?" Jeff told Ted. "You think he tells me shit just because he's my partner in this golden goose. It's mostly his money and he treats it that way."

Ted looked at Jeff expecting him to continue.

Jeff took a sip of his beer and after a minute said, "I'm not certain I heard him right, but I think I understood him say he was into them for a load and a half and that was before last night. He dropped a bundle last night same as you did, but a way bigger bundle. He may be into them for any number plus some since he split last night without ponying up a dime."

"He didn't pay for any of his losses from last night?" Ted asked Jeff.

"Nope, just up and walked out without saying a word or tossing any money into the pot. His chip count was big, too," Jeff said.

"No shit," Ted exclaimed.

"For all I know he could be into them for any number, any number at all," Jeff continued, "and if that's the case, the club may be gone, too."

Nolo finally said something after hearing Jeff's last comment. He practically whispered as if there was anyone else there to hear them when he said, "Well, shit, what the hell are we going to do about this? These guys can't just take our money, Joe's business, and the club, can they?"

"You got a way to stop them?" Ted replied. "Jeff?"

Neither Jeff nor Nolo had a reply for Ted.

"I'll be damned," Ted said.

"I think you already are," Nolo told him.

After a few minutes of silence Jeff said, "Ted, you get numbers from all the boys, real numbers and not any made up bullshit numbers, and I'll get Kurps to open up for him and his posse. We have to know how deep the hole is before we can figure out how to climb out of it, if we can."

"Okay, I'll try," Ted told Jeff.

"Don't try, do it," Jeff told him.

"Alright," Ted answered. "You gimme a day or two and then we can get together to pool what we come up with. But I'm telling ya, I don't think it's gonna be a pretty picture."

"Shit ain't pretty and we're all in it as deep as we can be, maybe deeper even," Jeff answered Ted.

"Even deeper than that if I got this thing pegged right and I'm pretty sure I do," Ted said as he got up and left the bar.

Chapter 104

Harry was sitting at Tom's kitchen table talking on his cell phone when Billy came in. Billy sat down at the table and waited for Harry to finish his call.

"Yeah, I think we got it laid out," Harry said into the phone. He listened for a bit and then said, "Billy just got here and Tom's out doing what we talked about. Your end straight?"

More listening on Harry's part; more waiting on Billy's.

"Good, then we're set," Harry said as he finished the call.

Harry turned his attention to Billy and said, "Where you been?"

"Sleeping," Billy told him.

"Sleeping?" Harry asked.

"Yeah, sleeping," Billy repeated. "I was at Nolo's until late and had some checking to do before I hit the sack."

"You played in the game at Nolo's last night?" Harry asked.

"Yeah, you could say that," Billy answered.

"You win?" Harry asked.

"I was doing fine until the normal game rules went out the window and the stakes went through the roof, as in unlimited. In the end I came out ahead, but the Rich Valley crowd took a massive beating. Fetts' guy Keough was there and he teamed up with Buddy. Together they hit Kurps for a bundle and a half."

"You help?" Harry asked rather cautiously.

"I didn't help anybody and I'm not sure Buddy and Keough were looking for my help. They didn't know I'd be there before the game started and I didn't know they were going to be there either. Buddy maybe, but Keough being there really surprised me. It caught me totally off guard," Billy told Harry.

Harry had to think on what Billy said for a minute. When he had his thoughts straight, he said, "If Keough is Fetts' big gun on the poker side, why send him to a Rich Valley game? Why try and fleece what could arguably be considered small time potatoes and risk blowing up his operation if something went totally wrong? Am I missing something here?" Harry asked.

Shaking his head, Billy replied, "I don't know, Harry. I've been asking myself the same questions since I saw Keough and I can't come up with a good answer. Well, one answer, maybe."

"What's that?" Harry asked him.

"I caught a whiff of a rumor Fetts was setting up for what he has always called the "big score" that would propel him to the big time in our game and with the Vegas big boys. The real players I'm talking about. The ones you never see and never will. If the rumor is true, maybe this is a dress rehearsal for that play. It's a nutty idea, but I got nothing else," Billy told Harry.

"But why here?" Harry continued.

"In case you haven't noticed, Harry, we are in da sticks of Pennsylvania. It ain't New York, Vegas, or most any other place you or I could name. Something goes down here who's gonna know, or care, other than the folks that get hurt. Fetts has his prime boys do their thing in preparation for the big one and gets out with none the wiser. Nobody in his world ever sees it happen, or cares," Billy expounded.

"Risky play though," Harry answered Billy.

"For who?" Billy says. "If it goes down as planned, great. If it scoots sideways on him, Fetts hauls his boys out and walks away with a fair payday just the same—fuck you so very much Mechanicsburg, PA. Hard for him to lose," Billy explains.

"What if there's trouble?" Harry asks.

"Harry, if what I think is happening is happening, you can bet every dime you have ever seen in your entire life Jon Francis Fetterman has exit plans well thought out and will have enough muscle close by to handle any circumstance. He's got too much invested and his top dogs in play to let it blow up on him. At the slightest sniff of trouble he doesn't think he can easily handle, he's pulling the plug on this operation and they're all long gone before the smoke clears," Billy said.

"You and I trouble?" Harry asked.

Billy smiled and said, "Harry, Fetts hasn't sniffed it yet, but you and I are a world of trouble that sucker will wish he never encountered."

Harry smiled right back and answered, "You got that right, kiddo."

Chapter 105

Billy was on the range at Rich Valley just trying to keep his "lefty" game sharp when his cell phone rang. When he practiced he never let shit like calls on his cell get in the way. You have to be disciplined and, since he hadn't been a regular on the range lately, he let it go to voice mail. Two minutes later it rang again and again he ignored it.

"Hey, you gonna get that?" the guy to his right asked Billy.

Billy just looked at him, shook his head and went back to hitting balls.

It rang again.

Billy never left his cell on when he was at the range but with shit going down, Billy was afraid he'd miss Harry's call.

With the guy giving Billy the mean hairy eyeball look, Billy put down his club and picked up his phone. Walking away from the range Billy looked at the number but didn't recognize it. Answering it he said, "Yeah, what?"

"Billy, Billy, Billy, is that any way to greet an old friend?" is what he heard.

Not sure he was hearing what he was hearing, Billy answered, "Friend?"

"Now that hurts me, Billy. After everything I did for you that's the thanks I get? No 'Great to hear from you' or 'I missed you so,' Billy boy?"

Keeping calm Billy responded, "It has been much too long after what you did to me, Old Friend."

"Billy..."

"Fuck you and your Billy, Fetts. You screwed me over and you owe me my cut. What could you possibly be calling me for?" Billy told Fetts.

"I had the feeling you might have some hard feelings, Billy boy. I'm here to make amends and get everything straight between us," Fetts answered.

Billy wasn't sure what to make of that remark. Fetts would lie to his mother's face while picking her pocket at the same time, so why should be believe anything Fetts said to him now.

Before Billy could say anything, Fetts continued, "I'm at Arooga's on Carlisle Pike right now, Billy. Jump on over here and we can get things right with each other again."

"Right how?" Billy replied.

"When we see each other, Billy, not on the phone," Fetts told him.

"You and who else, Fetts?" Billy asked him.

"Just me, Billy. I knew you'd freak if I had any of the boys with me, so it's just me," Fetts told him.

"I don't know why the hell I should trust you, Fetts, but give me fifteen and I'll be there," Billy told him and ended the call.

~ * ~

Billy immediately dialed another number from speed dial and the person picked up after the first ring.

"Hey, I gotta meet a guy at Arooga's on the Pike in fifteen. Go over there and make sure he's alone and there aren't any guys hanging around looking like they're with him. Call me if you see a problem."

Disconnecting Billy hit another speed dial number and got Harry right away. He told Harry, "You're not gonna believe this but I'm meeting Fetts over at Arooga's in fifteen. He called and said he wants to get things right between us."

"You trust it's not a trap?" Harry answered.

"I got a guy looking at it and he'll hang around just in case."

"Hit me if you need me and I'll be right there. I won't be far," Harry told Billy.

Billy replied, "Thanks Harry, that's why I called."

Chapter 106

Twenty minutes later Billy walked into Arooga's and found Fetts in a booth in the back. Billy's guy was sitting at the bar drinking a beer and watching a game on the TV. Feeling just a bit uneasy Billy walked over and slipped into Fetts' booth.

"Been a while, Billy," Fetts greeted him.

"Yeah, it has, Fetts," Billy replied playing it cool.

"You by yourself?" Fetts asked Billy.

"Yeah, I am," Billy lied.

"That's good, me too," Fetts lied right back.

The waitress showed up at the table just then and Billy ordered a beer. Fetts told the waitress he was good for now.

"So, why now?" Billy started.

"Now's as good a time as any," Fetts replied. "You were one of my boys and I don't like the way things ended between us."

"The way they ended was you stiffed me out of a chunk of dough and I hightailed it out of town while the getting was good. But I didn't forget; I never forget, you know that Fetts. Neither do you," Billy told him.

Fetts smiled and said, "It was a misunderstanding, Billy. Just a small misunderstanding that I want to make good on and fix things between us."

Billy just smiled at Fetts and said nothing.

Sensing it was on him, Fetts continued, "Some of the boys said they ran into you. I was kinda surprised to hear you where hanging out in this part of the country. Last time I heard you were running stuff upstate more."

"I get around," was all Billy said in response.

"You always did, Billy," Fetts replied.

Billy's beer came and the waitress left. Cute on exit Billy thought to himself.

"Let's cut the small talk and get down to it. If you want to make things right you owe me a bag-a-bills and something to account for the shafting like you did. And a "What the fuck" for this meet right out of the blue. And why now?" Billy threw at Fetts.

Fetts took a long pull on his beer while he eyed Billy. Safe to say he wasn't pleased with Billy's tone and he showed it.

Remaining remarkably composed, Fetts said, "Remember who you're talking to, Billy. You may have come up some since we split but you're still a punk kid in this business and I'm still Jon Francis Fetterman. I run where you only dream of running your penny-ante shit. Keep that in mind when you talk to me."

Billy smiled and sipped his beer.

They waited.

The Mexican stand-off ended when Fetts' cell buzzed. He looked at it, ignored it, and said, "You'll get the money coming to you, but first I have a job for you. Do your part and I'll double what I owe you."

"A job?" Billy queried.

"Yeah, a job," Fetts replied. We got something going as I know you figured out by now. My boys see you hanging around Rich Valley and working your way into the action going down there. Starting small and seeing your way to the bigger money angles. Sorry to spoil your action at the card game but I didn't know you'd be there. Once we're set I don't like to pull back unless it's absolutely necessary. You know how we run, don't you, Billy?"

"Yeah, I do," Billy went along.

Billy's guy sitting at the bar yelled at the TV along with the rest of the people watching the game. Neither Billy nor Fetts paid him any attention.

"You get much at Rich Valley?" Fetts quizzed Billy.

Playing it cool, Billy replied, "I was moving into some bigger action when Keough showed up with Buddy for the big game at Nolo's. I knew what was going down and took a few bucks with me but had to get out when the stakes got out of hand. You took them for a ride that night."

"We did," Fetts agreed. "It actually went to a place I hadn't expected and moved our action along much quicker than I thought. I expected to be another month or so before the end game went down, but we're closing in on the kill and I need another piece to finish it."

Fetts cell buzzed again and he looked at it longer than the first one. He said," I gotta take this. Get us a couple more beers and I'll be right back."

Fetts wedged his way out of the booth and walked toward the restrooms as he started talking on his cell phone. Billy grabbed his cell, hit a button, and when it connected he let it ring once before he disconnected telling Harry all was still cool.

Chapter 107

Fetts was gone maybe five minutes and returned just as the cute waitress was putting their beers down on the table.

"Thanks, hon," Fetts said to her as he slipped into the booth.

Hoping for a nice tip the waitress gave Fetts her best smile.

"Everything good?" Billy asked Fetts.

"Everything is always good in my world, Billy. You of all people should know that," Fetts replied with his eat-shit smile that Billy knew all too well.

Wanting to move things along Billy said, "Another piece you were saying."

"Yes, the final piece needed to put this operation to bed and move on to bigger and better things, Billy," Fetts answered.

"And what does this "final piece" have to do with me?" Billy asked him.

"You know how my operations work, Billy. You were a vital part of the previous take-downs and played your part to perfection. Our minor disagreements in the past were small potatoes and I'm sure we can fix them, can't we Billy?" Fetts replied.

Billy stared at Fetts and sipped his beer.

Fetts stared back and gave Billy a "what up" shrug of the shoulders.

The crowd in the bar reacted to whatever happened in the game that was on TV and they had to wait for some quiet before they could resume their conversation.

"Minor disagreement?" Billy threw at Fetts.

"Hey, I shorted you some money and you split," Fetts answered Billy. "You know I would have squared things up later on, like now."

"Bullshit," was all Billy said in reply.

Unaccustomed to subordinates catching an attitude with him, Fetts glared at Billy. He took a long pull on his beer and finally smiled at Billy.

Billy didn't smile back.

"Just for argument sake let's say I owe you some dough and

maybe we could have handled our disagreement differently. I got the money I owe you with a bit of interest on top to soothe your hurt feelings. That make it right, Billy?" Fetts asked.

Billy mulled over what Fetts had said and then replied, "Just for argument sake let's say I accept your offer and get the cash in hand with the interest thrown in. And again let's say just for argument sake this "another piece" you're talking about is what I think it is and I say I'm in. What's to stop you from screwing me same as you did last time and maybe even worse this time?"

Now Fetts was pissed. Billy could see it in his eyes and in the way he raised himself up in his seat with a body stiffness that always preceded an ass-kicking in the past. Billy had him where he wanted him now.

Calmly and evenly, Fetts said, "You had better watch yourself Billy boy. Just because I come here to this shit town and offer to buy you a beer doesn't mean you can disrespect me like you are. I'm still Jon Francis Fetterman and you're still little Billy Burns. I made you and I can crush you for no reason at all. Just because I can. You hear me little Billy Burns?"

Calmly and evenly, Billy replied, "You may still be the same Jon Francis Fetterman but I'm not "little" Billy Burns any more. I haven't been "little" Billy Burns for some time. I got my own thing going on and I'm Billy Burns now."

Fetts leaned back and shook his head at Billy.

Billy just stared at Fetts and waited.

The waitress came to the table, Fetts looked up at her and the waitress ran.

"Okay, just Billy Burns," Fetts started. "You got your big britches on and you got your own thing going on. My boys have this Rich Valley thing set up to go and it's time for the final takedown. I need the final piece to make it happen with no hitches and you know, just like I know, you are the last piece to the puzzle just like the previous jobs. You in?"

"You asking me?" Billy said.

"Yeah, I'm asking you," Fetts replied.

Billy sipped his beer and smiled at Fetts.

Fetts just stared back.

"What's in it for me if I do this one?" Billy asked.

"Same as before," Fetts replied.

Billy sipped his beer and smiled at Fetts.

Fetts just stared back.

"Yeah, I'm in," Billy said, "but not same as before."

"What the fuck!" Fetts snapped.

Calmly and evenly, Billy replied, "I'm in, but here's what I get: first, I get the money you owe me from prior jobs and fifty percent interest—up front, like now. Second, I get double the normal slice for this job to compensate for the pain and suffering you caused by your prior actions—up front, like now. Third, you can count me in and I get a piece of the "Big One" you got planned after this one, same slice, same time—up front, as in like now. All comes in one nice package and no chance we have a similar "disagreement" like we did last time around."

"You shitting me," Fetts spit at Billy.

"I shit you not, Jon Francis Fetterman. It's a take it or leave it offer. No compromise, no haggling. You agree and I'm in as the final piece to your puzzle—this job and for the "Big One" you got planned. I already got myself in perfect position to pull off this one and I'm the best guy to help you score big on the next one and make you a big man in Vegas, just like you always dreamed of. As I said, a take it or leave it offer. No compromise, no haggling." Billy finished.

Jon Francis Fetterman got up from the table and left.

Billy sipped his beer and waited. He knew Jon Francis Fetterman would be back.

Chapter 108

The waitress had just brought Billy another beer when she saw Fetts coming back to the table. As it was actually more like storming back to the table she scurried away lickety-split while she could.

"Have to take a leak?" Billy asked Fetts.

"Fuck you and your leak, Billy," Fetts answered. "Here's what I'm gonna do for you. I'll give you what you asked for, up front, just like you asked. You do the Rich Valley job and then you lay low until I need you for this other job I have planned for later this year. And this here is a take it or leave it offer. No compromise, no haggling. You hone those skills of yours and you had better not screw up or our next disagreement will be a permanent one. You get my drift, Billy?"

"I get you loud and clear, Fetts. Money up front, all of it. I do the Rich Valley job and your "Big Score" job and then we part ways permanently. No more jobs, no more disagreements. Should you ever think about coming after me, I'd recommend you think about it long and hard before you act on it. My people, people I trust with my life, they know all about you and all of your crew. Something happens to me or anyone I know and you go down. In the ground down, six feet under down. Never to be found again down and under. You get **MY** drift, Fetts?" Billy said with emphasis.

Sitting back, Fetts said, "It's all grown up Billy Burns telling me, Fetts, how it's going to go down. Threatening me, Fetts, like he's the big man now. Making demands of me, Jon Francis Fetterman, like it's his game and not mine. I'll play, Billy Burns, but you listen closely. You better do you part or I'll extract the up-front money you're getting and it will hurt, real bad. You get my drift, Billy?"

Billy just sipped his beer.

"I'll have your money in two days," Fetts told Billy. "The Rich Valley job goes down within the week, two tops, and then I'm gone. You do your thing and I do mine and later this year we both will be sitting on a pile of dough. Don't screw up, Billy."

With that Fetts got up from the table and left. Billy's guy threw some money on the bar a short time later and followed Fetts out the door. Two minutes later Billy's phone rang twice and he knew the coast was clear for him to leave.

Billy hit a speed dial on his cell, waited for it to connect and said, "It's done. I'll be there in fifteen minutes."

~ * ~

Harry was sitting in the corner booth at Nolo's sipping a Stella. He had been waiting for over an hour, all the time getting restless and a bit anxious until Billy's call came through. It seemed like things continued to move along according to plan but, as Harry knew all too well, plans can unravel in the blink of an eye.

Fifteen minutes later Billy strolled into Nolo's like he didn't have a care in the world. Truth be told, Billy always looked like he didn't have a care in the world and everything was cookies and ice cream with whipped cream and a cherry on top. Under the surface he could be a bundle of nerves with maximum uncertainty but you'd never know it.

Sliding into the booth across from Harry, Billy said, "Harry."

"Billy," Harry replied in kind.

Nolo happened to be passing by when Billy came in and he stopped to see if Billy wanted anything.

"Same as Harry's having," Billy told Nolo.

"Coming right up," Nolo told Billy and he left.

Billy looked around the rest of the room to make sure they were alone—they were. He was sure anybody that overheard their conversation wouldn't necessarily understand what they were talking about but there was no reason to take any chances. Both Billy and Harry were stout believers in 'Better Safe Than Sorry' all of the time.

"We're set?" Harry asked Billy.

"We're set," Billy replied. "Fetts was royally pissed but he finally agreed to everything I told him I wanted and how I wanted it. The money's coming in a few days and the job goes down within the week, two tops. He must have his end already set up and all he needed was me to fill in the final piece to the puzzle."

"No additional directions from him?" Harry asked.

"No, no additional directions," Billy answered. "Fetts knows that I know what to do and how to do it. He's seen me do my thing several times already and I do it to perfection."

"So, game on?" Harry asked.

"Game on," Billy replied.

"I got some things to finalize on my end but we are just about set. As soon as you get the day and time from Fetts, I will put things in motion from my side," Harry said.

"Piece of cake," Billy told Harry.

"I'll make sure there's a piece for me and a piece for you after we finish this thing off," Harry told Billy.

"Chocolate cake with chocolate icing," Billy replied.

"Is there any other?" Harry said with a big smile.

Chapter 109

Billy had time to think which had always produced some interesting results in the past. Having the time to think gave him the ability to wander around in his mind and conjure up images of the shit that got his ass in trouble time and time again. Not three squares a day trouble, but trouble none the less. Free time to brain-wander was not necessarily a good thing for Billy.

The reason he had the time was two hundred miles plus and nothing else to do. Billy was on his way to New York to take care of something he had been tossing back and forth in his head for a while now. It was Harry's fault and Billy had come to trust most of what Harry said when they talked seriously, in private, about serious "stuff" as Harry liked to call it. Stuff that meant something to Harry, and to Billy, and needed to be considered. Didn't happen often, but when it did, Billy listened. It was like having his own personal E. F. Hutton moment with whispering in his ear and the whole world wanted to know what Harry was saying.

Serious thinking was also something Billy took very seriously. When his mind locked-in on a target it was like a Vulcan Mind Meld kind of locked-in that Mr. Spock specialized in. Billy's focus was intense, crystal clear, and he could see past any and all obstacles that could potentially present themselves. He had a few hours to crystallize his thoughts and he was well on his way to getting there. He was beginning to think it had been there for a long time and he just hadn't brought it to his conscious surface to deal with it. Now, primarily thanks to Harry, and it was there front and center.

As he got closer to his destination Billy experienced a sensation that came upon him so rarely it took him by total surprise. He was used to being in control of his circumstances with little doubt he was headed in the right direction. In what Billy did, his life, his actions, control was paramount and loss of control in any situation could lead to devastating results. What you don't know, haven't thought through and seen, anticipated and visualized, considered and dealt with as a possibility can literally kill you in the end. Total calm and knowledge of what lies ahead was where Billy liked to be, had to be.

The sensation Billy was now experiencing was nervousness.

Billy was actually nervous.

He didn't feel totally in control. He didn't know what to expect nor what the outcome would be as a result of his pending actions. It made him feel unsure and Billy Burns was always sure only because he had to be sure. It was the number one requirement in the life he had chosen for himself. Well, maybe his parents had had a hand in his life's path, but that wasn't up for debate at the current moment.

Billy shook it off and drove on.

The voice on the portable GPS was beginning to annoy the living piss out of Billy so he decided to shut it off. He had a lock on the rest of the trip and needed the peace and quiet to finalize his approach. He had worked through in his mind what he was going to do, how he was going to do it, and what he was going to say. He had visualized all of it and it looked and sounded perfect to him. Then why in the name of all that was unholy was he so damned nervous!

As he closed in on his destination Billy grabbed his cell and hit a speed dial number. He needed to confirm all was in place as he had requested from the people he trusted without having to provide reasons. If Billy asked for something, his people knew it was important. Billy didn't ask much of anyone else and gave of himself freely to everyone in his circle, and his circle was large. Loyalty to Billy was a given and he could trust his people.

He was there. It was time. Billy had done so many things in his short life, good things and bad things, probably many more bad ones than good ones when you added them all up. He was sure no one thing had been more important than what he was about to do. It felt right, it was right, he was sure it was what he wanted in his heart and in his soul. All he could hope for was that it would be received in the same vein when he opened his heart and his soul as he had never, ever done before.

Yep, he was sure. He felt that calmness come over him that told him he was right. If not, he'd kick Harry's ass for pointing him in this direction in the first place.

Chapter 110

Harry was sitting up at Nolo's bar at Rich Valley. He and Tom had been nursing a beer for too long a time while talking quietly between themselves. Hope came over and asked Harry if he needed anything and Harry had told her they were fine. Hope got the message and went back down the other end of the bar to talk to Bonita.

"I think we got everything in place, Harry," Tom said.

"Dammit, you know thinking we got everything in place just isn't good enough, Tom. Either we got this puppy locked down tight or it's gonna bite us in the ass and everyone else that's involved. That's a bunch of folk, Tom. A bunch of folk that got a whole lot riding on us having this thing locked down solid as a rock. You got me, Tom?" Harry asked him.

"You think I don't know that, Harry. These people are my friends, been my friends for a long time and I'm not gonna let them down. No, I'm not gonna let them down one bit," Tom replied firmly.

"I know that, Tom. It's just what we do, you and me both, when we get down to the short strokes on a job and try and make sure we didn't screw up somewhere along the way. I trust you, Tom, and I trust the people behind us on this one. We're good, I can feel it. We're good," Harry told Tom.

"Yeah, me too," Tom agreed as he got up to hit the head.

Harry waved to Hope for two more beers. When she came over Harry pointed to the shelf behind the bar and said, "Hey, Hope, I've been looking at that thing up there since the first day I came in here and I still don't have any idea what the hell it is. Can you enlighten me?"

Hope turned and looked up at what Harry was pointing at. It was a rectangular glass jar with something fuzzy sticking out of the top that seemed to have a tail.

She let out a laugh and turned back to Harry.

"That's a Rat's Ass," she told Harry.

Harry gave Hope a look that said you better explain what the hell you're talking about.

"Our Friday afternoon mixed golf group gives out an award each week to the team that wins that day," Hope told Harry. "That's the trophy they give out and nobody gives a "Rat's Ass" about any trophy so they give it right back. It goes back on the shelf until the following Friday. And so on, and so on. Happens like clock-work each and every Friday."

Harry shook his head and laughed. Just then Tom came back and he asked Harry what he was laughing at.

"Don't worry about it, Tom, you wouldn't give a 'Rat's Ass' about it anyway.

Hope and Harry laughed their asses off while Tom sat there trying to figured out what he had just missed. When Hope pointed to the "Rat's Ass" trophy on the shelf Tom knew what he had missed.

~ * ~

Jeff Austin came into the bar and sat down on the stool next to Harry. Benita saw Jeff come in, brought him his usual beer of choice and went back to the end of the bar to rejoin Hope.

"Gents," Jeff addressed Harry and Tom.

"Jeff," was returned in greeting by both of them.

"Kurps called me and wants to meet. He says it's urgent. You guys know what's going down and when?" Jeff asked.

"I got an idea on the what, but I'm not exactly sure on the when," Harry told Jeff.

"The boys are shitting bricks right about now and asking me if I know what's going to happen. They appointed me the savior in this mess and I sure don't want to disappoint them, Harry," Jeff said.

"Jeff, it's just like we talked about before. Me and Tom got a handle on this thing, and if it goes down like we think it will, everyone comes out whole in the end," Harry told Jeff.

"Kurps and I have been trusting you all along, Harry, so I guess I don't have any choice right about now do I?" Jeff said.

"Jeff, I trust the people I'm working with and they are the best you could possibly get to fix the shit you and the boys got yourselves into. You need to trust me and Tom on this. If Kurps doesn't fuck up, everyone gets themselves right and life gets back to normal," Harry told Jeff.

"I sure hope so, Harry. This plan of yours goes south and a lot of good people are gonna be up shit's creek without a damn paddle, me included," Jeff told Harry.

"It's gonna work, Jeff, trust me on that," Harry told Jeff.

"I got another choice?" Jeff asked.

Neither Harry nor Tom could say anything in return.

"Then I guess that's it," Jeff said. "I'll know it's going down when it does, I guess."

As Jeff got up and left the bar Harry turned to Tom and said, "I sure hope we're right on this one, Tom."

"You and me both, Harry, you and me both," Tom replied.

"No reason not to have another coupla beers, is there?" Tom asked Harry.

"No reason at all, Tom" Harry replied.

Tom turned to Hope down at the end of the bar and yelled, "Do us again the same way, Hope."

And she did.

Chapter 111

Billy spent the better part of an hour making sure everything had been set up just as he had requested. He wanted it all to be perfect and he never left the important stuff to chance. If he did it himself, or if he checked and double checked to make sure it was done right, then he was satisfied and not an instant before.

Strangely eerie was what popped into his head as he finalized his preparations. He knew it was almost time and he wanted to be ready. He knew he was burning nervous energy with mindless activity but he couldn't help himself. Run out the door, jump in the car and head back to Pennsylvania as fast as he could was nudging him away from here.

Nudging hard.

Nudging real hard.

But no, Billy kept telling himself Harry was right, this was right, it better be right. If it blows up in his face it could all go to shit. It *would* all go to shit. Shit, shit, shit.

Billy stopped, took a long calming breath, and then smiled. He had gotten himself all worked up because he had never done anything like this before. Never, not like this. It was never important before and now it was. It is. It might be. He hoped it would be.

"*Shit, she's here,*" Billy said out loud and then he ran to put "*it*" in motion.

~ * ~

"Yes, sir," Harry said into the phone. "We have everything set on our end and we're ready to take care of business. I'm safe in assuming that your end is equally ready to take care of business when the time comes?"

Harry listened for almost thirty seconds and then said, "I wouldn't doubt you for a second. You have never steered me wrong before and I know you aren't going to do it this time either. When you say you're side is covered, it's covered. Period—end of discussion."

Ten more seconds of listening to the man and Harry hung up

the phone. He turned to Tom and gave him the thumbs up.

"I guess that means the man says we're set?" Tom asked.

"That would be correct," Harry answered. "You heard me make the stupid mistake of 'assuming' something he was to have accomplished would be done after he said he would accomplish it."

"That was pretty fucking stupid, Harry, wasn't it," Tom asked him.

"You heard my reply to him, so yeah, it was pretty fucking stupid," Harry replied.

"You gonna call Billy?" Tom asked him.

"No, Billy's busy," Harry told Tom.

"Busy? He's busy? We got huger than huge shit about to go down and you're telling me Billy's busy," Tom quizzed Harry.

"Yeah, he's busy," Harry repeated. "Billy's taking care of a different kind of business up north and it's important to him. He didn't realize how important it was until just recently and it needed to be tended to pronto. So yeah, he's going to be busy for a day or two. Not to worry though, he'll be back in plenty of time and his end of the game is already set."

"You sure about that?" Tom asked.

"Tom, I'm rock solid sure about what Billy's doing up north and I'm just as rock solid sure about what Billy's got set up down here. Trust me, Tom, we don't have to worry about Billy one bit."

"I guess I don't have much choice but to trust you, do I, Harry? You got the cards on this one and I ain't got nothing to say about it. You know I'm worried about this going down perfect and I'm in the middle of it with no say on how it goes down. If I had a part, I'd be concentrating on that and not on what everybody else is supposed to be getting done. Shit, I just want it done and my buddies back on solid ground again. You know what I'm saying, Harry?" Tom said.

"Tom, I know exactly what you're saying," Harry told him. "I ain't got much of a part in this either and if it turns into a clusterfuck you and I both will be looking at it from the outside in. We just have to trust the plan and the people we have doing the important parts for us. Trust the plan, trust the people. We have done it before and we'll probably do it again, Tom. You with me on this one, buddy?" Harry asked Tom.

"Well shit, Harry, you know I'm with you. Your people done us right every time and they're gonna kick some ass again this time for sure," Tom told Harry.

"Good. Let's get us some grub and a few cool ones and relax our bones for a bit," Harry told Tom.

Chapter 112

Frankie was sitting in the back booth of a Vegas strip dive waiting for his ten o'clock appointment to show up. He had never been in this particular dive before and he didn't like the place when he walked in. Now that he had been waiting fifteen minutes past ten o'clock, he liked it even less.

He was just about to leave when he saw him walk in the front door. The sight of him made him want to puke his guts up, but he was in too deep to him already and he still needed him.

"Jon Francis Fetterman sitting in *The Gents Joint*," the guy started. "I never would have thought I'd see the likes of you in a place like this."

"It's not where I would have set the meet," Frankie replied. "Your meet, your place, Germ, so let's get to it."

"What's your hurry, Fetts? We haven't seen each other in too long and I'd like to sit a while, have a few pops of their finest liquor, and chat some. That okay with you, Frankie?" Germ asked Fetts.

"If you want to pollute your insides with some of their rot-gut "finest liquor" you can go ahead. I'm good as is," Fetts told Germ. "You want to chat, go ahead and chat, but make it fast. I have things I need to get to and I can't do it sitting here watching you savor this top-of-the-line establishment's finest liquor."

The waitress came to the table and Germ asked her for a Chivas double on the rocks. She looked at him like he has just asked her for the combination to Fort Knox. Germ changed his order to a double scotch on the rocks with a water chaser and she went away.

They waited for the scotch to come in silence.

Drink in hand, Germ said, "You got your play set to go, Frankie?"

"Yes," was all Fetts said in reply.

"Your order the same as before?" Germ continued.

"Yes," was all Fetts said in reply.

"You wanna tell me what it is you got going down?" Germ

asked him.

"No," was all Fetts said in reply.

"Must be pretty big if you're here in person in *The Gents Joint* sitting with me as I enjoy this fine drink," Germ continued.

"Germ, answer me this. Have I ever told you one iota of my business dealings either before they were conducted or after they were done? Even once, Germ?" Fetts asked him.

"Well, no you haven't, Fetts," Germ replied.

"Then puzzle me this, Germ. Why the fuck would I tell you what I have going down this time if I never gave you a sniff of what I had going down before? You got an answer for that, Germ?" Fetts asked him.

Germ drained his glass and said, "Fetts, you have never told me shit before and you don't have to tell me shit now about your business. But you mark my words, Fetts, if your shit ever blows back at me I will make you wish you never set foot in this town. You understand what I'm saying, Fetts?"

Fetts looked at Germ but didn't say anything.

Fetts didn't like Germ.

Fetts didn't like being dressed down by Germ.

Fetts didn't like being threatened by Germ.

Fetts hated Germ more and more as each minute went by and he had no choice but to endure Germ.

Fetts needed Germ.

"I hear you, Germ," Fetts told him.

Germ smiled knowing what it took for Frankie to say those words.

"I'll have what I need when I need it?" Fetts asked Germ.

Germ smiled again and said, "Sure, Frankie, you'll have your stuff just like you ordered. That is, as soon as I get my money."

Fetts reached in his jacket pocket and pulled out a packet that he passed across the table to Germ. Germ picked it up and put it in his jacket pocket.

"You going to count it?" Fetts asked.

"No need to count it," Germ replied. "I know you wouldn't even think about short changing me or you and I would be done. And, you and I being done means you're done in this town for good. You know that, I know that, everyone in town knows that."

Fetts had no answer because he knew Germ was 100% correct.

　　With that, Germ got up from the table and left.

　　Fetts waived to the waitress and ordered a double scotch just to punish himself.

Chapter 113

Tips had had a bitch of a morning so far and came racing into the warehouse knowing her day was already way behind. She had a group coming in at ten and the overhaul on two of the golf simulators scheduled for the same time. Who the hell decided to put both of those together at the same time?

That's right—she did. What a stupid shit she was. And then there was the afternoon thing with...what the hell!

Tips stopped short and started in amazement at what was in front of her. If she had been out late the night before and still hadn't gotten her focus back yet this morning she might have understood better. At least it would have been a reason. A possible reason. But, since she hadn't been out late and had gone to bed stone cold sober, she couldn't get her mind around what she was seeing. And why.

"Good morning, Tips," Billy said in greeting.

"Um, good morning, Billy," Tips replied.

"Running a wee bit late this morning are we?" Billy continued.

"Um, yeah, a bit," she replied.

That's when the full realization of what she was seeing came into focus. Billy was there, in the warehouse, just after eight in the morning, dressed in an apron. Well, he had other clothes on, too, but he had an apron on. And he was shaking a pan over the burner on the stove with what looked like some kind of eggs. And already sitting there on the counter was a plate of bacon, and toast, and orange juice, and...again she thought, what the hell!

"Hungry?" Billy asked.

Hard to reply when you find yourself temporarily speechless.

"Come on over here," Billy told her.

Regaining her composure, Tips went around the counter and over to where Billy was standing. She stood by his side as he put the pan back on the burner, turner toward her, wrapped his arms around her and gave her the mother of all kisses right on the smacker. A long one that melted her body right down to the tips of her toes. A 7.2 on the Richter Kiss Scale.

When Billy let go Tips never moved.

Hearing Billy say, "The eggs are going to burn," was what brought her back to the here and now.

"What…" was all she could get out.

"The eggs are going to burn," Billy repeated.

"Not that," Tips said, "what the hell are you doing here?"

"Why, cooking you breakfast," Billy replied.

"But, why…here…now…like this…and the…," Tips mumbled out.

"Because I wanted to, in a warehouse I own and you take care of, at breakfast time, like I always make a big breakfast, and, um, that was to tell you…" Billy told her.

Tips looked down at and gestured toward the pan.

Billy jumped and said, "Oh crap, the eggs are going to burn."

Shutting off the burner, Tips said, "Screw the eggs, Billy, and screw me, too."

As any gentleman would, Billy complied as requested.

~ * ~

Thirty minutes later, Billy and Tips were sitting at the warehouse kitchen counter. The eggs were cold, the toast hard and the OJ was getting warm by the time Billy and Tips managed to get back to the breakfast Billy had prepared.

"I'll pop the eggs in the microwave and get some ice for the Orange Juice," Billy told Tips. "But we'll have to make some more since I can't do anything about the toast—it's hard."

"That's not the only thing that got hard," Tips told Billy.

Now wearing only the apron, Billy looked at Tips and smiled.

"You seemed to enjoy it that way," Billy told her.

"I think I read somewhere breakfast appetizers should always be served hard," Tips said with a smile.

Billy smiled back at that one.

"And from the looks of your apron, breakfast may have to wait a little longer," Tips said.

Billy looked down at his tented apron and said, "I believe you are correct in your assumption, my dear," as the apron hit the floor.

Chapter 114

Kurps was on the first tee of the local course near his house where he played with his buddies all the time. Rich Valley he owned and he played there enough to keep his presence felt and take money from the members; this is where he played for fun.

He had now played seven days straight and mostly by himself. He worked on the range before he played and had gotten in thirty-six holes every other day. His game didn't need all that work, but he wanted to be at the very top of his game for what lay ahead. He knew the boys at Rich Valley let him win, he being the owner and all. He paid them back in comps and free drinks up at Nolo's two times over. This was honing his game for keeps. It was for the biggest round of golf he would ever play in his life—at least up to now he told himself.

"You're up, Kurps," Ton told him. At six-five, two hundred and ninety-five pounds, they didn't call him Ton for nothing.

"Right nice of you, Ton," Kurps replied.

"Right nice my ass," Ton replied. "When was the last time you didn't have the honor on the first tee?"

"Coming up with that one may take awhile," Kurps replied as they all laughed.

"Rumor has it you've been working mighty hard on your game the past week or so," his buddy Burks told Kurps.

Somewhat surprised by that comment, Kurps said, "I've been playing some and maybe hitting some balls on the range."

Without giving them a chance, Kurps stepped up and unloaded his drive down the first fairway. He loved to play from the tips everywhere he played and this course played just over 7,000 yards from the back tees. He had been playing from the White tees all week that simulated fairly closely the Blue tees at Rich Valley. That's what they played today.

"Nice drive, Kurps," Ton told him. "You should be able to eat up this course from the white's."

"Plays pretty friendly from the white tees," Kurps said with a smile.

"You want our money now?" Burks asked him.

"Naw, you can hold it until we're done. You never know what can happen on any given day," Kurps replied.

"My ass," Ton said as he sailed his drive twenty yards to the right of the fairway into same gnarly crap. "Shit, twenty bucks gone already."

They played on through the front nine and his buddies were constantly surprised at how Kurps hit the ball. He mishit a few shots but on the whole, he ate up the front nine just as they had expected he would.

As they got to the tenth tee, Ton said, "My ass is fucking killing me. Killing me I'm telling you. Yours too, Burks?"

"Ouch, man, double ouch. I won't be able to sit for a week," Burks replied.

"What the hell are you two going on about?" Kurps asked them as he handed out beers all around.

"It's the result of you kicking our asses so bad on the front," Ton told Kurps.

"You planning on continuing the ass-kicking on the back, too?" Burks asked Kurps.

Kurps smiled and said, "I was taking it easy on you two bums on the front. After we're done I'll take all your cash and own your wallets too."

"With the way you're hitting 'em I might as well give it up now," Burks said as he took his wallet out of his back pocket and threw it at Kurps' feet. Ton did the same and tossed his at Kurps knocking his beer out of his hand.

"Now you owe me for the beer you just wasted as well," Kurps told Ton.

"Screw you and your wasted beer, Kurps," Ton told him. "I paid for the beers to begin with just like always."

"Oh, yeah, you're right," Kurps said.

"I'm going first," Burks told Kurps. "At least I can have the tee for one hole out of eighteen."

"You never know what can happen on any given day," Kurps replied for the second time today.

"Yeah, sure," Burks replied. "And gimme my wallet back."

Kurps proceeded to whip them even worse on the back nine.

Chapter 115

Billy was in his car headed back toward Central Pennsylvania feeling the best he had felt in a very long time. Maybe it was the best he had ever felt in his whole short life, or at least for as long as he could remember. The day had gone exactly as he had planned and Tips was overwhelmed from start to finish. The breakfast was salvaged after the new toast was prepared and they had cleaned themselves up for the rest of the day's activities that Billy had planned out meticulously. The new oversized showers Billy had designed and Tips had seen through the installation came in very handy.

The newest addition to the golf instruction team took Tips through eighteen holes at Pebble Beach and she loved every minute of it. Billy could see she had worked on her game some and, even though she could still be considered a beginner, she was hitting the ball much better than he remembered. They followed that with a thirty minute MMA (Mixed Martial Arts) workout in the gym that came within a whisker of repeating their early morning shenanigans, Billy let Tips pummel him just enough to make her feel good about her improving skills.

Tips knew Billy worked religiously on his MMA and straight boxing regimen and could kick most people's ass without breaking a sweat. With how they conducted their lives it was a necessary skill set to have and often came in very handy. It could save their lives in the worst of circumstances. When she asked him if he had let her whack him around like he did, Billy replied, "Do you actually think me, Billy Burns, would let a wimpy girl like you get the upper hand on him?" The swift smack to the side of his head Tips delivered gave Billy his answer.

The head chef Billy employed served them an unbelievable lunch topped off by a flaming Bananas Foster that blew Tips away. He knew she didn't have the time nor the inclination to eat anywhere close to what he was providing so he did it up real big for her. The demands of running the warehouse was a full time job for an army and Tips managed to juggle everything on her

274

own with minimal assistance from Billy. It took Harry to make Billy see it and when he did, it boggled his mind at what she could accomplish.

The afternoon he had planned for her was top of the line dynamite: half-hour in the sauna followed by a full body massage with the top masseuse he could find who had come very well recommended by one big time CEO in Manhattan. That would be followed by a facial, manicure and pedicure by their on-site staff who Tips already knew were top shelf. The day would be topped off by a limousine ride into the city to see the rave play on Broadway followed by a late dinner in her favorite Little Italy restaurant. Unfortunately, Billy wouldn't be able to join her for any of it.

"I can't do all of that," Tips told Billy after he had laid out the rest of his plans for her right through dinner. "Who's going to take care of the warehouse?"

"Well, they will," Billy replied as a dozen of their best friends and regular users of the warehouse came into the room.

Tips was speechless again.

"They know this place inside and out and each one of them has a specialty that will allow them to take great care of the facilities while you enjoy the time that has been coming to you for a long while. It's my gift to you. It's our gift to you. Please take it and enjoy," Billy told her.

His kiss told her he meant every word of it.

"We have more of our friends coming in later to make use of what we have created and lend a hand. And I do mean "we" when I speak of this place, Tips. I couldn't have done it without you and it wouldn't last a single day without you as well."

"What about you? Aren't you going to enjoy the rest of the day with me?" Tips asked him.

"I would love to but I have this thing I've been working on and I have to get back to it. The shit's gonna hit the fan real soon and we have to make sure we don't get spotted brown when it does. For a change there are a lot of people depending on me to help them out of a jam and I don't want to let them down," Billy told her.

Tips took Billy's face in her hands and kissed him deeply.

"You're coming back soon, aren't you, Billy?" she asked him tentatively.

"Tips, I'll be back real soon," Billy told her, "and forever."

Chapter 116

They were sitting in Tom's living room enjoying a few cool ones while they went over what was ahead of them. Tom went to take a call leaving Harry and Billy alone for the first time since Billy had gotten back.

"How was New York?" Harry asked Billy.

"It was good. Thank you, Harry. You were dead on right; it was there all along and I just didn't see it. It felt better than I could have ever imagined," Billy replied.

"Tips good with it?" Harry asked.

"Oh yeah, Tips was better than good with it," Billy answered with a big smile on his face.

"That good?" Harry asked.

"Yeah, that good," Billy replied.

"It's on hold for now?" Harry asked.

"Yeah, Harry, it's on hold for now," Billy replied.

"You good?" Harry asked.

"For now," Billy replied. "Got to get back to it soon, though."

"Yeah, I hear ya loud and clear," Harry replied.

Tom came back in and they got back down to business.

~ *~

Fetts had his boys together to go over the specifics of the Rich Valley job one more time before they actually went about their business. This was ritual and Fetts was one to stick closely to ritual. It wasn't as much superstition as it was to put his mind at ease that they all knew their jobs cold and no last minute hitches would put a kibosh on his well laid plans, not to mention the expenses already in play.

Fetts said, "I know you boys have your parts down cold and I don't have to worry about any of you for this Rich Valley job. You all know this one leads to a job I've been planning for a long, long time that will put mucho dinero in all of your pockets. For you, it's not fuck-you money, but it's 'I'm going on a long vacation and you ain't botherin' my ass no time soon" money. You dig?"

Nods all around told Fetts his boys were with the program and they all saw the light at the end of the tunnel. Pull off the Rich Valley job with no hitches and then they would make their way to the Promised Land. The Las Vegas Promised Land. Green back heaven. Rolling in the dough flat-ass loaded Promised Land. The "You be there, brother, Promised Land" they all had dreamed of since they started on their path with Fetts.

Fetts. The guy they had all hooked their wagon to and followed without question.

Fetts. The guy that showed all of them why, how and when to get it done.

The right way.

The Vegas way.

The kick ass and don't take prisoners way.

The gimme the money and tough shit on your ass way.

Plainly stated—Fetts' way.

Bringing them back to the here and now, Fetts said, "We put it in play, we set it up the way we should, we led them to where we needed them to be, and now, now we take them down just the way we always do. All the way down."

"Yeah man's," from all the boys put the fitting exclamation point on Fetts' little rah, rah speech.

"You know what to do now, all of you. Get your heads on straight, put everything in order, because we all go under now then we put this thing to bed. Then we lay low until I say so and when the time is right you get your share," Fetts told them.

He looked at all of them and gave them a knowing nod of approval.

"Know that we're the best and those at Rich Valley are gonna feel the full impact of what we can do real soon. Now get the fuck out of here and hear my words, *Be Prepared*, or the wrath of Fetts will follow your asses to hell for all eternity," Fetts told them.

~ * ~

Harry was sure Billy had his head in this like he had never centered in on anything before. Harry knew where Billy had been and gone before, or at least he though he did. He just knew this was different. This was personal. Billy's personal business to set things right. This involved Harry and Harry thought, or at least he hoped, Billy had moved to a place he hadn't experienced before. A place where it wasn't just yourself that mattered. You had to depend on other people to get a job done; a place where you wanted to be part of something that made things right. As they should be. As they ought to be.

For somebody else and not just for yourself.

To be part of something that was right.

To be part of something that helped other people and didn't just take from others.

To take because you could, but to give because you should.

Because you wanted to.

A different Billy and it scared the shit out of Billy.

Unfortunately, it scared the shit out of Harry, too.

Chapter 117

Jeff had gotten to every one of the "Rich Valley" guys who were deep into this mess and had a heart-to heart with every last one of them. Kurps had handled the "high rollers" that constituted both his posse at Rich Valley and his home course and had the same heart-to heart with every last one of them as well. When Jeff and Kurps put their heads together to see where they stood, they found out they were in what Jeff liked to call deeper than deep shit.

As they sat and compared notes, Kurps yelled over to Nolo for a couple of beers so they could think properly. They were the only ones in Nolo's Bar and that was good.

Beers delivered, the three of them talked it through.

"You sure you got your end of it right?" Kurps asked Jeff.

"Why are you asking me that, Kurps?" Jeff asked.

"Why? Well, that's a shit-load of money for a bunch of guys that don't have a shit-load of money to piss away," Kurps told Jeff.

"Yeah, it sure is," Jeff agreed. "They are all shitting bricks, some more than others. A few of the boys don't have any way to pay off their IOU's short of losing their businesses and probably their homes, too. And that won't even cover it for a few of them."

"This really sucks," Kurps said.

"Where are your guys sitting in all this?" Jeff asked Kurps.

"I think my guys can all cover their nuts but it is gonna hit a few of them real hard. It's a pile for me, too," Kurps told Jeff.

"How much total all in?" Jeff asked.

"You won't believe this shit but it's over three hundred fifty large for me and my guys," Kurps told Jeff. "And I can't be sure they are giving it to me straight, either."

"Are you shitting me!" Jeff exclaimed.

"I shit you not," Kurps said with a resigning sigh.

"That include golf and poker losses?" Jeff asked.

"That's all in," Kurps said.

"Well then, we're screwed," Jeff told Kurps. "With my guys

we're over a hundred fifty K and there's no way my guys can get it back. And same as you, it's probably some number north of that."

"We're all in the same boat I guess," Kurps said.

"If you and me can't fix this by ourselves we don't have any way out but to go with the plan on the table and hope it works," Jeff told Kurps.

"You sure with these guys?" Kurps asked.

Jeff thought for a few seconds before he answered, "No I'm not sure about these guys. I'm not sure about the plan either. I'm not sure about any of this shit from the first day those two assholes walked onto Rich Valley property and hit their first golf ball. A friendly poker game we run and look what kinda hole that dug us. No, I'm not sure about anything, Kurps. But if you have a better plan I'm all ears because I don't have one. I ain't got jack shit right about now."

"Then we go with the plan and we go with the guys who brought it. If they turn out to be tied to them mothers that swindled us then we ain't got no shot, cuz Slim is already on the bus and he be out of town days ago," Kurps said.

"If that happens," Jeff said, "then Slim never existed in the first place."

Kurps shook his head in disgust, finished his beer, and got up to leave.

"Go ahead and put it in motion and call me when it's set," he told Jeff.

"You got it, man," Jeff told him.

When Kurps was gone Jeff picked up his cell and hit a speed dial number.

"You sure this plan of yours is gonna work?" Jeff said when the phone was answered. He listened and finally said, "Let's do it and god help all of us if it doesn't work."

Jeff hung up and told Nolo, "Keep 'em coming."

Chapter 118

"How you doing?" Harry asked when Sherry answered his call.

Surprised it was Harry on the line, Sherry answered, "I'm good, Harry. What's the occasion?"

"Occasion?" Harry replied.

"Yeah, occasion," Sherry replied. "To what do I owe the honor of a call from the one and only Harry Mickey Shorts?"

"What the fuck?" Harry answered.

"No, when the fuck?" Sherry replied in return.

Harry had to laugh at that one.

"I was calling to see if Max was around," Harry told her.

"No, he's not," Sherry told Harry. "Are you bailing on them for your "Saturday with the kids" that's coming up?"

Harry hated it when Sherry got her shorts in a bunch, but she happened to be right in this instance. And, he also hated it when Sherry was right—it cost him every time.

"I'm not bailing on them," Harry started, "I just won't be able to make the date we already have set."

"Explain to me how that doesn't constitute *"bailing"* on them?" Sherry huffed.

Harry hated when Sherry did the huffy thing.

"This thing I'm involved with is getting down to the short strokes and I'm not sure exactly when it's going to happen. It looks like it's going to be real soon and I have stuff to finalize before it does," Harry explained.

"So you are bailing on them," Sherry said.

"Sherry, on the few occasions when I wonder why we aren't still married..." Harry started.

"I'm just yanking your chain, Harry," Sherry said with a laugh.

"Do you have to do that?" Harry asked.

"Of course not," Sherry replied, "but why wouldn't I when it's so much fun."

Harry would have replied but Sherry was laughing so hard she wouldn't have heard what he said anyway.

When she finally stopped, Harry said, "Sherry, would you kindly inform our children I regrettably will not be able to make our assigned day and time for our next Saturday outing. Please tell them I will let them know when would be a suitable replacement date and make it up to them at that time."

"Sure, Harry, I would be happy to oblige," Sherry told him. "And me?" she concluded.

"You?" Harry asked.

"Yes, me," Sherry replied.

"You what?" Harry asked.

"When the…" Sherry began to say before she realized Harry had hung up on her this time.

~ * ~

Just as he had hung up on Sherry, Billy showed up at Tom's house. Harry had been expecting him but not for another few hours.

"Everything good with you?" Harry asked Billy tentatively.

"Yeah, I'm good," Billy responded.

"I wasn't expecting you for another few hours or so," Harry told him.

"You don't have to worry about me, Harry. My shit's in order and I will answer the bell when I have to. Don't forget I been down this road before and I know what I have to do and I know what the other guys are going to do. Or at least what they are supposed to do," Billy told Harry.

"I'm not biting on your ass, Billy; I'm just saying I wasn't expecting you for another few hours or so. It has nothing to do with your shit being in order or you knowing what you have to do. If you don't, we're all screwed," Harry assured him.

"All right, I hear you, Harry," Billy replied.

"But now that you've said it, what do you mean you "know what the other guys are going to do. Or at least what they are *supposed* to do"," Harry asked Billy.

Billy gave Harry one of those curious looks Harry had learned the hard way to be very wary of.

"You heard me," Harry confirmed for Billy.

Realizing he had to answer him, Billy said, "Harry, I know

what has gone down in the past during one of these jobs because I was in on the job. I know what went down on the few I didn't participate in. They all followed the same MO and included the same guys in almost every one. But, and it's a huge but, Harry, Fetts is still Fetts and you never take Fetts for granted."

"And so?" Harry queried.

"And so," Billy went on, "you have to be prepared for anything. I'm back in on this job and I would expect it to follow the same scripts we used in the past. I hear from my people the same crew has been seen in Vegas and Fetts doesn't seem to be hanging with anyone new."

"But," Harry continued.

"But," Billy continued, "as I just said, Fetts is still Fetts and you never take Fetts for granted."

"Great," is all Harry said in reply.

Chapter 119

"A hot dog cart on the sidelines at a football game!" Harry repeated in absolute astonishment.

"Yeah, what's so wrong with having a hot dog cart on the sidelines at a football game?" Tom asked.

"Well, I don't believe there has ever been a hot dog cart on the sidelines at a football game. At least not a professional football game," Harry replied.

"And that means there can't be one?" Tom responded.

"Where in the world did you come up with an idea like that?" Harry asked him.

"Just came to me," Tom told Harry.

"Really?" Harry replied.

"Yeah, really," Tom said. "You watch a football game and you see people eating hot dogs and all kind of stuff in the stands. And you see all sorts of people on the field who aren't playing or coaching in the game. Those people need to eat just like the people in the stands, isn't that right, Harry?" Tom asked.

Harry thought for a few seconds and said, "Well, I guess so."

"Then it fits perfectly. You put a hot dog stand like they got on the streets of New York right there on the field and those people can get a hot dog and a soda any time they want. They're happy and I make some dough," Tom finished.

"You are serious?" Harry asked Tom.

"Well, there's some stuff to be worked out, but yeah, it could work. I'm going to call it the *Umbrella Club*," Tom replied.

"The stuff that needs to be worked out is the stuff that somehow gets up in your head and comes spewing out like this hare-brained idea. You got some serious delusion issues to deal with, Tom," Harry told him.

"My delusions bring in some hard cold cash and I don't give two shits about hare-brained issues or not," Tom said.

"Yeah, you work on that one and let me know how it turns out. Okay, Tom?" Harry told him.

~ * ~

Las Vegas can be an outrageous town at times; well, most of the time really. The expression "What happens in Vegas stays in Vegas" applies to so many things, so many times, it is actually an understatement when you get right down to it. The people that make Vegas go are also too many to count and too varied to pin down. It takes a whole lot to make that town hum like it does.

Sometimes a tiny blip occurs and Vegas gets lowered a notch with nobody the wiser. While he was sitting at his favorite bar enjoying his favorite refreshment, Germ found that out for himself.

A guy sat down on the stool next to Germ and asked him, "Mind if I sit?"

Germ gave him half-a-look and returned to his drink without saying a word. He thought that would end it, but it didn't.

"Thanks, don't mind if I do," the guy said seemingly not the least bit put off.

Germ didn't even twitch.

"You're the guy everyone calls Germ, aren't you?" the stranger asked.

That brought a small twitch from Germ, but not a word in response.

"Not needed, we know who you are," the guy said staring straight ahead now.

The "we" made Germ think twice about who this guy was. Still didn't bother him that much, but it did make him think twice.

The bartender came over and asked the stranger if he wanted anything.

"Short beer," the stranger told the bartender who left to fill his order.

When he was gone, the stranger turned to Germ and said, "You familiar with the expression *Every Dog Has His Day*, Germ? Not your most common expression mind you, but common enough I'd guess. You familiar with it, are you, Germ?"

With that Germ turned to the stranger on the stool next to him and snarled, "Who the fuck are you and what the fuck do you want with me?"

Smiling, the stranger reached into the breast pocket of his jacket, extracted his wallet, and placed it on the bar. Still smiling, the stranger said, "I'm your worst nightmare and best friend all rolled into one."

Germ was in the process of getting up from the bar when the stranger reached out and opened his wallet showing Germ the badge. Germ sat back down knowing this was going to be his day and he be the dog.

Chapter 120

"He wants to what? Where did you hear that from? Who did you hear that from? He wants to what? I don't get it, why? Did he ever do that before, ever? Like, when he was this close to the finale?"

"Harry, in case you don't know it, you're rambling. Yes, you are rambling incoherently for no reason at all," Billy told him.

"No *reason* at all!" Harry yelled. "No reason at all," he repeated in a somewhat milder tone.

"Yes, as I just said, for no reason at all," Billy repeated.

"Oh, I have a reason. You bet your ass I have a reason. We have this thing planned out to the smallest, most minute detail and Fetts goes and throws a monkey wrench into the whole fucking thing and now the thing's all ass backwards. The whole thing," Harry continued.

"You used the word thing four times with or without an "s" and I'm not sure which "thing" you are talking about in any of them," Billy told Harry.

"The whole thing!" Harry yelled back at Billy. "The whole damn thing!!!"

Tom sat on the couch observing the exchange occurring between Harry and Billy and was fairly sure he had followed Harry perfectly—from one thing to the next thing. All four things—with or without the "s". Since Billy didn't know Harry like Tom did, he could understand why Billy wouldn't know exactly what Harry was talking about. Just as Tom now did.

"Spell it out for me word for word just as you heard it. What, from who, when, and how," Harry told Billy. "Don't leave out a single detail, not one smidge of a freakin' detail."

"Something tells me we are going to need more beers," Tom said as he got up and headed for the kitchen.

"Beers, we don't need more beers," Harry yelled at Tom's back. "We are gonna need a barrel of something much stronger than a few beers. You hear me, Tom? A barrel, maybe two…" Harry trailed off.

"Sit, Harry, sit," Billy urged Harry. "As I have tried to tell you many times before there is no such thing as *the normal* with Fetts. He will do the same thing, in the same situation, every time it happens until he decides to do something else. And don't think for a single second it's on a whim. If you think that then you have underestimated Fetts terribly and that's the formula for getting your head handed to you and your balls kicked in, all in one neat little package. Sit down and we can talk this through."

Harry refused to sit and continued to stalk around the living room looking for something to smash into smithereens. To say the least, Harry was beside himself.

"I'll stand if you don't mind," Harry told Billy just as Tom came back into the room and handed Harry another beer. He took a long pull on the beer and then said, "I'm calm. Look at me, I'm calm. Go ahead and tell it to me and Tom slowly and don't leave anything out."

Billy took the beer Tom was trying to get him to take and remained quiet for a full minute. He took a long pull on his beer just as Harry had done before him. He was now ready to spill the beans.

"As I said before, nobody ever knows for sure what Fetts is going to do. Follow the same pattern, deviate slightly from that pattern, or go off in a totally new direction he has never traveled down before. That's Fetts. That's his M.O. and he is famous for it. You can't pin him down or anticipate what you should do because you never know what he is going to do. It's probably what makes him so good at what he does and, trust me, he knows it.

"Tips called me and said there's scuttlebutt Fetts wasn't in Vegas. No big deal I thought because Fetts travels all the time whether it's for business or just to get out of town for a spell. He always told me "Static is bad, Billy, don't ever remain static" and he has kept to his word for as long as I've known him."

"So where did he go?" Harry asked Billy.

"That's the weird part. A guy that uses the warehouse and that we trust without question, told Tips he heard from a guy who's part of the "in crowd" in Vegas, who can usually be trusted, Fetts was headed East."

"East. Just east?" Harry asked.

"No, not just East," Billy answered. "East as in east coast and he thought it was somewhere in Pennsylvania."

"Why'd he think that?" Tom asked.

"Because his source at the airport said Fetts had boarded a plane headed for Philadelphia," Billy told them.

"Philadelphia? Why would he be going to Philadelphia? And why now? Why this close to the end game at Rich Valley?" Harry asked. "Has he ever been a part of the final operation before? And why's he travelling commercial? Big shot like him and he doesn't fly private?"

Billy cocked his head to one side, thought for a moment, then said, "Yes, I don't know, I don't know, I don't know, not that I'm aware of, he does long distance and private on shorter trips like to LA."

The look on Tom's face was priceless. If Billy had said. "Green grass grows faster than blue grass when it rains for three days straight," Tom would have understood it better.

Harry's face just showed quizzical in its broadest terms.

Before either of them could say anything, Billy added, "He wants to meet."

"He who? Fetts?" Harry asked.

"Yup," Billy confirmed.

"Meet who, why, when," Harry continued his pursuit.

"Jeff and Kurps I would guess. I'm not entirely sure who else, if anybody, and immediately from what I know," Billy answered.

Fully exasperated with all this, Harry said, "Fuck me."

Billy quickly dispelled that thought with a, "I don't think that is on Fetts itinerary for this trip."

"Fuck you," Harry threw at Billy.

"That neither," Billy replied.

"I'm going outside," Harry said and he left.

Not knowing what Harry's leaving meant, or what to do, Billy turned to Tom and said, "Do you think it was something I said?"

"Well yeah, you might be able to figure that from the conversation I just heard," Tom told Billy. "But don't take no heed from it. Harry gets himself all flustered and he just needs a spell of fresh air to cool his jets. Don't happen often, but when it does he needs it and it's best for everyone if he does it. He'll be right back pretty soon, I think."

"What do we do in the meantime?" Billy asked.

"I don't know about you but that last exchange and Harry's departure didn't hurt my thirst none. Another beer?"

"Might as well," Billy agreed as he followed Tom into the kitchen to do just that.

Chapter 121

Tom and Billy were sitting in the living room enjoying their beers when Harry returned from his "air trip" outside. He looked calmer, but not totally back to his normal Harry state.

As if nothing had interrupted their prior conversation, Harry looked at Billy and said, "What else do we know?"

"That's about it," Billy replied.

"So, what do we do now?" Tom asked.

"Now, we wait, I guess," Billy replied.

"For how long?" Tom asked.

As if on cue, Billy's cell phone rang. After looking to see who was calling him, he said, "Not that long I guess."

"Hello, Mr. Fetterman," Billy said into the phone.

Billy listened for a full minute before he said, "I think I can facilitate that. When would you like to meet with them?"

At that point Billy hit the speaker button on his phone while putting his finger to his lips indicating for Harry and Tom to remain silent. Fetts told them, "There's no hurry but we should probably get it over and done with. Day after tomorrow, ten am, the Rich Valley restaurant would be good."

"And who do you want there?" Billy asked him.

It didn't take long for him to answer. They heard him say, "I don't care how many of them losers you bring, but make sure the money man is there and his partner so I can tell them how this is going to go down and what will happen immediately afterward." With that Fetts disconnected the call.

As soon as Fetterman had hung up, Harry said, "Are you sure he's never done this before, Billy? You have been involved in a few of these golf course steals Fetts perpetrates. If he knows, or at least thinks he has it locked up, why meet? Why not come in, kick some ass, and walk away with all the money and the course. Why show himself and let everyone know who's behind it, especially when he has the big score coming up after this one if you have this pegged right. I don't get it,"

"I don't know, Harry," Billy told them. "As I have tried to tell you, Frankie is Frankie and you can never anticipate what he is going to do in any given situation. Maybe he wants to gloat for some reason. Maybe he wants to get involved personally since this is the dress rehearsal for the big one. Or, maybe he won't even show up to the meeting. Anything could happen when Fetts is involved."

"Well, shit on a shingle," Harry replied.

Billy looked at Tom as if to say, "What the hell does that mean?"

All Tom did was shrug his shoulders and take a slug of his beer.

Without waiting Harry said, "I'm going to call Jeff and get him and Kurps over to Nolo's now so we can plan this out. If Fetterman wants a meet, we give him a meet. But we orchestrate how it goes down and we don't give Fetts a chance to dictate terms and conditions and stick them right up our asses. We need to get aggressive and make sure we have the upper hand when this fuster cluck goes down. Agreed?"

"No," Billy told Harry.

Shocked. That is the only way to describe the look on Harry's face after Billy's one-word response.

Tom took another slug of his beer and waited for what was to come next.

Staring down Billy with a look that would scare the bejesus out of most people, Harry said, "No?"

"Yeah, no," Billy replied.

Trying to remain as calm as possible, Harry said, "Can you expound on that a small bit beyond *no*," Harry asked.

"Sure," Billy told Harry.

Harry waited but Billy didn't say anything else.

"Now," Harry said with a little more enthusiasm.

"Sure," Billy told them. "If you try and take the initiative Frankie will know something's up. He set this up. He took everyone's money and he knows he is holding all the cards. You try pushing him and he will turn around and say, screw you—gimme my money."

"So we just let him have his meet, have his way, and eat shit in any way he says," Harry asked.

"First off—this ain't a we, Harry. Fetts doesn't have me, or you, or Tom by the balls. He has Kurps and his guys, Jeff and his guys, and probably some guys we don't even know about. That's whose balls he's got. We don't get involved in this meeting and we don't direct the meeting. Fetts believes he has Jeff and Kurps' asses in a sling and that's who he expects to put in their places at the meeting. Scare the living piss out of them and tell them he is taking their golf course and they can't do shit about it. And listen carefully, Harry, they had better look scared. If they don't, Fetts walks out of that meeting and every IOU is called in and his guys can do it in spades if necessary."

"And us?" Harry asked.

"Us?" Billy asked.

"Yes, us, Billy. What do *us* do while all this is going down?"

"Us, Harry, us makes sure we get our part handled and I mean handled with no screw ups by anyone involved. Us? We save the day, Harry," Billy told him.

"True that, Billy," Harry replied. Turning to Tom, Harry said, "Well don't just stand there, get us some beers so we can think this thing out appropriately."

"Oh yeah, what are you gonna do in the meantime, hotshot?" Tom answered.

"Me, I'm going to call Jeff and start saving the day."

Chapter 122

Jeff was sitting at the bar with Nolo when Harry, Billy and Tom came into Nolo's. The rest of the bar was empty and would remain that way until at least eleven that morning. Jeff had made sure of that. What would happen the rest of the day would be decided once he met with Harry. All seemed to depend on Harry and the team he had assembled.

Nolo went around the bar and poured everyone a cup of coffee. There would be plenty of time later for beers—right now they needed to focus on what was before them and how to make everyone whole again.

"Where's Kurps? Harry asked Jeff.

"Well, I'm not exactly sure," Jeff told the group. "He said he would be here before nine but we haven't heard from him yet. Now that you are here I can give him a call and see what's up with him."

"Hold off on that for a bit," Harry told Jeff. "We want to make sure you are on board with what we discussed last night and you don't have any reservations on how it's going to go down. After all, the course is half yours and a good bit of the money that's owed comes from your guys here at the club. If you aren't one hundred percent comfortable with the plan, we have laid out you can still say no and let everyone else fend for themselves. Your piece of the actual lost/owed money is small compared to the group in total. We can probably manage some way to let you keep the course, but that means Kurps has to settle up as well as the rest of his high rollers. And your guys would have to pony up for your collective piece and that would mean some of them lose their companies, their homes and who knows what else."

"That's not how it was drawn up and what we had agreed to," Jeff told everyone. "Nolo has a say in it and my guys are important to me. Plus, Kurps did his part perfectly once we knew we, as a group, were in trouble and I'd never hang him out to dry. Never. He's my partner and always will be. He lost a bundle to these guys on purpose to help set up where we are today and I know for a fact it killed him to play the drunken asshole at the card game and lose all that money to the fucking professional card cheats Fetterman sent into our game. A friendly game we ran for years and Fetterman and his guys turned it into a mockery of everything we believe in here at Rich Valley."

Jeff stopped there and looked over at Nolo. "You think me and Nolo serving Kurps water instead of vodka at the poker game and taking all his shit came easy for me, for Nolo. One tiny slip up and the cat's out of the bag and we all go into the shitter. No, we all got ourselves into this mess and together we will fight our way out of it. We trust you, Harry, and your team as well. Billy here has to come through too and, if it all comes together like you told us it can, then we come out of it whole and as lucky as pigs in a whole pile of shit."

"Lot to lose if it doesn't come together the way we think," Tom told Jeff.

"I know that, but deserting my friends when they need me most would cost me a whole lot more. It would cost me everything," Jeff said for everyone there to hear. "Everything. You hear me, Tom, everything."

"Morning, boys," Kurps said to everyone in attendance as he entered the bar.

They turned in unison to see Kurps striding toward them, a wide smile on his face as always. His usual mondo cup of java looking small in his huge hand with seemingly not a care in the world as you looked at him. They all knew nothing could be further from the truth but that was Kurps.

"Nice of you to stop by, Kurps," Jeff said in greeting.

"Had a bit of free time and you know I'm always pleased to see my partner and his boys. And there's Nolo's food that keeps bringing me back time and time again. Wouldn't miss that for the world."

"Yeah, yeah…yada, yada," Jeff replied. "Grab a chair and let's get started on trying to figure out how we want this to go down. That is if we have any choice in the matter when it comes down to it. Harry and Billy have some new info and we need to figure out what it means."

"That right, Harry?" Kurps started. "And it's good to see you, Billy. I'm assuming you're one of the good guys playing on our team full time now?"

Billy wasn't sure if he should say anything in response or whether he should keep his mouth shut and let Harry carry the ball for the team to get things started. He teetered back and forth for fifteen seconds before he decided to say, "Might depend on how you hit 'em when the shit starts hitting the fan. A twenty buck Nassau is hefty money for some and they would shit themselves just thinking about it. Having to carry the load for every member of the group when there's close to a million bucks, probably much more when you consider the club's at stake too, plus people's livelihoods are on the line, it's a whole different thing all together."

Stunned silence would probably sum it up best. The bar was dead quiet and all eyes were now on the eighteen-year-old kid who could con your balls from between your legs without you knowing your nuts were gone.

Billy let them hang for a minute and then he smiled and said, "I'm just playing with you, Kurps. First off, I like you guys and what's happening to you is all wrong in so many ways. Second, me and Frankie have some unfinished business that needs to be settled. And third, nobody other than my parents, and I mean nobody, treated me like I was somebody and not just some punk kid hustler trying to con your ass but good until Harry came along. He's done right by me and I owe him more than I can ever repay him and his family, too. So yeah, you can count on me. I'm all in on this one and there's no way we are going to let Fetts and his boys take Rich Valley. That just ain't gonna happen. No way, no fucking how!"

Kurps looked Billy straight in the eye and said, "Do I need to check my back pocket to see if my wallet is still there?"

"Nah, you don't need to, Kurps," Billy told him. "But it is still early in the day."

Finally, there were some smiles evident in the room.

"So, tell me where we are," Kurps said to the group.

"All yours, Harry," Jeff told him.

"Alright, I'll get us started and everyone can jump in whenever you have something to add," Harry told them. "The plan hasn't changed much from when I first laid it out for all of you. My connections have confirmed everything that we need to fall into place has been arranged and the necessary back up will be here whenever it goes down. As Billy has said over and over again, Fetts is Fetts and you can never count on him doing what you expect him to do. That being said, my people, people I trust with my life, are ready for whatever goes down. As long as we all hold up our end we will come out on top and Fetts and his boys will be done, now and forever."

After hearing Harry deliver his spiel to the group, Kurps had that look in his eye Jeff knew very well. He had seen it before and knew not to question him when his mind was set and his vision was clear. Kurps was ready. Kurps was determined. Kurps was dead set on getting what he wanted, what he needed, what they all needed, and nobody, not Fetts, not his boys, nobody was going to get in his way.

"You feeling it, Kurps?" Jeff asked him.

Nodding his head, Kurps replied, "I'm more than feeling this one, Jeff. More than ever before, I'm feeling this one. And not just for me, and you, and everyone who has a stake in what happens. It's the principle and honor that's involved. Shouldn't happen like this—it just isn't right."

Heads were nodding all around the room and you could feel the "we got these assholes" vibe exuding from every one of them. All but one that is. Billy just sat back and took it all in. The extreme confidence. The bravado. The "we'll kick their asses right back to where they came from and show them they can't mess with us." Not in our town. Not on our course. Our turf. Our territory. Our home.

"Jon Francis Fetterman."

They all turned at once, frozen, and stared. Stared at the one who had uttered the words and waited for more. All a bit afraid at what might come next.

What they heard was more of the same; just "Jon Francis Fetterman."

They remained frozen in place, afraid to speak. Afraid of what they might hear in return. Afraid of what he knew, what he had experienced, what he had seen, what he had done. Afraid.

Finally, he spoke again.

"Jon Francis Fetterman, gentlemen. Las Vegas Jon Francis Fetterman. Not some hick from the sticks of Mechanicsburg,

Pennsylvania but Jon Francis Fetterman from where it all goes down, all day and all night. Every day, of every week, of every year. You can expect the unexpected and God help you if you don't. He is Fetts with all the world behind him and we ain't. As big as you think you are, you ain't, and he is. Bigger than you can possibly imagine and much, much more. He is FETTS!"

With that having been said, Billy walked around behind the bar and started pulling beers from the tap for everyone.

Chapter 123

The ability to launch a golf ball off a tee high and far is not a unique trait. Lots of guys, and gals for that matter, can step up to the golf ball, address the ball, maybe add a waggle or two, and send it off on its way to distances the average golfer can only dream of. It's a different game than the weekend duffer plays. But, and it's a mighty big but, being able to control how high it goes and how far it goes, moving it from right to left or left to right when the need arises with unending consistency, that is what separates the "can doers" from the "always does." With ease like they aren't even trying. Over and over again like clockwork.

The Player could do that and more, much more. All of it in fact. From tee to green he had all the shots and could manufacture a game most people don't even see as possible. A deft, soft touch around the greens and a pure putting stroke rounded out a game that every pro would give their right arm to possess. He was known as the Player to the few that knew of him, and he belonged to Fetts. The Player was his.

Growing up he wasn't the sharpest tool in the shed but he was no dummy by any stretch either. Book learning came hard for him, real hard. His parents worked a farm from sun up to sun down just like their parents had done before them. And their parents before them and before them and so on. They lived in the heartland of the country and there was no time for schooling when there was land and livestock to be tended to. An only kid doing the work of the brothers and sisters his parents could never have.

The coaches in the local school had seen him run and jump and knock other kids out of the way on the off days when he would hook up with his cousins to play in the monthly Sunday town games held on the high school grounds. If ever there was a natural born athlete, Healey was it. But the farm came first and last. Occasionally they would hold a long drive contest to show-case the kids on the high school golf team so the rest of the town could see why they were supporting their trips to play in tournaments around the state. Healey would utilize his free swinging "grip it and rip it" style and win by a country mile every time. And when the day was done he would go back to the farm and get back to his chores just like he did every other day of the month.

Until Fetts came into his life. The same Fetts who dropped five thousand dollars on his parent's dining room table and told them Healey was going to college. The same Fetts who paid Po-dunk Junior College to admit Healey to play golf for the coach he had personally selected for the job. The same Fetts who was told this kid had the game that few had and nobody knew anything about it. Not just the bomber who could hit it a mile. No, the kid who could hit it long and straight and do it with all the clubs in the bag. That is if he had a bag, which he didn't. But that is why he is Fetts and better at what he does than anybody else. He just knows that kind of stuff because he pays well to be told that kind of stuff.

It was now six years later and Healey was now The Player Jon Francis Fetterman used to close out his golf course steals. He counted on him to show up on the final day of the deal and destroy the other team with a game that could match up with most of the best on the PGA tour on any given day. There was only one small problem that got in the way on occasion. Healey learned how to win at golf while at the Community College and also how to be a college kid. The good and the bad, mostly the bad, when it came to being a college kid. It nearly killed him twice.

Fetts was watching him hone his game at an out-of-the-way range at some small golf course in Central Pennsylvania. He had two of his guys watching him day and night for the past two weeks to make sure his college educated ability to put away any type of booze in large quantities until he passed out was kept in check at least until he was done presenting Fetts with Rich Valley Golf Course on a silver platter. So far it was working.

"You good to go on this one, Healey?" Fetts asked him.

"Yeah, Boss, I'm cool," he replied.

"It's going down day after tomorrow and when it's done I'll put you up on the strip for the weekend and you can party until you drop. But, not one ounce of anything until you walk off the eighteenth green and I own that patch of land. You hear me, Healey?" Fetts told him with a bit more emphasis than was probably needed.

"Yeah, I hear you loud and clear, Frankie," Healey told him. "I'm clear on the when and the how is a piece of cake no matter who they throw out there. I played the course twice and I could handle them myself with no problem. Me and Billy will be done with them long before we get to the eighteenth green and you will have your crappy piece of land in wherever the hell it is. Summpin like Mechensburger or whatever it's called. And me, I get my share and then I go off for a while and have some fun, Player style like you know I can."

Fetts didn't like the attitude on this kid and would rattle his cage when need be if he went too far. But not when he was this close to closing out one of his deals, just like on this occasion. And he needed him for the big one that was right around the corner. After that he'd be done with him and he could go off to some dark place and drink his sorry ass to death if that's what he wanted to do with himself. For now, he was his and he was a very valuable commodity to have in his corner.

"Just be ready when I say so and everybody will get what they want, you included, kid," Frankie told him.

Healey gave Fetts the look he used when someone had pissed him off for no reason. He didn't like being called kid and not even Fetts should be doing that, not even now. But the money was more than he would ever see again in his lifetime and he liked having it more than anything else. Being called kid by Fetts was okay for now, but only until he got his piece of the big one that wasn't very far off.

"You bet, Boss, you bet," he answered him.

Fetts waved to his boys to come on back and resume their 24/7 watch on The Player. As he walked away he took out his cell and hit the speed dial number that would begin the process that would put the final play into motion. Rich Valley would be his before long.

Chapter 124

The boys had been in Nolo's for several hours now going over the plan that would free everyone from Fetts' grip and allow them to breathe easy for the first time in weeks. Kurps had lightened up the mood for a time replaying his drunken escapade at the Nolo's high stakes poker game where he had lost a bundle to Fetts' guys. They laughed long and hard at Kurps re-enactment and had applauded him on his stellar performance.

"None of us were sure you could pull it off," Jeff had said. "We had no idea you had the acting chops to give a performance like that."

Smiling broadly, Kurps had told them, "To tell you the truth, neither did I. I knew we had no choice and we had to put the number over the top to get the final act into play. But keeping it together for that long without falling out of the 'drunken asshole mode' was a lot harder than any of you knew. I may take the act to Broadway if we get our asses out of the sling we are now in."

"It was good, but not Broadway good," Billy told him.

"Yeah," Nolo chirped in. "I'd keep the day job if I was you."

"Well, it was good enough to convince them bozos and we got the job done. But we have one more job to do and we had better get that one right or we are all out of a job," Kurps told them. "And a lot more than only a job," he added.

Before anyone could respond, Billy's cell chirped and the room went instantly dead quiet. Nobody said a word and all eyes were on Billy. Billy just sat there like he didn't even hear his cell ringing.

"You gonna get that, Billy," Jeff asked him.

"Not yet," Billy replied.

"What if it's Fetterman?" Jeff asked.

Looking down at his cell, Billy casually said, "It is."

"Well?" Jeff replied for the group.

"Not yet," Billy told him as the cell went silent.

Not used to seeing Billy as he was being Billy, Kurps, took the lead and said, "This isn't the time to be playing games, now is it Billy?"

The only person in the room who knew what was going on was Harry. He knew for sure Billy wasn't playing any game and knew exactly what he was doing. He put up his hand and said, "Billy's got this. Let him handle it his way."

They all looked from Harry to Billy and then back at Harry. Before anyone could question what Harry had just said, Billy's cell rang again. After three rings, Billy answered it. Whoever was on the other end of the call was letting Billy know what he thought of the size of Billy's balls and that he didn't like being treated that way by anyone, let alone Billy.

Billy just sat there and listened to the person rant on.

When it got quiet, Billy said into the phone, "Sure, tomorrow at ten would be fine. Same place?"

After listening for another minute, Billy answered, "That works for us. Looking forward to seeing you again," as he disconnected the call. Billy placed his cell on the bar and picked up his now empty beer class. "I think I'll have another if you wouldn't mind, Nolo."

Not knowing what else to do, Nolo got Billy another beer.

Again taking lead for the group, Kurps said, "And?"

Billy sipped his new beer as if the question hadn't been directed at him.

Kurps waited a beat before he again said, "And?"

Looking up at Kurps, Billy replied, "The meet's still on for ten tomorrow morning. Fetts will call me at nine to tell me where and who should be there. He said he wasn't sure who he wanted to meet with now and he'd decide where overnight."

"That's it?" Jeff asked.

"Oh, he did say he was pretty sure he wanted the two soon-to-be ex-owners of Rich Valley to be there," Billy told him.

Kurps was nodding his head as he said, "Ten it is then. Let me know where," and he got up and left the bar.

"Man's kinda casual considering what you all have on the line; wouldn't you say?" Tom said.

"That's Kurps," Jeff replied. "Calm and casual on the outside no matter what's going down. On the inside, well, on the inside he wants to rip Mr. Fetterman's heart out and crush every last one of his posse. But that's what makes him Kurps, though, and we love him for it."

Nolo thought about it before he decided to add, "At least some of the time."

Jeff just smiled.

~ * ~

Harry, Tom and Billy were sitting out on Tom's deck enjoying a few cool ones while they tried to think of what Fetts could do to screw up their well laid out plan to rescue Rich Valley and everyone else who had an interest in getting whole again. Most of what they tossed about was rejected as too far out there even for Fetts, but a few resonated as distinct possibilities.

"And if Fetts doesn't bring this "Player" guy as his top gun, then who?" Harry asked.

Billy had considered this one before, several times before in fact, but he just couldn't see it happening. The Player was too good and he could eat up Rich Valley on his worst day. Turning toward Harry he said, "I still can't see Frankie bypassing him for someone else. I've seen all his hidden sources and when it comes to golf The Player is it, hands down, not even in the same state, never mind ballpark."

"And the last time you saw the full corral of resources Fetts has at his beckon call was when, Billy?" Harry asked him.

Billy's face got that "good point" look and he sat back in his chair. After considering Harry's question for too long, Billy replied, "Well, it's been too long I guess."

"So there could be another guy ready to eat our lunch and we wouldn't know it, would we?" Harry continued.

"Yup," was all Billy said in reply.

"And you can't take him one-on-one?" Harry queried.

Billy told them, "Straight up, both of us sober as a judge, on my best day, not even a small chance."

"Really?" Tom asked.

"Really times infinity," Billy qualified. "Not a chance in hell."

"Well sheeeeeeeeet," Tom drawled.

"Forget that," Harry stopped them. "Our plan doesn't call for Billy to kick The Player's ass or anybody's ass single handed. Our plan kicks their team's ass and Fetts' ass right along with them. Eighteen holes and we win any way we have to. Rich Valley stays in Jeff and Kurps' hands and all of Jeff's and Kurps' guys get whole again. Well, mostly whole. I'm still not sure we can recover the money that has already passed hands on the golf course, but we are going to give it the old college try."

"Hey, Billy, let me ask you a question," Tom asked. "I've seen you draw the ball and fade the ball on command. When you say go left five yards, it goes left five yards. When you say hey, yo ball, go five yards right, it goes five yards right. But can you actually hook it and slice it like the rest of us do on command? I'm talking one fairway over either direction or dump it in a trap like you walked over and dropped it in?"

"Interesting question, Tom," Billy replied. "Most people don't try and do those things you know. On purpose I mean. But to answer your question, we will find out real soon, won't we."

"Then let me ask you another question. When's the last time somebody told you to fuck off on purpose?" Tom asked Billy.

"If I got this one right it was just now," Billy answered.

"That would be absolutely correct, Billy my boy," Tom said with a smile.

"Are you two about done now?" Harry asked them.

"I would guess so," Tom told Harry.

"Then if you don't mind can we finish what we were discussing so we can head on over to Nolo's and get some grub? We haven't eaten since that crappy breakfast we had this morning and I'm starving," Harry told them.

"Sure, Harry," Tom told him. "And by the way, you can get awful grumpy when your poor little tummy says it's time to feed me."

"When's the last time somebody told you to fuck off on purpose, Tom?" Harry asked him.

"Um, just now?" Tom answered.

"Correct. Let's get out of here and feed my hungry little tummy."

Chapter 125

Breakfast was ancient history and their third cups of coffee were getting cold waiting for Billy's cell phone to make some noise. It had rung ten minutes earlier and they had all jumped out of their seats anticipating that was the call they had been waiting for. Billy had listened for a full two minutes without speaking before he turned to Harry and said, "Wrong number."

"Remind me to kick your ass but good when we are done with this thing," Harry told him.

Finally, it came. Exactly at nine as Fetts had said.

Billy answered on the fifth ring which surprised Harry. He had expected him to let it ring out and wait for the recall like he always did when Fetts called. They went back and forth, Billy saying very little when he did speak, and then the call was done.

"So?" Tom asked.

"So, Fetts wants to see Jeff and Kurps and their lawyer at ten just like he said. Just as unpredictable, he said Nolo's would be fine," Billy told them.

"On their turf?" Harry replied. "I never would have guessed that would be the meeting place. I was sure he would flip-flop and pick a place much more to his advantage."

"Me neither," Billy agreed. "But, as I have said over, and over, and over again—that's Jon Francis Fetterman being Fetts. You just never know what the hell he is going to do."

"Nobody else?" Tom asked.

"Nope. Jeff, Kurps and their mouthpiece as Fetts called him. He said the rest of them don't matter."

"The damage has already been done. Fetts has their money and their IOU's and to him he doesn't need them anymore. They fulfilled their piece of this puzzle for him and now it's up to Jeff and Kurps to do the rest," Harry said.

"And Billy," Tom reminded them.

"Yeah, and little Billy Burns now all growed up," Harry agreed.

"Well, you better get on the horn and tell Jeff and Kurps to get their mouthpiece on his horse and hightail it over to Nolo's. We don't want Fetterman hanging around waiting for him when he already told us he wanted him there," Tom told Harry.

"I'm going to do that right now, Tom. And by the way, you calling the shots on this deal now?" Harry threw back at Tom.

"Just being my useful, helpful self," Tom replied with a wide smile

Even Billy laughed at that one.

Harry dialed Rich Valley and was transferred up to Nolo's. He got Jeff right away. He relayed Fetts' instructions and told him to get his lawyer on the phone and have him at Nolo's before ten.

"He already knows about it and he's just waiting for my call. He doesn't know why he has to be someplace at ten, but he knows he has to be there. Here. Someplace. Shit, I don't even know what the hell I'm saying now."

"Jeff, calm down and take a few breaths. We have been over this and we have a plan in place to get you and everyone else out of this mess. It will work and you and everyone else will be breathing much easier come late tomorrow afternoon," Harry told him.

Harry could hear Jeff taking a few deep breaths just as he suggested. Unfortunately, they didn't achieve the desired result Harry was hoping for. When Jeff spoke again it was obvious he wasn't calmed down.

"Harry, Harry, you still there, Harry?"

"I'm here, Jeff."

"You didn't say anything so I thought you bagged off."

"And what, I took my toys and went out into the yard to play? Jeff, get your shit together or Fetts will eat you alive before you even get a chance to go out onto the course tomorrow. He's a master and he'll get inside your head and have you handing him the keys to Rich Valley on a silver platter. Is that what you want, Jeff? Well is it?"

Harry could hear Jeff take a long slow breath before he said, "No, Harry, that isn't what I want and you know it. There is too much on the line and we're dealing with pros that steal shit for a living. I run a golf course and play golf for fun, Harry. Kurps plays life for fun. I don't play for my golf course and other peoples' livelihoods. And their families, too. It's a shitload to handle, Harry."

Two beats and Harry said, "I know it is Jeff and lord knows you didn't ask to be put in this spot. But you're in it and I'm here and the team behind me, who are the best in the world at what they do, are here, we are all here for you, Jeff. Don't you forget that and know we won't let you or Kurps or the team at Rich Valley or all the rest of the guys involved down. Hear me, Jeff, we got them right where we want them and tomorrow we are going to show them who's boss around these here parts."

"I hear you Harry and I sure as hell hope you are right."

~ * ~

The 2009 Honda Civic turned into the Rich Valley Golf Course entry road, proceeded down the hill and into the parking lot. It moved to the back of the lot, parked, and the ignition was shut off. Nobody got out, nobody did anything. The car just sat there for ten minutes with no signs of movement.

It was now ten minutes past ten.

Jeff saw the guy come into Nolo's and wondered how the hell he got in. The door was locked and only he, Kurps and their lawyer were in the building. When he took out a wand and starting moving around Nolo's waving the wand back and forth, Jeff knew what was up. The asshole was checking the place for bugs.

"Who are you?" Jeff asked him.

"Don't matter who I am, buddy. I'll be done in two minutes and I'm out of here. All yous just sit tight and stay out of my way, you hear me?" he told Jeff.

Nobody said a word in reply.

Two minutes later the guy was done with what he came in to do. He took out his cell and hit a button. When the party he had called came on the line he said, "It's clean," and then he hung up and left. Immediately the car in the back of the parking lot started up and headed back to the exit road that would take them out of the Rich Valley grounds. But before the car left the grounds it made a right into the small parking lot that fronted Nolo's Bar and Restaurant. The car stopped as close to the door as possible and shut down. It was now time.

Fetts waited for the driver to open his door before he got out and headed for the entrance to Nolo's. His lawyer got out of the

309

car from the other side and followed him into the building. The guy who wanded the place was waiting just outside the entrance and followed both of them in. He was obviously the designated muscle as well.

The driver stood at the entrance to Nolo's and you could bet any amount of money nobody was getting into Nolo's without his say so.

Fetts stopped just inside the doorway to the bar and took stock of what he saw. Mostly he was looking for what he didn't want to see and was satisfied he could proceed with the meeting.

Jeff took the initiative and stood to greet Fetts.

"Sit down, Jeff" Fetts told him. "We ain't here for no fun and games so let's dispense with the pleasantries and get down to business." Pointing to Jeff and Kurp's lawyer, Fetts said, "Him I don't know so that must be your lawyer. Kurps over there I recognize."

Kurps still hadn't moved a muscle or said a word.

"Let's get started," Fetts said as he took a seat at the table. His lawyer stood behind him and he also hadn't said a word as of yet.

"Here's how this is going to go down. Don't try and argue with me or tell me what you want should happen, it isn't, so don't waste my time. You understand?"

Jeff didn't know whether to answer or not so he remained quiet. Kurps didn't move a muscle or say a word. He just continued to stare directly at Fetterman.

Fetts looked at his lawyer and nodded. With that, his lawyer spoke.

"The total amount of money that has already changed hands plus what is owed to my client via IOU's by all parties concerned comes to a total of seven hundred twenty-three thousand, four hundred seventy-three dollars. That includes all accumulated interest on the outstanding debt."

Jeff and Kurps looked at each other in amazement. Once his amazement had ceased slightly to the point where he could speak, Jeff said, "Interest?"

Fetts' still unnamed lawyer answered, "Mr. Fetterman's schedule for interest on outstanding funds is in line with the going rate within the Las Vegas community. If those involved did not inquire as to the specifics of said schedule that is not Mr. Fetterman's concern."

Jeff was about to say something when Fetts put up his hand and said, "Don't bother. In all we are talking seven hundred large and then some. Your little club here might arguably be worth more, but that don't mean shit right now. I get my money today or the club's your collateral for the whole tab. What's it going to be?"

When no response was forthcoming, Fetts continued.

"Yeah, that's what I thought. So, here are my terms:

One: The total amount including money already changed hands plus IOU's against Rich Valley Golf Course and everything included—restaurant, land and anything else connected is part of the deal.

Two: A contest of one round of golf—eighteen holes—to be played here at your home course. Two players on each team, best ball of team on each hole, match play scoring for eighteen holes wins. You and Kurps over there against my two guys.

Three: Everybody walks, no riding in a cart, you provide the caddies for your team if you want them. I provide caddies for my guys. One cart will travel along for the refreshments which I will provide for all players, caddies, etc.

Four: You designate one person to serve as score person and I will be the score person for my team. We agree on low score for each team after each hole is completed.

Five: At the end of eighteen holes we meet right back here in this room, at this table. Empty the bar and restaurant—you make it happen.

Six: My guy will have two sets of papers—a cashier check for the seven hundred plus g's and a letter you and your lawyer sign saying you got the check and all IOU's are voided. The second set will transfer Rich Valley to my company and you will vacate the premises. It's mine as of then if I win.

Seven: Last point: you try and play any games, anything at all, and the deal is off. I walk plain and simple. Then the IOU's are due and I collect any way I have to."

When Fetts was done nobody said a word. The silence in the room was deafening. Fetts' lawyer finally broke the quiet and said, "Any questions, gentlemen?"

When Jeff and Kurps remained silent for a full minute. Fetts stood and said, "Good. See you guys tomorrow. Please sweep up my place if you get a chance tonight, will ya."

With that Fetts turned and left the bar. His lawyer trailed behind him followed by the muscle.

When they were gone, Kurps said, "Call Harry and get him over here. Tell him it's on and we need to get our shit in order so we can destroy that fucker but good."

Chapter 126

Mr. M. Randle Trundle was not normally one to frequent small town bar/restaurants attached to rural semi-private golf courses. Trundle Industries has a Sports and Recreation Division that included in its portfolio of holdings several major golf courses and numerous slightly lesser known tracks in which they are either full owners or partial owners. Rich Valley Golf Course was not a part of their portfolio.

Never say never when it came to what Mr. M. Randle Trundle would, or would not, do on any given occasion.

On this given night Randle found himself sitting in a side room at Nolo's preparing to kick some ass. Well, not him exactly, but as part of the Harry Mickey Shorts team that was going to take down Jon Francis Fetterman and save the day. Randle would have helped Harry in any way he could just because Harry asked him. Harry actually worked for Trundle but that's another story for an earlier book. No, someone pissed Trundle off. Someone pissed Trundle off beyond where he couldn't look the other way and chalk it up to blind stupidity. That someone was Fetts and he had stepped in the biggest shitpile of his entire life.

You see Fetts didn't know cardinal rule number one—don't fuck with M. Randle Trundle. He had and now he had to pay.

Nolo came up to the table and asked Trundle if he could get him anything else right then. Having been told by Harry how good the food was at Nolo's, Randle exaggerated a bit and said, "Harry's been bragging to me about how good your food is here at Nolo's so I probably should find out for myself. We may be here awhile so why don't you bring out whatever you think we would enjoy and we'll see for ourselves. That okay with you guys?"

Oh yeahs from everyone at the table sealed the deal and Nolo went off to put together a feast for the CEO of Trundle Industries...and his friends. But mostly for Trundle.

"So, we have a plan to stop this bullshit Fetterman and his guys have been perpetrating on you and your buddy? Harry, were there any surprises at the meet this morning?"

Harry didn't want to take lead on this since he really didn't have a dog in the fight, but Trundle was his guy and he figured he could get it started and then let everyone jump in when they could. He wanted Jeff and Kurps to be exposed to Trundle since you never knew what might come down the road in the future.

"From what Jeff told us there weren't any real surprises at the meeting. If anything, I guess it was the finality of how it is supposed to end. Somebody wins and they either get all their money back or they lose and no money is returned and the golf course and everything that comes with it belongs to Fetts. We really didn't expect him to return the non-IOU money," Harry told Trundle. "All in, one match on one day, and it's over—good or bad."

"Interesting," Trundle commented. "And the game itself, the rules, the set-up, no surprises there?" he asked.

Jeff took that one and replied, "It was pretty cut and dried. Just as Billy described it beforehand is how Fetts laid it out for us. Two of us against two of them and eighteen holes later, or sooner, somebody wins."

Just as Jeff finished Nolo came up to the table with several plates of what looked like appetizers to Trundle. Nolo explained what he had brought and told them Mitzi would be right out with several plates of entrees for them to start on.

"Family style sharing if that is okay with you, Mr. Trundle?" Nolo asked him.

"Nolo, it's Randle, not Mr. Trundle. The Mr. is for business; Randle is what my friends call me."

"Yes sir, Randle," Nolo replied. "Another Magic Hat #9 for you?"

"Sure. This isn't a bad beer. And if Harry likes it, it can't be all bad, can it now?"

A few laughs at Harry's expense was a good interjection right about then.

Trundle looked at Jeff and Kurps and asked, "Are the two of you comfortable with the way this is going to go down? I've never seen either of you play but I understand you both can play fairly well."

Jeff let Kurps take that one and sat back to listen to what he had to say. Of the two of them he was probably the better player and much more of his money was tied up in the club, so Jeff though he deserved to answer for the both of them.

Kurps cleared his throat and said, "Comfortable, no I wouldn't say comfortable would be the word to describe how Jeff and I are feeling about tomorrow. Or this whole thing to tell you the truth, Randle. We can both handle ourselves out there on the course, but this is for our business and a hell of a lot of money; both ours and that of our friends. Plus, we've never seen who we will be playing against and that is never a good idea when money is at stake. Two bucks or a million. We are counting on Billy to help us out and from what Harry has indicated, you have a hand in how this may turn out as well. That's a lot of maybes that need to come out our way for this "thing" to turn out as we want. No, make that the way we need it to."

Trundle listened to what Kurps said intently. He turned to Jeff and asked, "Do you have anything to add to what Kurps just said?"

Jeff thought for a bit, shook his head no and said, "No, I don't think so. Kurps summed it up pretty well and we both feel confident in what we can do. Having the rest of it out of our control is surely not comfortable by any stretch. We don't have any choice but to rely on Billy's help, and your help, Mr. Trundle. We haven't known Harry very long but we've known Tom for ages and he vouches for Harry one hundred percent. That's good enough for me."

Randle took it all in and sat for a minute. Turning toward Billy, he said, "We got this, Billy?"

Billy smiled that "little Billy Burns" con artist smile of his and said, "With you and your team on our side how can we lose, Mr. Trundle."

Flashing the "I Never Lose" M. Randle Trundle smile, he replied, "You got dat right, Billy. We got these succas!"

Mitzi appeared at the table with a boat-load of food and the pre-victory feast began in earnest.

Chapter 127

It was a long night for all parties involved. Harry, Tom and Billy hunkered down at Tom's house trying to make sure they hadn't missed anything while also running different alternative scenarios around and around to see if any of them seemed plausible. As Billy had continually drummed into their thick sculls, he is Fetts and there is no normal when it comes to Fetts. Once they decided they had planned for everything they could realistically envision happening, they ceased making themselves crazier and relaxed with a few cool ones.

Jeff called them multiple times doing exactly the same thing. "Did we forget anything? Are your guys ready? What didn't we think of? My guys are shitting bricks and I can't tell them what's going down or they will string me up from the nearest tree. And Kurps, where's Kurps, have you heard from Kurps, where is he? I got three calls asking me the same thing—where is Kurps and what is he doing? Me, personally, I'm not worried about Kurps in the least bit. He can flash that "I'm Kurps" bravado shit all he wants, but when it counts, I'd bet my life on him every day of the week. Outside versus inside is a totally different ballgame with Kurps. His priorities are family and friends first, and last, and you had better not get in the way of that or you will have the fight of your life on your hands. Kurps, he'll be there tomorrow and kick some ass—and there will be no taking names necessary, either."

In answer to all of Jeff's panicked questions all Harry could say was relax, we are going to come out of this just fine. We have a great plan and the best people in the world helping us get through this. If only he could convince himself they would. Finally, at a bit past eleven, they said good night and hit the sack. Sleep was hard to come by even though Harry didn't have one single dime at stake in the whole fucking mess. He couldn't even imagine what the rest of them were going through. Harry had his own struggles throughout has checkered past, but losing businesses, homes and possibly families trumped anything he had been through. Well, except for his own immediate family but that's for

316

another day, another time.

Harry must have dosed off eventually and was awakened when somebody, namely Tom, came into his room and yelled, "Wake the hell up you asshole. We got shit to do and people to save and you're sacked out like you ain't got a care in the world. And where is that son-of-a-bitch Billy? He better not be screwing us or I will personally track him down and skin him alive. Get the hell up, Harry."

Shaking himself awake, Harry said, "Huh?"

When he realized Tom had already left the room, it hit him—"…where is that son-of-a-bitch Billy?" Had Tom actually said those words? If he had, well then holy shit is what Harry thought of that. He better get up and find out what the hell was going on. He threw on some clothes and hurried into the kitchen to find Tom at the stove scrambling up eggs while bacon sizzled in the pan next to him.

"What the hell do you mean 'where is that son-of-a-bitch Billy?'" Harry asked him. "Isn't he here?"

"If he was here why would I ask you where the son of a bitch is?" Tom answered him.

"Shit," was all Harry said in return.

"Yeah, shit it right. You better call that kid and find out where he is. Right now, Harry, call him right this fucking now," Tom replied.

Before Harry could get out his cell the front door opened and in walked Billy. "Morning, Harry. Morning, Tom," was all Billy said as he walked over to the fridge and got out the orange juice container.

Trying to act as calm as he could, Harry said, "Morning there, Billy. Tom was just wondering where you had gone to when he didn't find you in the house when he got up."

"Out," was all Billy said as he walked over to the kitchen cabinet and got out a glass for his orange juice.

"Out?" Tom repeated slightly less calmly then when Harry had addressed Billy just before.

"Yeah, I went out for a walk," Billy told them. "I couldn't sleep so I decided to take a little walk and get my head ready for today. I feel great and ready to go now!"

Tom turned off the burners on the stove and turned around

to face Harry and Billy. Again, speaking as calmly as was possible for Tom to do at that moment, he said, "Oh, you decided to take a little walk and get your head ready for today. You feel great and ready to go now. I'm here having a freaking panic attack with my head ready to explode thinking you did the adios and left us to clean up after you when you didn't have the balls to go through with the plan. The freaking plan that has you as the key ingredient to make it work. To save my friends, and Rich Valley, and Jeff and Kurps and every other god damn thing tied to this god damn freaking mess of a, of a, of a thing. A walk. I'll be damned."

Tom turned around and started cooking breakfast again. His breathing was to say the least a tad less than steady right about then.

"I like my bacon on the fatty side," Billy said to nobody in particular.

Tom just sighed.

Harry smiled.

And Billy, well Billy headed for the back of the house singing a very respectable version of Van Morrison's mega-hit Moon-dance. Harry was definitely rubbing off on the kid.

~ * ~

Harry and Tom were waiting for Billy out by the car when he emerged from the house. When Tom saw him he took a quick double take before he said, "Harry, what the hell is the kid doing? Has he gone completely off the deep end, or what?"

"I'm thinking 'or what'," was what Harry said in reply.

Not knowing what else to say, Harry asked, "What the hell is it you are doing, Billy? Have you gone completely off the deep end, or what?"

Stopping short after hearing what Harry had said, Billy replied, "What are you talking about?"

"First you take a walk and we don't know where you are. And now, now you come out looking like that," Harry told him.

"Like what?"

"Like that," Harry said pointing to what Billy had on. "Cutoff jeans, a ratty old golf shirt that's at least one size too big, and those socks. What the hell is up with those socks?"

Billy smiled as big a smile as was humanly possible. Obviously feeling quite proud of himself, he replied, "Pretty neat outfit wouldn't you say? Do I look like a piece of crap, good-for-nothin' kid who couldn't hit a golf ball with a telephone pole never mind a gold club? Oh, and the socks, I've had these forever. They're the sock my parents had me wear when they took me on a job so I'd catch everybody's eye as they pulled off whatever con they were doing at that time. They were huge then and they are still big on me now. I refer to then as my Pistol Pete socks."

"Maravich?" Harry asked.

"You got it, Harry. He wore the same kind of floppy socks, same look when he played in college and the pros. Pretty cool, huh?"

"And why today?" Harry asked.

"It's the outfit I wore for all the jobs I did with Fetts. He wanted me to look like a range rat and not a plus two golf hustler when we applied the finishing punch and stole the clubs."

"You're a plus two handicap you little lying bastard?" Tom spat at Billy.

"Only right handed," Billy clarified for him.

"Well I'll be a…" Tom started to say before Harry cut him off.

"Yeah, you are that and much more, Tom. Let's get in the car and get over to Rich Valley so we can get set up before Fetterman and his guys show up. I have to meet with my team and lock everything down as well. We good to go?"

"I'm all set," Billy told him.

"God help us if he can," Tom said as he got in the car.

Chapter 128

There was still an hour before the match was to begin and Harry and his team were holed up in a closed off section of No-lo's going over what was to be done item by item. Trundle was not there mainly because he didn't have to be there. Yes, he was the main driver behind this portion of the plan. And yes, it was his guys who would make sure the plan came off without a hitch. But now it was time for other individuals to do their jobs and help ensure *the plan* worked and Rich Valley was saved.

"Why is he doing this?" one of the team members asked Harry.

"Who, Trundle?" Harry asked in return.

"Yeah, Trundle. Why is he so interested in this Rich Valley Golf Club and a bunch of guys from Central Pennsylvania?"

Harry thought about what to say and how much he could divulge before he replied, "Two reasons. The first one is because I asked him to after I explained what was going on and what had happened. The second reason is personal to Randle. It seems Mr. Fetterman has made the worst mistake of his entire life and will have to pay for it with everything he has to his name and then some. The golf club Fetts has his eyes set on as the last piece to his master plan will turn out to be the death of him. A corporation that has a very minor interest in that club became aware of some unusual interest in the club and began to make inquiries. The long and short of it, Trundle Industries is that corporation and the club happens to be one of Trundle's favorite places to play eighteen when he can find time to do so. And those times are rare. Someone trying to take that away from him is both a professional and personal affront to the man. That is the worst thing anyone could possibly do to M. Randle Trundle. As a result, Fetts will have to pay dearly for doing so."

"And for that reason he has assembled the accumulation of what waits here for Fetts and his boys today?"

"No, actually the main reason is because it is a favor to me and also something he will enjoy watching go down. He does enjoy a well thought out and executed piece of revenge," Harry said to the group.

Nobody said a word in reply.

"So, are we ready?"

Ten people nodded their heads affirmatively in unison which was all Harry needed to see. He looked directly at Mueller and asked, "As the designated caddy for Kurps may I assume you and your guys are ready for anything that may go down?"

"Harry, me and my guys would like nothing better than for something, anything, to go down. You don't have to worry for one second about me and my guys. A word to the wise though—if it does go down you had best head for cover and quickly if you know what's good for you," Mueller assured Harry.

"Mueller, a G-Man don't have to tell me twice to head for the hills if the fur were to start to fly," Harry told him.

"Who's driving the refreshment cart?" Harry asked.

The cute blond in the back spoke up and said, "That would be me, Mr. Shorts. I have everything under control and don't you worry, I'll be packing a lot more than refreshments in my cart."

"I bet you will," Harry told her.

"Anybody have any questions?"

"I do have one question," the big Irish looking guy in the back asked.

"Yes," Harry queried.

"Once we take down these assholes will Nolo's be open for a victory celebration?"

"You bet your collective asses it will!"

~ * ~

There were only a handful of golfers on the practice range hitting balls when Harry got downstairs to check on the course-side preparations for the match. Jeff and Kurps were there with two of their guys to make it look like all was normal. Jeff had made sure to put the word out to the regulars to stay clear of the course for the day. The course wasn't closed, but someone was up at the top of the driveway quietly urging anyone who came that way to come back tomorrow if they wouldn't mind. The website had a "Nolo's is closed for the day" message posted.

Billy and a few of Jeff's guys were on the putting green looking like they were just wasting time honing their short games. The grounds crew was busy doing what grounds crews do, but it was a well-orchestrated routine thanks to Jeff's coaching the day before.

All was ready for their arrival.

At nine forty-five a three car caravan came down the hill and parked in the middle of the parking lot. For a full five minutes no one exited the cars. Finally, the driver went around and opened the rear passenger door and Fetts emerged. Simultaneously another individual exited the car from the rear driver's side door giving Harry and the rest of those in attendance their first look at Fetterman's main guy—The Player.

Billy looked up, saw him, and went back to missing putts one putt after another. Left handed.

Having seen the entourage enter the parking lot, Jeff and Kurps hit a few more balls then gathered up their clubs. They slowly made their way toward the first tee to begin what was to be the most important round of golf they would ever play in their lives, bar none.

As they walked, Jeff turned toward Kurps and said, "You nervous?"

"We're gonna play a friendly round of golf—what's to be nervous about. We've done this before, haven't we, Jeff?" Kurps told him.

"I guess you are right, Kurps. Maybe a little more on the line than a twenty dollar Nassau, but all we have to do is play golf the way we can and hope for a little help from Harry's team should we need it," Jeff told Kurps.

Kurps smiled at Jeff and said, "All we can do is take care of ourselves, Jeff. The other guys are going to do the same thing and somebody has to win. We play good and together with the other shit that is supposed to be in play we walk away with all of us whole again. You, me, our Rich Valley family and all of our friends. We are going to kick their collective asses today. You ready for a good old fashion ass kicking, Jeff?"

Now it was Jeff's turn to smile. After a quick peek back at The Player, Jeff said, "Like you never saw before, Kurps. Like you never saw before!"

~ * ~

Mueller and Nolo were waiting at the first tee quietly chatting between themselves when Jeff and Kurps got there. They all looked at each other not exactly sure what they were supposed to do. Thirty seconds later Harry appeared on the apron in front of the pro shop and walked over to where they were standing.

"Morning, gents," Harry said in greeting. "We all ready to go?"

"Not to ask a stupid question, but what do we do now?" Kurps asked.

"It seems Fetts is having a heated discussion with one of his guys and I'm pretty sure it involves someone not being here on time. The Player is here but Fetts' number two player isn't," Harry told them.

"Just as we expected?" Jeff asked.

"Just as we expected?" Harry confirmed.

"You set, Mueller?" Harry asked him.

"We are ready, Harry," Mueller answered. "Jeff, Kurps and Nolo can handle the golf part of the plan and I've got everything else covered. If you guys see anything at all starting to go down, you hit the ground and stay down until I tell you to get up. We should have smooth sailing all the way through if everything goes as expected; but, as Billy said yesterday, Fetts is Fetts. First, don't worry—we will have enough fire power scattered around to take care of business no matter what happens."

Just as Mueller finished, Fetts and his entourage were approaching the first tee still deep in discussion. As they got there Fetts' lawyer separated from the group and headed for the pro shop entrance.

Without as much as a good morning or a how-do-ya-do, a mighty pissed off looking Fetts said, "We got a problem here. One of my guys isn't here and he isn't coming. We will have to forget it for today and try again tomorrow."

Right on cue, Harry said, "I believe the rules were set by you and today, now, is when the match was to take place. The fact you don't have a full team isn't our problem. You have other guys here, let one of them take the place of your missing second."

"They're here to caddy not play no fucking golf. And who made you their mouthpiece anyway?" Fetts replied.

Pointing toward Jeff and Kurps, Harry said, "They did. The

match is set for now, ten am today, and the match will be played as scheduled. If you can't, or you don't want to field a team, the match will be forfeited and you will lose. Everything will be returned to Jeff and his people and all IOU's will be null and void. Their attorney is waiting up in Nolo's and will finalize the details with your "mouthpiece" as you call him."

As the now stocked beverage cart pulled up to the first tee, Fetts said, "Gimme a minute," and walked away with his boys.

With just the hint of a smile starting to form on his face, Harry said, "I do love when a plan comes together just as you expect it to."

Chapter 129

After a five-minute verbal explosion of Las Vegas rage directed at his entourage, Fetts stormed back to the first tee with fire in his eyes and steam coming out of his ears. Well, maybe the "steam coming out of his ears" quip might have been a slight exaggeration.

Pointing at Harry, Fetts spat, "You! Are you still in charge of this clusterfuck?"

Looking slightly taken aback at Fetts crudeness, Harry answered, "Yes, I continue to represent the Rich Valley interests for the time being. And if I may, what clusterfuck is it you are referring to?"

The fire intensifying in his eyes, Fetts said, "Don't play with me whatever your name is. Don't you dare play with me! Do you have any idea who I am?"

Smiling broadly now, Harry replied, "Well yes, I surely do. You are Fetts. Jon Francis Fetterman. Frankie. And, you're the guy who is going to lose today and return the money you have cheated Jeff, Kurps and the rest of their friends out of. I know exactly who you are."

Fetts took one step toward Harry before one of his boys stopped him from going any closer.

As a calmness seeming to take over, Fetts said, "My guy can kick both of these losers' asses all by himself all day long. We don't need no second to **WIN** this match and take this piddly little excuse for a golf course right away from them. But, just to make the teams even, I'll pick somebody that's here and name him my second."

Harry was about to object when Kurps put up his hand and said, "Hold on, Harry. The man is entitled to a second, so let him choose somebody to fill out the teams."

Fetts smiled the look of a winner and said, "I'll take that kid over there," pointing to Billy standing around on the putting green.

"Him?" Jeff said in mock amazement.

"Yeah, him. I'll take him," Fetts replied.

"The kid with the socks and the, ah, whatever the hell he's wearing?" Harry said in exaggerated shock.

"Yup," Fetts replied. "The kid and my Player are gonna whip your asses so bad you're gonna cry uncle before we even get fifteen holes in. But to ease the pain I brought along plenty of Coronas for you to drown your sorrows, Kurps. That is your beer of choice, right, Kurps."

"Yes, it is," Kurps confirmed.

"Sorry, Jeff, you'll just have to endure some of his Corona to cry into," Fetts told him. "My guys are going to enjoy some of your local Yuengling brew during their victory parade around **MY** course."

"Give me us a couple of those Coronas and let's quit the bullshitting and get this thing started," Kurps said. He threw a tee up in the air and it came down pointing at Jeff. "Looks like we're up."

Billy had made his way over from the putting green and was introduced to everyone who would be participating in the match. Fetts explained what was going on and Billy immediately tried to bow out, wanting no part of what the match meant. Fetts quickly informed him that choice wasn't available if he knew what was good for him.

"Joey there is gonna caddy for you, Billy. He's got your clubs and anything else you will need," Fetts told him.

"But those are right handed clubs," Kurps pointed out. "I played with the kid before and he's a lefty swinger."

"Not today he ain't," Fetts answered as he slapped Billy on the back and said, "Go get 'em kid."

On hearing what Fetts had just said, Jeff shook his head and said, "Oh, shit, we've been had, Kurps." Pointing to the blond driving the beverage cart, Kurps said, "If we are gonna get our asses handed to us today, give these two guys a coupla Yuenglings so we can all have some fun out here."

She did and the match was on.

Harry stepped up and said, "To make it official, I'm going to throw a tee up to see which team will be up first. You have any objections, Mr. Fetterman, on behalf of your team that is?"

Still feigning intense hatred for Harry and everything that was

Rich Valley, Fetts replied, "No, be my guest. Won't make a damn bit of difference who hits first on the first tee cuz my guys will own the tee from here on in."

Harry turned and tossed a tee in the air. It pointed at Jeff; he and Kurps would have the honor on hole #1. Pointing at Jeff and Kurps, he said, "You have the tee, gentleman. May the best team win."

Jeff went first and would try and put it in play allowing Kurps to "let the big dog eat" as they say. Even from the tips where they would be playing from today, he could hit his driver 300 plus yards when he got ahold of one and birdies would fall into line, when he could find his tee shot that is. If Jeff wasn't in good position off the tee, Kurps would drop down to his 3 wood and still hit it 270-280 yards and fairly straight. Again, that's on a good day.

It was a good start for the Rich Valley team when Jeff's ball came to rest just off the neck of the fairway which turned slightly right to an uphill green. Perfect position and green light time for Kurps to unload one. Which he did cutting the dog-leg perfectly and landing just short and right of the green. Picking up his beer which he had placed a yard to the right of his tee, Kurps gave Jeff a fist bump and said to his opponents, "I believe you are up," as he took a large slug from his beer. "Drink up Mr. Player. There's plenty of beer in the cart and we don't want it to go to waste, now do we?"

Healey glared at Kurps, raised his beer to his mouth and drank it dry. "You're gonna need it after me and this kid here are done with you two," The Player replied.

Fetts was about to say something to him when he threw the empty at Fetts' feet and said, "Don't need you to say shit, Frankie. Let's get this thing done and get the hell outa this place."

The Player grabbed his driver and strode onto the tee. Billy looked at Fetts knowing the plan was always for him to hit first, just as Jeff had done for their team, and allow Healey to do just what Kurps had done for their team. Fetts put one hand up as if to say, "Let him blow off some steam and then we can get on with it."

Healey took a monster swing and let one rip high and long. Unfortunately, it went exit stage right, short and into the wet area to the right of the fairway. Seeing where it went he was shocked and was just about to let his driver fly high into the air when Fetts yelled, "Hey! Don't you do it! Get the hell over here and settle your ass down. We have a long way to go and you're gonna need that club."

Hearing Fetts, The Player stormed over to the drink cart and grabbed another beer. Knowing their beer was non-alcoholic and the Rich Valley beer was spiked to 10% alcohol content, more than double the normal amount, Fetts didn't care how many beers Healey downed. They would have no effect on him or Billy, while the Rich Valley guys would be drunk on their asses long before they knew what hit them. Thanks to Germ, Fetts was able to set up every match his guys played the same way and almost guarantee a win no matter how good or bad his guys played. Germ was worth every penny Fetts had to pay him.

"What the fuck? That ball didn't go anywhere, Fetts," Healey quietly said to Fetts when he had calmed down enough to speak. "It should have been up on the green no problem at all."

"You get all of it?" Fetts asked him.

"I hit it exactly the way I wanted to," Healey replied. "It should have carried that shit with plenty to spare and been right up there on the green. It just didn't go nowhere I'm telling you."

When Billy hit his tee ball and it ended up in the fairway but twenty yards short of Jeff's ball, Fetts took notice. Unless both The Player and Billy miss-hit their drives, something wasn't right and Frankie had no idea what it was. The balls his guys were hitting were supposed to be jacked up to go ten percent farther than the normal ball. Germ had gotten them from his manufacturer and supplied them to Fetts for every golf game either he or his guys played for as long as Fetts could remember. Something wasn't right but he'd wait a few holes to determine if it was a two shot fluke or there was an actual problem with the balls his guys were playing.

The caddies grabbed the bags for their players and they all trudged down the first fairway to continue the match. Healey had hit into a "red-staked" area so he was allowed to drop a ball next to the marshland with a one stroke penalty. He grabbed a club and hit it right on line but again it came up short. He was on the closely mown grass just off the green about five feet to the left of Kurps' ball. Unfortunately for him, Kurps was there in one shot and he was there in three.

He looked at his club, then at Fetts who was standing ten feet behind him, and shrugged his shoulders as if to say, "What the hell is going on, man?"

Fetts shrugged his shoulders back at him and starting walking toward Billy. They were still in play and he needed Billy to come through for their team. Healey would have to figure out his shit all by himself.

Billy had played the course enough times and knew how to adjust for the elevation of the green plus play for its undulations. He didn't want Jeff and Kurps to get off to too quick of a start and also give Fetts something to be happy about, too. Soon enough he'd realize the balls they were playing with weren't jacked up but were "deadened" by about ten percent courtesy of Germ's manufacturer. Billy knew another of Fetts' famous explosions was not far off.

He was 100 yards from the middle of the green with the pin slightly toward the back. His caddy was about to hand him a sand wedge when Billy said, "No, the pitching wedge."

Slops, who was known for his less than sartorial splendor, hence his nickname, balked at first but relented and handed him the wedge. Billy flew it just short of the pin, one bounce and it skidded to a halt two feet below the hole. A kick in birdie for Fetts' team.

Jeff saw where Billy's ball had stopped and wanted to give Kurps a free run to try and chip his ball in for a two and take the hole. He hit a good shot but a bit long and left stopping ten feet above the hole. Not dead like Billy's but good enough to allow Kurps to take a run at it. Since he was lying three already and out of the hole, Healey picked up his ball and walked toward the 2nd tee.

They gave Billy his putt for a birdie and surveyed what they had. Jeff had almost the same line as Kurps so they decided he would putt first and give Kurps a read. His putt was right on line but moved slightly left at the hole and stopped a foot past. Kurps played for the slight break but left his uphill chip two inches short giving him a matching birdie—no blood on the first hole. Fetts and Harry marked their score cards agreeing to matching birdies. As they walked to the second tee Harry told Mueller to watch out for The Player's caddy. Unless Harry was dead wrong that bulge in his jacket wasn't a bunch of extra golf balls.

"Already got that one and Judy has the other caddy," Mueller told Harry.

"Judy?" Harry asked.

"Your favorite good looking beverage cart girl, Harry. She's one of mine and a much better shot than me, too," Mueller told him.

Chapter 130

The second hole was a short par three with a carry over the hazard that found Healey's ball on the first hole. Nobody hit it close to the pin tucked in the front right portion of a severely sloping back to front green. Jeff had his guys double cut and roll the greens that morning so they were running like lightning. His and Kurps' knowledge of the greens, along with Nolo's, would be a major advantage for them throughout the round. Billy needed to sink a three-footer to halve Jeff's par and he did. As they came around the turn toward the third tee there seemed to be a small but growing crowd around the pro shop apron and in the parking lot. Those who had their lives on the line had begun to congregate at Rich Valley hoping to catch a small glimpse of the match with their future at stake.

The third hole was a tricky shortish par four with a fairway that swung to the right about 160-170 yards out. It was a deceiving driving hole with a string of small but getting bigger all the time pine trees all along the right side rough, a "you lost your ball in the high grass" area on the left, and an elevated green similar to the first hole. It was very easy to lose your ball right off the tee and that's exactly what The Player did; landing smack in the middle of the first fairway. Growing increasingly irritated he hit the cart girl up for another beer and trudged off to find his ball with his caddy and Fetts close behind him.

The other three players were bunched together roughly seventy yards out after playing it safe off the tee all hitting three and five woods instead of driver. Billy looked at Harry and signaled it was time to start their move toward saving Rich Valley and its slew of IOU's. Healey went first and came up short in the bunker guarding the right side of the green. He screamed at his caddy and blamed him for misjudging the distance to the flag when it was probably the dead ball that made him come up short. Fetts truly didn't know what the hell was going on and was beginning to think there might be something wrong with the ball Healey was using. He instructed the caddy to give him another ball for the next hole.

Jeff was away and hit his ball a bit thin. He one hopped the green and stopped in the short rough behind the green. Billy was next and he hit his fat and right—a pop-up that joined Healey's ball in the sand trap. When Kurps hit his ten feet below the hole, Fetts was livid. He told Billy to get his head out of his butt even though Billy had saved their asses on the first two holes.

Harry looked over at Fetts and just smiled.

Billy's ball was stuck up against the grass that hung just above the trap and he was lucky to get it out leaving him fifteen feet from the cup on the green apron. Healey was excellent out of the sand. His ball was sitting up perfectly in the middle of the trap and he showed why he was The Player by hitting it to within three inches of making it. Jeff made his four-footer for par and Kurps now had his putt to win the hole. Never in doubt, he drilled it into the middle of the cup and the Rich Valley team was now one-up in the match. The cheer that erupted from the growing crowd in the parking lot and practice facility added to the anger Fetts was now feeling. Not wanting to make matters worse, he let loose with a violent tirade directed at his two caddies who had them scurrying to the fourth tee way ahead of everyone else.

The fourth hole wasn't long but it had trouble in and around it. A narrow fairway with out of bounds right into the neighbors' yards down the length of the hole and out of bounds left over a hill and back onto the third green. Two hundred and forty yards out was a sand waste area with fifty yards of carry to a false front that played havoc with your yardage calculations. With Mueller wisely staying out of the conversation, Nolo convinced Jeff and Kurps to play safe and lay back well short of the waste area. With tee honors they both did exactly that and had roughly one hundred and twenty yards to the flag from the middle of the fairway. Billy followed suit leaving himself in the right rough ten yards behind his competitors opening it up for Healey to hit his driver and try to fly the waste area. He had no trouble doing it when he had played there earlier coming up just short of the green. He had no doubt he could do it again. With Billy in good position Fetts finally told him to let it fly. After a healthy slug from his beer he addressed the ball but seemed to stand over the ball an extraordinarily long time. Finally he stepped back and took another practice swing before he again got into position and gave it a powerful whack. It flew high and long, dropping down at the very end of the waste area, thirty yards short of his prior efforts on the hole. The new ball his caddy had given him did him exactly shit good.

"What the hell is the matter with you?" Fetts barked at his Player. "I didn't bring you here to do shit like that. Get it together, or else."

"Or else what?" The Player growled back at him.

Again the caddies had to restrain Fetts from going after Healey while Billy looked on knowing it was all over but the shouting—he hoped.

Neither Jeff nor Kurps was able to hit the green from A#1 position in the middle of the fairway leading to a half on the hole. Billy missed a ten-footer that would have won the hole and cursed his way to the fifth tee.

Harry was impressed with the kid's showmanship.

After halving the fifth hole with routine pars, Harry said to Fetts, "I have Rich Valley one up, Mr. Fetterman. Do you agree?"

"Yes, but not for long," Fetts replied.

The sixth hole was tailor made for the Player. Just over three hundred twenty yards and straight as an arrow with a slight breeze behind them. Again the Rich Valley boys played it safe and left their tee shots just short of the bunker on the left side of the fairway. It was a fairly new addition to the hole Jeff had placed there two winters ago to annoy the mid-range hitters who aimed left to avoid the corn field on the right. The same bunker Billy's high draw found on the fly leaving him with a buried lie. Knowing his partner could hit the green, Billy was surprised he could actually carry his drive into the bunker on a fly. The Player didn't even hesitate and wailed away with his driver, long and straight, but a full fifteen yards short of the green.

"Shit, shit, shit. I flew that fucking green last time with the wind in my face," he yelled loud enough to be heard two counties over.

With a straight face, Kurps told him, "Have another beer, kid. It will give you the extra oomph you'll need to give us a match."

Taking Kurps advice, he drained his beer and headed straight for the beverage cart. Judy the cart girl was more than happy to oblige. Even though The Player's tolerance for alcohol far surpassed most mere mortals, the juiced beer he was consuming would have to get to him sooner rather than later. He looked and acted fine now, but the end wasn't far off.

Jeff had the grounds crew place the cup on the very front of the sixth green that sloped back to front and very severely the closer to the front of the green you got. Knowing this, he and Kurps hit their approach shots just beyond the cup leaving themselves a slippery downhill putt but still on the green. Billy blasted his shot out of the bunker, a thirty-yard bunker shot over a five-foot front lip, to the back of the green leaving him two options: either lag his first putt making sure he stayed at least ten feet short of the cup or try and make it and run the risk of having it race right off the front of the green. Either option was less than desirable which is exactly why he had intentionally played the bunker shot in the way he did.

Fetts watched all this transpire before confidently saying to The Player, "Throw this up there close and we get out of this hole all even. This is why I brought you here and continue to have confidence in your ability to be the man and seal the deal for us. Birdie this puppy and let's get back on track and finish off these losers."

"You got it boss," Healey replied.

After two practice swings with his sixty-degree wedge, each gently brushing the grass, The Player stepped up and lofted the shot three feet short of the pin only to watch it roll back down the slope to the edge of the green. Only an old pitch mark saved it from rolling completely off the green and right back to where he was standing. After Billy boldly rolled his putt off the green, a trio of two putts left the Rich Valley team one up going to the seventh hole. Two par fives lay ahead of them followed by a tricky dog-leg right ninth hole to finish the front nine.

Billy needed to make sure Fetts didn't suspect anything so he easily birdied the seventh hole which halved the hole when Jeff drained his five-footer. Kurps and Healey both had eagle chips but they each ran them well past the hole. Fetts began to get a little worried when his Player either slipped or lost his balance after hitting his chip. He was downing beers like they were going out of style but being non-alcoholic Frankie was sure that had nothing to do with it. Billy wasn't matching Healey beer for beer, but he had downed a few and looked perfectly fine. Little did Fetts know Billy was secretly pouring beer out of his can every chance he got. Kurps also was hitting the beers fairly hard so as not to give Fetts anything to bitch about. Fetts had expected them to have some effect by now but he also looked perfectly fine, the same as Billy.

It would only get much worse for the Player and it wasn't that far off.

Chapter 131

The drives on the eighth hole proved to be a troublesome affair for everyone. It isn't a long par five but there is enough trouble all around to make it much harder than it should be. Jeff
pulled his drive and went far enough left to find himself stymied
behind one of the many pine trees he had planted throughout the
course. A chip out was all he had leaving him with a 220 yard third
shot to a tricky green. Kurps just missed his and ended up in the
right fairway bunker. A 210-yard bunker shot is no picnic for anyone and not one Kurps exceled at. Thinking he needed to acceler-
ate their downfall, Billy hooked his drive into the tall grass left of
the fairway which prompted another outburst from Fetts. Billy
hung his head as if the effects of Fetts' tongue lashing was having
some effect on him. Nope, not happening.

As The Player prepared to tee up his ball, Fetts told him,
"You had better get your game together and start producing or
you will regret what I will do to you for the rest of your life you
low life piece of shit." After glaring at Fetts, The Player proceeded
to miss-hit his drive short so far right it ended up all the way
across the adjacent seventh fairway. This time it took both caddies
to restrain Fetts from killing Healey right there on the eighth tee.
Again glaring at Fetts with a look that could kill, Healey dropped
his driver where he stood and walked off the tee.

They spent the allowable five minutes looking for Billy's ball
but they never found it. Instead of going back to the tee to hit another drive which would have been his third shot, Billy declared
himself out of the hole. Fetts wasn't happy about it but he still had
The Player in play and it wasn't a long par five. With both Jeff and
Kurps in some trouble, he was confident Healey could save the
hole for them. His confidence was buoyed even further when Jeff
hit a low screamer right and Kurps came up fifty yards short out
of the trap. Unfortunately, his confidence was shattered when
Healey's second shot was chunked so bad it barely made it back to
the eighth hole rough some 175 yards from the green. A few more
mediocre shots from all three combined with two-putts all around

and Kurps halved the hole with a bogey. They halved the ninth hole and made the turn with Rich Valley holding on to a slim one-hole advantage.

By now Healey was showing further signs of the effects the pumped up beer he was consuming was having on him. Just off the ninth green Fetts pulled him aside and asked, "What the hell's going on with you? You drunk or something?"

"Whatcha mean? I'm fine. The balls you gimme suck and hows me suppposded ta play with dems suckee balls?" The Player slurred back at Fetts.

Before Fetts could reply his franchise player turned and walked away from him on legs that looked a long way from steady to Fetts. Billy asked Fetts, "What's up with him? He's killing us and I'm trying as hard as I can to make up for it but it's messing up my game trying."

"Just play your game and you better start doing it a whole lot better or else," Fetts told Billy. With that they took off to catch up with Healey and hopefully get back on track on the back nine. Fetts had everything tied up in this match and losing would ruin all his plans for the big one that was to follow. Come hell or high water that wasn't going to happen.

To get to the tenth tee you had to walk right past the first tee and the club house on your way back up the hill. One of the two outside decks attached to Nolo's overlooked the first tee. As Fetts passed he looked up and saw two guys in suits sitting there, flanking what to him had to be an apparition. Could that be Germ sitting there on the deck to Nolo's with two official looking suits keeping him company? It couldn't be. It better not be. Fetts couldn't fathom any reason for Germ to be here at Rich Valley, flanked by what looked like G-Men if he had ever seen two G-Men before. All at once it hit him—he had been fucked over! He had been had by a bunch of amateurs and he never saw it coming.

The true life apparition called down to him as he stood there gawking up at them. With the snarliest smile Fetts had ever seen, Germ yelled, "Hello Frankie. How's your game going?" If there was anything that could have been said in reply Fetts could not manage to conjure it up. The words spoken by Germ were surpassed only by the sounds coming from The Player who was at that moment bent over barfing his brains out into the waste can next to the first tee. The capital T and capital P clearly no longer applied when referring to Fetts #1 player.

The entire Rich Valley scene seemed to freeze like a singular shot from a movie in super slow motion before Fetts regained his equilibrium and shouted at Germ, "Fuck you, Germ. I'll get you for this, you double-crossing maggot."

Fetts now grasped it all as if the light finally shone through the darkness: the balls his team were using weren't jacked up as Germ had provided for every other job before this one. If anything they were most likely ten percent or more deader than a regular golf ball you could get off the shelf in any sports store. The beer his guys were guzzling down like soda water had the 10% jolt added to them and Jeff and Kurps were drinking the non-alcoholic version. The Player, who was an alcoholic waste of a human being to begin with, was driven down that path without him even having to lend a helping hand.

Germ could be heard laughing hysterically as he was led back into Nolo's bar no doubt about to pay for being everyone's "go-to" guy in Vegas for too long a time. Selling Fetts down the river for the golf jobs he helped perpetrate and every other underhanded scheme Fetts pulled off with Germ's help was a rock-solid, 100% given. No doubt about it!

Fetts did a three-sixty standing in place before his vision narrowed on the only person on the earth who could save him—Billy Burns. Maybe not from the eventual shit-storm that would descend down upon him, but maybe he could at least salvage the Rich Valley job and stash away a small bundle in case it would be awhile before he ever saw the light of day again after the Feds were done with him. Seeing an angle when there was none to be had was what had made Fetts who he was and he wasn't about to go down without one last fight.

While Fetts' two caddies were attempting to keep Healey from passing out altogether, Billy had stood around with the Rich Valley team watching Fetts' demise play out right before their eyes. He was fairly certain his payday, if there ever was to be a payday at all, was going right down the drain along with Jon Francis Fetterman's future. It caught him by surprise when he heard, "Billy, get over here. Yeah, you, get your ass over here right now. You're still part of my team and we ain't done with this match just yet."

"What are you talking about? Look at your boy over there puking his guts out in front of all these people. He can't even stand up never mind hit a golf ball. I can give it my best but two against one is going to beat us every time," Billy told Fetts.

Fetts put both hands on Billy's shoulders, looked him straight in the eyes and said, "Me and you, kid. Me and you are gonna kick their loser asses and take this club right away from them just like we planned all along. Me and you, together, my team."

Billy looked right back at him and said, "Yeah, you and me boss. You and me are gonna kick their asses but good."

Fetts said, "Yeah, kick them where it counts." With that he turned, yelled at the two caddies to "Pick up them bags and let's get going" as he headed for the tenth tee leaving the player to take care of himself. He was as good as dead to Fetterman now.

Billy turned to Jeff and Kurps and said, "This is going to be more fun than I have ever had in my life and trust me, I've had some pretty good times up to now."

Chapter 132

Everyone had arrived at the tenth tee, a 165ish yard par three that played a half-club longer all day long. It required a full carry over a small waste area with a severely sloping apron in front of the green that would propel your ball back down twenty yards to the bottom of the hill if you came up short. Balls that landed on the front of the green had been known to roll back off and down the hill. A slight left to right breeze complicated the club choice.

"Me and Billy are done with the beers," Fetts informed the group. "We need to put all our concentration on these nine holes and we don't need no Healey scenario to fuck it up." Pointing at Jeff and Kurps, he said, "You two have at it, but me and Billy are done."

"That's fine by us," Kurps told him. "But, just so you know, since you're changing the rules and replacing one team member mid-round, me and Jeff will provide our own beer should we care to imbibe from here on in."

Fetts was about to object when Harry stepped in and said, "Mr. Fetterman, if I was you, I'd let that one go; if you know what's good for you."

When Fetts looked like he wasn't going to let it go, Harry said, "The Player and Germ."

Looking at Jeff, Fetts said, "You guys are up."

Maybe it was beginners luck, but Fetts hit his tee shot to within ten feet. Trying to make it look like he was trying, Billy was just outside Fetts and would be able to give him a good look at the line. Kurps flew it into the left side trap and Jeff was hole high just off the green on the apron. Advantage Vegas.

"Maybe this is just what I needed," Fetts told his caddy loud enough for everyone to hear. "That putz Healey shit the bed and I'm going to have to save my own bacon just like always."

Ignoring Fetts all together, Kurps blasted to within eight or nine feet and Jeff chipped his approach a few feet inside Kurps' ball. They would have two makeable putts for par if neither Billy nor Fetts drained their birdie putts.

With the two caddies right behind them, Fetts asked Billy, "What do you think, kid?"

Kneeling behind the ball, Billy replied, "Left edge or maybe a half-a-ball outside."

One of the caddies though it was a bit more outside the hole and the other agreed with Billy. Neither of them could get inside a twenty handicap ever but Fetts listened to them anyway. When Billy's putt grazed the left edge and ran on two feet past the hole, Fetts said, "Gotta be on the left edge. I got this one." He was a ten handicap and no slouch on the greens, but he wasn't used to the Rich Valley greens that could fool the best of them. When his ball moved right more than he thought it would and just missed the right edge, he said, "I'll be a son-of-a-bitch."

Kurps drilled his in the center of the cup and Rich Valley remained one up moving to the eleventh.

Two of the next three holes were halved with Billy sinking a ten-foot side-hill par putt on eleven and a snaky three-footer for a birdie on the par 5 thirteenth. He missed what looked like a routine five-footer on twelve to give the hole to the Rich Valley boys. Kurps gave him a look when his birdie dropped, but Billy winked right back at him telling him not to worry. As they approached the fourteenth tee with Jeff and Kurps now two holes ahead, Harry exclaimed, "Gents, the fun is about to begin."

Fetts, who had been of no help whatsoever to his team so far, either smacking his ball all over the lot or missing easily makeable putts on every hole, said, "What the hell is that supposed to mean?"

"Oh, you'll see," Harry told him.

Billy explained to Fetts that the fourteenth hole was a three-hundred-yard hole—one hundred and fifty yards straight out and one hundred and fifty yards straight left from there. With their two caddies looking totally perplexed, Fetts said, "Say what?"

Nolo gave Jeff a six iron and he lofted one through the tunnel of trees right into the middle of the fairway. With the hole set up perfectly for his power fade and the team now safely in play, Kurps told Mueller, "Three wood my good man if you would, please." The lefty started the ball right on target well inside the tree line on the left and it headed left as it cleared the trees. It ended up fifty yards from the green right in the middle of the fairway—perfecto position.

After seeing both of their drives, Harry told them, "Gents, I believe the Fat lady has begun her warm up."

Fetterman was now beside himself with growing rage. The match was crumbling before him no thanks to his inept play and the shadow of Germ and the G-Men hung firmly over his head. In a last ditch effort to salvage something from the unfolding disaster, he told Billy, "Kid, I need you to do this for me. I need you to do your magic like you did on the other jobs and pull this one out. You can do it; I know you can. Do it for yourself and do it for me."

Billy smiled at Fetts and replied, "Sure boss, this is for you." He promptly swung and missed and said, "That's one." He took another swing and missed the ball by a foot. "That's two." After repeating his wayward attempt at striking the ball for the third time, Billy said, "I guess that makes three." As Fetts looked on in disbelief, with his fourth attempt Billy hit the ball directly left into the trees. Turning toward Fetts, Billy said, "Jon Francis Fetterman, Frankie, Fetts, I don't owe you shit. You owe me more than you can imagine and I have provided you with my thanks. I'm out of the hole—you're on your own on this one now, boss."

With surprising calmness Fetts turned to the two caddies and said, "It's time, boys. You know what to do."

The two caddies reached over to the golf bags they had been carrying, unzipped one of the pockets, and pulled out a gun. Before they could do anything with the guns, Judy the cart girl pointed a very large firearm at them and said, "I wouldn't if I were you boys. Step away from the bags, drop the guns, and be good boys for me and lie down on the ground, face down, hands over your heads."

Mueller pulled his weapon and had it pointed at Fetts who had produced a small .22 handgun from somewhere. Mueller said, "Why don't you give me a reason, asshole."

Fetts wisely surrendered his weapon to Mueller. Simultaneously a caravan of golf carts came screaming down the thirteenth fairway with enough backup to corral a small army. Screeching to a stop next to Judy's beverage cart, the G-Men assumed control of the situation and hauled the caddies away. Fetts they left to Mueller, Judy and the Rich Valley boys.

The silence that ensued on the fourteenth tee was deafening. Deciding he should help move things along, Harry said, "Okay then. Now that we seem to have things under control we still have a golf match to finish. The Rich Valley team is currently two holes ahead with five holes to play including this fourteenth hole. They have concluded their tee shots and Billy Burns of the Fetterman team has declared himself out of the hole, and mercifully so I might add. Mr. Fetterman, you have the tee. And be mindful, if you get yourself shot you may not be able to finish the match, so I'd be careful how you conduct yourself from here on out. Swing away, sir."

Billy was now standing between Jeff and Kurps smiling broadly at Fetts.

Not knowing what else he could do, Fetts grabbed his driver out of his bag and teed up his ball. He swung as hard as he could and hit the best shot he had hit so far. Unfortunately, he picked the wrong hole on which to hit it. It flew high and straight through the trees, over the 150-yard marker and across the fairway, completely over the rough and directly into the bunker that was out of play 99.9% of the time. You have to work hard to hit a shot that bad, for that hole, and Fetts had done it. "Motherf..." he started to yell before Judy jumped up.

"Uh, uh, uh Mr. Fetterman."

Unfortunately, Fetts would now have to play on without his driver after twirling it deep into the woods.

After leaving his first attempt to get out of the trap in the trap and sculling his second into the waste high grass to the right of the elevated green, Fetts walked out of the trap, picked up his bag and trudged to the fifteenth tee. He forfeited the hole and he and Billy were now three down with four holes to play.

The fifteenth was an uphill par four with a nasty, grassy hill all along the left side and trees and all sorts of trouble along the right. Jeff ended up in the left rough but safe, 150 yards out. Kurps tried to muscle his drive and power-sliced one over the hill on the left and out of play. Seeing a tiny slice of light in the darkness of defeat Fetts decided to go first and hit a mediocre drive down the right side of the fairway about 165 yards from the green. Billy wanted to remind Fetts what he could do so he smoked one a country mile right down the middle leaving him only 110 yards from the pin. Turning to Fetts he said, "Nice drive, huh boss?"

Fetts just glared at Billy and walked away.

Billy hit his approach to within three feet and birdied the hole to bring their team to within two down with three to play. Fetts had a renewed bounce in his step as he walked over to the sixteenth tee while trying to convince himself they actually still had a chance in the match. Mueller interrupted his reverie when he said, "Fetts, should you get any ideas, just look over at the clubhouse. The guy on the roof who looks like he is pointing a fancy looking scoped long gun at us is actually a sharpshooter who could pop the button off the top of your golf hat if you as much as twitch the wrong way. So be advised, behave yourself."

Fetts glanced over his shoulder, stared in the direction Mueller had indicated, and then continued walking toward the tee.

Chapter 133

The sixteenth hole could easily be described as "a bitch of a hole" by anyone who has ever played it. A long carry is needed to reach the fairway with out-of-bounds down the entire left side that then turns sharply around the corner and continues on for another 150 to 160 yards. The approach shot needs to carry a smallish waste area thirty yards below the green with a bunker ten yards beyond that at the base of a severely elevated green. Add in additional trouble spots all around the hole and it plays much harder than it sounds.

With the honors for the first time, Fetts promptly deposited his tee ball out of bounds left by twenty-five yards. Now playing his third shot from the tee he left it wide right short of the curve leaving himself no chance to reach the green with his fourth shot. Seeing Fetts botch the hole entirely, Billy played safe and left himself a 210 yard shot over the crap—not ideal. Utilizing their prior course knowledge and the opposing team's position off the tee, both Jeff and Kurps deposited their tee balls in the middle of the fairway roughly 180 yards to the pin. Result—advantage Rich Valley.

Fetts proceeded to help his team immensely by hitting a duck-hook left that quacked its way out of bounds thus rendering him out of the hole. Billy shook his head and hit a high draw that came to rest twenty-five feet left and above the hole. Not an easy putt by any means. Again, course knowledge prevailed and both Jeff and Kurps hit their approaches below the hole leaving them much easier putts. Result—continued advantage Rich Valley. If Billy missed or either Jeff or Kurps sink their birdie putt the match is over. Rich Valley would be saved and everyone would become whole again. All miss and the match would go dormy— Rich Valley would be up two with two holes to play.

As they walked toward the green, Fetts grabbed Billy and said, "It's up to you now. As slim as our chances may be, if we are going to stay in this match you have to come through for us right here on this hole. The team is counting on you. I'm counting on

345

you. I'm asking you…do it for us!"

Billy kept on walking like he never heard a word Fetts had just said.

Billy stalked his putt looking at it from all sides. Fetts followed him around the green like a lost puppy dog looking for a new owner. It was one of the tougher greens to read and Billy never saw the degree of break in the putt; or, he did and he just missed it. Maybe on purpose, maybe not. He tapped in for his par and stepped aside to await Jeff and Kurps' putts. If one of them dropped, Fetts would have to clean out his tidy-whities and resign himself that he was most likely going to be taken away by the feds and be out a ton of money as well.

Jeff built the course, played it a million times—well maybe not a million but a whole lot for sure—and was known for his putting. He knew every inch of the greens. Kurps read greens as well as anybody and his putting stroke is as pure as they come. Two shots at a ten- footer from the same angle would produce a birdie nine times out of ten but that's why you putt the balls. Two misses and when the second one didn't fall Fetts practically passed out right there on the sixteenth green.

With continual reports being sent to the pro-shop during the round by Judy, a large crowd slowly gathered up and down the seventeenth fairway. By the time the contestants rounded the corner to head back to the seventeenth tee, the fairway was packed with onlookers. Jeff and Kurps waved and urged them on while Fetts stared at them as if they were a mirage. Billy, well, he just smiled as did Harry. The conclusion of a well thought out and executed plan was about to come to fruition.

Seeing Fetts' state when he became aware of the crowds lining the fairway, Mueller said to him, "Don't get any ideas or this won't end well for you. Just finish the round and let us do our jobs and when it's done we will make sure to take you safely where you need to go."

Once they had reached the tee area Harry gathered the four players and the Rich Valley caddies together and said, "So there is no confusion, here is what we're looking at. The Rich Valley team is ahead by two holes and there are two holes to play—the seventeenth and eighteenth. If either hole is won by the Rich Valley team or a hole is halved, Rich Valley will be declared the winner.

Should the Fetts team win both holes the match will be tied and we will have a sudden death playoff starting at hole number one. Do both teams agree with what I have just said?"

Jeff spoke up for his team and said, "We agree."

When there was no response forthcoming from Fetts, Harry looked at Billy who took it upon himself to speak for the Fetts' team and said, "Agreed."

"Fetts?" Harry asked.

Finally, he replied, "Yeah, sure."

"Okay then, the Fetts' team has the tee. Play on," Harry told them.

"You want to hit first, my capitan?" Billy asked Fetts.

By the look of resignation on his face, Fetts was now a beaten man. Grabbing his 3 Wood from his bag since his driver was sitting comfortably in the woods where he had thrown it, he replied, "Yeah, sure." Considering the circumstances, he hit a fairly good shot clearing the water at the end of the tee box and landing on the right side of the fairway approximately 200 yards from the green. Showcasing his skill level, Billy hit his drive to within five yards of Fetts' ball.

Seeing where Billy's ball ended up, Fetts looked at him with a large degree of suspicion. Harry, who was standing behind Mueller, smiled the smile of a knowing man. Jeff and Kurps both hit their drives safely in the fairway with Kurps ten yards closer to the green than Jeff. The Fat Lady could now be heard warming up her pipes in the distance.

Fetts was the first to play and tried to muscle up resulting in a low screamer that went right and ended up short of the green and right in three-inch-high rough. "Fuck me with a broomstick," was his opinion of his shot. Billy drew his club back slowly and hit a high fade just off the edge of the fairway five yards from Fetts' ball. After admiring his shot, he calmly walked past Fetts and inserted his club back into his golf bag.

Fetts could be seen storming down the fairway before Jeff or Kurps even hit their second shots. Mueller followed closely two steps behind Fetts playing shadow to the big bad man. When both Jeff and Kurps lofted their second shots onto the green the crowd on both sides of the fairway erupted in cheers as they raced to the green to get a good spot not wanting to miss seeing the final nail being placed in Fetts' coffin. Billy walked toward the green with Harry high fiving everyone along the way. He saw a good dozen of "his people" among the crowd all there to protect their guy and enforce the code. The word must have gotten out—Billy was our man.

Fetts couldn't get out of the rough and in a fit of absolute rage fired his club across the thirteenth tee and into the woods. With Fetts' eyes burning a hole in Billy's back, he hit a great shot to with a foot of the cup. Turning to Fetts, Billy said, "Payback is a bitch, ain't it Frankie boy."

Rushing toward Billy, Fetts yelled, "I'll get you ya son-of-a-bitch." Judy's gun in his face convinced him that wasn't going to happen here, not now, maybe never. She produced a pair of handcuffs and slapped them on Fetts causing a thunderous roar from crowd. A military style jeep screeched to a halt next to where they were standing and Fetts was gone.

When they had all gotten to the green, Billy went over to the flag and removed it from the cup. He turned to Kurps and asked, "My putt good?" When Kurps told him it was he looked at both Jeff and Kurps and said with a huge smile on his face loud enough for everyone around the green to hear, "So are yours."

As you might guess, pandemonium ensued. Rich Valley Golf Club had been saved along with the livelihoods of many of Jeff and Kurps' friends.

Chapter 134

It took a good fifteen or twenty minutes for everyone to get back to the clubhouse and up to Nolos. Drinks were flowing and congratulations were offered all around as they entered the bar. The lawyers were waiting in the front dining room to conclude the business at hand—officially declare Rich Valley belonged to Jeff and Kurps free and clear, tear up the IOU's, and replenish the funds for everyone who had been swindled by Fetts crew. Government presence was there to ensure all went as planned and Randle Trundle was also there to conduct business as only Randle Trundle could.

Harry grabbed Billy before they entered the bar and guided him toward the men's room door. "Get in there," he told him and then stood guard to make sure nobody else went in. One of the G-Men was nearby to help if needed. Unsure why he was doing it, but trusting Harry like he had never trusted anyone before, Billy cautiously entered the men's room. Shocked would be a major understatement at what, or rather who, he found waiting for him.

"Hello, Billy."

Billy stood there frozen in place absolutely unable to speak.

"Hello, son."

Billy finally stammered out, "Mom, dad."

"Bet you never expected to find us standing here in the men's room of Rich Valley Golf Course," his father told Billy.

"Well, this may top anything you have ever done before and we all know the two of you have concocted some real doozies," Bill replied.

Billy's mom then said, "You may be right at that, Billy. And make that three, not two."

Billy's father stepped forward and extended his hand toward Billy. Still slightly unsure of exactly what and why, this was going down, Billy bypassed his father's hand and hugged him as if he hadn't seen his father in a very long time. In actuality, he hadn't. When they disengaged, Billy looked at his mother and said, "May I?"

Billy's mother opened her arms and said, "You're my son, of course you may."

Wiping away a tear, Billy asked, "What are you both doing here?"

His parents looked at each other before his mother responded, "Billy, just because we weren't there with you these past years doesn't mean we abandoned you entirely. We have had eyes and ears on you the entire time. The people we work with have been very kind to us when it came to knowing exactly what you were up to."

"People?" Billy asked.

"Best not to go there, honey," his mother told him.

"So why are you here, now?" Billy asked.

"As you are aware it is good to know people, the right people, at the right time, Billy," his mother started. "Your people, the ones you trust with your life and similarly theirs with you, who were once our people, your father and I that is, don't ever let them leave your life. And Tips, she's the one for you, Billy. But the people we deal with now, they appreciate what you have done here today. That's a bad man you helped take off the streets and they appreciate your help. Your past is now your past and they will help make sure it stays as just that—the past. These people you are associating yourself with now, this Shorts fellow and Mr. Trundle, stay close to them, Billy. They can be your future and a good future it will be. But never abandon our people, Billy; never forget who you were and what they have meant to you. To us. At the end of the day they are all we need in times of trouble. Trust them, Billy, and trust yourself."

"Can't you be with me as well?" Billy asked.

"We will always be there for you, Billy, but our lives, your father's and mine, take us in a different direction right now. Someday it may be different and who knows, we may get the chance to work together again. But for now, no, we must be going now."

Billy didn't know what to say. Why wasn't available to him and thanks wasn't necessary. It never was needed and it wasn't needed now. They hugged, the three of them together, and Billy turned and left the room. Harry was waiting for him when he came out and asked, "You good, Billy?"

"Yeah, I'm good, Harry" Billy told him. "For now at least.

Let's get a beer and join the celebration. And Harry, are they going to be okay?"

"Yeah," Harry told him. "They will be fine."

"You have anything to do with them being in there?" Billy asked.

"Me," Harry replied. "Who could I possibly know who could help me get your parents into the men's room at Rich Valley Golf Course at the same time you would be there?"

Billy smiled his own knowing smile.

They waded through Nolos' Bar greeted by high fives, back slaps and shouts of 'You da man' and 'Way to Go' plus much more. When they finally made it into the front dining room they found everyone seated around a large rectangular table covered by what looked like reams of legal papers. Upon seeing them, Trundle got up, shook Billy's hand, and then Harry's as well. He said, "Billy, you sit over there with the official looking guys for now and we will talk in a little while. Harry, you come and sit next to me."

When everyone was seated again, Trundle said, "Okay, where were we before we were rudely interrupted," which prompted a good laugh from everyone at the table. Rich Valley's lawyer said, "We were just about to complete the paperwork that would effectively negate any and all IOU's that are in Mr. Fetterman's possession for anyone connected in any way to Rich Valley plus either Jeff and/or Kurps personally. With Mr. Fetterman's legal representative's signature in his unfortunate absence, that will have been accomplished. The last piece to complete our business for today is the transfer of funds from Mr. Fetterman's personal off shore account to an account here in Mechanicsburg, PA that will accommodate the "making whole" of anyone involved in this nasty affair. Signatures were affixed to the two documents and effectively all was now right with the world, or at least the Rich Valley, etc. world.

Trundle called to Nolo and said, "A round for the room and everyone at the bar as well if you would, please."

"Coming right up, Mr. Trundle," Nolo told him and bodies hastened to fulfill his wishes with due speed. When the drinks had been served, Trundle stood and said, "I don't like to meddle in other people's affairs if I don't have a dog in the fight. To begin with I didn't until Harry called and explained what was happening and what was at stake, and then I did. For those of you in this room, and I would like it to stay in this room, that will give you some indication of my relationship with Harry Mickey Shorts and, much to my benefit, that of one Billy Burns. We all know the part Billy played in making this come out the way it did and in helping put a rat-bastard away for a long time. Please raise your glasses with me to thank Harry and Billy for all they have done."

"Here, heres," were heard and drinks were drunk.

"Next," Trundle continued, "my people tell me we have had cursory dealings with Kurps on a few occasions in relation to some of his many business endeavors. As he has decided to consolidate some of his empire, Trundle Industries will be purchasing his interests in Rich Valley Golf Course with Jeff's blessing. We will remain in the background and supply Jeff and his team with some added financial backing so they can implement numerous plans they have for the course and the restaurant/bar facility. Trundle Industries is thrilled to be a part of Rich Valley going forward."

Jeff stood and thanked Kurps for his unending support towards Rich Valley and his long-time friendship. He then said, "And perhaps we can get something done around here now that we finally got rid of his deadweight ass!" He then walked over and hugged Kurps as true friends do.

Trundle retook the floor and said, "And finally, thanks to Mueller and his people for their back-up and handling of that scum-bucket Fetts and his minions. And of course many thanks to Mr. Barry Potts, aka Germ, for telling the necessary tales and placing the knife in Fetts back for the Feds to turn any which way they choose. May he rot in his cell for the rest of eternity." Mueller and Judy took a bow and promptly exited with the rest of their team. The lawyers took the cue and headed out as well leaving the old and the new Rich Valley team alone in the room. Harry waved Billy over to the table and they all sat again. Nolo had a feast delivered to the table, gathered up a few of the staff and sat down to join the others at the table. Disaster had been averted and a lesson was learned that would not soon be forgotten.

Chapter 135

The long day was winding down and Nolo's bar area was now empty save for Randle, Harry and Billy who were having one last drink out on the side terrace. Nolo and Aaron were tidying up the kitchen and told Harry to make sure the door locked behind them when they left.

"I'd say everyone here at Rich Valley was more than pleased with the outcome, wouldn't you agree, Harry?" Randle asked.

"More than pleased," Harry told him. "And I'd bet dollars to donuts Kurps and his entire crew are breathing a very large sigh of relief as well. Kurps would have come out fine after all the assistance he lent in setting up our version of a sting, but you never know what's going to happen until it does. Stranger shit has gone down than this thing going sideways and he and his boys would have been out a pretty bundle."

"Billy?" Randle asked.

Having been caught by surprise when Trundle asked him his opinion, Billy quickly regrouped and replied, "From my perspective it couldn't have ended up any better. Everyone was made whole, Jeff keeps his club and picks up a huge backer in Trundle Industries, and I'm sure Kurps made out pretty well also. Harry got to have some fun setting it up and doing his thing and I got my satisfaction with Fetts that was a long time coming. Maybe the motherload of cash I was promised would have been nice, at least a motherload by my standards that is, but as they say the "greater good" won out this time. Yeah, Little Billy Burns talking about other people's "Greater Good," that's a good one. The guys back at home will get a real kick out of that."

Trundle had been listening intently to how Billy answered his query after he had put him on the spot. What he was looking to hear was exactly what he got and it made him both proud and quite pleased, too.

"I wouldn't worry about that "motherlode," Billy. You never know how things will turn out in the future," Trundle told him.

Billy frowned and Harry just smiled.

353

Trundle stood signaling their little chat had come to an end. Before he left them he said, "I have pressing business in Europe that needs my immediate attention. I'll be away for several weeks I'm afraid but perhaps we can get together for a Bayport Schooners game when I get back. What do you think?"

"Hot dogs, beer and a Bayport Schooners baseball game—need I say more, Randle?" Harry replied.

"I would enjoy that very much, Mr. Trundle," Billy told him.

"We have a give-away afternoon game coming up in about three weeks that might work. I will reserve an entire section that sits about one hundred fans—do you think you could entice one hundred or so of your fellow compatriots to join us for a game? My treat all the way, Billy?"

Smiling from ear-to-ear, Billy replied, "That would be beyond great, Mr. Trundle. The gang would love it to death," Billy replied.

"Excellent," Trundle told Billy. "One condition though. Please ask them to take the day off if they would. Okay, Billy?"

"I'm sure I can convince them to do that," Bill assured him.

"Great. I have to leave and one of my people will be in touch with the details. Nice work as always, Harry. You too, Billy," and Trundle was gone.

Once they were alone, Billy asked Harry, "Is he really going to do that for me, for us, for my people I mean?"

"Billy, you will learn that once you become part of M. Randle Trundle's inner circle the sky is the limit and it's always blue," Harry told him.

"And Harry, you can't imagine how much it meant to me to see my parents again. I will never be able to thank you enough for that," Billy told him.

"First, I have no idea what you are talking about. Parents? You? But for your information, Billy, buds do for buds. You don't have to ask and there is no need for thanks either. That's another one you will learn hanging around Randle and me."

Chapter 136

The sun was shining, the dogs were plentiful and the beer was flowing. Billy's crew had been overwhelmed when they learned they would be M. Randle Trundle's guests at a Bayport Schooner's game. That is as soon as they were told who and what the Bayport Schooners were and what was up with this mystery man who went by the moniker of M. Randle Trundle. Their entire section was rocking and the rest of the stadium was rockin' right along with them.

Sherry, Max and Briande were right in the middle of the entire circus and having the time of their lives. Sherry would have to keep her eye on Max to make sure he didn't disappear when Billy's crew headed out. He was already producing quarters from behind Briande's ears while laughing his ass off. Jeff and his entire team from Rich Valley had made the trip from Mechanicsburg to Long Island to join in on the fun.

Randle was holding court in his box with Billy seated next to him and Tips next to Billy. Harry and Ms. Timmons, who had made the trip in to enjoy their success and do a little business as well, were seated right behind them. When the message appeared on the scoreboard out in centerfield in big bold letters "WELCOME BILLY BURNS AND FRIENDS TO THE HOME OF THE BAYPORT SCHOONERS" the place exploded with cheers throughout the entire ballpark that went on for a full five minutes.

They were now seated again with a new round of dogs and beers for everyone. Trundle took a good swallow from his cup, turned to Billy, and said, "So, now that we have completed the Fetterman/Rich Valley caper, what's in store for you, Billy?"

Still feeling his way around the world and ways of Randle Trundle, Billy said hesitantly, "I'm not really sure, Mr. Trundle."

"It's Randle, Billy. No more Mr. Trundle if you wouldn't mind," Randy told Billy.

Harry, who had been chatting up Ms. Timmons in his usual Harry way, heard what Randy just said and smiled knowing Billy was truly one of them now.

"Yes, sir Mr. Tr..." Billy said before catching himself mid-word. "Ah, Randle, I, no we, Tips and me that is, we have work to do in the warehouse that needs to be attended to as soon as we can raise some additional capital to cover it. Then, there's me and Tips that I need to attend to and that's going to be a top priority. It's been long overdue and that's on me."

"Without "spilling all the beans" Harry has told me a small amount about your warehouse and I must admit, the little bit I do know, I find it most intriguing as I do your friends who seem to be taking over my ballpark today with no problem at all. If we didn't already fill the park for every game as we do now, I'd have to consider bringing them back occasionally to generate some buzz. I just might do it anyway. Ms. Timmons," he said as he turned to look in her direction.

"Duly noted and as good as done," she replied.

"Good," he told her. "Now, back to Billy Burns. And Tips—my apologies my dear. Trundle Industries has its fingers in every pie that exists and some most people don't know exist. The borough of Brooklyn is an area where we were severely under represented and has been a priority for me, hence for Trundle Industries as well. For a small percentage interest in your warehouse we would be willing to provide the "additional capital" you just spoke of and hasten your ability to work on the enhancements you have in mind. And trust me Billy, I can guarantee you the terms and conditions Trundle Industries will propose will be very attractive to both Tips and yourself. What do you say?"

Harry was all ears now after hearing that offer from Randy to Billy and Tips.

Billy looked at Tips and asked with his eyes what she thought of Trundle's proposal. Receiving the answer he thought she would give him without saying a word, Billy turned back to Trundle and said, "Randle, there isn't a single person in this world I would allow entry into our warehouse and expose the outside world to my people. That is what I had always thought of as a golden rule never to be broken. Harry and his family took me into their world and taught me rules truly can be broken. You, sir, are the second person to pierce my impenetrable armor and make me want to have you as a part of our family. With great joy, Tips and I, and our entire family of friends, welcome you into our world."

It took much, way beyond much, to move M. Randle Trundle. Upon hearing the words Billy had just spoken, he was truly moved. Even Ms. Timmons could tell from his body language Billy had touched his heart and that just doesn't happen.

"You and Harry put something together and get it to Ms. Timmons. Whatever it is, consider it done," Randle told Billy.

It caught Billy by surprise when Tips grabbed him and practically knocked him over with the hug and kiss she laid on him. Harry considered congratulating Ms. Timmons in a similar manner but thought better of it in the end.

"Now, one more thing," Randy told Billy. "The shortstop on our lower level rookie team broke his hand and it seems we are need of a middle infielder for a month or two. Ms. Timmons has a short-term contract with her that you may sign right now and become a part of the Schooner organization if you are agreeable. Care to play some ball for me, Billy?"

It was Tips who was caught by surprise this time when Billy grabbed her and practically knocked her over with the hug and kiss he laid on her. Again Harry considered congratulating Ms. Timmons in a similar manner but again he thought better of it in the end.

Composure regained all around, Billy said, "Mr. M. Randle Trundle, consider yourself in possession of one part-time fill-in middle infielder as of this very minute." Simultaneously the bullpen doors opened to allow the Schooner relief pitcher to enter the game and finish off the last few innings of another Schooner rout. The park exploded again when Grubby exited the gates, horns blaring, lights flashing as it made its way around the field to deliver the Schooner pitcher.

Billy turned to Harry and asked, "Will it always be like this?"

Harry smiled and replied, "Billy, the world has just begun to open up for you and Tips."

It was Harry who was caught by surprise this time when Ms. Timmons grabbed him and practically knocked him…

Imagination can be a wondrous thing.

About the Author

Rich Kisielewski has spent thirty plus years in the insurance industry and currently works in New York and Philadelphia. An uprooted New Yorker, he lives in Central Pennsylvania with his wife and collection of dogs and cats.

Visit his website at: www.richkisielewski.com

Other Books by Rich Kisieleswki
from WolfSinger Publications

da sticks

Not long ago, Harry moved back to the town where his ex-wife and kids reside and was trying to rebuild his life. The "work hard and play hard" attitude that carries Harry through life is balanced by the softness evidenced in his dealings with his children. Once again, he was going to have to be away from them and the new life he had been trying so hard to establish.

Going undercover at MechInsCo, Harry gets exposure to executives within the company including his lifer accounting boss, the psycho senior finance executive and a frantic company president. They all paint the same picture-a company losing money with no idea how, or why. His stint at MechInsCo supplies Harry with some raucous times: large amounts of information, booze and ladies provide him with much more than he signed on for.

da bug

Harry Mickey Shorts gets a call from M. Randle Trundle, a New York business tycoon, who is in need of Harry's help. Without a thought, Harry drops what he is doing and races off to help his benefactor, and his friend.

Trundle is a part owner in Board Room Farms—a horse racing stable—which is run by his brother, Danny Trundle. He informs Harry the stable's stud breeding stallion was found dead in his stall and Trundle feels something is wrong. Harry agrees to help Trundle with the case and does what he does best by going undercover and begins digging into the world of thoroughbred horse racing. Having bet on more than a few nags before in his lifetime, Harry is comfortable around the track and blends in very smoothly.

During his investigation, Harry forms an alliance with the ranch's female vet—in more ways than one. She agrees to provide needed intelligence on the current and prior goings-on at Board Room farms. Along the way, she becomes a serious love interest in Harry's life. Unfortunately, that conflicts with Harry's renewed part-time interest in his ex-wife that may prove to be a "pick one" dilemma, sooner, rather than later. His love for, and continued attempt to become part of his two children's lives, remains paramount in Harry's thinking.

da nuts

Harry Mickey Shorts, street wise private detective, gets a call from Max who just happens to be his favorite as well as his only son. Max doesn't ask his dad for much but he and his buddies are in need of Harry's help. Without a thought, Harry drops what he is doing and races off to help his son and his friends.

Max informs Harry he would like him to investigate the untimely events that prohibited Clint, their current cult hero, from participating in a first ever poker tournament. Clint had played over a quarter of a million hands of poker by the time he had reached his eighteenth birthday and, as evidenced by the size of his bank account, he had won a lot more of those hands than he had lost. All of that meant nothing when he turned up unconscious in his hotel room on the morning of the first day of the inaugural "Under 18 World Championship of Poker" tournament.

During his investigation, Harry uses his expertise that sets him apart from other private investigators and goes undercover to explore the world of internet poker. The twist with this version is only kids between the ages of sixteen and eighteen can participate and all winnings may only be paid to higher institutions of learning for the kid's college education. Harry's renewed part-time interest in his ex-wife and his love for and continued attempt to become part of his two children's lives complicates his own life but remains paramount in Harry's thinking.

Investigate these other Mysteries
from WolfSinger Publications

The Dolmen – Matt Bille

When attorney Julie Sperling's fiancée is murdered while re-searching a controversial museum exhibit, she calls on her ex-lover, science writer Greg nightmarish pursuit as very real preda-tors from ancient folktales try to hunt down anyone with knowledge of their existence.

For Greg and Julie, the City of Angels has become the gate-way to hell...

In Adam's Fall – Phoebe Wray

Old New England towns are infamous for their odd murder stories, but that had never happened before in Halton, Massachu-setts.

When history teacher Nikki Sheridan trips over the dead body of a young Muslim girl in her backyard she finds herself at the center of a murder mystery. A mystery that will take her on a perilous journey with the police, the FBI, a nervous town ready to point fingers at neighbors who seem different, and a man calling himself 'the Patriot': a dangerous zealot whose hateful agenda could destroy the small town or bring them even closer together as they face a homegrown terrorist in their midst.

Murder Most Howl – Margaret H. Bonham

Dog Mushing Can Be Murder

For Stephanie Keyes, noted sled dog racer in Colorado, sled dog racing can be dangerous enough. But when a fellow musher and rival is found murdered and she's a prime suspect, Stephanie races to find the killer before he can strike again.

Missing sled dogs and deadly goals abound in this super sleuth tale—or is it tail?

Blind Eye – F. Lynn Godfriaux

Mattie Lamont Tyler loses both parents in an apparent car accident, then finds herself estranged from her only sibling when her sister Angela elopes with a new boyfriend. But Mattie, a photojournalist with (ironically) a phobia of guns and violence, is blind to dangers around her until Angela ends up on the critical list in an ICU six hundred miles from home and Mattie's husband, a Southern Ute who appears to be a quiet, unassuming weather forecaster, stops answering his cell.

Before she can figure out what's going on, Mattie is kidnapped by Hawk, a ruthless stranger with accusations Mattie does not understand. Her own survival and the lives of her loved ones depend on whether Mattie can see beyond her "blind eye" into unknown inner strength.

From the plains of Oklahoma to the mountains of Southwest Colorado, Blind Eye sweeps the reader into a frantic race against greed, lies, and pre-meditated murder.

www.ingramcontent.com/pod-product-compliance
Lightning Source LLC
Chambersburg PA
CBHW060931030726
47503CB00003B/557